Until All The Stars Fall

Tim Frankovich

Books by Tim Frankovich

Heart of Fire

Until All Curses Are Lifted
Until All Bonds Are Broken
Until All The Gods Return
Until All The Stars Fall

Dragontek Lore

Viridia
Incarnadine
Auric (coming soon)

Until All The Stars Fall

Heart of Fire, Book Four

Tim Frankovich

WARPSTEEL
PRESS

Cover Design by Rofiatul Adawiyah
Map Design by Alexandra Lindgren

For Denise
My one and only

N
Drusa's Crossing
Ch'olan
Mandiata
Efesun
Wogan
Tenjkidi
Djatan Desert
Great Plains
Reman
Zes Sivas
Arazu
Varioch
Sandu-Emuq
Simbala
Kuktarma
Lake Titanu
DISPUTED
Rasna
Raeton
the Six Lands of Antises

(((1)))

Eniri opened the door but paused before stepping out. The streets of Intal Eldanir looked empty at the moment. It should be safe. It had been safe all her life. It had been safe yesterday.

But that was yesterday. Everything changed this morning. The wardens had failed. Six Durunim entered the city and did as they wished for almost an hour before being caught and killed. Other Durunim had been seen just outside the city, as if waiting to enter as well.

The entire incident happened before Eniri left home and came to work. She hadn't even heard of it until much later. And now that her work shift was over... she no longer trusted the empty street.

Eniri's life had been without fear for almost all of her twenty-five years. Only once could she say she had experienced fear: when Lady Siratel spouted such a frightening prophecy it almost incapacitated the old seer. When Eniri heard it, her heart raced, a weakness filled her joints, and she wanted to hide.

Today was different. Her heart did not race; it seemed like it moved slower than ever. Her fingers holding the door open grew cold. A sour taste filled her mouth. This was fear, but not the same kind of fear.

"Eniri? Are you all right?"

She shot a smile at the co-worker who spoke. Ensirha had just arrived to take over from her. Working with the patients here, like Lady Siratel, required full-time observation. "I'm fine, Ensirha. See you in the morning." She stepped out onto the street.

Mornings were an illusion in the Starlit Realm, of course. But like all Eldanim, Eniri could see the sun setting in the primary world, just as she would see it rising after she slept.

The walk to her home normally took only a few minutes. Tonight, those few minutes stretched on and on, far beyond what should be normal. She could feel each step with excruciating detail, her heel touching the ground, followed by the roll of the ball of her foot. How strange to notice something like that.

She stopped walking.

Three figures walked down the center of the street. Like all Eldanim, they stood immensely tall. But Eniri knew right away: they were Durunim. They could not be anything else. Even from here, she could see their dark faces absorbing all color around them, yet crackling with energy. They wore dark armor in composite pieces across their bodies, including tall helmets.

Even without the visual evidence, Eniri's other senses warned her. The three figures radiated malice like a living thing that writhed through the air around them. The malice spread apart and broke into three distinct sources as the Durunim spread themselves across the road. Eniri would not be able to get past them.

She took a step backward. Almost at once, she felt new malice behind her. She took a quick look. Two more of the dark figures stood on the street near the hospital.

Where were Intal Eldanir's defenders? Though the outer wardens had failed, the city still boasted thousands of Eldanim, many of whom would be able to deal with these intruders. Yet the streets were empty. Eniri did not even see anyone at the windows of nearby homes.

Her hand reached inside her bag. She carried no weapons, but she had one hope. She wrapped her finger around a Ranir Stone and murmured a desperate plea for help. Only one person would hear it, if the stone were working properly, but that one would be enough.

She moved toward the center of the street, giving herself as much space as possible. The silent enemies came closer from both directions. If she had no other choice, she would turn and try to get past the ones behind her. She had little hope of success, but two might provide slightly more of a chance than three.

The stone street beneath her feet rumbled and Eniri breathed a sigh of relief. He had heard her.

Another figure appeared behind the three enemies in front, approaching them at a rapid pace. Even from this distance, she recognized him. Harunir. Her father. While everyone knew her mother, Indala, as a member of the High Council, not as many knew her father's true profession.

The three Durunim drew their curved swords and dropped into defensive stances to meet this threat. That would do them no good. Eniri ran forward, wanting to see what happened, and staying ahead of the two behind her.

Harunir, mightiest mage of the Eldanim, carried no sword. But almost as he reached the first enemy, he gestured, and a long, golden staff appeared in his hand. He swept it through the legs of the first Durunim, upending it. The second one charged him, sword high.

Eniri glanced back and saw the other two breaking into a run also. She swerved toward her father's side of the battle.

Harunir blocked the downward slash of the sword with his staff and pointed at the Durunim with two fingers. *"i hatel nirhatal!"* he cried. The enemy warrior flew backwards through the air as though a mighty force had slammed into its chest. It smashed against a column and fell.

Harunir swung his staff down and smacked the prone Durunim in the head as it tried to rise. It collapsed unconscious. "Are you hurt?" he called to his daughter.

Eniri ran past him and turned around. "I'm safe!" And she genuinely believed it now. Her father stood between her and the remaining three Durunim.

Having seen the prowess of this attacker, these three advanced with caution. They fell into a formation, not too close, but not too far from each other. They readied their swords and stepped closer.

Their silence was baffling. Why didn't they speak? Eniri had witnessed many duels and training exercises among the wardens. They often spoke while fighting, or shouted battle cries. Or laughed. The Durunim never opened their mouths. Had the dark gods stolen their tongues?

"These three will trouble no one else," Harunir said. "That much is certain."

Her father pointed his glowing staff toward the stars and swept his other hand in a half-circle toward his assailants. "In the name of the One Beyond," he breathed.

Eniri could not see her father's power, but she could sense it. Her hair fluttered back and a warm breeze swept her skin. The three Durunim stopped advancing. They seemed frozen for a moment. Then all three dropped their swords and reached for their own chests.

"Close your eyes," Harunir warned.

Light exploded from within the Durunim. Eniri shut her eyes a moment too late. The warm breeze turned into a hot wave of power sweeping over her body. She gasped. When it ended, her eyes flew open. She looked down at herself quickly, but everything seemed all right. She would not have been surprised to see the edges of her clothing singed or starting to burn.

She looked up. The three Durunim were gone. Nothing remained of them save a few tattered shreds of clothing that floated to the ground beside the dropped swords.

Harunir turned and pulled her into his arms. "I came as soon as I got your message," he said into her ear. "I will always come when you call."

"Thank you. Thank you." Eniri realized her heart was racing again, like the first fear she had experienced. She took a deep breath and composed herself.

Harunir released her and looked down at the unconscious Durunim on the street. "This should never have happened." The tone of his voice changed; anger radiated from him now. "To think that enemies would walk the streets of Intal Eldanir openly! I will speak to the Council about this."

"Can we go home first?" Eniri asked.

"Of course, my daughter." Harunir waved to a trio of Eldanim who had just come into view. "Let me arrange for this one to be taken somewhere secure, and I will walk with you every step of the way."

Eniri wanted nothing more than that, though it troubled her. Enough of fear. She would need to learn how to protect herself. It seemed all of Intal Eldanir might need to do the same.

•••••

The chamber of the High Council of Intal Eldanir resonated with Harunir's voice. Eniri couldn't help wondering if her father might be enhancing his voice with magic. If so, he did it only for the High Council. No one else had been permitted in the chamber today to hear his complaint.

"It is outrageous that this was allowed to happen!" he thundered. "That my daughter should be threatened by Durunim on the very streets of Intal Eldanir is unthinkable! Yet it happened. How could this be?"

Eniri's eyes went to her mother who stood behind one of the twelve podiums as a Council member. Indala kept her face impassive, trying not to react in a personal manner. It was a talent all Council members were forced to adopt.

"As you no doubt know by now," one of the other councilors said, "a large number of the Durunim attacked the city on the west side. The five you faced snuck in from the east while most of our defenders were occupied."

The stars cast multicolored light through the domed glass ceiling. Imbued with magic, the hexagonal glass panels magnified the differing lights, filling the chamber with light in its many forms. Eniri loved the effect. No other building in Intal Eldanir could boast the same. It was almost enough to distract her from the seriousness of the moment.

"Two hundred thousand of our people live in this great city," Harunir declared. "At least five thousand of them are trained wardens, warriors, or mages. How is it that four thousand, nine hundred and ninety-nine were all required to repel one invasion?"

"Your sarcasm is not necessary," the councilor replied. "Of course not all of them were there. Many were going about their own business. No alarm was raised, as the High Warden saw no need to frighten the rest of the city."

"If these five had not come across my daughter, what then?" Harunir gestured with an open palm. "Suppose they had kept going, broken through to the interior of the city and the gardens? Five Durunim could cause untold damage to our food supply."

"What good are these hypotheticals?" another councilor asked. "What is your point, Harunir?"

"The High Warden is not doing his job," Harunir said. "The exterior wardens should have discovered these Durunim long before they reached the city. And once they did, our defenders should have been there to stop them at every point around the city. We have an entire series of failures here." He gestured again, a broad stroke with both hands. "They have grown lax! This is nowhere near the size of Durunim invasions we have repelled before now. Our enemy has mostly given up on attacking our city. Yet now we let them in?"

"What do you propose, then?" To Eniri's surprise, that question came from Indala.

"One man, no matter how talented he is, should not be in charge of the entire city's defense. The High Warden should share that responsibility with the High Mage and the High Champion." Having made his point, Harunir stepped back from the speaking podium.

Eniri's eyebrows went up, as did those of most of the councilors. Her father was nothing if not audacious. She waited for the obvious response.

"We do not have a High Mage position."

Harunir stepped back up. "And why don't we? Even the humans have Master Mage positions for each of their lands. Why do we not have a similar position? The mages defend the city as well as the wardens and warriors. We should at least have a chain of command to organize around."

"And I suppose you would be the top candidate for this new position," one of the councilors observed.

Harunir spread his arms. "I would be honored to serve, if chosen. But there are other mages who could serve just as well."

"Your modesty is noted," the councilor replied. "The Council will consider your proposal." He glanced around at the other councilors. "While I cannot say for certain, I believe there will be little objection. You raise points that perhaps should have been dealt with a long time ago."

"In that case, I would like to make one more proposal," Harunir said. Eniri could have sworn her mother stiffened at that.

"Proceed."

"Since the High Warden, the High Champion, and perhaps the new High Mage are in charge of the city's defense, it would seem prudent that they would also have a voice in the High Council."

"Preposterous!" snapped another councilor. "The High Council has always consisted of twelve members, chosen by the people."

Indala raised her hand. "Are you proposing that we expand the Council to fifteen members and give each of these three a position here?"

Harunir gave a short bow to his wife. "Ideally, I would prefer that solution. But if it proves too drastic of a change, perhaps only one position could be added, occupied by a rotation of the three city defenders."

Eniri heard grumbles from some of the councilors. The fact that she could hear them showed how much Harunir had thrown them off balance. The members of the Council prided themselves on their stoicism during meetings.

"We will consider this suggestion," a councilor said, in a tone that implied the exact opposite.

Harunir bowed again. "That is all I ask."

He stepped down from the dais and beckoned to Eniri. Together, they walked out of the chamber. None of the councilors spoke while they exited.

Outside, Harunir chuckled. "What did you think of my performance?" he asked.

"Performance? You mean, you didn't mean what you were saying?"

"I meant every word." Harunir patted her on the shoulder. "In politics, Eniri, always ask for far more than you actually want. Then your primary goal will seem reasonable."

Eniri considered. "Then you only wanted them to create the High Mage position and arrange a new way of defending the city?"

"Yes. Of course, I would love to have the other proposals as well. It seems only right to me. But I will be content if they only do what I asked for in the first place."

Eniri shook her head. "All this time, I thought Mother was the politician in our home."

Harunir's eyes twinkled. "Ah, perhaps I have learned from her over the years. Or maybe she got it from me."

Eniri laughed. "I'll tell her you said that."

"Then I truly will be in trouble!" Harunir joined her in laughter.

As they continued on their way home, Eniri thought over the rest of what had been said. "Do you think the Durunim threat will return?" she asked.

"Many of them have left the Starlit Realm and invaded the primary world. That's why we have seen so few lately. At least one of the ancient portals has been opened."

Eniri's eyes widened. "I've heard nothing of this! Then they are attacking the humans?"

Harunir nodded. "And we are foolish to ignore it. For should they conquer Antises, they will return here, more powerful than before. And if we do not strengthen our defenses and how we control them, we will not be ready."

"So you used the attack on your daughter to spur the High Council in the direction you already wanted."

Harunir bent his head. "It worked out that way, yes. I was genuinely outraged on your behalf. But good came from it. Or will come from it. I hope."

Eniri had no doubt her father's words would sway the Council. Then again, she had thought the same before and been surprised by their rulings. She could not always tell what they would do, not even her mother.

"Come. Let us find a place to dine," Harunir suggested. "I am hungry after all that postering."

Eniri chuckled again and followed her father.

(((2)))

"Curse Boy. That's what they used to call me." Marshal looked over the map of Antises inside his tent. How far he had come from those days.

"Who did?" Tich sat on the floor, peeling an apple.

Marshal snorted. "The people I grew up with," he answered. "In a little town called Drusa's Crossing, right about here." He pointed to the map.

Tich got to her feet and looked. "Well, that's a stupid name for a town. You should go back there sometime. Let them see what you are now."

"What good would that do?"

Tich shrugged. "I just like to see bullies get what they deserve." She took a bite of her apple. "You want some, Talinir?"

The Eldani warden, who stood behind Marshal, shook his head.

Marshal thought for a moment. Of course, part of him would love to parade through Drusa's Crossing and show everyone his power. His tormentors, like Titus, would be shamed. Would they get what they deserved? Maybe.

"Maybe people shouldn't always get what they deserve," he said aloud.

Neither Tich nor Talinir responded. Marshal didn't expect them to. He knew his philosophy was difficult for some to grasp, though Talinir at least should agree, since the Eldanim were no fans of the Laws of Cursings and Bindings. In fact, he had been thinking about that very fact for quite some time.

"Talinir, I know you promised to stay by my side…" Marshal began.

"And I will continue to do so," he said quickly.

Marshal turned to him. "But I need you elsewhere. I need you to do something for us. It's not directly protecting me, but it will protect my people, which is sort of the same thing."

"No. It isn't." Talinir folded his long arms and stood resolute.

Marshal fought with the usual perception problems of looking directly at one of the Eldanim. He needed to look Talinir in the eyes for this. "Yes, it is. I've accepted my role as King of Antises. It's my job now to defend the six lands and their people."

"And even a King needs someone to protect him."

Marshal spread his arms. "I'm surrounded by people wanting to protect me. After we left him behind last time, I don't think Victor will leave me again. I'm going with Seri and Dravid to Zes Sivas. And for now, we have half the army of Kuktarma surrounding me. If all of that, plus my own power, can't protect me, what does it take?"

"I made a promise."

Marshal pointed to the map. "The ancient gods have brought an army of Durunim through the portal. They're not far even now."

"All the more reason that you need protection."

"And," Marshal went on, "they're bringing more troops through in Varioch and Rasna, since that portal is still open. I may have to deal with that myself sometime soon. But in the meantime, these armies are here, and human armies can't stop them."

"Are you trying to terrify us?" Tich asked. "Because you're heading in that direction."

"The point is: we can't stop them!" Marshal insisted. "We need help. More help than we can find here. Even if I assemble all the remaining Lords and mages and we stand together... maybe we could halt the gods and their armies. Maybe. But we can't count on that happening. And I need them all at Zes Sivas to make things right, to end the system that created all of this problem."

"You want the Eldanim," Talinir said without emotion.

"I want the Eldanim." Marshal nodded and pointed to the map again, this time on the west side of Varioch. "I want you to go back to Intal Eldanir and persuade the Eldanim to join our fight."

"They will not come. You saw the Council. They would not stoop to help you, even when your mother made an impassioned plea. Why would they risk their lives to help the rest of humanity?"

"Because it's in their best interest! You admitted—they admitted—that the Durunim are their enemy. They've been fighting them. And the Durunim are Eldanim, aren't they? Twisted by the gods?"

Talinir did not reply. Marshal gritted his teeth. The Eldanim had some sort of pride thing which wouldn't let them admit that simple fact to outsiders.

"Well, now your enemy is here, in our world. We need your help to stop them. We can fight together and defeat them, once and for all."

Talinir's demeanor shifted from unyielding to dubious. That was progress, at least.

"And my ultimate goal is good for them too!" Marshal pressed. "If I can undo the Laws of Cursings and Bindings, magic will return to the way it used to be. More of it will flow back into the Otherworld, right? And maybe heal the land on that side as well."

"It could use some kind of healing, that's for sure," Tich observed.

Talinir shook his head. "Your arguments are good, and make sense to me. You know I agree with your quest. But the High Council is adamant. You remember. No interference with humans. No exceptions."

Marshal reached out and grasped Talinir's arm. "When we stood before them last time, my mother made the case. It was a human making the argument, on behalf of another human. You… you are not human. You're one of them. They'll listen to you."

"I wish that were true, Marshal." Talinir sighed. "I am young. I am one of the least of the wardens. And by aiding you, I have left behind my usual duties. They will not look on that with approval."

"You are uniquely suited for this job. You are Eldani. Yet you have walked with humans for the past year or so. You have a job, a title from the Eldani. And I am giving you a job and title from the humans." Marshal straightened. "As King of Antises, I hereby appoint you, Talinir, as my personal ambassador to the Eldani people. When you speak to them, you speak in my voice. You have my authority to tell them whatever they need to know, and persuade them to join us against the Durunim."

"I…" Talinir hesitated. "Your words move me, Marshal. I will not deny it. And I am honored by your faith in me. I do not think it is as well placed as you do."

"You've proven yourself to me time and time again. I will never forget what you have done for me, Talinir."

Talinir bowed his head. "Then… I will travel to Intal Eldanir and speak your words. Perhaps… perhaps there is a chance. We have a few allies. I will consult with them before I speak to the Council. Maybe they will listen."

"That's all I ask." Marshal turned back to the map. "Along the way, you can check on the status of the other portal. If you can, find a way to get word back to me at Zes Sivas."

Talinir laughed. "Do you have any other impossible tasks for me?"

Marshal grinned. "No, I've saved those for Seri and Dravid. They have to figure out how to end the Laws of Cursings and Bindings."

"And what impossible task do you assign yourself?"

"Besides actually doing whatever they come up with? I've also got to figure out how to persuade the other Lords to join us." He lost his grin. "And maybe persuade them to give up their power. Maybe forever."

Talinir considered for a moment. "It is hard to decide who has the more impossible task, then." He gave a short bow. "I'll prepare to leave immediately." He exited the tent.

Tich yawned. "You two are so grim sometimes. You've been doing impossible things for months, from what I've seen. How else can you explain a scar-faced 'Curse Boy' becoming King of all Antises?"

"How about a cynical sailor diving through a portal to the Otherworld because she was bored?" Marshal asked, smiling again.

"Nah, that's completely normal." Tich took another bite of her apple. "You've seen how boring it can get out on the water. Besides, that turned out all right, didn't it? Maybe Theon is watching out for us, making all these impossible things happen."

"Let's hope so," Marshal answered, looking back down at the map. "Because right now, I don't see how we can win. I'm just trying to do what I can. Every move I make is a complete gamble. I'm keeping Volraag around and sending Talinir away."

"I take it back," Tich said. "You're crazy."

• • • • •

Talinir considered his mission. Despite his positive words to Marshal at the end of their conversation, he did not see much hope for success. The High Council of the Eldanim were set in their ways. It would take a monumental shift in thought for them to change their minds.

He would be crossing almost all the way across Antises, and speed was of the essence. As a warden, alone, he could move much faster than any of his recent travels with humans. Even so, he would need to alternate between the primary world and the Otherworld for different parts of the trip.

Marshal wanted speed, and he would have speed. But first, as he left, Talinir needed a quick stop in the Simbala marketplace. He could certainly find some sugar there. Tea just hadn't been the same since he ran out.

(((3)))

Marshal handed the rolled scroll to the messenger. The young man snapped a quick bow and hurried out of the tent.

"I don't think I'll ever get used to that," Marshal said. He walked to the table and poured himself a drink. This morning, only Victor sat with him.

"The bowing?" Victor chuckled. "You've come a long way, huh?"

"It doesn't feel real." Marshal took a sip of water. "I feel like I'm going to wake up at some point and be back home with Mama. Or… in our tent with Volraag's army." He put his hand up to the tent's ceiling to feel the material, so much finer than the army tents.

"That would be a nightmare."

"Would it? I suppose. But maybe then some people would still be alive."

"And people wouldn't be bowing to you."

"That too."

Victor shook his head. "You're always looking at the dark side of things, Mars. We've won a victory. The portal is sealed. You healed Antises, at least for now. And now we're all working together. Plus, you're King of all Antises."

"Ugh. Don't remind me." Marshal slumped down in his camp chair. "I can put on a mask in front of the others, but not you, Victor. Even Talinir: I had to be King in front of him to get him to go on that mission. I hate this."

Victor leaned forward. "Look, your goal is to get rid of the power, right?"

Marshal rubbed one of his scars. "I suppose. I mean, I want to end the Laws of Cursings and Bindings. I'm only guessing that will mean the Lords and I all lose our powers. I can't know for sure."

"Let's say it does." Victor rolled his hand, palm upward. "Then you only have to be King until that's done. After that, you won't have any power. Nobody will insist you stay King. Hailstones, maybe we won't have a King any more. Or Lords."

"You're right." Marshal sighed. "I haven't… I mean, I guess I just haven't had the time to think about what might happen after all this is done. What will I do if I'm free of… everything?"

Victor spread his hands. "I have no idea what I'll do. And that's the beauty of it. We can do anything! Go anywhere! Without any assassins or soldiers or gods chasing us!"

Marshal smiled. "Thanks, Vic. Without you, I don't think—"

The tent flap swept open and Adhi entered, followed by his brother Nijamu. Marshal lost the smile and straightened up. Time to put on the mask again.

"I saw the messenger leaving," Adhi said. "Was that the last one?"

"Yes." Marshal stood. "The one to Lord Tyrr. It was the hardest of the letters to write. I don't know how he'll respond."

"If he is a true Lord, he will come," Nijamu said.

"You don't know much about Lord Tyrr, do you?" Victor asked.

Marshal looked down at the map of Antises again. He had stared at it every day for weeks now. "We need all of them if it is to work," he said. "Your father will come. Lord Rajwir, I am sure, will come."

"Throw in you and Volraag, and you've got four," Victor said. "See? Things aren't that bad."

"If even one doesn't come, it will fail," Marshal argued. "Lord Tyrr hates Varioch with a passion. I can only assume that includes me. Plus, he's no doubt still at war. The Durunim will be invading Rasna, if they haven't already."

"The army here still has not moved," Adhi reported. "We do not know what they are waiting for."

"Every day they give us is one day closer to winning," Victor said. "Right?"

Marshal nodded, though it certainly didn't feel that way.

"What of Arazu?" Nijamu asked. "Who possesses the Lord's power now?"

"Seri's trying to find that out," Marshal said.

•••••

Seri tossed the stone in the fire and waited. Ixchel stood nearby, as always, but no one else came close. Dravid still slept, and Jamana watched over him. Marshal and the others were busy making plans. The rest of their Kuktarman escorts were frightened of Ixchel. Seri didn't blame them. But it did mean she had a lot of time to herself lately.

Her father still traveled with them, and she could see him at any time. And she could join Marshal's planning meetings. Yet he would always ask questions, questions she couldn't answer yet.

"What is it, my daughter?" The voice of Lady Lilitu came from the fire. Or the stone. Seri still hadn't decided which.

"Good evening, my Lady," Seri said. She did not know if she would ever call the Lady "mother." It did not feel right, not when she had spent her entire life calling another woman by that title. "We continue on our way toward Simbala. We should arrive within a week."

"That is good, but hardly news requiring a special report," Lilitu replied. "What is troubling you?"

"How are the repairs going?" Seri didn't want to get to her main questions yet, and she was genuinely anxious about her home.

"It is slow work, but the people are eager to rebuild. I will not lie to you: it will take many months, perhaps many years, before Sandu-Emuq is restored to its previous glory. We had only begun to repair the damage done to the palace by Volraag before the earthquake struck."

Seri winced. The reference to Volraag could not fail to remind her of Lord Enuru's death. She knew Lady Lilitu remained in mourning, even through all that had happened since. It felt like a lot of time had passed, but it had only been two months. In her mind's eye, Seri could see her sitting beside her Lord's throne, clothed in black.

"While I delight in our conversations, Seri, I do have limited time available."

"Oh. I'm sorry. Sorry." Seri gathered her thoughts. "The King wished me to ask you again if you have any new information regarding the lost power of Arazu's Lord."

"Should I learn anything else, I will let you know immediately, Seri." The Lady's voice grew colder. "You know this."

"Yes, I do. I just... he asked, and I promised I'd ask you again. It's weighing heavily on his mind, you know."

"As it does on mine." The Lady sighed. "I do not yet know this young King of yours, Seri. He acquitted himself well enough during the earthquake, but it was a narrow thing. I hope he is strong enough for what must come next."

"We all do."

"Will there be anything else, my child?"

Seri shook her head, then remembered the Lady couldn't see her. "Oh, uh, no, my Lady. That's all for now. I will check in with you again when I, um, have any other news."

"Farewell for now, child." The voice ended.

Ixchel reached into the fire with a stick and pushed the stone out of the embers. Seri watched it cool. She never knew if the connection with the Lady ended at her decision, or not until the stone grew cold again. She had examined the stone many times in the past few weeks, with both her regular vision and her star-sight. But she still had little understanding as to how the magic worked. She wondered if the Master Mages used something similar for their communication from Zes Sivas to the six lands.

"Have you checked on Dravid?" she asked, the thought suddenly occurring to her.

"A few moments ago," Ixchel said. "There is no change, though perhaps you could tell something different."

Seri nodded. Ixchel never said it, but she somehow expected Seri to heal Dravid, to wake him from his sleep. But like the stone, it was a magic beyond her understanding. Or if not magic, something with Dravid's body the doctors did not grasp. The thought pained her.

When they reached Zes Sivas, she would beg the Master Mages to investigate Dravid's condition. The old King claimed Dravid was necessary to fix Antises. With that as their motivation, surely the Masters could solve this problem.

Of course, she still had no idea how to fix Antises. It had something to do with the Passing, and what had occurred when Marshal stopped the earthquake. But beyond that, she felt ignorant. Marshal expected her to figure it out, and she would... somehow. The book Jamana talked about would probably help, once she got a look at it.

Seri picked up the communication stone. At least she had some time to think about the problem. They would not reach Zes Sivas for at least a week, depending on how long they paused in Simbala.

"At least we're getting to see all different parts of Antises," she said aloud.

"I've seen little to impress me thus far," Ixchel said.

Seri whirled on her, mouth open and about to snap something... and saw the beginnings of a smile on Ixchel's face. She closed her mouth and chuckled. "Careful, Ixchel. You might develop a sense of humor."

"If my Lady requires it."

•••••

Marshal fell into his cot, exhausted. It seemed to be happening virtually every day since leaving the high place. When they weren't traveling, his time became eaten up by meetings of various kinds: discussing scout reports or troop movements, trying to decide on methods to appeal to the other Lords, or just visiting those who wanted to meet the new King. When he could find the time, he also checked on Dravid, or talked with Seri about their plans. And at least once a day, he insisted on taking some time alone to work on his magic.

Tomorrow, they would arrive at Simbala. Then he would need to spend time with Lord Meluhha before setting out on the final journey to Zes Sivas. At least on board the ship, he would be able to rest. Maybe.

He longed for the days when his exhaustion came only from physical exertion. The hard work he did back home in Drusa's Crossing. The days of walking with Aelia and Victor. The hours of training with Talinir.

Come to think of it, he needed to spend some time in sword practice. He had neglected that particular skill lately. And he even had a new sword! He couldn't believe he had barely glanced at it since the battle with Curasir. He would correct that in the morning. Right now, he needed sleep.

But his thoughts wouldn't leave the sword. Where had Curasir found it? Was it forged by the Eldanim? He should have shown it to Talinir and asked him before sending him away. He chided himself for overlooking the obvious.

If he hadn't been awake thinking about the sword, he might not have noticed the assassin in time.

The blade came down at his neck. Almost without thinking of it, Marshal triggered his power, not from his hands, but from his neck and the surrounding area. The blade was repelled, but did not go far.

Marshal rolled out of his cot and scrambled to his feet. He looked back to see his attacker.

One of the Durunim stood in his tent, holding a strange dagger. In fact, everything about this assassin felt wrong, confusing Marshal's senses, both physical and magical. Like all the Eldanim and Durunim, the attacker looked taller than his physical body appeared. But in addition to that, this one did not seem to be in one place at a time. His body shifted back and forth, but Marshal couldn't tell where it physically stood. Magically, Marshal couldn't sense him at all, as if this particular Durunim held no magic within him. Yet that couldn't be true.

The dagger, forged of some sickly green metal, vibrated on its own. Some kind of liquid dripped from its tip. If the blade managed to cut him at all, it would probably be a very bad thing.

"Victor!" he shouted, then remembered his friend would be guarding Volraag at this time. Still, some of Adhi's guards would be close enough to hear him.

He directed a burst of power at the Durunim. And punched a hole through the side of his tent, missing the assassin completely. As his attacker moved, Marshal had even more trouble identifying its location. The confusion of his senses grew worse with the motion. Queasiness threatened his insides.

The dagger swept in towards his stomach. He fell back into one of Talinir's defensive stances and managed to shove the attack to the side, but not by much. Up close, he caught a glimpse of the Durunim's eyes. They glowed with a dim red fire in the midst of his colorless face.

Voices approached outside.

Marshal needed space, but too much power would harm those who rushed to help him. He released a burst of magic in all directions. It should be enough to drive the assassin back without damaging anyone else. "Stay back!" he yelled.

His attack worked well enough, but only for a moment. The assassin fell back to the tent wall before falling to the floor. The fall confused Marshal. That shouldn't have happened. And then the assassin rolled across the ground with blinding speed and stabbed.

The dagger pierced through the top of Marshal's left foot. Pain lanced up through his body, but it also gave him focus. In that exact moment, he knew the precise location of his attacker. He unleashed a massive burst of power straight down at him, not holding anything back. A cloud of dust filled the tent. After a few seconds, Marshal allowed a tiny burst of power to radiate out from himself, pushing the dust away.

His attacker lay completely still, driven into the ground by the force of Marshal's power. He could not possibly have survived. Marshal grabbed the dagger and pulled it free from his foot.

Before he could contact those outside, Marshal felt something climbing up his leg. In a horrific instant, he realized it was not climbing up his skin, but inside it. The dagger had delivered some kind of magical poison which was already working its way up. He didn't want to think about what would happen if it reached his vital organs.

But Marshal's control of his own power had been growing in leaps and bounds since they left the Starlit Realm. He dropped the dagger, grabbed his own leg above the knee and focused. Vibrations ran through his lower leg and foot. At first, it did nothing to halt the rise of the poison. The toxin twisted through his shin and approached his knee.

Marshal concentrated. If the Durunim had used a traditional poison, he might not have been able to stop it. But this poison consisted of some kind of magic, and it vibrated. Every vibration could be countered, Seri said. Marshal cycled rapidly through various patterns until he found the right one. He let a gentle surge of his power flow through his leg until it pushed back on the poison. He amplified its power and pushed. The toxin retreated down into his foot, which still hurt like fire.

With one last burst of power, Marshal drove the poison back out through the wound. It erupted from the stab in his foot and flowed onto the floor. It pooled into a small circle, where it continued to tremble.

"Come in!" Marshal called to those waiting.

Nijamu burst into the tent, followed by two of his soldiers. He stared at the crushed assassin for a moment, then noticed Marshal's bleeding foot. "Send for a healer," he ordered, and one of the soldiers slipped back out.

Marshal picked up his camp chair and sat down. He lifted his foot and put pressure against the wound. He could hold it there until someone arrived who knew what they were doing.

"I am sorry, my King," Nijamu said. "We should have anticipated that the enemy would try to strike at you."

Marshal looked at the dead assassin. "I don't think…" He paused. "I don't know if they thought this would actually work. I think they did it just to show me they could, and to test our abilities."

"Our?"

Marshal nodded, thinking. "I got lucky here, but what if they send these kind of assassins against the other Lords?"

The soldier returned with a bustling healer who hurried to Marshal's side. As he bent and took over dealing with the wound, Marshal lifted his head.

"Put more guards around Volraag," he ordered. "And find some more messengers. I have new letters to write to the other Lords." He looked down at the floor. "Find someone who knows how to handle dangerous things. I want to send them all a sample of that poison to show them what we're up against."

He reached for paper and ink. It looked like he wouldn't be getting a good night's sleep after all.

(((4)))

Talinir came to a stop and looked out over Lake Litanu. From here, travel would be easier in the Starlit Realm, though not without danger. He would have to pass near Zes Sivas, always a hazardous location. But if he stayed in this realm, he would need a ship.

Talinir disliked ships. In fact, he disliked the entire concept of traveling on water. He would never tell Marshal or the others this, of course, but Eldanim did not like water at all. Talinir could swim, a rarity among his people, but he didn't like it.

He could not open doorways to the Otherworld, like Marshal could, with his warpsteel sword. That very act fascinated him, but he needed no help. He had his own method for shifting himself, though it wasn't as easy.

He sat on the shore and crossed his legs. Then he closed both eyes, shutting himself off from two worlds. He took several deep breaths, steadying himself. And then he opened his right eye.

The Starlit Realm filled his vision. A part of him was always there. The Eldanim walked between worlds, and their essence always occupied both to some degree. It had always been so, except for that time Marshal dragged him into the Otherworld completely.

The trick now consisted of shifting his essence more into the Otherworld than this one. It took time, little by little. But once he passed the halfway point, it would happen almost at once. It was like a balancing beam that, once shifted enough, flipped over.

Talinir kept his focus on the stars, the true stars that lit the realm. Marshal always wanted to know more about the stars, but Talinir would never tell him all. To the Eldanim, the stars were sacred, a part of their existence, and not something to be discussed with humans.

Despite his fascination with them, Marshal would never truly understand. He couldn't.

Ah. Talinir felt the tipping point. His essence flowed now, shifting, shifting… done.

Talinir, the Eldani warden, stood to his feet and opened both eyes. The desolation and beauty of the Starlit Realm stretched out before him in all of its color, while the primary world faded. He strode forward. No time to waste now.

● ● ● ● ●

The sound of a horn woke Marshal after far too little sleep. Despite spending days with the Kuktarman army, he still hadn't seen that horn or its blower. Why did he have to start the day so early?

He groaned and swung his feet over the side of his cot. As soon as they touched the ground, he yelped. It would take some time for the wound in his foot to heal. And he faced one more day of walking. He didn't look forward to it.

He reached down and picked up the sword which always lay beside his bed. He had promised himself to look at it again. Maybe he had enough time before the soldiers came to take down his tent.

Finding a scabbard to fit the sword had been difficult. Adhi managed to locate a broadsword's scabbard, not the usual style for Kuktarman soldiers. Marshal's sword fit into it for the most part, but not very well. After examining it, Adhi summoned a craftsman who took careful measurements of the sword. He was sent on ahead to Simbala to arrange for a custom scabbard.

The sword did resemble a broadsword in that it was straight and long, tapering to a point. A double fuller ran down each side of the blade. It did not look exactly like the warpsteel swords Marshal knew, but he was convinced it must be similar, Eldani-made at the very least. After all, it channeled magic even better than warpsteel. When Marshal rested his hand against the blade, he could feel power stored up inside it, vibrating back against his palm. If he hadn't seen what the sword accomplished back at the high place, he would have worried it might shatter itself.

He turned the blade and looked at the hilt again. The leather grip looked fairly new, much newer than the sword itself, certainly. It felt comfortable in his hand, but could be better. The craftsman had muttered something about re-wrapping it.

The cross guard curved upward in a gentle arc. It looked like steel with gold inlays. The gold might have formed letters at one time, but use had worn them down. Marshal couldn't make out what they might be.

The pommel, though… he remembered seeing it when he first fought Curasir in the Otherworld. Even then, broken and battered, he wondered about it. Gold coated the round pommel, but he didn't believe it to be solid gold. He studied the image of a strange creature carved into the gold, still distinct and visible, unlike the cross guard. Marshal touched it, tracing the creature's curved neck and sinuous body, almost like a snake. But no snake he knew possessed a pair of wings like this beast. For some reason, the image looked familiar. He couldn't imagine where he would have seen it before.

Victor pushed into the tent. "Coming with us today, Your Highness?"

"Please don't call me that. Not you, Vic." Marshal groaned.

"All right, You can address me that way instead." Victor looked at the sword in Marshal's hands. "That's the one you took from Curasir, right?"

Marshal held it up and let Victor take it. "It's got to be Eldani made, but it's not like anything I've seen."

"Huh." Victor swung it through the air. "The balance is incredible. And it almost seems like it's vibrating."

"It's storing magic," Marshal explained. "It can hold an unbelievable amount. Even with all we did back there, I don't think we reached the limits of what it can do."

Victor pointed the sword, closed an eye and stared down the blade. "Maybe the Durunim made it. They used to be Eldanim, right?"

"I don't know. That doesn't feel… right. If it had been made by evil hands, I think I would feel that. And I wouldn't like it."

Victor raised his eyebrows, then handed the sword back. "Too mystical for me. Maybe you should have Seri look at it."

"Have you ever shown her your flail?"

"No, never thought of it."

Marshal got up and gingerly put weight on his injured foot. It was not pleasant. He took a step and grimaced. "How much do I have to walk today?" For much of the trip, he could ride in one of Adhi's chariots, but some walking would still be involved.

Victor made a face. "That doesn't look good. I'll go get the healer. Maybe he can wrap your foot up enough to—I don't know—make it easier to walk on?"

Marshal took a few more steps and sat down on his camp chair. "I'll take whatever I can get."

Victor nodded and left the tent.

Marshal looked over the sword one more time. No, it could not be Durunim-make. In fact… he hefted the sword and moved it around in the air again. No. This had been made for human hands.

Well, wherever it came from, it was his now. And with luck and maybe Theon's blessing, he would use it to save Antises.

●●●●●

Talinir arrived on the far shore of Lake Litanu without significant incident. The journey past Zes Sivas had been tense at one point: no less than four tunaldi roamed near the island for some reason. But he made it through without even drawing his sword. Amazing what a warden could do while alone and at the height of his powers.

A new stage of the journey lay before him, though he remained in the Starlit Realm for now. The open portal was only about a day's journey ahead now. He didn't know which world would be the most hazardous. Durunim probably prowled on both sides.

Marshal wanted to know what was happening here. Talinir could think of only one way to get him the information, but he hoped not to use it. Perhaps the portal had collapsed on itself. Maybe the Durunim didn't have the numbers to invade on this side, as they did at the Kuktarma portal.

His hopes proved groundless. One day later, he looked out over his worst fears.

The Durunim had not merely marched an army into Varioch and Rasna. They had come to stay. The portal on Talinir's side appeared little different from the other two portals. But in the primary world, a huge construction project had been underway.

The Durunim and their human slaves had excavated the portal completely and built a wide road down to its opening. The road led up into a fortress.

Talinir knew his own people's construction capabilities, but even he was impressed with how much the Durunim had built in such a short time. The portal had been open for a few months, but the fortress looked like something that would take a couple of years to construct under ideal conditions.

Then again, to the Durunim and their masters, these were almost ideal conditions. The armies of Varioch and Rasna, weakened by their own battles, could not stand against these invaders. And with Volraag gone, only Lord Tyrr remained with enough power to cause them any problems. If he brought his full power to bear against this enemy, he could do significant damage. Yet Talinir saw no evidence that he had done so.

The fortress looked to be at least equal to the citadels of Zes Sivas in size, but with much more open space. Within that space and also in large sections outside the fortress, dozens of tents had been erected. If each tent supported two-to-four of the Durunim, then the army… must be at least fifty thousand strong and growing. Within the Starlit Realm, Talinir watched more soldiers approaching, carrying more equipment and building supplies. The city he and Marshal's grandfather had seen must be emptied out by now. Between this army and the one in Kuktarma, surely there could not be more Durunim.

Talinir watched the enemy carefully, then shifted to another point where he could see from a different angle. So far, he had not seen any of the so-called gods, the golden-skinned rulers of the Durunim. They had to be here somewhere. Perhaps inside the fortress.

Talinir considered entering the fortress in the Starlit Realm, then crossing over into the primary world inside an empty room. The only difficulty with the plan would be escaping. If he were seen, he could not escape back to the Starlit Realm fast enough to avoid being caught. Fighting his way out of an entire fortress of Durunim and potentially one or more of their masters would be an impossible task, even for him.

Based on his understanding of troop readiness, it looked like this army was about to march any day now. The capitals of both Varioch and Rasna would not be able to stand against them. Lord Tyrr might be able to hold off for a while, but if he were confronted by a god even remotely like Murdak, he would have no chance.

Talinir had seen enough. Marshal needed to know about all this.

(((5)))

Lord Meluhha bent over backward to make Marshal welcome in Simbala. In addition to his sons' testimony, he had heard from many of his officers regarding Marshal's actions at the high place. When Marshal and his company arrived at the city, the Lord came out himself, along with his remaining four sons, to meet them at the gates.

For his part, Marshal found the whole thing ludicrous. He was tired, dirty, and limping from the stab wound in his foot. But Lord Meluhha and his sons actually bowed to him.

"I don't know how to react to this," he whispered to Adhi.

"Just say 'thank you for your welcome' and keep going," Adhi answered.

Marshal tried that. But Lord Meluhha would not allow him to enter the city without first proclaiming his presence to all of the crowd. Dozens, maybe hundreds of Kuktarmans gathered along the street, applauding and pushing each other, straining to get a glimpse of the new King.

By the time they finally reached the Lord's palace, Marshal was dead on his feet, even though he'd ridden the chariot for most of the trip. He begged for time to recover from the journey. Fortunately, Lord Meluhha accepted his plea and did not press for immediate conferences. He did insist on seeing his two sons at once.

After being guided to a (far too lavish) room, Marshal tumbled into the bed. The servant promised a hot bath would be ready for him in a few minutes, then scurried away.

The few minutes turned out to be less than two, and Marshal found himself led into a side room where a steaming tub awaited. The bath soothed his aching muscles, though it took some time before he could bear to put his wounded foot into the water. He completely forgot the scar on his back until he sat back and water flowed over it. While not as recent as the foot injury, it was much larger. The shock of water against it almost made him jump out of the tub.

When he finally did emerge from the water, the same servant offered to dress him. Marshal ordered him out of the room. The servant retreated, suggesting Marshal join "his Lordship and sons" for dinner once he clothed himself. A few minutes later, Marshal regretted his hasty order. The torn and stained clothes he had been wearing since the high place were gone. In their place, he found new clothes, made of finer material and brighter colors. The loose-fitting pants were obvious —at least they came with a belt—but he despaired of understanding the rest of them. He had just managed to find a place to put his arms inside what he assumed to be a kind of shirt, when a soft knock came from his door.

"Come in!" He turned, hoping it would be the servant coming back to check on him. He yanked on the shirt, but it did not come down, leaving most of his torso exposed.

Instead, the door opened and Seri stood there, Ixchel behind her.

"Oh, ah…" Seri stammered and looked away.

"I'm sorry," Marshal said. "I'm having trouble figuring these clothes out."

She looked back for a brief instant. "Well… you're halfway there, at least."

"I don't think so." Marshal furrowed his brow. "I don't seem to have this shirt right, and there are two more things here. Are they more shirts? I don't understand this at all."

"Oh dear." Seri put her hand to her mouth. "I don't… I mean…"

"You got to keep your mage robes. Why couldn't they leave my old clothes?"

Seri stepped into the room at last, but her eyes darted every direction but at him. "Because they were falling apart! Even after Adhi gave you new clothes, you still ended up tearing them up." Ixchel moved in behind her, a half-smile on her usual stoic face. Her clothing remained the same, of course. Marshal couldn't imagine her wearing anything different.

"I was practicing my powers," Marshal complained. Could this get any more awkward?

"Marshal! Are you ready yet? I'm hungry!" Tich sauntered into the room. She still dressed like a sailor, lacking only her usual coil of rope.

Marshal could tell her clothes had been washed at least, if they weren't completely new. She stopped on seeing Seri.

"Marshal is… having difficulty with his wardrobe," Seri said, fighting a smile.

"So I see." Tich pushed past Seri and went to Marshal's side. "For starters, you've got the pants on backward."

Marshal looked down. "I do?"

"And this thing goes on after the others." Tich took hold of the shirt and yanked it off. "Go ahead and flip the pants around first."

"Uh…"

Tich rolled her eyes. "You too? Where were you men raised? Fine. I'll turn around." She spun and faced the door. Seri's eyes almost exploded out of her head before she whirled around also. Ixchel was the last to turn.

"It's not like I didn't see you in the Otherworld, with your clothes in shreds," Tich grumbled. "And then when you finally bathed in the stream."

Seri gasped.

"You weren't there when I bathed!" Marshal exclaimed.

"That's what he thinks," Tich said, elbowing Seri.

"Ugh. I've got the pants right now. Show me how to do the rest of this."

Tich turned around and came back to him. Seri kept her eyes on the door.

"All right, you put this on first…" Tich helped him into something like a thin vest. "Then this one." The second shirt had long sleeves, but no front to it, and only half a back. "And this one goes over all of them." The third, which he had thought to be the more normal shirt, had short sleeves, half of a front, and no back. "These aren't the most traditional Kuktarman clothes, but I'm guessing they tried to find something at least vaguely similar to your Varioch sensibilities." She tugged on the last shirt a little and stepped back to look at him. Marshal slipped on a pair of surprisingly comfortable sandals to complete the outfit. Even his wounded foot felt good.

"I'm good, Seri," he called. She turned around and looked him over too. Ixchel gave him a cursory glance.

"You look… good," Seri said. Marshal looked down at himself and almost agreed. To his surprise, the clothing felt comfortable. He had expected the multiple sleeves and odd combination would be much more awkward. He flexed a little and looked up to see Seri watching him. Had she been blushing? It was hard to tell with her darker skin.

Tich noticed him looking at Seri and put her arm through his, almost like she was claiming him. Was that how this situation was shaping up? He had so little experience in relationships.

"He needs a shave and a haircut," Tich said. She reached up and brushed his facial hair where it grew across one of his scars.

"No question," Seri agreed.

"Are you two done evaluating my appearance?"

"You're the King now," Seri pointed out. "Your appearance matters, especially in a place like this."

Marshal sighed. In all his worries about being seen as the King, his personal appearance hadn't even occurred to him. "I feel like Forerunner," he griped.

"You look nothing like him," Seri assured. And to be fair, the colors weren't nearly as outrageous. The pants were black, and the shirts were combinations of dark crimson, gold and deep blue.

Two more items remained lying on the bed. His sword lay next to a new scabbard. Marshal lifted it and stared. Made of black hardened leather, it began and ended with polished steel. In fact, looking closely at the steel, he saw a pattern in the steel itself, like raindrops. At first, he thought the black leather had no design, but when he turned it, the light glinted off gold. He peered closer and saw that somehow, an artist had replicated the flying creature carved in the sword's pommel. The design was pressed into the leather, with some kind of gold thread embedded in the lines. Marshal picked up the sword and slid it into the scabbard. The cross guard fit perfectly against the top, almost snapping into place. A black sword belt completed the design. He attached it to his pants, letting the sword hang on his left.

"Now can we go eat?" Tich asked.

The servant returned at exactly that moment. "I've come to escort Your Highness to dinner," he announced. He glanced over the three girls. "And your, ah, companions."

Marshal opened his mouth to say something, but Tich elbowed him. "Let's go, Your Highness." Somehow, she made the title sound even more ridiculous.

Seri fell in on Marshal's other side as they walked. Ixchel followed. The servant led them through several far-too-wide hallways until they reached an enormous dining hall. Marshal stared about him at the crowd of people, both official and servants, tables filled with food, and elaborate tapestries hanging on every wall. He tried to get a look at some of them, but Lord Meluhha rushed to greet him.

Marshal found himself pulled away from the girls and led to the main table. Lord Meluhha re-introduced his sons, as well as a number of officials. Marshal was sure he would never remember any of their names. The Lord made Marshal sit in the seat of honor, between himself and a young woman whom Marshal had not met. Meluhha's wife and sons, including Adhi and Nijamu, occupied the rest of the table's seats.

"May I present my daughter, Kumara," Lord Meluhha said, taking her hand and smiling. "Daughter, this is our new King."

"I am honored, Princess," Marshal said, bowing his head.

She giggled. "I'm not a princess," she protested. Kumara looked remarkably like Adhi in her facial structure, though she wasn't quite as slender as he. Marshal thought her quite attractive. Maybe this meal wouldn't be as awkward as he'd feared. Then again, he was sure his own awkwardness would be enough.

He looked about and saw most of his friends at another nearby table. Tich gave him a jaunty wave. Victor had something in his mouth, but was talking away with Jamana. Seri sat beside her father and Ixchel. Marshal wished he were sitting at that table, in poorer clothes. He almost wished he still possessed his curse. At least he wouldn't feel so awkward. No one had ever cared if he ignored them back then.

"Where are you from, Your Highness?" Kumara asked.

A servant placed a plate of food in front of him before he could answer. Lord Meluhha sat down and insisted Marshal eat something before answering the question. He obligingly took a bite of something he didn't recognize. Flames exploded in his mouth, or so it seemed. He struggled to keep a straight face and not spit the food out. Moisture gathered in his eyes. He smiled and swallowed.

"Tasty," he gasped through the pain.

Lord Meluhha laughed and clapped him on the back. After that, he allowed Kumara to take over the conversation, though he steered it away from anything negative. Kumara inquired about Marshal's family, his home, how he had been raised, and so on. Between bites of food far spicier than he was accustomed to, Marshal managed to answer most of them. He knew he must sound like an uncultured peasant to these people, especially with his awkward voice. Victor told him he was getting better, but he still struggled with pronunciations at times. At least they didn't expect him to give a speech.

When the meal finally ended, Marshal pleaded exhaustion and was allowed to return to his room, though Kumara appeared disappointed. Once there, he struggled to remove the fancy clothes. He tossed them on a padded chair and climbed into the bed.

Being King was too complicated.

•••••

Talinir looked around. The office and hallways surrounding him were empty. Now was the time. He sat cross-legged on the ground of the Starlit Realm and closed his eyes. Once again, he began the process of shifting his essence across the worlds.

This time, he opened his left eye and embraced his presence in the primary world. In this particular instance, he appeared inside the Lord's palace in Reman.

He timed his transition perfectly. He had only just stood and dusted off his clothes when the office door opened. A man in a red cape stopped in the doorway, mouth hanging open.

"Greetings," Talinir said. "I am Talinir, warden of the Eldanim. I am familiar with your Lord Volraag. I have an urgent message to deliver." He recalled all that Marshal had told him of Varioch's military. "You are Otioch, yes?"

The officer's mouth closed. He looked up and down the hall before answering. "I am Otioch. Did Lord Volraag send you to help us? Where is he?"

"Your Lord is on his way to Zes Sivas even now, on a mission to save all of Antises. But you are threatened by an implacable enemy. I have seen their numbers and must report it."

"We have scouts watching them at all times," Otioch said, a look of annoyance crossing his face. "How do I know you aren't in league with them?"

"Because you are not dead," Talinir responded. "I have no desire to harm you. And my report is not for you, but for your Lord and those with him that will be arriving at Zes Sivas shortly."

"I still have only your word to go on." Otioch's hand had slipped to his sword hilt. "And our invaders look an awful lot like you do."

"Then you are blind." Talinir spread his hands. "Again, if I wanted to cause you problems, I would do so. All I want to do is send the message, and then I will leave. You can even hear the message yourself and add to it, if you like."

Otioch nodded slowly. "I will summon a messenger and have a

swift boat prepared."

"That will not be necessary." Talinir took a step toward Otioch. "And far too slow. For now, please take me to the highest-ranking mage in this palace."

(((6)))

"Time is of the essence," Marshal insisted. "We must leave for Zes Sivas immediately."

Lord Meluhha spread his arms. "I cannot drop everything and go, not when this deadly enemy stalks our land."

"The enemy army won't even matter if we don't heal Antises. It has to be our first priority." Marshal nervously pulled one of his shirts straighter. The outfit today differed only slightly from yesterday's, but he still didn't fully understand it. He glanced around the council room at the others gathered around the table. They made an eclectic group outside of the Lord and four of his sons. Seri, Ixchel, Victor, and Jamana all crowded in with him.

"We have just received word that the enemy is starting to move," Nijamu reported. "Right now, it looks like they might be heading this way, but it's too early to tell for sure."

"Let them come!" another of the sons (fourth?) declared. "We have now assembled the largest army Kuktarma has ever seen! Ever since the earthquake, we have been gathering." He pointed to the map on the table. "Arazu has agreed to send troops as well. We should outnumber this other world's army by three or four to one!"

"It could be ten to one and it wouldn't matter!" Victor stepped up from behind Marshal. "The Durunim are ferocious fighters. Do not think of them like human opponents. And beyond that, you have to deal with the gods. And some of them are worth thousands of your soldiers."

"They can't be all that powerful," a military leader argued.

"Have you seen your Lord in action?" Seri asked. "He is easily worth several hundred soldiers or more, if he unleashes his power, isn't he?"

"Yes, of course, but—"

Seri pointed to Marshal. "The King's power is over three times that. And one of these gods, Murdak, defeated him."

No one spoke. They all understood the implications.

"And there's another one that kills with a mere touch," Victor said. "And another who controls… plants, wasn't it?" He looked to Seri.

"Yes, plants. And we don't even know how many more there are, or what their powers might be. We don't stand a chance in a straight-up fight right now."

Lord Meluhha placed a palm on the table. All eyes turned to him. "On the one hand, you tell me the enemy army doesn't matter, but then you tell me we cannot defeat them. Which is it?"

"It's both," Marshal said. "If Antises falls apart on its own, then they won't matter. But if we heal Antises, then maybe we can—"

"Do what? If I understand your plan aright, won't we be abandoning our power, at least temporarily? What will we use to fight them then?"

Marshal closed his mouth. He hadn't thought of that.

"If I may…" Adhi spoke up. Everyone looked to him. "Only a few hours ago, I was informed of another faction in play to fight against the gods. Jamana and I will be joining with this faction and doing what we can to slow the enemy down or defeat them outright."

"What is this faction?" his father demanded.

"I have been asked not to discuss it in public, but I will enlighten you further in private, father."

Lord Meluhha did not look convinced. He stared at his youngest son for a few moments before turning back to Marshal. "Here is what I propose: you may depart tomorrow, if you so desire. I will come and join you, but not until I have a better idea of the enemy's movements, our troop disposition, and this… faction. I cannot consider giving up power or taking it away from my people while they are under attack."

Marshal tried to hide his disappointment. He had been counting on Lord Meluhha to be the easiest to persuade. He was the only one of the Lords Marshal would be able to see in person. And he'd failed completely to convince him.

The plan was off to a rocky start.

•••••

Jamana met Adhi in the hallway. "Faction?"

Adhi glanced around to be sure no one could hear them. "What was I supposed to say to everyone? That a thousand-year-old mage has come to fight the gods?"

"It is not that much crazier than everything else that has happened, I am thinking."

Adhi sighed. "In some respects, you are correct. Yet I could not tell my brothers and the military leaders that our hope of defense lies in one old man."

"And two acolytes. And an assassin." Jamana chuckled.

"I will try to explain it to my father later, but I think I'll leave out the part about the assassin. Father must be persuaded to go to Zes Sivas." Adhi glanced around. "For now, let us go and check on… our faction."

The two acolytes descended to the palace's lowest level and made their way to a particular room no one else seemed to know about. When they entered, they found Kishin the assassin sitting by the fire, along with Nehesy, the thousand-year-old mage.

Kishin looked up at Adhi. "Can you take me back to my cell? At least there, I didn't have to listen to this old man go on about grace and mercy."

Nehesy shook his head. "You still do not understand. So sad."

"You told me I had choices and to seek redemption. So I did."

"By turning yourself in to the father of one of your victims?" Nehesy shook his head. "Redemption is a gift, Kishin. Not something you can earn."

"Then why do you want my help?"

"You can still do some good with your life." Nehesy raised a finger. "It does not erase the evil you have done, but while you still live, you can make a difference in the lives of others."

Kishin snorted.

"I will be telling my father about you," Adhi said to Nehesy. "Knowing you are fighting for us is the only thing that may persuade him to go to Zes Sivas."

The old man nodded. "It is well. You may do that. But do so quickly. Unless I miss my guess, the gods are on the move again. We shall have to leave as soon as possible."

"How do you know that?" Jamana wondered.

"I can feel many things in ways that are too hard to explain."

"Admit it," Kishin said. "You enjoy being mysterious."

"When you have lived as old as I have, you find enjoyment where you can," Nehesy said. "Sometimes what I consider hilarious will only baffle you young people. And the reverse is true, I'm sure."

Seri and Ixchel burst into the room. "Oh good," Seri exclaimed. "You're still here."

"You'll be leaving before we do," Jamana said.

"I meant him," Seri said, pointing at Nehesy.

"You wanted to see me?"

Seri stopped next to Jamana. "You were there, weren't you?"

"To which 'there' are you referring?"

"Oh, ah, when they created the Laws of Cursings and Bindings." Seri looked ready to jump on whatever answer she received.

Nehesy fingered the arm of his chair. "I was not," he said after a moment.

Seri took a step back. "But I thought… your mother was part of it, wasn't she?"

Nehesy nodded. "Yes, she was. But unfortunately for all of us, I was not yet a part of things. In fact, I was traveling, on my way to Antises from a distant land."

"You've been outside Antises?" Jamana asked.

"All of us in the early days came from outside Antises." Nehesy looked off into the distance. "Akhenadom led us here, all of us. I returned to let others know of this wonderful land. Most would not listen to me, but I brought a few more back."

"So you don't know how they did it," Seri said. Her shoulders slumped.

"I was not there… but I do know much of what took place." Nehesy's gaze returned to her. "You are on the right path already, you and Marshal. You came near to it at the high place."

"I thought so!" Seri exclaimed. "It just seemed to work so well!"

"The Lords must give up their power," Nehesy said. "That will not be easy. And then, you must guide Marshal into the Heart of Fire."

"Guide him to the Heart of Fire? But he's already seen it now."

"I did not say 'to.' I said 'into.'"

Seri wrinkled her brow. "I… don't know what that means."

"Nor do I. I am not a King. Or Lord, for that matter."

"But you're a Master Mage. A High Master Mage! The only one alive, apparently. Surely you can tell me more!"

"Alas, I cannot." Nehesy picked up his staff and pulled himself to his feet. He walked to face Seri and placed a hand on her shoulder. "But I do not believe you need my help any further. You will solve the problem."

"I... I don't know that I can."

"Have faith." Nehesy smiled and turned back to the others. "Gather your things. We leave at dawn."

(((7)))

Compared to all their other travels, the trip from Simbala up the river to the coast was nothing. Even so, Marshal chafed at the slowness of the barge's progress. When he finally saw Lake Litanu stretching out before them, he let out a sigh of relief.

"That anxious to get back to those mages?" Victor asked.

"You know why I'm anxious." Marshal turned to him. "I want to get this all over with."

Victor snorted. "You don't fool me. I've known you too long."

"What are you talking about?"

"You're feeling the weight."

Marshal looked around the barge, then shrugged. "The weight of what?"

"Responsibility." Victor sat on a crate. "You don't just want to get things over with. You want to help people. To save Antises."

"Well, yeah. I mean… I want to do that." Marshal frowned. "But I want to do it soon, and be done with it."

"Because if you don't, people will be hurt." Victor pointed at him. "Your people."

"I don't have any people. I'm—"

"The King of all Antises. We're all your people now."

Marshal ran his hand along one of his facial scars. "That still doesn't feel real, you know."

"Even after the way they treated you back at the palace?"

"Now that was crazy. I'm glad to be out of there."

"You're still wearing the clothes."

Marshal looked down at himself. "What else am I supposed to wear? I never got to steal my clothes from a Remavian Guard."

"Ohhhh, that's wrong." Victor touched his red cape. "This thing is my favorite part of this entire adventure!" He looked up at Seri and Ixchel emerged from the cabin where Dravid lay. "Well, maybe second favorite."

Marshal looked at the two girls. "Really? Good luck with that."

Victor shrugged. "Girls aren't throwing themselves at me, you know. I'm not royalty."

"You should be." Marshal laughed. "So instead you decide to go after the most inaccessible woman in all Antises."

Victor jumped to his feet. "I like a challenge." He moved past Marshal, said hello to Seri, and nodded to Ixchel. He drew his sword and showed her something on the blade. She examined it while Victor kept talking.

Seri glanced back at them before joining Marshal. "I don't know what to think about that," she said softly.

Marshal shook his head. "Neither do I. How's Dravid?"

"No change. He still sleeps. He takes water and a little broth each day. If they cannot wake him at Zes Sivas, he'll… waste away. He can't keep living like this."

Marshal nodded, but didn't know what else to say. He watched Victor and Ixchel talking for a moment. His eyes wandered the rest of the barge. Near the back, Volraag paced, shadowed by four Kuktarman guards. Marshal frowned.

"Have you seen Tich?"

Seri giggled. "She's with Dravid. Before I left, she was telling him a story about a sea monster. Honestly, Marshal. Dravid told a lot of stories, but with her… it's like…"

"Like she'll come up with the most outrageous thing she can think of, just to see how you'll react," Marshal finished. "I know. She's different."

Seri looked up at him. "And she's smitten with you."

He hesitated. "We're both broken people, Seri. I think that tends to pull people together, sometimes. I don't know."

"What do you mean by 'broken'? Your scars?"

Marshal touched his face again, then sat on the crate. "No. I mean, that's part of it. Just one more pain in my life. I've lost so many, Seri. My mother. Nian. All of my soldiers. My grandfather, even though I barely met him. And I've been beaten, tortured, stabbed, poisoned. A lot of it never really heals. I have pain every day." He looked toward the back of the barge. "I can't… I don't believe I'll ever be 'normal.' Or have a normal relationship with someone."

Seri put her hands on her hips. "You have completely normal relationships with us. We're all your friends! You're not alone, Marshal."

"I know, I know." He put his face in his hands. "And I value that, more than you know. But it doesn't change all the broken parts inside." He looked up. "Theon help me, Seri. Part of me hopes that whatever happens on Zes Sivas, it kills me. No, not just part of me. Most of me."

She studied him for a few moments. "I don't know what to say, Marshal. You're not the only one who has hurts in your life, you know."

He smiled a little. "That's why Tich gets along with me. She's lost a lot too, you know."

"No, I don't know." Seri glanced toward the cabin. "She doesn't talk much to me. I think she thinks… that you like me."

Marshal didn't answer. He didn't trust himself to answer. In many ways, he did like Seri. Maybe he even loved her, if he even understood what that meant. But so did Dravid. And Seri loved him back. Marshal would never get in the way of that.

Seri shot him a quick look, as if she suspected some of the truth by his silence.

Victor and Ixchel separated with brief farewells. Victor headed toward the back of the barge to resume guarding Volraag. Ixchel joined Seri with a brief glance at Marshal.

"Listen," Seri said. "We're young. The world is falling apart around us, and bad guys are trying to kill us. If we can't enjoy the company of our friends, what do we have left?"

"A worthy death in battle," Ixchel said, patting her sword hilt.

Marshal snorted.

● ● ● ● ●

Volraag watched the interactions between Marshal and the others. Uneducated fools, all of them. Except Seri, of course. She continued to intrigue him.

His least favorite of the group arrived and dismissed the other guards. Ugh. At least the female warrior was pleasant to look at.

"How are you doing, Volraag?" Victor took a seat on a supply crate. Wonderful. He was in a cheery mood. Just as well. Volraag derived some pleasure, at least, in bringing him down.

"Tell me, Victor. Why is your friend determined to hand Antises over to the gods?"

Victor rolled his eyes. "You're not going to turn me against him, big guy. You've tried six or seven times by now."

Ten, not that Victor had noticed. "I'm serious. We should be focusing our attention on the invaders, not claiming a throne."

"Last I remember, you were the one who let the invaders in," Victor said. "And Marshal doesn't want a throne."

"Yes, I was deceived and let them in. I do not deny it. But I'm wise enough to know that I made a mistake, and to look for a way to correct it."

"Didn't you give a big speech about how the Lords were corrupt and we needed to end their rule?" Victor toyed with his flail. "Seems like you'd be happy Marshal is doing the same thing, in a way."

"Taking the power from the Lords and giving it to the gods is not my idea of solving our problems." Volraag pointed back toward Simbala. "Lord Meluhha understood that, or he'd be with us now."

Victor swung his flail back and forth like a pendulum. "He'll be coming later."

"When the Durunim army approaches Simbala, do you really think he'll leave it and run to Zes Sivas instead?"

"You talk and you talk and you talk," Victor observed. "And in all this time, you still haven't learned the basics about me."

Volraag folded his arms. "Fine. What are the basics about you, Victor?"

Victor grinned and yanked the flail chain up, bringing the swinging to a stop. "First of all, I'm just a fighter. I don't worry about the big picture stuff all that much."

"And yet—"

Victor held up his hand. "Second, Marshal's my best friend and I won't do anything against him. You'd think you would have picked up on that by now. And then there's the third thing. You of all people, should know that one."

Volraag glared. "What is it?"

Victor cocked his head. "You got some of my friends killed. Because of that, and a long list of other reasons, I will never, ever believe a single word you say." He leaned in a little. "I don't like you."

Volraag narrowed his eyes and turned away. Victor was right in one regard: trying to manipulate him was pointless at this time. But they would arrive at Zes Sivas before long. And there... he would have plenty of people to manipulate. Marshal thought he was taking Volraag to his judgment. In reality, he was taking him to his deliverance, and hopefully… his domination.

•••••

Seri spooned broth into Dravid's mouth. Some of it dribbled out of the side of his mouth and into his beard. Frustrated, Seri wiped it off as best as she could.

"He needs a shave," Ixchel observed. "When we are back on solid ground, I will find a razor and take care of it."

Seri nodded. Dravid's facial hair seemed like such a minor issue, but it was something they could control. She sighed and placed the bowl of broth on the table beside her. It rocked gently with the ship's movements.

"Ixchel, do you mind giving me a few minutes alone with him?"

"Of course, my Lady. I'll be out on deck." Ixchel paused, then patted Seri on the shoulder before leaving the cabin.

Seri had to get up to allow the door to open. Kishin's ship was much smaller than Volraag's. At least they wouldn't be here for long. With the wind back, the voyage to Zes Sivas would take no more than a day or two.

She bent over Dravid and brushed a stray bit of hair out of his face. In the last couple of weeks, he had lost so much weight. And he couldn't have been very well fed during his time in the Otherworld, either. Marshal and Tich had told Seri what they knew about it, but no one really knew all that Dravid had experienced there. She had him back, but he couldn't talk to her, couldn't make her laugh, or, or…

Seri tried not to cry again. The Master Mages would know what to do. No one achieved that level of wisdom and power without knowledge, after all.

"Dravid…" She kept her voice low, even though they were alone in the cabin. She still felt some paranoia about being overheard. "Come back to me. Please. We're doing everything we can, but you've got to do your part."

She found his hand and grasped it. As always, his hand did not react.

"Evander said we needed you to fix Antises. So you've got to wake up. I can't do it alone."

She didn't expect a response, but waited a moment, just in case.

"But maybe that's not what you need to hear: that your world needs you." She sighed again. "How about this? I need you. You're my friend and… so much more. I haven't forgotten, you know. I haven't forgotten the… kiss."

She pulled his hand up and kissed the back of it. "Or what you said to me."

She said the words back to him then, but she didn't know if he heard them. "I love you." She still didn't know if he heard. "If you wake up, I promise I will say it to you where you can hear me. See? There's another reason to wake up. Now you have to!"

She imagined his hand grasping hers with sudden strength. But it didn't happen.

"This is kind of like one of your stories of the sons of Lord Meluhha, isn't it?" She chuckled. "Only, if you were telling it, the seventh son would walk in, dispense some wisdom, and then the sleeper would awaken. True love triumphs." She glanced at the door. "Unfortunately, we left Adhi behind. You'll have to wait for Zes Sivas to hear any more wisdom."

She buried her face against his hand. "I know I don't have any."

(((8)))

Marshal watched the dock draw near. He had been inclined to sail around to the northern dock again, where the King should land. But Seri persuaded him to use the southern dock. It would be much easier to unload Dravid here and get him to the Master Mages and the healers. Everything else would be simpler too. They wouldn't have to trek all across the island just to meet people.

Instead, the people came out to meet them. A crowd of mages stood at the end of the dock, wearing several different shades of robes. At their front stood some in purple. Those were the Masters, if he remembered right.

"Back again," Tich said at his side. "Our last visit didn't last long."

"You decided that," Marshal reminded her. "I don't know if I'll ever fully understand why you jumped into my portal."

"I haven't regretted it yet." Tich leaned against him. "I do have a bad habit of jumping into things, though. Usually, it doesn't go so well. I jumped into this tavern in Woqan once…" She paused. "No, wait. I jumped out of the tavern. That's right. Someone started a fight by insulting the Lord of Ch'olan's fashion choices. I can't imagine why they'd defend such a silly thing. I had to jump through the window to escape."

"Are you sure you don't know who made the insult?" Marshal asked, smiling.

Tich looked thoughtful, then shook her head. "No. No, I don't think I do. It was a long time ago. Probably some drunken sailor I was working with at the time. What's a girl to do?"

"Not work with drunken sailors?"

"Ha! All sailors are drunk at some point. It's an occupational requirement, I think."

"I've never seen you drink anything… strong enough to get drunk."

"You haven't been around me very long. I used to…" Tich trailed off.

"Yes?"

"You know, it doesn't much matter what I used to do, does it? I drank to forget things, and now it seems some god took the memories away. What would I drink for now?"

"I can't imagine." Yet in some ways, Marshal could imagine it. He remembered his experience with Talinir's starshine drug, and what it took for Talinir to stop taking it. The Eldani warden hadn't been trying to forget anything; he just enjoyed the feeling it gave him.

"Neither can I. Oh, here comes Seri."

Marshal turned to see his favorite mage approach. "Ready to go back to your second home?"

Seri looked toward the dock. "I haven't been here in so long. It feels like… a strange place, not a home. Without Master Hain…"

Marshal winced. He had forgotten that Seri lost a mentor.

"Oh, they've been rebuilding," Seri observed. "It's looking much better than when I left."

"Time to lower the longboat," Tich announced. "Let's get moving."

With great care, the crew moved Dravid into the longboat. Marshal, Seri, and Tich joined him along with two other sailors to man the oars. Victor and Volraag would come in a second trip.

As they neared the dock, Seri smiled. "When Master Ganak arrived here, he showed off by jumping high into the air." She looked at Marshal. "It was so impressive then, but it's nothing compared to what you can do now."

Marshal nodded. He had no desire to show off, but the Masters would probably demand more evidence from him. As if opening a portal to the Otherworld in front of them hadn't been enough…

Four Masters walked out onto the dock to greet them. Marshal frowned. There had been only three the last time. He didn't remember them well enough to tell which one might be new. Arazu had not sent a new Master, from what Seri said, and Master Korda of Mandiata had disappeared, possibly victim to the wrath of one of the gods. Lord Bakari had appointed a new Master, but he apparently hadn't arrived yet. That meant these four were from Ch'olan, Kuktarma, Rasna, and Varioch.

"Let me go first," Seri whispered as Tich tied off the longboat.

Without waiting for an answer, she climbed (awkwardly) out and approached the Masters.

"Greetings, Masters!" she called. "Some of you know me. I am Seri-Belit, mage of Arazu. I was sent out by Master Hain of Arazu and Master Korda of Mandiata, in search of the lost King of Antises. I am pleased to report that my journey was a success. He has been here briefly already, but now let me formally introduce you to Marshal, King of all Antises!"

Marshal groaned inwardly, but climbed onto the dock and joined Seri.

"Welcome back, Marshal, son of Varion," said the largest of the Masters, the one from Kuktarma, Marshal thought. "We are most eager to learn all about you. Our last meeting was… far too short."

Marshal inclined his head. "Grave situations required it so," he answered. "And even graver situations bring me here now. We come from Kuktarma, where the ancient gods have invaded our world. Have you received my messages?"

"We have," said a shorter Master.

"Marshal, that is Master Plecu of Rasna," Seri put in. "This is Master Ganak of Kuktarma, Master Tzoyet of Ch'olan, and…" She paused, looking at the fourth Master, a young-looking bald man with pale skin.

He stepped forward and gave a short bow. "Your Majesty. I am Master Magnus of your home land of Varioch. Lord Volraag appointed me to this position months ago, but, ah, grave situations at home delayed my arrival until only recently."

Marshal's eyes shot back toward the ship involuntarily. A new Master appointed by Volraag? As if things weren't complicated enough.

"We have many, many things to discuss," Seri said in a rush, "all of them vitally important, but foremost, we have a friend here who needs both medical and magical attention." She pointed to where Tich and the others were bringing Dravid onto the dock.

"We will have him taken to the infirmary," Master Ganak said.

"Your pardon, Master, but his difficulty is related to magic more than to a physical infirmity," Seri explained. "I have tried everything within my power to help him. I am hoping you can do more. He is… important to all of us."

"He is one of my truest friends," Marshal declared. "If you help him, you are helping me, and I will not forget it."

Master Tzoyet stepped forward. "Bring him. I will go with him and examine him. Mage Seri, if you could come along and describe the circumstances that led to his condition?"

Seri agreed. Two younger mages took Dravid on a stretcher and they all left together. Marshal still stood on the dock, facing the remaining three Masters. Tich slipped up beside him, adjusting her coil of rope over her shoulder. "Cheerful bunch," she whispered, a little too loud.

"Come!" Master Ganak boomed. "We will gather in the council chambers and discuss your arrival. Is there anything you require first?"

Marshal gestured to the longboat pushing away from the dock. "They will be returning with another friend, and a dangerous prisoner. Do you have a secure place to keep him?"

"What is the nature of this prisoner?" Master Magnus asked.

"I prefer to discuss that with all of you in more comfortable surroundings," Marshal answered.

Master Ganak summoned another mage with a wave of his hand. "This one will await the prisoner's arrival and make arrangements on our behalf. Let us leave this place. Zes Sivas awaits its King!"

Marshal and Tich followed the Masters down the dock and onto the island. The instant Marshal's foot touched the ground of Zes Sivas, he experienced the same sensations as the last time. His foot hit the ground harder than he intended. He felt a rush of magic within, flowing down to his legs, pulling at the magic of the island. The impressions paralyzed him for a moment, until the island and his body reached some kind of equilibrium. He lifted his foot and took another step. The power swirled up inside him, making him feel invincible.

"You all right?" Tich asked, touching his arm.

"It's this place," Marshal said. "It makes me feel… overwhelmingly powerful."

Tich glanced around. "Good for you. It kind of makes me overwhelmingly depressed. These people need new tailors." She shook her head. "Robes."

•••••

The council chambers of Zes Sivas had seen better days. Marshal looked around at cracked walls as the Masters took their seats at the front. He tried not to laugh. It looked so small and pathetic compared to the council chamber in Intal Eldanir. Yet even there, the councillors stood before the people. The Masters sat, as if they were all kings.

Tich stood behind Marshal. The rest of the mages filed in and found seats.

Marshal spread his arms and looked at the Masters. "Is this how you treat a King? Make him stand before you while others watch?"

"We are not yet convinced that you are the King," Master Plecu snapped. "You have yet to provide the requested evidence."

"Some are not convinced," Master Ganak clarified. "Not all."

"What will it take?" Marshal demanded. "Have you not heard of everything that happened in Kuktarma? I know messengers have come. And what of your own communications? Do not the eyes of Zes Sivas see all?"

The Masters exchanged looks. He must have hit on something there.

"Perhaps we should wait until Master Tzoyet joins us," suggested Master Magnus.

"We can settle some preliminaries," Master Ganak said calmly. "Your Highness, we have heard conflicting reports, but not everything. Can you tell us where you have been and what has occurred since last we saw you?"

Marshal sighed. In as few words as possible, he told of traveling in the Otherworld, rescuing Dravid, fighting the gods, and returning to the primary world. He took more time in explaining what happened at the high place in Kuktarma, from the gods' arrival to the earthquake and his work with Seri and Dravid to stop it.

Toward the end, Master Tzoyet and Seri arrived, to his great relief.

"Seri-Belit, do you confirm this man's account of the earthquake and its ending?" Master Ganak asked.

"Of course I do. I was there." Seri paused. "I mean, with respect, sir, I witnessed all of it as well. I am sure the King has rendered a faithful retelling."

The Masters asked several pointed questions about the events. Marshal allowed Seri to answer most of them. All of it was tiring. Victor slipped in at one point and nodded to him. He must be satisfied with Volraag's accommodations. Coincidentally, the conversation turned to his half-brother soon thereafter.

"Am I understanding correctly that you have brought Lord Volraag here as a prisoner?" Master Magnus asked.

"That is correct. You have heard the list of his crimes. Some of you were witnesses to some of them."

"It would be preferable to allow his own people to judge him," Master Tzoyet suggested.

"Volraag himself insisted that no one could judge him except the other Lords," Marshal said. "Yet another reason I have sent messages summoning them all here. And once we complete a new Passing, Volraag will lose the power he has stolen, if I understand correctly."

"It makes logical sense," Master Ganak said. "But you are wanting more than just a new Passing, aren't you?"

Marshal hesitated. Up until now, he had not told the Masters of his full plans. "First I must know if you recognize me as King," he responded.

"These things take time," Master Plecu hedged.

"How much time? Antises has two enemy armies within its borders even now. Do we debate my credentials some more while they kill and enslave our people?"

"That is not our intent..."

"No, but it is the outcome. What will it take to confirm my identity? Let's get it over with now."

"Form the Heart of Fire," Plecu demanded.

"It doesn't work that way!" Seri exclaimed. "You only think that because Tezan did it, and he wasn't the real King! The Heart of Fire forms when the King surrenders his power, not when he uses it!"

"Mage, you are out of line addressing a Master in that manner," Master Ganak warned.

Seri ducked her head. "I apologize, Master Plecu."

"Nevertheless," Ganak said, "you make a fair point. None of us alive have witnessed the Heart of Fire in truth. Except, of course, the two of you, if your story is true."

"That being the case, how do I confirm my identity?" Marshal asked again.

"We can all sense your power," Master Tzoyet said. "It is clearly greater than that of a Lord. I do not have any questions."

"Nor do I," Master Magnus said. Marshal did not expect that one.

"With the testimony I have received from two of Lord Meluhha's sons, I must concur," Master Ganak said.

All eyes turned to Master Plecu. "I am still uncertain."

"It's because he's from Varioch, isn't it?" Tich said. "Politics. It ruins everything."

"Master Plecu," Marshal addressed him. "It is true that I was born in Varioch, but outside of my home village, I have no attachment to the rest of the land. I want to be King for all of Antises and its people."

"Master Plecu is entitled to his opinion," Tzoyet said. "But it does not matter now. A majority of existing Masters have ruled. Marshal, the Council of Mages recognizes you as King of Antises, pending full recognition by the Council of Lords, of course."

"Thank you." Marshal gave a short bow.

"But what now of your other plans?" Master Ganak asked. "The acolyte Jamana informed us that you wished to change or remove the Laws of Cursings and Bindings."

Oh. Jamana told them. "I do. I feel they are unjust, and allow no room for mercy."

"What need is there for mercy?" Master Magnus asked. "If someone commits a crime, they deserve their punishment. The Laws determine their guilt or innocence and act appropriately."

"Was it appropriate for me to be born with a curse?" Marshal clenched his fist, but kept himself under control. "It was my father who committed the crime, not me."

"The twisting of the Laws by the Lords did create this unfortunate side-effect," Lord Tzoyet agreed. "Perhaps, with enough research and study, we might be able to correct that one error."

"It's not enough," Marshal argued. "Suppose someone committed a crime in their youth, but has truly changed later on. Do they still deserve a curse for their entire life?"

"It is justice," Master Plecu said.

"But without mercy. And mercy is not something that can be left to magic to determine." Marshal patted his own chest. "It requires a human heart."

After a moment of silence, Master Tzoyet gave a single nod. "This is something we will consider carefully. It is not something that can be rushed into."

"Very well," Marshal said. "I only ask that you investigate how this can be accomplished."

"And what of this lifted curse?" Master Ganak said. "We would hear more of this."

"You've heard all there is to tell, I believe. My mother, Aelia, gave her life to lift my curse."

"And this took place at the temple of Reman?" Master Magnus asked.

"Yes."

"You had been cursed from birth, correct? What was the nature of the curse itself?"

Marshal made an exasperated sound. "Is this relevant right now?

There are enemy armies in Antises. We need to deal with them."

Master Tzoyet lifted his hands. "The King is clearly tired from his journey. Let us adjourn for now and discuss these matters more at a later time."

Marshal breathed a sigh of relief and turned to Seri. "What about Dravid?"

Seri glanced at the Masters. "Master Tzoyet has some ideas he is willing to try. We will attempt them tomorrow morning, after we've all had a little rest."

Marshal nodded and turned back to the Masters. He had so many things on his mind, so many things to keep track of. One more popped into his head. "Have you received any messages from Varioch or Rasna lately? I am expecting word from… a scout I sent in that direction."

"Our communications have… failed recently," Master Tzoyet said.

"If he is the King, then he may be able to help," Master Magnus pointed out.

"That is a distinct possibility," Tzoyet agreed. "Will you come with me, Your Highness?"

"All right. In the meantime, please find accommodations for my friends here." He pointed to Tich and Victor. "Seri, I want you to come along. If this is magic, I want your insight." He moved toward the door.

"Your pardon, Highness," Ganak said, "but this secret is reserved for Masters, and the palace Mages of each Land."

Marshal looked from Seri to the Masters. "Shall we consult with the Lady Lilitu? I am sure she would approve of Seri having the authority of a palace Mage, um, whatever that is."

"I think we can make an exception in this case," Tzoyet said. "We have had enough disagreement for now."

(((9)))

Seri followed Master Tzoyet and Marshal, her head spinning. So much was happening at once. Dravid could be awakened tomorrow. Marshal had been recognized as King by the Masters. And now she was about to learn the secret of how the Masters communicated with the mainland. Finally.

Master Tzoyet led them through several hallways, some of which showed signs of recent repair, into the Citadel of Kings. The last time Seri had walked these halls, she had been trying to stop Volraag and Rathri's murderous rampage.

"Has the Inner Sanctum been restored?" she asked.

"Unearthing the chamber was our first priority in the rebuilding effort," Master Tzoyet answered. "We made great progress, but the most recent earthquake buried much of it again. As more Masters and other mages have been returning, we are again making good progress."

"If I can help in any way, I would be glad to," Marshal offered.

Tzoyet nodded. "It is not a matter of raw power, Your Highness, but careful work. We will have it ready in time."

He found a door and fumbled through a large ring of keys. "These will belong to you, once we have everything re-opened," he told Marshal. "In the meantime, should you need a door unlocked, do not hesitate to find me."

Marshal didn't answer. If he were like Seri, he was wondering what doors in this place could be locked, and why.

Master Tzoyet found the right key and unlocked the door. He took an oil lamp from a nearby sconce and lit the flame. Then he led the way down a curving stair, at last entering a hexagonal room with an odd pedestal in the center. On each wall hung a tapestry depicting the symbol of one of the lands of Antises. The entrance to the room brought them in between Ch'olan and Mandiata.

"Be careful," the Master Mage warned. "Do not touch the magic."

Seri and Marshal stepped up beside him for a better view of the pedestal. Shaped like the room in a hexagon, it stood about three and a half feet tall, with a flat surface on top. On each side, facing the walls, polished metal plates were mounted. From each of the plates, a narrow beam of light extended about two feet outward, ending in a dark pinhole which appeared to spin in the air.

Master Tzoyet pointed to the nearest of the pinholes. "Each of these are portals, for lack of a better word, to the palaces of each of the six lands. When I first came to Zes Sivas, they were as big as my fist. Master Hain"—he glanced at Seri—"told me they were twice that size when he first arrived. This is how messages have been exchanged between the island and the palaces, for hundreds of years. But as you can see, they have shrunk to a size where not even a tightly-rolled scroll can fit through them."

Seri walked around the room, staring at the portals in fascination. "How big were they when this was first built?" she wondered.

"It is said they were large enough for people to walk through," the Master replied. "The King maintained them. It allowed him to keep in close contact with all of his realm." He folded his hands together. "We were hoping you might be able to restore them, at least large enough for messages to pass through again."

"Seri, what do you see?" Marshal asked.

"The same thing you do—oh!" He meant with her star-sight. She blinked and examined everything through her special vision. "It... it appears that magic flows from beneath, up into the pedestal, and out to the, uh, portals."

"How are you able to discern this?" Master Tzoyet asked, watching her with narrowed eyes.

"I can, ah, I can see the magic," Seri answered. "I will explain it to all of the Masters later."

The beams of light appeared pale and transparent with normal vision. With her star-sight, Seri saw a pulsing cable of many multi-colored beams entwined together. Most of them ranged from dark blue to purple, the part of the spectrum she generally associated with greater power.

She stepped between the portals and stared down at the pedestal from above. Something about it drew her attention. She reached out and placed her palm atop it. Vibrations. Of course.

"Marshal, come here." He obliged, being careful to avoid the beams of light, standing between them opposite from Seri.

"If I'm understanding this correctly, it pulls power from Zes Sivas below, but also from above," Seri explained. "Without a King, um, 'priming' it, I guess, it's been losing its pull on the island as well."

"We suspected as much," Master Tzoyet said. "Though it is impressive that you determined the same so quickly."

"Place your hand on top," Seri instructed. Marshal obeyed, centering his right hand on the pedestal's peak. "Do you feel the vibration there?"

"Yes. It's very faint."

"I want you to release magic into the pedestal, but… try to match that vibration. I don't think just throwing power at it would work. Otherwise, I'm guessing the Masters would have done it." She glanced at Master Tzoyet, who nodded. "It has something to do with the King's power. Maybe you're the only one who has enough? Or can match this particular vibration?"

"I'll do my best." Marshal closed his eyes and focused. "All right, I can feel it. Give me a minute."

Seri watched. Colored light began to flow from Marshal's hand into the pedestal. The color alternated between multiple shades, again mostly dark blue and purple. The light descended within the pedestal. To her surprise, it passed by the portal generators and continued down into the earth below.

"That's curious."

"What is?" Marshal asked, opening his eyes.

"Keep going. Don't stop." It looked like… yes, the magic flowing up from Zes Sivas into the pedestal was increasing… slowly.

"This is… difficult," Marshal said. He braced his right arm with his left hand.

"I think it's working, though." Seri was certain now. The power grew within the pedestal and started to affect the beams and portals.

"Yes, I can see it now," Master Tzoyet said excitedly. "The portals are beginning to grow again!"

There could be no doubt. All six portals expanded from pinholes to about an inch wide. Seri looked to Marshal. Sweat beaded on his forehead and scars. His arm trembled. Could this simple device really be causing him that much of a strain?

Simple device! What was she thinking? This device powered actual portals across all of Antises! And kept them open perpetually! The power requirements must be enormous.

Marshal gritted his teeth and poured more power into the pedestal. It flowed down, and then up again. The pinhole portals sputtered, then expanded until each reached the size of a handspan. Marshal jerked his own hand back from the pedestal. At the same time, a dozen or more envelopes and scrolls poured out of each portal and fell to the ground. From one of them, something larger came through and clanked as it hit the floor.

Seri blinked, turning off her star-sight and backed away. Marshal did, as well.

"Magnificent," Master Tzoyet declared.

Marshal put his hands on his knees, bending over and trying to catch his breath. "That… that took a lot out of me. Whew."

Seri looked at the papers lying around the room now. "So whenever I wrote to my parents, Master Hain tossed those letters into this little portal to Arazu?"

Master Tzoyet nodded. "Without this, it can take days or weeks before messages can be carried to and from the six capitals."

"And these used to be large enough to walk through?"

"That is what the records show."

Marshal wiped sweat from his face. "If I work on it a little each day, I might be able to get them large enough after a while."

"That would be incredible!" Seri exclaimed. "Can you imagine it? Being able to step through to Sandu-Emuq, eat lunch with the Lady, then come back and step through to Woqan for supper!"

Marshal chuckled. "Why does it have to involve a meal?"

"Because I'm hungry. We kind of skipped lunch after we got here."

Master Tzoyet began to gather up the envelopes and scrolls. Marshal stepped in front of him to the pile beneath the Varioch portal. "Excuse me. I believe one of these is mine." He reached down and picked up a thin metal case.

"What's that?" Seri wondered.

"It's from Talinir. I told him to find out how the mages sent messages and use it."

Master Tzoyet made a disapproving grunt.

Marshal looked over the case. He showed Seri a script on the top. "That's Eldanim writing. I saw it a lot in their city." He put his thumb on what looked like a lock and released a tiny burst of power. The lock popped open. Marshal took out a sheet of paper and read it. Then he handed it to Seri.

As she read Talinir's report, Marshal walked in a circle around the portals. "I'm going to have to get these open faster. Unless we do something about that third high place, our plan has no chance of succeeding."

●●●●●

"This is ludicrous," Kishin said. He stopped walking and looked at his three companions. "Worse, it's foolish."

"You've said this before," Jamana grumbled under his breath. After traveling by chariot for miles, they now walked through a rougher area of Kuktarma, filled with woods, ravines, and steep hills. Based on earlier scout reports, the enemy army would not be far.

Nehesy turned to face the assassin. "What is your complaint this time, Kishin?"

"What is my complaint?" Kishin spread his arms. "What are we doing here, old man? What can we four do against an invading army complete with gods as their leaders?"

"I have told you this already," Nehesy answered mildly. "Yet still you doubt."

"Of course I doubt! Only an idiot wouldn't have doubts."

"Nehesy has been right about everything else," Jamana said. "I have faith in him."

Kishin pointed at Jamana. "Why is he here? You're supposedly this all-powerful ancient mage. I'm an assassin. I even get him,"—he pointed at Adhi—"since he provided transportation up to this point. But why the acolyte? He's not a warrior. He has no magic power of his own. What good can he do?"

"He is here to bear witness," the old man answered. "Beyond that, only Theon knows."

Kishin snorted. "If he tells you, be sure to let the rest of us know." He glanced at the sword hanging from Adhi's belt. "You haven't even given me a weapon."

Nehesy leaned on his staff and cocked his head. "I thought you were Kishin the famous assassin. You are a weapon. Or so I've been told."

"You've been known to kill people with a piece of string," Adhi pointed out.

Kishin rolled his eyes. "It doesn't mean I don't prefer to use a blade when I can." He scowled and folded his arms. "This has gone on long enough. Why should I stay with you?"

"Because I asked you to," Nehesy said. "And you said yes."

"It was the only way out of Lord Meluhha's dungeons."

"I thought you were willing to stay there, as penance for killing my brother," Adhi said, his eyes flashing.

"I got bored." In truth, Kishin had almost killed himself after a month alone in Simbala's dungeon. When Adhi freed him on Nehesy's instructions, he would have said or done anything to get out.

Nehesy rubbed his beard. "All will become clear in time. When you need a weapon, Kishin, one will be provided for you."

"Your staff again?"

Nehesy chuckled and tapped the staff against the ground. "Why not? It's a good staff. It's served me longer than you've lived."

"So it's an ancient stick. Wonderful."

Nehesy shook his head. "Why don't you ask the question you really want to ask, Kishin? Why try to veil it in all of these complaints?"

Kishin growled. How did this old man always know? Maddening. He glanced at the two young men. He did not prefer to discuss things in front of them, but it seemed he had little choice. "Why do you want me to kill again?"

"Ah, there it is." Nehesy nodded. "I told you once before that if you must fight, let it be for a cause greater than yourself. This is one of those causes."

"I don't like being controlled."

"When have I controlled you? I've given you advice, and you haven't taken it. In fact, not once did you do what I expected you to do!"

"What did you expect me to do?" Kishin unfolded his arms, curious.

"For one thing, I expected you to help Marshal much more."

"He has my ship and crew. I'm still helping him."

Nehesy shook his head again. "It matters not. Not any more, anyway. Marshal is beyond our help, other than what we can do to slow his enemies." He gestured with his staff. "Shall we move on?"

Kishin sighed and followed the other three. Ludicrous. All of it was still ludicrous. And the old man still hadn't answered his question.

(((10)))

Talinir traveled on through the Starlit Realm. After sending the message to Zes Sivas, he made the transition again. Intal Eldanir stayed in the Otherworld right now, only a few days away.

He circled around an outcropping and gazed across the wasteland. With one eye he saw the barrenness of the Starlit Realm, and with the other he saw the fertile forests of Varioch. Such a dichotomy.

He patted the rock. At least he would be able to sleep in his favorite campsite tonight. He had discovered it four years ago, during some of his earliest warden duties. Since then, he had found many such hidden spots, but the first one always meant more, somehow.

Talinir glanced around once more. He wasn't worried about other people, but the occasional predator still roamed this region. With no movement in sight, he pushed aside a couple of smaller rocks to expose an opening below the large outcropping. It was just wide enough for him to slip into. He smiled, sat down, and pushed off.

Feet-first, he slid down a narrow passage, far too small for the tunaldi and other creatures. Only a couple of seconds later, he came out of the passage and landed on his feet in his favorite spot.

The broken rocks here formed a natural hollow about twelve feet in diameter. Far above his head, jagged openings let the stars bathe the hollow with their multi-colored light. The hollow provided shelter from animals, wind, dust, and anything else that might disturb a warden's rest.

Over the years, Talinir moved rocks and dirt to make it even more comfortable. Natural shelves provided places to store extra food and water. He opened a large container and sniffed. The smell brought an even bigger smile to his face. Tea.

In the center of the hollow lay the usual spot for a fire. Talinir reached toward his woodpile and froze. It was smaller than it should be. Someone else had been here.

Another warden? It was possible, but this spot lay outside the usual patrol area. With the Durunim activity as it had been lately, there would be no reason for another warden to travel this far. Talinir himself wouldn't be out here if not for his promise to Marshal.

He looked around the hollow with a more critical eye. Now he saw evidence everywhere. Someone had camped here, and recently. Someone with extensive talent. Anyone else might not have even noticed. They had hidden their presence well: no footprints or anything resembling any physical remainders.

The more Talinir examined everything, the more convinced he became that a warden had been here. And yet… something still did not feel right. A warden would know another warden's shelter and respect it, perhaps even leave a message behind. Whoever had been here tried to disguise their presence on purpose.

It was a mystery beyond Talinir's grasp just now. But it left him unsettled all through the night. His place of refuge had become a place of suspicion, and he had no idea why.

● ● ● ● ●

Seri's impatience grew as Master Tzoyet arranged his robes. He directed two of the island's healers to either side of Dravid's bed. It felt like she had been waiting for this day for years, but she hated every moment Dravid remained in this state.

"All right. I think we're ready to begin," the Master finally declared. He looked over Dravid's sleeping body. "The problem seems to be that he channeled too much power for too long. His body simply could not take the stress."

Seri bit her tongue to keep from answering. She knew all this; they had been over it.

"For the most part, then, his sleep has been his body recovering," Master Tzoyet went on. "But it has gone on too long. Something is… stuck, for lack of a better word."

He took one of Dravid's hands in his own. "We speak of the body channeling magic. This is a fairly accurate representation. Magic flows through the human body, following any path it can find: the bones, the blood vessels, nerves, or some other structures we do not fully understand yet."

Seri nodded. That made sense to her; she often felt the magic flow through the parts of her body, following some kind of paths.

"I am going to gently push small flows of magic through each channel of Dravid's body, to be sure nothing is… stuck, as we said."

"Will it matter that the magic he wields is different from ours?" Seri asked.

"I don't know for certain, of course," Master Tzoyet answered, "but it seems to me that power is power, regardless of its form. You said Dravid described side effects in his throat and chest. I will focus my efforts in those areas."

He took Dravid's other hand as well. "Seri, please monitor my magic use. Should I grow low in power, I want you to feed more into me, as I will not have the ability to find and absorb more myself while I am busy with him." She nodded. "Healers, please keep a close watch on Dravid's physical reactions to what I am doing. Should his body react unfavorably, please let me know. I'm sure there will be some difficulty, but if it appears it is becoming too dangerous for him, we will stop the process."

"Yes, Master."

He looked again at each one of them in turn, nodded and closed his eyes. Seri activated her star-sight and watched. Tiny beams of red light flowed from Master Tzoyet's hands into Dravid's and wove their way down his arms. Seri marveled at the control it must take for the Master to release such gentle magic, and then to keep it going.

Fascinated, she watched the light beams criss-cross back and forth. Soon dozens of them made their way to his shoulders and from there, began to spread out through his torso. Some faded away as the distance between the source in Master Tzoyet increased. Many more kept moving. Some wrapped themselves around his rib cage, following the outline of his bones. Others followed his blood flow into his heart, spiraling into it and his other internal organs. A few beams continued on down into his legs.

A dozen or more beams, fading in and out, flowed up Dravid's neck. And then only two of them continued up his chin and into his face.

"Oh!" Seri exclaimed. "Something… it's getting blocked at the top of his neck. Um, in the back."

"Turn him over," Master Tzoyet instructed the healers. With gentle care, they rolled Dravid over, and positioned his pillow so as to elevate his head, but not obstruct his breathing.

"Watch carefully," the Master told Seri. He placed his hands on Dravid's shoulder blades and released the delicate flows of vibratory magic again. Seri imagined it to be a pleasant feeling and resolved to learn it herself someday. She moved closer and stared at the beams that came up the back of Dravid's neck and stopped.

She placed a finger where the beams stopped, right where Dravid's neck connected to his head. "Here," she said. "The magic stops here."

Master Tzoyet increased the flow of magic ever so slightly. Some of the beams turned more orange. "Look!" he commanded. "Can you see anything there?"

Seri bent down and scrutinized the stopping point. She couldn't be completely sure, but… "I think there's a tiny piece of his gold magic right there."

Master Tzoyet nodded and stopped. "Healers, does that make sense for his condition?"

They looked at each other. "From there, it would be blocking his brain's control of much of his body," one of them said. "From what we understand of the brain's functions, that is."

Master Tzoyet tapped his chin. "I am a little unsure on how to proceed here. Have you witnessed the magic of Antises against his power before?"

"His power usually blocks it," Seri said. "Marshal shattered through one of his constructs once. He was very angry at the time. Dravid couldn't understand how he did it."

"I see." The Master considered for a few moments. "I am reluctant to use too much power on him, especially at such a critical juncture. If we are not careful, we could break his neck, or damage his brain, or any other of a myriad of possible dangers."

Seri's heart sank. Was Dravid doomed to stay like this? Maybe only someone with similar powers could heal him, like one of the gods.

"However," Master Tzoyet declared, "I do not think we need use extreme power like the young King did. If I am right, it is only a matter of finding the right vibrational frequency."

"Do you really think so?"

He nodded. "When the King exerted himself, you said he was angry. It is very likely it was not the overwhelming force of his power that shattered the magical construct. Instead, his angry burst of power likely included dozens of different frequencies all at once, and one in particular was the one needed to disrupt the magic."

Seri thought about it. When she had watched Marshal or others use tremendous amounts of power, she often saw it as every color possible, all flowing and interwoven together. If each color represented a different frequency, Master Tzoyet's theory made sense. "I think you're right." She explained what she had seen.

"Very well." Master Tzoyet placed only his forefinger against the back of Dravid's head. "Let us see if I can find it."

A thin beam of light lanced out of his finger and into Dravid's head, stopping abruptly at the obstruction. Receiving confirmation from Seri that he was in the right spot, Master Tzoyet took a deep breath and closed his eyes. Seri did not take her eyes away from the beam. As she watched, it slowly shifted from red toward orange, then on into yellow. Once again, she stood in awe of the Master's absolute control of his power.

She also noticed the glow of magic within him was dimming. She pulled magic from Zes Sivas and poured it into Master Tzoyet, restocking his supply until it glowed brighter and brighter. He grunted in thanks, but continued to concentrate on his work.

Seri looked back at Dravid. The beam of light now shifted into the green spectrum, gradually moving away from yellow into a dark forest-type green. Dravid's body suddenly flailed. The healers moved in and seized his left arm and his legs. Seri caught hold of his right hand. It trembled beneath her touch. "Something's happening!" she cried.

"We appear to have found the right frequency," Tzoyet said. "Now…"

The green beam increased in size only a tiny bit, but Dravid's whole body shook in response. "Master," the healer on his left said, "His heart rate is accelerating." Seri could feel the same in his right hand.

"Tell me if it becomes dangerous." Sweat stood out on Tzoyet's brow as he continued to hold the beam in place.

Seri's star-sight showed the beam continued to be stopped in the same place. But as she stared, she saw something different. At first, she thought her vision was blurring. She blinked a few times and looked again. Master Tzoyet's beam, about the width of her little finger, stopped at the blockage. But now she could tell: a tiny beam, almost imperceptible, continued past the blockage and flowed down Dravid's neck. She reported it to the Master.

"It's working, then." He wiped the sweat from his brow with his left sleeve and kept concentrating. Seri couldn't fathom the toll this must be taking on him.

Bit by bit, the beam of light continued to grow as more of it pushed through the obstruction.

"His heart rate is now dangerously high," the healer reported.

"You've almost got it!" Seri insisted. She glanced at Master Tzoyet and saw his teeth clinched and sweat continuing to bead up and pour down his face. His hand trembled.

"Master," the healer warned. "This is too much. For both of you."

The beam burst through the rest of the way and flowed down Dravid's neck and into his torso. He gasped out loud and coughed.

"You did it!" Seri cried.

"Indeed." Master Tzoyet stepped back and stumbled. The healer nearest him reached to give him support, but he waved her away. "I will be all right."

Seri assisted the healers in turning Dravid back onto his back. He gasped again and opened his eyes. "Wh-wa…" He coughed.

"Give him water," a healer instructed, handing Seri a glass. The other lifted Dravid's head and held him up while Seri brought it to his mouth. He drank a couple of swallows, paused, then drank a few more. They let his head back down. He closed his eyes and took a deep breath, then looked up again.

"Seri."

"Dravid." Her eyes glistened, she knew, and not from magic. "You're awake."

"I will take my leave," Master Tzoyet announced. "Do not overburden him with talk. He still has a long way to go to recover."

"Master?" Dravid looked at him. "Are we on Zes Sivas? How long have I been out?"

"Yes, and… weeks. I've lost count," Seri answered. She seized his hand again and squeezed it. He smiled, but then his head shook and his eyes rolled back momentarily. He blinked and re-focused.

"He will need to get some real rest now, and then eat," the healer said. "You can stay, but no more questions and answers just yet."

Seri nodded and sat down. She didn't trust herself to say very much, anyway.

The healer adjusted Dravid's pillow. "Go to sleep now. Real sleep. You should recover in time."

Dravid blinked in response, already fading.

"Wait… I have to know one thing."

Seri smiled and glanced at the healer. "One question, then."

Dravid's voice slurred, but he got the words out: "Is Adhi *really* the seventh son of Lord Meluhha?"

(((11)))

Marshal gathered everyone into Dravid's room. He had a decision to make and he needed their advice. Seri sat by Dravid's bed, holding his hand. Ixchel stood behind her. Victor and Tich sat on the other side of the bed, waiting for him to speak. They wouldn't like what he was going to say.

"All right, thanks for coming, everyone. Dravid, it's good to see you awake."

"It's good to be awake," he answered hoarsely.

Marshal glanced at the door. "Seri, can any of the Masters listen in on us here? And would they?"

"I don't think so," Seri said, wrinkling her brow. "I don't know of any technique which would allow that. Then again, until two days ago, I didn't know of ways to open portals across the world. Still, I don't think they would. At least I hope not."

"Portals?" Victor asked.

"It's how the island communicates with the six lands," Marshal explained. "Right now, the portals are only small enough to send notes, but with a lot of work, they could become big enough to let people walk through them."

"That could save a lot of time."

"But then you wouldn't get to enjoy the experience of sailing," Tich argued. "You'd miss out, I say."

"You can keep it," Victor said. "I've had enough of ships."

"This is what I wanted to talk about," Marshal said.

"Ships?" Tich asked.

"No." He smiled. "The portals. I'm thinking of using one as soon as possible."

"What for?" Dravid asked.

Marshal gestured broadly. "Now that the messages are moving faster, the Lords are starting to listen to us. Lord Rajwir is on his way. Lord Meluhha will be coming soon. The big problem remains Lord Tyrr."

"No surprise there," Seri said. "We always knew that he'd be reluctant to come."

"Talinir sent a full accounting of the Durunim invasion over there," Marshal explained. "We can't leave that high place portal open. As long as the enemy continues to grow in strength, I can understand why Lord Tyrr wouldn't want to leave. He's the only one who can defend his people."

"You want to use the portal to go persuade him in person?" Victor asked.

"No. I want to use the portal to go help him. We'll close the high place, stop the Durunim army, and then come back for the Passing and the end of the Laws."

No one spoke for a few seconds. Then Victor and Seri spoke at once. Victor stopped and gestured to her to go on.

"We need you here," she said. "Lord Tyrr doesn't even recognize you as King. What's to stop him from arresting you when you arrive?"

"Do you think his ordinary guards can keep me from doing what I want?"

"Ugh. This is why Talinir didn't want to leave you," Victor complained. "You're not going without me."

"No. I need you here to keep an eye on Volraag. Besides, how far would you get through Rasna while wearing half a Varioch military outfit?"

Victor slumped. "Hailstones. I like my cape. Fine. I'll change clothes."

Marshal shook his head. "Sorry, Vic. Not this time. It's going to be hard enough for him to accept me, since I'm from Varioch. If I bring along a warrior from Varioch with me, it will only add tension."

"Good thing I'm from Rasna," Tich said. "When do we leave?"

"It's going to be dangerous, Tich. When we go to the high place, Lord Tyrr and I will both have to be throwing out tremendous amounts of power. You wouldn't be able to do anything but watch."

"I don't mind watching you."

Marshal wondered if his blush could even be seen around his scars and facial hair. "I just... I don't want to put you in danger. And if I have to worry about you…"

"I can take care of myself!"

"You're worried that if Lord Tyrr understands how much she means to you, he might threaten her to control you," Seri broke in.

How did she do that? "Um, yeah. That's basically it."

"That's sweet," Tich said. "But I'm still coming."

"We'll talk more about it in private," he said, without agreeing. "For now, I want to talk about how this would work, and what the rest of you would be doing while I'm gone."

"Wasting more time watching your half-brother," Victor grumbled, arms folded over his chest.

"What do you mean by 'how it would work'?" Seri asked.

"That's what I wanted to ask you. Do you think I could use the pedestal to open just one of the portals all the way? It would take days to feed enough power in to open all of them, and I don't want to waste any more time than I have to."

Seri frowned. "I'll have to examine it some more. There may be a way to block off some of the other portals so all the power goes to the one you want."

"All right. Let's assume we can do that. While I'm gone—"

"While we're gone," Tich corrected.

"While… Um, Seri and Dravid, I want you to get that book Jamana brought back, and read every word of it. I'm counting on you to figure out how we're going to finish things."

"Reading isn't a strenuous activity. I can do that," Dravid said.

"I'll bring the book in here," Seri agreed, "assuming Master Ganak will allow it."

"If he gives you trouble, I'll order him to do it," Marshal said.

They discussed the Passing and other magic issues. Seri explained what Nehesy, the old mage, had told her. Victor and Tich eventually grew bored and left the room.

"Let me walk through this," Marshal said. "At the Passing, when the Lords release their power, it creates this… cube of light, you said."

Seri nodded. "Dravid and I both saw it."

"And when the King adds his, it forms the interior of the cube, and that's the Heart of Fire."

"Which we also saw when you stopped the earthquake."

"So maybe that's when I'm supposed to enter it?"

"I think we might both have to." Seri looked at Dravid. "And maybe do something similar to what we did before?"

"Where I channel your power?"

"I hope not," Marshal said. "That's what put you in that bed."

"Your grandfather said Dravid had to be a part of it," Seri pointed out. "Somehow, he's involved, and we enter the Heart of Fire, and then…"

"And that's all we know."

Seri nodded.

"Let's hope the book gives us a little more to go on." Marshal sighed. "I guess I'd better go try talking to Tich."

"You're going to lose that argument," Dravid said. Seri laughed.

"I'm glad you both have such confidence in me." Marshal moved to the door.

"We have confidence in you," Seri replied. "We also have confidence in Tich. She's going with you, and you know it."

"We'll see."

• • • • •

Marshal and Tich watched Seri examine the pedestal with the portals again. "I'm not sure about this," she said.

"What do you mean?" Marshal stepped closer.

"I don't see any way to control the flow of power," she answered. "Your magic flows down into it, and then flows back up into all six portals."

"Can we temporarily block the other ones?"

"I don't see how, without breaking it." Seri stepped back from the pedestal. "And anything I try might break it, anyway." She put her hands on her hips. "Marshal, this is an ancient magical device from a time when the mages of Antises knew a lot more than we do now. I'm honestly terrified to tamper with it."

Marshal took a deep breath. "All right, then. I guess I have no choice."

"What do you mean?" Tich asked.

"I'll have to pour in enough power to open all of them."

"Can you do that?"

"I don't know. Guess we'll find out." He stepped up to the pedestal and put his hand on top again.

"Take it easy," Seri said. "Again, this thing is ancient. You don't want to overpower it."

"What would happen if he did?" Tich asked.

"We have no idea. It could just stop working, or it could release all of its power in, uh, some kind of violent way."

Tich took a step back. "Maybe I should wait in another room."

"If something happens, I'll protect us," Marshal said, but he didn't feel very confident about it.

As before, he let the vibrations of the pedestal speak to him. The combination wasn't complicated, a regular rhythm, far simpler than when he tried a counter-vibration to the earthquake. It took only a few moments to understand it and begin to create it himself.

This was so much different than how he usually used his power. In battle, he threw the power out of himself, letting it run wild and reckless. This technique required concentration and skill. The bursts of power had to match the specific vibration the pedestal used. As such, it took a lot more out of him than simply blasting away at something.

"Good. The power is flowing," Seri said, keeping watch on everything with her star-sight.

Marshal grunted. He wanted to push harder, shove more and more power as fast as possible into the pedestal, but it wouldn't work. It could only handle so much.

"The power's starting to come back up into the portals," Seri reported. "You know, in the past, the King probably only had to walk in here and give the pedestal a little boost every so often. That's probably how it was designed, and why it's so hard to get it working now. I wonder if it hits a certain point if it just runs by itself for a long time."

"Do you always talk this much?" Tich asked.

"Only when I'm nervous," Seri said. "Or angry. Or frustrated. Or… it's working, Marshal!"

The portals expanded, maybe an entire inch.

"Keep at it, and maybe I could stick my head through," Tich said.

"You know, she's got a point," Seri said. "You don't have to get them large enough to walk through, necessarily. Just big enough to crawl, I guess."

Tich bent to peer at one of the portals. "More like dive."

Marshal didn't answer them. He had already reached the point where his arm grew tired from all the power flowing through it. He braced it with his other arm.

Tich and Seri continued talking, but he paid little attention. Keeping the rhythm correct while continually pouring power into the pedestal took more and more concentration and energy. Sweat began to trickle along his scars. The new one on his back became a persistent itch as his sweat-dampened shirt rubbed against it.

"How long has it been?" he asked after what seemed like hours.

"Oh, um, about twenty or thirty minutes, I think." Seri looked to Tich, who nodded.

Marshal released the pedestal and staggered back. "I need a break." He found the wall and collapsed against it.

"Are you all right?" Tich moved near him, her hand reaching out like she might touch him, but couldn't decide.

"I just need to rest," he answered, waving her back. "So hot…"

When Tich moved back to the side, he got a good look at the portals. They were definitely larger than when he started, but the progress seemed so little for all his effort. As Tich observed, a person's head could fit through now, but not much more.

"I'll get you some water," Seri offered. She hurried up the stairs.

Tich examined the portals again. "This is going to take a while."

"Yeah." Marshal wiped his face with his shirt. "Maybe we aren't going today."

Tich cocked her head at him. "When you do get it big enough, you're going to need to rest and change clothes, anyway."

"You don't think I should greet Lord Tyrr looking like I just fought a battle?"

"You don't look like you just fought a battle. You look like you just climbed out of the lake." She squatted down near him. "We once pulled a guy up on board, out of the lake. We were way out in the middle too. Craziest thing. He couldn't have swam that far, and there were no other ships around. I never could figure out how he got there."

"He didn't tell you?"

"No." Tich eyed him. "That was part of the crazy. He didn't have a tongue."

Marshal rolled his eyes. Footsteps down the stairs announced Seri's return with an entire bucket of water and a ladle. Marshal drank two full scoops, then dumped a third over his head. After another ten minutes of rest, he decided to try again.

He repeated the process four more times. He poured magic into the pedestal for around half an hour, though each time got a little bit shorter due to his exhaustion. Then he rested and hydrated, each time taking longer. At the end of it all, the portals had changed quite a bit.

While initially square, once they reached around two feet wide, the portals started elongating vertically. Their new shape, once they reached full size, looked much more like doorways. When Marshal quit for the day, they were two feet wide and about three and a half feet tall. Marshal felt confident they could step through now.

Seri offered to test one, but he turned her down. "If you get through, but then can't get back, it would take you days to return," he explained. "If I have to get back in a hurry, I can move faster than you can."

"And leave me behind?" Tich asked.

"Um, only if necessary."

"I see."

Marshal staggered to his feet. "I think I need to go to bed."

"First you need a swim in the lake," Tich said. "You're a mess."

"Thanks." He took the first step and wavered. "On second thought, maybe I'll rest here for a little bit longer." He sat down on the stairs.

(((12)))

After the hollow, Talinir kept a close eye on the land, watching for any more signs of the mysterious trespasser. Every so often, he found a trace, a hint of another person's recent passage. A disturbed stone, the barest hint of a print in the dust… things only an Eldani warden would notice. But to Talinir, they screamed a message: someone had traveled the same path he was now taking, someone who did not want to be noticed. Someone… on their way to Intal Eldanir.

His concerns about the mystery traveler faded as he came within sight of the city. He stopped and drank it in. Intal Eldanir never failed to take his breath away, followed by a swell of pride. This was his city, the work of his people, and there was nothing like it in two worlds.

White stone made up the majority of the buildings and paved the streets. Dark polished hardwood, harvested from the forests of Varioch, created contrast. All of the stone came from quarries far to the north, in the same region as Ch'olan in the primary world. Most of the city had been built there before being moved to its present location.

Talinir, though he knew much of magic in both worlds, still marveled at the power it took to float the enormous city in the air. Since the city could shift between the two worlds, much like the Eldanim themselves, the original Eldani designers created the magical devices which kept the city floating well above the ground. In that way, when it shifted from one to the other, there was much less chance of materializing into something or someone else. The ground might shift through the years, but the city's foundation remained solid… in the air.

He passed another warden, acknowledging him with a nod. The other warden had shifted to the primary world, but kept a close eye on the approach to Intal Eldanir. At least a dozen of them would be stationed at equidistant points around the city.

Talinir approached, trying not to run. A platform separated from the street above and descended to the ground for his convenience. Either someone saw him coming, or some new magic technique detected his presence. He stepped onto the platform and it rose again, joining seamlessly with the white stone street above.

His first task would be to report to the High Warden. After that, he would seek out Indala, the council member most likely to be favorable to his proposal. He squared his shoulders and started down the street. Home at last.

•••••

Marshal straightened his shirts. He had chosen to wear the clothes he'd been given in Kuktarma. It would not make Lord Tyrr forget he came from Varioch, but it might send a subtle message about his loyalties. Every little bit could help.

He glanced at Tich. "Are you ready?" Despite suggestions from Seri, she had chosen to wear her usual sailor clothes, low neckline and all. She saw no need to dress up for the man responsible for her parents' deaths.

"I've been ready. Just waiting on you to get done napping."

"Right." He stepped in front of the portal to Rasna and stopped.

"What are you waiting for? You've gone through portals to the Otherworld back and forth."

"I can see through those," Marshal countered. He knew these portals worked, since the mages sent messages and packages through on a daily basis. But it was still disconcerting. The portals appeared as nothing more than thin rectangles of light floating in the air.

Master Plecu entered the room. "Oh, good. You haven't left yet."

"Is there a problem?" Marshal frowned. Plecu had been reluctant to recognize his Kingship, but hadn't complained since then. "Didn't you let the palace mage know we were coming?"

"Yes, yes, I did." Plecu fumbled his hands together. "I was just thinking… maybe I should be going with you, to introduce you to Lord Tyrr."

Marshal blinked. He hadn't expected that. "I… appreciate that, Master Plecu, but I don't know if it's necessary. Don't you need to be here for the arrival of the other Lords?"

"If these portals work, then I can come right back," Plecu said, gesturing at the glowing rectangles. "Isn't that correct?"

"Yes." Marshal nodded. "Then I accept your offer." It might actually smooth things over with the first impressions.

He turned back to the portal. "I'll go first." He ducked his head, and stepped into the portal without taking any more time to think about it. A sensation of motion flowed over his body, almost like a powerful wind suddenly impacting him. And then it was over. He stood in a small, bare room, save for a duplicate portal behind him now, and a mage in blue robes staring at him wide-eyed.

Marshal stepped to the side, narrowly getting out of Tich's way as she burst through the portal also. Her short hair whipped around her face as she came to a stop. "Whoa. That was... something."

"Make room for Master Plecu," Marshal said. He grasped Tich's hand and pulled her to the side next to him. But the Master Mage took a few more moments before he finally arrived, robes fluttering.

"Oh, my." Plecu bent and put his hands on his knees. The palace mage stepped forward in confusion. "Master! I didn't know you were coming as well!"

Master Plecu waved aside his help. "I'm all right. How exhilarating."

The palace mage turned his eyes on the other two. Like most people, he immediately stared at Marshal's scars.

"Where will we find Lord Tyrr?" Marshal asked.

"Oh, ah, he is in conference with his generals," the mage replied. "I informed him that you would be arriving today, but he..."

"He did not wish to sit around and wait," Master Plecu finished for him. "Our Lord is not known for his patience."

"Inform him that we have arrived," Marshal ordered.

"Ah, he did ask not to be disturbed." The palace mage shifted his weight from one foot to the other.

Marshal considered for a moment. A strong part of him wanted to barge into Lord Tyrr's meeting and demand his attention, but he knew that would not win any favors. He could sit here and wait, which might show weakness, or...

"Master Plecu, would you please inform his Lordship that the King of Antises has arrived and wishes to speak with him?"

Master Plecu's face paled a bit, but he nodded. "I will do so at once. Cipen, would you please escort His Majesty and friend to the Lord's reception hall?"

The palace mage nodded and gestured for them to follow. He led Marshal and Tich down a long hallway to a pair of double doors. The hallway, built of painted wood planks, showed no decor of any kind. That changed once Cipen opened the doors. Lord Tyrr's reception hall was ornate in the extreme. Elaborate tapestries covered almost every inch of the two longest walls, portraying images of Rasna's sea ports, cities, and landscapes. At the opposite end of the two doors, Lord Tyrr's throne stood, an uncomfortable construct of wood and metal, sandwiched between two marble pillars. Behind it, a red silk tapestry decorated the wall.

"Promise me you won't have a throne room like this," Tich said. She sashayed up to the throne and knocked on one of the metal armrests with her knuckle.

"If I have my way, I'll never have a throne room," Marshal answered. He nodded to Cipen who left the room as quickly as he could. Marshal sat down in the throne. "Not very comfortable."

Tich walked around behind the throne. "I think he was going more for intimidation than comfort. Typical man."

"Is that so?"

"Oh, yes." Tich leaned over the back of the throne. "Ask most any man: 'do you want to be comfortable, or do you want to impress people?' And he'll choose intimidation. Every time."

Marshal patted the arm of the throne. "Are you intimidated by me sitting here, then?"

"More than you would believe. I wouldn't dare come before you with any requests." She swung around one of the pillars, back in front of the throne.

"No requests at all?"

"Maybe one or two, if Your Highness isn't too busy." She grinned at him.

Marshal laughed.

At that moment, the doors burst open and Lord Tyrr entered. A powerfully-built man with an impressive black beard, the Lord stood at least a few inches above six feet. Master Plecu looked tiny coming in behind him. Tyrr looked at Marshal, cocked his head to the side, and placed his hands on his hips.

"Not exactly what I was expecting, Plecu," he proclaimed in a loud voice.

"Your Lordship, may I present His Highness, Ki—" Master Plecu began.

"I see a boy pretending to be a man sitting on my chair and flirting with his favorite whore," Tyrr interrupted.

Marshal stood to his feet. "Lord Tyrr, you will apologize to the Lady Tich at once."

Tyrr snorted. "It's not an insult, boy. You're just like your father. He had a problem with the whores too."

"I will not ask again," Marshal said coldly. He had come expecting to be insulted and questioned by this man, but he would not sit by and let him talk about Tich that way.

"Good. Then I don't have to waste time listening to you." Lord Tyrr walked across the hall. "My chair, if you please."

Marshal released a burst of power, blowing the throne apart into shards of twisted metal and splinters of wood. "You can sense my power, just as I can sense yours. You know I have far more than you do."

"Marshal…" Tich whispered. "Don't."

"Are we comparing manhood here?" Lord Tyrr looked over the ruins of his throne. "That was petty, boy. Hardly the diplomatic actions of a King."

"You threw out all diplomacy when you sullied my companion with your coarse words," Marshal snarled. "Apologize. Or else I'll be negotiating with the new Lord of Rasna, assuming you have a son to take your place." He lifted his hands, feeling the vibrations build up within them.

Tich grabbed his arm. "Marshal, don't stoop to his level. Not for me. Please."

"Your lady is wiser than you, boy." Lord Tyrr gave a short bow toward Tich. "I apologize, young lady. Maybe this scar-faced brat is King and maybe he isn't, but you clearly have a better head on your shoulders."

Marshal let the power fade, but continued to glare at the Lord of Rasna. "I came here in good faith, Lord Tyrr. Together, we can end the threat to your land. If you want my help, you might want to show a little more respect."

"Respect for what?" Tyrr snorted again. "You invade my hall and destroy my throne. I'm not seeing much to respect. Or should I be intimidated by your mess of a face?"

"I am the King of Antises. I came to help you. In return for defeating the army on your borders, I expect you to return to Zes Sivas with me."

"I read your letters," Tyrr said. "You think another Passing will stop the earthquakes, even though we just had one."

"You did not have my power in that Passing," Marshal pointed out. "Together, we can do it. We can heal Antises." He held out his hand.

Tyrr shook his head. He bent and picked up a broken piece of his throne. "And who will be paying for this?"

"I… don't have any money," Marshal said. "But I hope to serve you and your land by defeating our mutual enemy."

"A King without gold?" Tyrr straightened. "Hmp. I suppose I can let the chair go. But make no mistake, boy, we do have a mutual enemy, and it's not these magic creatures running around at the border." He waved the piece of metal toward the side.

"Who do you mean?"

Lord Tyrr's eyes narrowed. "Volraag, of course. Plecu!"

"Y-yes, my Lord?"

"Didn't you say that Volraag is now a prisoner on Zes Sivas?"

"He is, my Lord. King Marshal brought him there."

Tyrr nodded. "And that is the only reason I'm willing to give you any kind of hearing. You caught Volraag. So I have one question: when do we execute him?"

Marshal tried to stand straight and tall, but knew he looked puny next to the Lord. "My… that is, Volraag will lose his stolen power after the new Passing. Following that, we will hold his trial before the assembled Lords. You, of course, will be there to list your grievances against him."

"Is that so?"

"Yes." Marshal nodded. "We already held one trial for him in Kuktarma. Lord Bakari and others presented their charges. Because of that, I brought him to Zes Sivas where he will lose his stolen power."

"And do you think that is enough to make up for the damage he's done? The lives he's cost?"

"That will be for the Lords to decide," Marshal said. The longer the conversation went on, the more awkward he felt, standing among the shards of the throne.

"Theon's pillars! You claim to be the King!" Lord Tyrr leveled a finger at him. "You should make these decisions!"

"What do you want from me?" Even as the words left his mouth, Marshal knew it was a mistake. Behind him, Tich groaned.

Tyrr smiled and folded his arms again. "I want all of the disputed territory, including the town of Kanna, ceded to Rasna."

"That is not… I do not have the authority to do that. The Lords must decide, and Varioch—"

"Who will rule Varioch?" Tyrr demanded.

"What?"

"Volraag will never sit on the Lord's throne again. So who will rule Varioch in his place?"

"I, I don't know. These things will have to be decided later."

"If you want my recognition of your Kingship, you'll decide some of it now. Those are my terms."

Marshal looked past the Lord to Master Plecu, who did not offer any help whatsoever. On the contrary, he looked frightened to even be there. What could he do, though? He needed to work with Lord Tyrr to save Antises. A King thinks of all his people. How could he serve all of the people best here?

"Well?"

"Your recognition, while desired, is ultimately not necessary at this time," Marshal said as he realized it himself. "I am here to help you fight the Durunim. Whether you see me in that fight as King, Lord, or just a young man who happens to wield enormous magical power is inconsequential. What matters for Antises is that we do fight together."

Lord Tyrr nodded slowly. "Now that I can agree with."

● ● ● ● ●

"Talinir. You, young warden, have a lot to answer for."

Talinir got to his feet and gave a respectful nod to the High Warden of Intal Eldanir, Tiranel. The High Warden summoned him with a gesture and turned around. Talinir followed him from the antechamber where he had been waiting into a spacious office. Tiranel had held the position for longer than Talinir had been alive. In fact, Tiranel might be older than anyone Talinir knew.

"You left us months ago in the company of humans," Tiranel said as he took his seat behind a desk made of the same hardwood which formed so much of the city's architectural accents. "Since then, no one has heard from you except in vague rumors. Explain yourself. And take your time."

Talinir nodded. Placing his hands behind his back, he began a recitation of his actions, beginning with the most important point: his oath to Marshal. From there, he described their journey to Reman, his strange journey to the Ch'olan high place, and learning about the gods and Durunim. He pulled his sleeve up and revealed the dark spots on his skin left there by the brief contact with one of the gods.

Tiranel did not show any surprise at this revelation, which puzzled Talinir. "Haven't we believed that the Durunim are created by those who chose to remain wholly within the Starlit Realm?" he asked.

"Many have believed that theory, but not all," Tiranel said. "Some of us have known the truth for some time, though it is difficult to persuade others. Continue with your narrative."

Talinir told of the battle with Volraag, the journey with Marshal in and out of both worlds until they arrived at the Kuktarma high place. He told of the army that breached the primary world, Marshal's actions in stopping the earthquake, and his current plans to heal Antises.

"And so, on his request, I have returned to speak to the High Council," Talinir concluded. "Marshal hopes to enlist our aid in fighting the Durunim in the primary world."

"That will be a difficult sell," Tiranel said. "But we'll come back to that. Let me be sure I understand you fully: all that you have done during these past months happened because you gave your word to a human, correct?"

"I gave him my oath," Talinir said. "I had promised no harm to him or his mother, and I failed in that. Since the promise was broken, I gave him an oath instead. I have held to that ever since."

Tiranel nodded. "Your word required nothing less, though it is highly unusual to give one's oath to a human. I do not recall anyone else doing so in my lifetime."

"Did I do wrong?"

"No, no." Tiranel shook his head. "Not directly. You did what was right for you. But in doing so, you did leave us with fewer wardens than I prefer. I had to rush two trainees through faster than I'd like. The Durunim have been harassing us with small incursions lately. Not long ago, a handful of them entered the city itself."

Talinir's eyes widened in horror. "Inside the city?"

"They were dealt with. We have one of them prisoner, but we haven't gotten a single word from him." Tiranel sighed. "If what you say is correct, these small bands were probably left behind for the sole purpose of keeping us distracted from what the Durunim are doing elsewhere."

"They have two armies in the primary world even now. The humans are ill-equipped to fight them."

Tiranel stood. "And you want to persuade the High Council to take action."

"That is why I am here."

"You'll go see Harunir and Indala, I assume."

Talinir nodded. "That's my next stop."

"Good. You show wisdom. But there is more you need to know. Thanks to the Durunim incursion I mentioned, and the persuasive words of Harunir, things have changed somewhat." Tiranel smiled. "Harunir is now High Mage. The High Champion, the High Mage, and the High Warden together now have a voice in the Council. We have a single vote, assuming we all agree. But our word will be heard, regardless."

Talinir felt a surge of hope. He had more allies than he expected.

Tiranel raised a finger. "But… the Mage, Warden, and Champion have one voice. Only one. And so we must be in complete agreement before we speak to the Council. If you want this voice to speak on your behalf, you must do one more thing: persuade the High Champion of Intal Eldanir to join the humans' cause."

(((13)))

Talinir knocked on the door and waited. After a few moments, he heard movement inside the house. The door swung open and Harunir stood before him. Talinir fought a lump in his throat. Seeing Tiranel had been emotional, but tempered by the duties required by their positions. Now, seeing a friend, one of his people, after so long… it pushed him almost to tears. With no family of his own still alive, Talinir treasured friendships such as these.

"Talinir." Harunir did not act in the least bit surprised to see him. "Come in, come in. Indala and Eniri should be home any minute now."

In a short time, the rest of the family arrived and gathered together for dinner. After giving thanks and insisting Talinir fill his plate, Indala asked the question they must all be dying to hear about: "Tell us, Talinir. How did things fare with Marshal and Aelia?"

"There is much to tell," the warden said. In between bites, he told the story. Since these friends knew Marshal, his recitation took a much more personal tone than his report to the High Warden. They joined in his sorrow over Aelia's death, the confusion over his journey through the Starlit Realm without being in both worlds, and the thrill of seeing Marshal come into his own in power and authority.

"And so, King Marshal sent me to seek the help of the Eldanim again," he finished.

"In fighting the Durunim and these so-called gods?" Indala asked.

Talinir nodded, his mouth full.

"It would be in our best interests," Harunir said, "but I doubt the Council will see it that way."

"Some will. Some will not." Indala tapped her chin thoughtfully. "Your recent maneuvers may help."

"Tiranel told me about the changes," Talinir said. "I guess my next move is to visit the High Champion. And then move on to the individual Council members. I could use an introduction, perhaps?"

Indala nodded. "I am not sure whether it would be better for it to come from me, or from our three defenders." She smiled at Harunir.

"Why not both?" Eniri asked.

Harunir chuckled. "Why not?"

"Rest here tonight, Talinir," Indala offered. "In the morning, you may visit the High Champion. And we will draft letters of introduction to the other Council members."

"Ah, the High Champion may not be as you remember him," Harunir said. "The struggle to defend the city has… worn him."

"What do you mean?"

"He struggles to remember things at times, and often repeats himself. But do not mistake his failings for stupidity. He is still very intelligent. He simply has trouble expressing himself at times."

Talinir nodded, but winced inside. The High Champion was his best option to gain support. If his mind was in question, that would not make him as much of an asset as Talinir hoped.

"Shift in ten." The voice echoed through the entire house.

"Already?" Eniri grumbled. "We just did one last week."

The announcement meant Intal Eldanir would soon shift from the Starlit Realm to the primary world. The shifts used to happen on a regular basis, with the city spending days or weeks in each world before changing. Now, the city spent almost all of its time in the Starlit Realm, only shifting when needed to take on supplies or to do other business.

"We will prepare ourselves," Indala said, rising from the table. When the city shifted, the Eldanim within had to shift as well, just as Talinir had done multiple times in his trip across Antises.

The others got to their feet. "In the morning, Talinir." Harunir nodded and followed his wife out of the dining room.

●●●●●

Lord Rajwir was the first of the Lords to arrive. As Marshal's representative, Seri felt obligated to greet him on arrival, though she would rather be studying the book with Dravid. The Lord came with only one servant, much different from his grand arrival for the previous Passing. Seri spent a full two hours speaking with him, explaining all that had occurred at the high place in his land. Between Lord Rajwir and all her interactions with the Masters as well, she didn't get back to Dravid for an entire afternoon.

When she finally got back to his recovery room, he was full of enthusiasm. "It was Akhenadom and Aharu!" he exclaimed.

"What about them?" Seri took a seat beside his bed, pleased to see he had more color and roundness to his cheeks. It would take some time to regain the weight he lost during his long sleep, but he was on his way.

"They did all of it," Dravid said. "Dividing the power among the Lords, the creation of the Laws of Cursings and Bindings: they did all of it."

Seri frowned. "Are you sure? I've always heard it was the mages of the time, uniting their abilities."

"The mages helped them, but those two did the real work," Dravid insisted. "And Aharu was the High Master Mage, anyway."

"That's true." Seri reached out and took Dravid's hand, as she had done so many times while he slept. He smiled back at her, and her heart skipped a beat. She blinked and tried to refocus. "Did you find that in the book?"

Dravid released her hand and pulled the huge book from the table at his bedside. "It doesn't say that exactly," he admitted, "but if you read between things, you can see it."

"Read between things?"

"You know storytellers don't always tell everything exactly as it happened."

"I seem to have encountered a storyteller or two like that."

"Or two?"

"Maybe just one." Seri laughed. Whatever else happened, at least she had this now. She had Dravid. Ixchel even left them alone together for hours at a time, though Seri knew she couldn't be far away.

Dravid paged through the book. "Aharu talks about their plans in great detail, about their hopes and what they wanted to accomplish with this new land. But when it comes to the actual execution, she… skips over things."

"Like what?"

"Well, she describes the gathering: all the most powerful mages along with the six men chosen to be the Lords. Obviously, it took place here, in the same chamber as the Passing is held today, if I'm reading right."

"Makes sense."

"And then they… siphoned the power below Zes Sivas, binding it to the blood of the King and the Lords."

"But how?"

Dravid shrugged. "Like I said, she skips stuff."

"I can understand the siphoning," Seri mused. "It's not that much different than what we do, just on a larger scale."

"Much larger."

"But how did they bind it those particular people? And then, even crazier, how did they bind it to enforce the Laws? I know they got the idea from the binding that holds our two worlds together, but having an idea and doing it are two different things."

"And then the Lords betrayed them on that somehow."

Seri threw up her hands. "How did they even know how to betray them, much less do it?"

"It might still be in here," Dravid suggested. "The book is not… written in order. She bounces around from time to time. Also, I think some pages were torn out and then replaced, but not in the right places."

"As if this could be any more confusing."

Dravid gestured. "It's a huge book, written by hand. It takes a while to get through it all."

"Keep trying." Seri sighed. "I wish Jamana were here. He already read it. I should have asked him more while we were together."

"You didn't know at the time. What about the Masters? Haven't any of them read it?"

"Master Korda did, but he's… we don't know what happened to him. Master Ganak has been reading it the most lately, but he said we should draw our own conclusions."

"That's helpful."

"He's willing to talk about it once we've read the whole thing, but not before."

Dravid pulled the book closer. "Guess I'd better get back into it, then."

Seri nodded, a little disappointed. Once again, their personal time came second to the urgency of their mission. At least she wasn't alone in the work now.

An apprentice mage in green robes appeared at the door. "Mage Seri? Your presence is urgently requested in the communication room."

Seri patted Dravid's hand and got to her feet. She might not be alone, but the demands on her time seemed to be growing.

(((14)))

Seri hurried to the communications room. Was that really what the Masters called it? They were so unimaginative sometimes. Seri could think of several other names, all of them more interesting.

Ixchel joined her along the way, seeming to come out of nowhere. Seri no longer questioned her bodyguard's movements. Ixchel came and went, occasionally taking a turn watching Volraag. Sometimes, Seri suspected, she spent time with Victor, though she'd never admitted it. Seri made a mental note to ask her about it again when they were alone.

"Where are we going?" Ixchel asked as they crossed into the Citadel of Kings.

"The com—portal room," Seri answered. Simple but still better than "communications room."

Seri led the way, smiling as she remembered her first days here. She got lost so many times in these hallways. Now wherever she went, she instinctively knew whether it was right. Perhaps it was a side-effect of her growth as a mage.

They descended the stairs to the portal room, no longer locked, where they found all four Masters waiting. Seri paused at the entrance, intimidated. What had gone wrong now?

"Ah, Mage Seri-Belit. Good," Master Tzoyet said. "Send the message." The latter instruction he gave to Master Magnus, who tossed a note through one of the portals. Seri sought out the banner to see… it was the Arazu portal.

"What is happening?" she asked.

"She insisted you be present," Master Plecu grumbled.

"What?"

87

The Arazu portal crackled. Ducking her head low, Lady Lilitu emerged through the portal and straightened in front of them all. She wore a black gown, in recognition of her widowhood, but with the Lady, no gown could be simple. It left her shoulders bare, but she wore black gloves that reached past her elbows. Her only jewelry this time was a frontlet with a green gem.

"My Lady!" Seri exclaimed, delighted both to see her, and to know the portals to the other lands worked. Once Marshal returned with Lord Tyrr, they could fetch Lord Meluhha without difficulty.

The other Masters gave short bows to Lady Lilitu. "Welcome, Lady of Arazu," Lord Tzoyet declared. "While your presence is certainly welcome, we were not expecting you at this time."

Lady Lilitu regarded him with a tilt of her head. "The Passing is set to occur soon, is it not?"

"It is, Lady."

"Then it is necessary that the power of Arazu be here."

The Masters exchanged looks of confusion. "Your pardon, my Lady, but... we were told that the power of Arazu is lost," Master Tzoyet explained.

A vibration rippled through the floor. Lady Lilitu lifted her hand. "The power of Arazu is mine, Masters."

Seri stared along with the Masters. How had this happened? When she last saw the Lady, the power was indeed missing. Where had it gone and how had it passed to her? Seri strained her magical senses. The Lady glowed with power, but far more and far different from their last meeting. She possessed both her own mysterious power and the power of a Lord.

The Masters could sense the same thing as Seri. They exchanged looks again, then bowed their heads.

"It appears to be true," Master Ganak said. "This is a year for new and unusual occurrences. Welcome, Lady Lilitu, the first woman to wield the power of a Lord."

The Lady nodded in return. "Your recognition is appreciated. There is another matter that requires immediate attention, which is why I requested all of you to be here."

"How may we be of service?" Master Tzoyet asked.

"Arazu has been without a Master Mage since the death of the greatly-lamented Master Hain," she answered. "My Lord Enuru had every intention to rectify that problem, but as you know, he was killed before the task was complete. I wish to finish the job."

"The Lords of Antises have always appointed the Masters from among their land's mages," Master Tzoyet agreed. "As you are, by default, the Lord of Arazu, it is your right to make this appointment. Will your new Master Mage be joining us then?"

In one swift movement, Lady Lilitu stepped up beside Seri and placed a hand on her shoulder. "She is already here."

●●●●●

Marshal and Tich were escorted to a waiting room where they spent a frustrating hour. At last, a steward appeared to inform them that Lord Tyrr had arranged a mid-day feast in Marshal's honor.

"You can't be serious," Marshal said.

The steward bowed. "Oh, yes, sir. It is all in readiness and waiting for you."

Tich gave Marshal a gentle push toward the door. "Never turn down offered food, I say. Let's eat."

They followed the steward down another hallway to another set of double doors. Marshal began to wonder if he would ever see outside Lord Tyrr's palace. He hadn't seen so much as a window yet.

The steward threw open the doors and gestured toward one end of the room. An enormous table waited there, elevated above the rest of the room, intended for the Lord and whoever was fortunate enough to dine with him. Six smaller tables filled the rest of the room, all of them already full of people engaged in eating and conversation. Everything fell silent as Marshal entered.

He hesitated for a moment, then followed another servant who indicated where he should sit. Lord Tyrr sat in the very center of his table, eyeing Marshal as he approached. Three of his officials sat on the other side, leaving three seats empty as Marshal approached. The servant pointed Marshal to the middle seat, leaving an empty seat between him and the Lord. Tich sat on his right.

The room's activity resumed. Faces turned away from Marshal, to his relief. He accepted a glass of wine from the servant and looked over the table. Here was food he recognized: roast pork, toasted bread, boiled potatoes with just enough seasoning. Rasna's culinary traditions adhered very close to Varioch's. Marshal felt much more at home with this fare than he did in Kuktarma.

Tich agreed. "Finally, some real food," she exclaimed, piling it onto her plate. "Between Talinir's trail cooking and the spices of Kuktarma, my stomach hasn't been truly happy in weeks."

Marshal glanced at Lord Tyrr, who seemed to be ignoring him. Why the empty seat between them? He tried to remember details about Lord Tyrr's family, but couldn't recall anyone educating him on that particular topic. He should have asked Master Plecu about it before coming.

Marshal took a bite of the roast pork and sensed movement next to him. He looked up to see a young woman his own age slipping into the chair next to Lord Tyrr. She was slim, blonde, and strikingly attractive. "The young King, I presume?" she asked, giving Marshal a pleasant smile.

Marshal swallowed his food and wiped his mouth. "Marshal," he said. "And you are?"

"Aluri," she answered with a nod of her head. "My father rarely holds such mid-day banquets. Either he honors you greatly, or he has some scheme in mind, and this is the start of it." She looked at Lord Tyrr, who deliberately turned toward the official on his left.

"Oh, you're his daughter," Marshal said, then felt dumb for stating the obvious. "I'm sorry. My education on the families of the different lands has been sorely lacking so far."

Aluri placed a few small servings on her plate and took a delicate sip from her wine. "I would be happy to instruct you, if you like. As it turns out, I'm somewhat of an expert on this land's ruling family."

Marshal chuckled. "I wouldn't mind hearing about it. I know far too much of Varioch's ruling family, and have just come from visiting with Kuktarma's." He didn't know why he had told her that.

"Kuktarma. Ah, that explains the clothes, then," Aluri observed, her eyes glancing down over him.

"Hailstones and coals of fire," Tich muttered in a low whisper on Marshal's right.

"I am the oldest of Lord Tyrr's children," Aluri said before Marshal could respond to either comment. "My next oldest brother, Ziv, is naturally next in line for the Lordship. He is currently away, monitoring the invasion along the border."

"That's why I'm here," Marshal put in.

Aluri nodded and continued. "I also have two younger brothers, Zal and Huth. They are currently staying with our mother in the summer palace by the sea." She took another sip of wine. "They were evacuated in case this city comes under attack." Her blue eyes gazed at Marshal over the rim of her wine glass. "Do you think that a likelihood?"

"Do I think what?"

"That Raeton itself will be attacked."

"Oh. No. At least, I hope not. I am here to work with your father to stop these enemies. I think between us, we possess the power to do it."

"That is good to hear." Aluri took a bite of her food. Marshal blinked and did the same. What was he thinking? He was here to help stop an invasion, not exchange pleasantries with a princess, however gorgeous she might be. What a contrast from Kuktarma, where Lord Meluhha's daughter badgered him with questions during the banquet of way-too-spicy food. Here, at least, was someone he could talk with who shared a similar culture. Except, of course, that he grew up a "curse boy" while she grew up a princess.

"Tell me, King Marshal, have you seen the pillars yet?" Aluri asked a few moments later.

"Uh, no. We came directly here from Zes Sivas, and I actually haven't seen anything outside the palace yet."

"Kuktarma to Zes Sivas to here. You have traveled a lot in a short time, it seems." Aluri demurely patted her lips with a cloth napkin. "Even so, you should see the Pillars of Raeton as soon as possible, as it is our only real claim to fame. Once the meal is over, I would be delighted to show them to you and your… companion." She cast a quick glance past Marshal at Tich.

"I would, um, be equally delighted to see them," Marshal said, "but I am anxious to discuss the invasion and our actions with Lord Tyrr."

The Lord abruptly leaned in front of his daughter, as if he had been listening all along. "I've arranged a meeting with my generals and advisors for two hours hence," he said. "Plenty of time to walk outside and see things." He pulled back and returned to eating.

"There you have it," Aluri said, though she gave her father a look of annoyance. "When we're all ready then."

Tich tugged on Marshal's sleeve. He turned to her and she whispered, "You aren't falling for this, are you? He must have ordered her to be nice to you. He's playing both sides."

"What do you mean?"

Tich rolled her eyes. "He knows you're really the King, but won't admit it. So he throws his daughter at you, thinking maybe he can get some control over you that way."

Marshal hoped Aluri couldn't hear Tich's words. "I'm not marrying a Rasnian princess. Besides, I won't be King for long, remember?"

"They don't know that."

"Is there a problem?" Aluri asked.

"No, not at all," Marshal said. "We were just discussing the urgency of the situation. I'm a little troubled that your father seems to be delaying action so much."

"Rasnian culture moves slowly in all things," Aluri explained. "We work hard on obtaining the mineral deposits that fuel our land: iron, gold, silver, and so forth. Just as it takes time to extricate the wealth from the ground below, so we take time in all our major undertakings. It is our way."

"And it's one of the reasons I left," Tich grumbled. "This place is as slow as Kishin's ship in the summer doldrums."

"But we don't have to move that slow," Aluri said. She got to her feet, despite having eaten less than half of the small servings on her plate. She reached out a hand to Marshal. "Come. I'll show you now."

Marshal glanced at Tich, but couldn't really argue. They had walked into that one. He took Aluri's hand and stood. He had meant to only take it while he got to his feet, but she held his tightly and led the way to the exit. Tich scrambled to keep up. Despite his observations to Tich, Marshal realized how this would appear to the dozens of other guests: the princess and the King leaving the banquet early, holding hands. Lord Tyrr was not an idiot, and neither was his daughter.

"Are the pillars far?" he asked, extracting his hand.

"Not at all." She smiled. Now that she wasn't half hidden by the table, Marshal got a good look at all of the princess. Despite his earlier impression of her height, he looked down at her eyes, but only slightly. She was very close to his own height, but so much thinner. Not too thin, though. Her feminine curves were quite evident from the tight blue dress that flowed with her body like water.

Aluri gave an inviting gesture and proceeded down the hall. She turned a corner and led them toward still another set of double doors. This time, when she pushed them open, sunlight and fresh air flowed in. Marshal breathed a sigh of relief. Claustrophobia had never been a problem for him before, but the stuffiness and stress of Lord Tyrr's palace had been closing in on him.

Stepping outside the palace doors, they entered an enormous courtyard. A stone paved path led straight ahead to the outer wall and gates, but to either side, a well-tended garden stretched upward in three tiers. Willow trees were arranged in a pattern on each tier, their weeping branches hanging down, sometimes over the edge down to the next tier. Flowers, most of which Marshal had never seen before, filled planters and circled each tree.

"This is the last thing I expected in Lord Tyrr's palace," he said, turning in a circle to take it all in.

"Do you like it?" Aluri's smile grew and her posture relaxed.

"It's beautiful." Marshal meant it.

"This is my mother's pride and joy." Aluri reached out and ran her fingers across a low-hanging branch from one of the willows. "While she is gone, I do my best to keep up with it for her."

Marshal followed the stone path. "You're doing a great job, from what I can see."

"If you like flowers," Tich mumbled.

"Come." Aluri moved on toward the gates. "You need to see the pillars before my father requires your presence."

Two guards opened the gates as Aluri approached. Marshal took one last look at the gardens, before turning and stepping outside the palace. For a second time, he stopped and stared in awe.

The palace stood on top of a very high hill, looking down at the city of Raeton spread out below. Marshal couldn't be sure, but the city looked larger than either Simbala or Reman. No walls surrounded this city, but at the foot of the hill, an enormous open space stretched out through the middle of the city. Pairs of enormous stone columns marched down the open space, two by two, at least a dozen. From his vantage point at the top of the hill, Marshal's eye level was still several feet below the massive capitals on the two nearest columns. The bases and capitals of the columns were carved of dark granite, while the primary surfaces appeared to be a lighter marble shot through with black.

"The Pillars of Raeton," Princess Aluri announced.

"Impressive every time," Tich said. "Gotta admit it."

Marshal took a step forward and continued to stare. "Who built them?"

"One of the earliest Lords of Rasna commissioned their construction," the princess explained. "Since then, every Lord has either spent time repairing them or adding to the decor down below."

Marshal spared a look for the ground level, noticing winding pathways through smaller columns and fountains. It looked pleasant enough, but his eyes immediately went back to the pillars themselves. Such a monumental feat of construction. He couldn't even imagine how much each of the pillars had to weigh.

"Good to see they survived the earthquake," Tich said.

"Two of them near the end are badly damaged," Aluri admitted. "We have restricted people from that area while the damage is assessed. They could fall at any time."

"What a loss," Marshal said. As he continued to admire the pillars, he remembered Nian. The priest had traveled to five of the six lands of Antises. His last desire was to see the Pillars of Raeton, but he had died trying to protect Marshal from Volraag's soldiers.

"They're every bit as incredible as you imagined, Nian," he whispered. "I never thought I would see them and you wouldn't."

"What was that?" Tich asked.

"Just remembering a friend who wanted to see these."

Aluri walked forward and spread her arms. She stood framed by the two nearest pillars with the midday sun shining down on them all. She turned in a slow circle with her eyes closed.

Marshal took a deep breath. Rasna had been the enemy of Varioch. He had even fought against their soldiers in the army. He never expected to find such beauty here, especially not in the home of Lord Tyrr, a scheming villain in every description of Rasna he heard.

Tich sighed beside him. "I grew up not far from here, but I've never seen the view from up here. Be a real shame if those Durunim make it this far."

Her words reminded him of his mission. "You're right. Maybe we can admire the beauty later." He looked past Aluri at the winding pathways below. "I would love to walk there some day, when all of this is over."

Tich took his hand. "I'll take you sometime." She looked from him to Aluri. "Unless you'd prefer her as a guide."

"She's just being hospitable." Marshal rolled his eyes.

"Remember who her papa is," Tich said in a low voice as Aluri came back.

"Thank you," Marshal said. "It's quite a view. I'll have to come back when things aren't so desperate, and take a stroll through them."

"Now that you've opened the portal between here and Zes Sivas, you can come any time," Aluri pointed out. "I will look forward to your next visit, then."

Tich nudged him.

"We'd better head back," Marshal said. "Your father and I have a lot of work to do."

"As you wish." Aluri walked past them, not even glancing at their clasped hands, and led the way back into the palace.

Marshal took one last look at the Pillars of Raeton, thought of Nian, and smiled.

(((15)))

Seri's face had to mirror the shock she saw on those of the Masters. Lady Lilitu could not possibly be serious.

"With all due respect, your Ladyship," Master Ganak said at last. "Mage Seri-Belit has not even had a full year of training yet. Her promotion from acolyte was done by the late Master Hain—"

"To allow her to travel," Lady Lilitu interrupted. "Yes, I know. But in that time, she has grown exponentially in both power and understanding. In some areas, she exceeds some of you. In others, she lags far behind, it is true. But as she is young, she will have plenty of time to grow in those areas."

After Marshal opened the communication portals, Seri had been forced to explain her star-sight to all of the Masters. It was yet another of the many long distractions keeping her from Dravid and the book. For their part, the Masters had been fascinated by her abilities and demanded numerous illustrations of them, as well as explanations of what different magical events had looked like during her travels.

But even so... the Masters would never approve this. It was inconceivable.

"We will... take consultation on this," Master Tzoyet said.

"Is that common practice when a new Master is chosen by a Lord?" the Lady asked.

"There is no precedent for..."

"Outrageous," Master Plecu muttered just loud enough to be heard.

"Is this because she is a woman?" Lady Lilitu demanded. "Or because I am?"

"It is a combination of factors," Master Tzoyet tried to explain. "It is quite unprecedented."

"It's never been done," Master Plecu added.

"Aharu was the first High Master Mage!" Seri burst out. "And she was a woman!"

"Do you compare yourself to the sister of Akhenadom?" Master Ganak exclaimed.

"No, I—"

"It seems my wishes as sovereign of Arazu are not to be honored, then," Lady Lilitu interrupted. She turned to face Seri. "Did you not say that Lord Rajwir is here? I will speak to him at once about the intransigence of his Master Mage and how that will affect our current trading agreements."

Master Tzoyet's eyes widened. "Lady Lilitu, please be reasonable. We are all dealing with unusual circumstances, and—"

The Lady, guiding Seri with her, headed toward the door. "And now I am accused of being unreasonable. Arazu feeds your lands, gentlemen. These insults will be remembered."

"My Lady," Seri whispered as they started up the stairs. "I do not think—"

"Wait, my child." The Lady took the steps at a glacial pace, while voices argued in rapid words below them.

Before they reached the top stair, Master Tzoyet hurried after them. "My Lady! Please wait!"

Lady Lilitu stopped, turned, and looked down on the mage, arms folded.

"We apologize, my Lady. The stress of recent occurrences. The presence of that criminal Volraag. These things have upset us, so that we are not ourselves." Master Tzoyet's words spilled out in a rush. "We accept your nomination, and will schedule an induction ceremony for your chosen, ah, Master, as soon as possible."

The Lady gave an imperious nod. "Very well. But I want to hear the words of apology from the esteemed Master Mage of Rasna now."

Master Plecu sputtered, but ascended the steps and bowed. "I apologize, my Lady."

"You called my choice 'outrageous,' Master Plecu. I expect you to apologize to her, as well." She placed her hand on Seri's shoulder again.

Plecu, trembling with a combination of rage and fear, no doubt, gave a very short bow to Seri. "I apologize… Master Seri-Belit."

Lady Lilitu nodded. "Very well. I accept your apologies. Do you, Seri?"

"Ah, I do, my Lady."

"Excellent." She turned and ascended the final step. "I will take the same rooms my Lord and I stayed in last time. I know the way," she said over her shoulder. "When next my new Master Mage reports to me, I expect to see her in the proper robes."

Seri watched her depart, heart racing. On the one hand, this was her dream come true. The first female Master Mage since the founding of Antises! On the other hand… the Lady had forced her into the position by essentially blackmailing the rest of the Masters. They would never accept her for her true worth now.

She turned slowly to face the Masters as they ascended. "I, I want you to know that I had no idea she would do this," she said. "I am just as surprised as you are."

Master Plecu snorted but said nothing.

"It cannot be helped," Master Tzoyet said. "It is the law of Antises. The Lord of each land—in this case, the Lady—chooses the next Master from all the full mages in service to the land. No other requirements have ever been laid on the appointment."

"Yet it has always been assumed that only the most qualified mage would ascend," Master Ganak declared, his eyes flashing.

"Now, now," said Master Magnus, climbing the stairs behind the others. "We all know that politics has always played a role, for good or ill. The Lords choose from their mages, yes, but rarely do they make that decision based on ability or training alone." He stopped and spread his arms. "Lord Volraag chose me, not necessarily for my great skill as a mage, but because of my relationship with his family." He shrugged. "My sister Cyra is his concubine."

Seri swallowed. At least she had not told the Masters of her familial relationship to the Lady.

Master Plecu pushed past the others. "I will not take lessons in diplomacy from Volraag!" He stormed down the hall.

Master Tzoyet sighed. "Master Ganak, will you arrange the induction ceremony. Tomorrow morning should be soon enough. The day is growing late."

One by one, the other Masters passed by Seri and returned to the Citadel of Mages. She stood alone for several minutes, unable to process all that had just happened. The mixed feelings continued to wash over her, but as she considered them, one feeling above all rose to prominence. She didn't want to call it pride. But wasn't it appropriate to take pride in one's accomplishments?

Seri-Belit, Master Mage of Arazu. One of the six highest mages of all Antises. Whatever the circumstances might be, she had made it. The annoying little man who had rowed her to shore that first day popped into her mind. "Do you think they'll let a woman be a mage?" she said out loud. "Ha!"

Then she rushed to tell Dravid.

•••••

"The enemy army is on the move," Lord Tyrr's general reported. A tall man with a dropping mustache, he stood firm at the end of the conference table.

"All of it?" Marshal asked. He stood to Lord Tyrr's right. Why did all these different groups insist on standing around a perfectly good table when chairs existed?

"We do not think so," the general said. "It is difficult to gauge the exact numbers of these…"

"Durunim," Marshal supplied.

"Yes. Durunim. Since they come and go through the portal, and they have built this fortress, we cannot say with certainty how many of them exist."

"How big is the army that is moving? Where are they going?" Aluri asked. Marshal had been surprised when she joined the strategic meeting. She stood to Lord Tyrr's left.

"We counted five hundred," the general said. "They are moving southeast, following the flow of the Amnis. They will reach the village of Fasena in two days."

"And from there, it's only a few days' march to Raeton, following our new road," Aluri said. "A road, I might add, that was built specifically for the passage of our armies to fight against Varioch."

"I do not regret the road for one moment," Lord Tyrr growled. "It served us well."

"So this army is between us and the high place," Marshal said. "Lord Tyrr, between the two of us, we wield more than enough power to deal with five hundred."

Tich mumbled something behind him, but he didn't catch her words.

"Truly?" Aluri asked. "You think your power that sufficient?"

"Seri… um, one of the mages explained to me that the King's power is roughly equivalent to three of the Lords. Since I also possess a Lord's power, I have four times that. Do you think the equivalent of five Lords can handle an army of five hundred?"

"A Lord's power far exceeds an army of a hundred," Lord Tyrr agreed, "if it's the right Lord. Not all who bear the title know how to use their power."

"The point is that we should set out at once," Marshal argued. "You and I. We can stop this army, then proceed to the high place and shut it down."

"A wise man goes into battle only when he possesses all possible knowledge of his enemy," Tyrr said.

"That's… actually pretty smart," Tich said

"What other knowledge do we need?" Marshal asked, irritation sharpening his words. It had taken far too long just to get to this conversation. How much longer would it take to get to action?

"Who leads this army? What are his powers? What magical defenses do these creatures possess? Do they die as humans do, or are they harder to kill? Are we truly seeing all of them, or might others be hidden from our scouts?" Lord Tyrr bent over the table, leaning his fists against it. "These are just some of the questions we could ask. There is much knowledge to be gained yet."

"Ah, our scouts do report a frightening number of eidola in the region of the, ah, Durunim army," the general said.

"Eidola?" Aluri frowned. "More magical enemies?"

"I've encountered them," Marshal said. "An eidolon is the shadowy form here of a Durunim in the Otherworld."

"Can they harm us in our world?" Aluri asked.

"Yes. And they are difficult to fight against, as they can remove their shadow form in a moment." As he recalled his previous fights with them, Marshal had to admit things might not be as easy as he hoped.

"Then how do you propose we fight them?" Lord Tyrr asked.

Marshal thought for a moment.

"If they're in the Otherworld, wouldn't it be easier to fight them there?" Tich asked.

"Yes, of course." Marshal nodded. "I can cross into their world and deal with them."

"You can do that?" Lord Tyrr asked, but all eyes in the room had fixed on Marshal.

"I can. I have traveled back and forth multiple times." Every time he did it, it grew easier to do. Yet every time he did it, it grew harder to leave. He hadn't tried it with his new sword yet, but he felt sure it must be the equal of a warpsteel blade.

"Let me be sure I understand," Aluri said. "Your proposal is that you and my father, just the two of you, meet this army and destroy hundreds of them with your magic, crossing into the Otherworld if necessary to hunt them all down and slay them."

"I do not want to kill them," Marshal said. "But they have invaded Antises. As its King, I am responsible for the safety of its people. I will do what I have to do."

"And what of their leaders?" Lord Tyrr wanted to know. "General Thesan, have you seen any of these so-called gods the mages have been warning us about?"

"Not as such, your Lordship. But this advancing army is led by a large figure in golden armor. We have not been able to see much of him to know whether he is one of their own kind, or something else."

"Have you seen him wield any magic?" Marshal asked.

"Not specifically, no."

It could be one of the gods. After all, they wouldn't all have gone to the eastern portal. For that matter, there could be an equal number here, already in Antises, as Marshal had seen with the eastern Durunim army. The thought did give him pause.

"How does that impact your plan?" Lord Tyrr asked. "What kind of powers might this leader have?"

"We'll have to be prepared… for anything," Marshal admitted. "The gods we've encountered so far have had a wide range of powers. All of them, at the very least, are exceptionally strong and resilient."

"And beautiful," Tich added.

"Some have shown power over nature. One was able to kill with a touch."

"Do our powers even work against them?" Tyrr wondered.

"Yes… for the most part." Marshal winced. "The leader of the gods in Kuktarma was able to resist my power."

Silence fell over the room. Aluri and the generals stared at Marshal. Lord Tyrr's fists grew tighter. At last he lifted them and slammed them back against the table.

"This is preposterous! You come here promising help, and suggest a quick and easy battle plan to defeat this enemy. Yet all the while, you knew their power might be more than we could handle!"

"I think, between the two of us—" Marshal began.

"No, you didn't think. That's the problem here!" Lord Tyrr straightened up and fixed his gaze on Marshal. "What chance do we have against the odds you've just listed? What if one of these gods is equal to the one you already fought?"

"Again, I think—I believe—the two of us together can succeed," Marshal insisted. "Alone, you might fail. Alone, even I might fail. But together, we can do this."

Tyrr glared at him, before finally nodding. "Very well. We leave tomorrow at noon. We'll take along some warriors to watch our backs." He raised a finger. "When we encounter this army, we test our strength against their leader. If he proves too much for us, we retreat. If we stop him, we can consider moving on to the portal."

Marshal hesitated. He hated every delay, but he couldn't get Lord Tyrr to Zes Sivas without taking care of this. "Agreed."

"Noon then." Lord Tyrr left the room. Marshal was sure at least one of the generals breathed a visible sigh of relief.

Aluri waited until the generals filed out, then turned to Marshal. "I will find rooms for you and your friend."

"I think we'll return to Zes Sivas for the night," Marshal said. "I've realized that I need something I left there."

Aluri nodded. "Then I'll see you when you return."

As Aluri left the room, Tich looked quizzically at Marshal. "What did you forget on Zes Sivas?"

"Victor."

<h1 style="text-align: center;">(((16)))</h1>

Marshal straightened up after stepping through the portal back to Zes Sivas. He stretched his back, feeling old pains from his many injuries complaining. Then he noticed Tich, her arms folded, glaring at him. "What is it?" he asked.

"What is it? Are you really that oblivious?"

"Apparently…"

"First you ignore me for that snobby princess, and now you want to take Victor along instead?"

"What?"

Tich spun and started up the stairs. Marshal lunged after her and caught her arm. "Tich, wait!'

She pulled away from him. "I know when I'm not wanted."

"Of course you're wanted!"

She stopped and glared at him again. The half-light of the stairs made it difficult to see her face. "You have a strange way of showing it, if that's true."

"I don't… I told you I'm not marrying a Rasnian princess, even if Lord Tyrr throws her at me."

"When she was around, your eyes never left her."

"That's not true. I, I looked at the Pillars. I examined Lord Tyrr's battle map. I wasn't watching her!"

Tich snorted, but didn't move.

Marshal spread his hands. "Look, she's pretty. I won't deny that. But I'm not interested in her. Not in… that way."

"Oh, there's another way?"

"I don't understand what you want from me."

"What I want?" Tich shook her head. "You told me…"

"I told you what?"

"You told me I didn't have to be alone any more." She pointed back at the portals. "I felt alone from the moment that whore sat down next to you."

"Tich, I… I'm sorry." Marshal swallowed back several more arguments that popped into his head. "I didn't mean to make you feel that way."

"Then why did we come back here so you could dump me off for Victor?"

"What? I didn't say anything about dumping you off!"

Tich didn't answer.

"I need Victor," Marshal explained. "He's my best friend and backs me up wherever we go. But more importantly for this, he's got that flail, which we know can hurt the gods. I want him there in case Lord Tyrr and I run into trouble."

Tich didn't answer again. She wiped something from next to her eye.

"Just because I want Victor along doesn't mean I don't want you there."

Tich sighed. She sat on the stairs and stared back at the portal room. Marshal awkwardly sat next to her.

"I won't do you any good if I do go back," she said at last. "I didn't do anything today."

"No, you, um, you kept me… you reminded me of who I was supposed to be. All day."

Tich's brow wrinkled. "How do you mean?"

"Even when you were annoyed, or when you would toss in comments in the middle of things… it helps." Marshal was sure his words sounded pathetic. "I mean, in the middle of all that fancy stuff, with Lords and princesses and generals… you were there. And it reminded me that I'm not a part of that. I don't want to be a part of that. Back in Kuktarma, when I had to sit with Lord Meluhha at the banquet, and all of you were at another table… I was miserable. But the longer it went on, the more I got caught up in it, and I actually started thinking of myself as a King. I don't want that."

"So… I remind you that you're not a King?"

"You remind me that I'm human. That I came from a small village up in the mountains. And that's who I want to be. Not a fancy King who wears fancy clothes and flirts with princesses and—"

"You admit you were flirting!"

"No! I'm saying I don't want to be that person."

"And you need me to remind you that you're pathetic like the rest of us."

"Something like that." He grinned. "My mother always reminded me that I was loved, valuable, and had a purpose in this world. Now that I have all this power, maybe I need someone to remind me of the opposite."

"That you're hated, worthless, and have a pointless existence?"

"Hailstones, I didn't mean that. Just… that I'm not as important as I might be tempted to think I am. I can't get arrogant. Then I'd be just like those gods."

Tich nodded. "I was hoping to be a little more useful, but if that's all I'm good for…"

"That's not all."

"Oh? There's another reason to keep me around?"

Marshal stood and held out his hand. Tich took it and let him pull her up. He looked down into her eyes. "You make me think there could be a reason to go on after all of this is over."

"I don't understand."

"Over and over, I keep getting hurt. I've been healed by magic several times now. Some other wounds have healed more slowly."

Tich reached up and touched one of his facial scars. He nodded.

"The more this goes on, the more I've thought I won't live through it all. That when I finally release all this power and change Antises… it'll kill me."

"No…"

"I don't know. It might. But… having you around… It makes me want to live past that."

Tich shook her head. "I can't be your reason for living. Don't put that on me."

"Wh-why not? I can't hope for a life after this?"

"I can't handle that." She pulled away. "I'll run. I'll hop on a ship and lose myself again. It's what I do. I always disappoint people."

He caught her hand again. "Then there's another reason to keep you close." He looked down at her. "Tich, I… I don't know much of anything about… love. Except that my mother loved me. So I don't know if… if I love you or not. But I want to find out."

"Idiot." Tich grabbed the back of Marshal's head and pulled his face down to hers. Before he understood what she was doing, she put her lips on his and kissed him. And before he could respond the way he wanted to, she pulled back, turned and hurried up the stairs.

●●●●●

Talinir hesitated before knocking on the door to the High Champion's home. The last time he had even seen Haruta in person had been the day Talinir graduated from his warden training. Haruta told him never to neglect his sword training, something Talinir took to heart. The High Champion of Intal Eldanir was chosen only when the previous one died or gave up the position. Though he did not command any troops, the High Champion was the greatest warrior of the Eldanim, recognized for his skill and bravery.

The sun shone brightly on the white stones of the city. Though Talinir loved its appearance beneath the stars of the Otherworld, he had to admit the city held a different sort of beauty beneath sunlight.

He took a breath and knocked. "I'll be right there," a loud voice called from inside.

Talinir waited. Several long minutes went by. No one came to the door, and no other sounds came from within. Hesitantly, Talinir knocked again.

A moment later, the door opened. Haruta stood looking down at him. He had always been tall, even for the Eldanim. "Ah… Talinir, wasn't it? Come in, come in. I always have time for one of our wardens." He beckoned and turned back into the house, with no explanation of his delay.

Talinir followed him into a wide living area sparsely furnished. An enormous vaulted ceiling lined with crossbeams made the room feel even larger. Haruta took a seat in a well-worn, but substantial teak chair. "Sit, sit. Tell me of your duties outside the city."

Talinir found another chair and licked his lips. How to begin? "Haruta, it is an honor to be in your home—"

"None of that." Haruta waved his hand. "I got to be High Champion by strength and skill, not by any fancy honor or something."

Talinir smiled. "Of course. I am sure you are aware of the recent Durunim attacks."

"Yes, yes. We drove them from the west side without difficulty. Annoying, but no one was seriously hurt. They don't seem to have the numbers they once did."

"That's because most of them have traveled here, to the primary world," Talinir said. "They are led by those who call themselves gods and are attacking the humans."

"Eh? Well, I suppose it's better than them attacking us."

"I have been traveling many months with the humans." Talinir inched forward on his chair. "I've spent a lot of time with their new King, and have come back to Intal Eldanir with a request from him."

"They have a King again? When did that happen? Seems like I would have heard of something like that."

Talinir patiently explained everything, step by step. Haruta looked off in the distance a few times, as if he had lost connection with the conversation. Each time it happened, Talinir waited a moment, then resumed talking, picking up from a few sentences earlier.

As he drew near the end, describing Marshal's request, Haruta jumped to his feet and paced around the room. "This is monumental. There is no question about it. We must help. We know how to fight the Durunim."

"I hoped you would agree." Talinir also got to his feet. "Between you, the High Warden, and the High Mage together, you will have a strong voice in the Council."

Haruta's eyebrows arched. "The Council? Why would the three of us have a voice in the Council?"

"Ah, High Mage Harunir told me that the three of you together now have a voice…?"

Haruta stood still, looking down. Talinir waited, not knowing what else to say. At last, he opened his mouth to speak, but Haruta jerked and looked at him suddenly.

"Yes. We will take this to the Council. With the recent changes, I now have a voice, along with the High Mage and High Warden. We will make them listen to us. This is an area ideal for us to speak on, after all."

"Yes, it is." Talinir sighed with relief. "I will be visiting the other Council members prior to the next meeting. May I tell them of your enthusiasm?"

"Of course! In fact, I should go with you. I haven't asked the Council for anything in years. They should listen to me now." He looked around as if he needed to find something before rushing out the door.

"If you think it wise," Talinir said. "I will have recommendations from High Mage Harunir and Council member Indala when I go to the other members—"

In the middle of Talinir's sentence, a dark figure dropped from one of the wooden ceiling beams, landing right behind Haruta. Before either of the Eldanim could react, the stranger whipped a blade across Haruta's throat. He grabbed at the cut, eyes wide. Blood gushed around his fingers. He stumbled, and collapsed to the floor.

Facing Talinir, his blade dripping, stood Rathri, the leper assassin.

"How…" Putting aside his shock, Talinir managed to drop into a stance and draw his warpsteel sword.

Rathri bent and wiped his blade on Haruta's shirt. "Come, Talinir. Cutting someone's throat is not all that difficult. I'm sure you've done it before, warden of the Eldanim."

"How are you here?" Talinir demanded.

Rathri stood again. "Back at the high place, Volraag knocked me into a crevasse… and I tumbled through the portal into the Starlit Realm. Once I eluded the Durunim gathered there, it was a simple matter to make my way to Intal Eldanir." He gave a mock bow. "I am, after all, a warden like you."

Talinir's mind spun. While back in Kuktarma, he had seen Rathri stumbling around in the Otherworld, but hadn't considered that he might come this way. The assassin must have been the other traveler whose existence he'd discovered. But… things still didn't make sense. Why did he still look like a human leper, if he'd made it into the Otherworld?

"Going through the portal did not heal me," Rathri said, as if reading his thoughts. "The abominable curse of the humans still restricts my body."

Talinir sidestepped, making sure he had plenty of room for any move he might need to make. Rathri mimicked him, stepping in the opposite direction. Haruta's body lay still now. He could not have survived.

"Why?" Talinir asked. "Why kill the High Champion?"

Rathri took a step backwards. "I want the humans to suffer. And your actions could help them. It's really not much more complicated than that."

"And so you kill your own people to hurt another?"

Rathri's eyes narrowed. "I tried to come to them for help, before you arrived here. They refused. I suppose no one has visited that particular hospital in the past day, or the bodies would have been discovered."

A deep sense of horror seized Talinir. Over the past year, he had seen much in the way of death and bloodshed, but not here. Not Intal Eldanir. This place was a sanctuary, a shelter from the dangers of the worlds around them. Rathri violated that sanctuary. And unless he was stopped, he would go on violating it.

Talinir leaped forward, sword moving like a blur. Rathri dodged and shoved Haruta's teak chair into Talinir's way. He staggered back, off balance.

Rathri did not take advantage of his plight. "I won't kill you yet, Talinir." He dashed to the nearest window, then paused. "Not yet. Your hope for the humans must be totally dismantled first." He saluted with his sword. "Intal Eldanir's streets will run red, starting with anyone who supports you." He disappeared through the window.

(((17)))

Talinir rushed out of the High Champion's home. He saw no sign of Rathri on the sunlit streets. The assassin threatened anyone who supported Talinir. That meant Harunir and Indala.

Where would they be at this time of the morning? And would Rathri even know? Talinir ran down the street, heading toward their home. Either of them might be there now. Harunir came and went at odd times. His duties as a mage involved eclectic work, much of it at home, but some throughout the city. Indala held an office near the High Council Chamber, and would probably be there now. Eniri would also be at work at her hospital.

Three locations. Which one would Rathri seek out first? The Council Chamber would be closest, but in the opposite direction from the home. The hospital was even further. Talinir wavered a moment, then dashed in the direction of the Chamber. Indala was his most significant supporter, and the most ideal target for Rathri.

Halfway to the Chamber, Talinir spotted something lying on the street ahead. His heart sank as he drew near. Bodies. Two of them. He paused long enough to confirm they weren't anyone he knew. Two passers-by, one male and one female, lay with their throats cut. Their bodies had been arranged in a crude arrow, pointing on down the street. Rathri was toying with him. He ran as fast as he could.

Talinir burst into Indala's office only to find her in conference with a young couple. Their eyes widened at the warden's sudden entrance.

"He's not here?" Talinir gasped, trying to regain his breath.

Indala stood. "Who? Talinir, what's going on?"

"Assassin. Killed the High Champion. Said he was coming for you."

Indala struck a bell hanging on the wall. "Two wardens will be here in moments," she said. "I will be protected. Talinir, report this to the High Warden immediately."

Talinir shook his head as he backed out of the door. "No. If he's not here, then he's going for your husband. Is Harunir at home?"

"Yes, he—"

Talinir was out of the building before Indala finished her answer. Rathri must have doubled back after killing the other two. Either that, or Talinir had just abandoned Indala to her doom. But he couldn't think that way. Harunir's safety mattered now.

The High Mage would be well capable of defending himself, if he saw the attack coming. But assassins rarely announced themselves, as Rathri had demonstrated in killing Haruta.

Talinir cut between two houses and ran through a park, trying to narrow the distance to the house. He knew the city somewhat well, but Rathri had been here several days studying his routes. He could be very far ahead by now.

The trip across this side of Intal Eldanir seemed to take an interminable amount of time. Talinir ran as fast as his long legs could take him. Surely Rathri's human legs would move slower. But the assassin seemed possessed of incredible power and resilience. Talinir could not underestimate him, no matter what.

He threw open the door to the house and screamed "Harunir!" at the top of his lungs. In seconds, the High Mage appeared at the top of the stairs to the second floor, looking down at him. "Talinir?"

Talinir bounded up the stairs and swept through every room in the house. No sign of the assassin anywhere.

"What is happening?" Harunir asked.

"We have an assassin loose in the city." Talinir put his hands on his knees to catch his breath. "He killed the High Champion in front of me, and said he was coming for those who support me."

"Indala!"

"She's safe." Talinir lifted his hand in reassurance. "I checked her before coming here. But if he's not here, then…"

Harunir bolted down the stairs. "My daughter!"

•••••

"Two of the patients will need to be shifted back before the city returns."

Eniri nodded at her co-worker's words. The magic of the hospital allowed individual rooms to be shifted back into the Starlit Realm. Some older patients, like Lady Siratel, could not stay away from the stars for lengthy times. It also came in handy when someone was seriously injured and needed healing.

"I'll check on them first," Eniri said. She made her way to the patient rooms, first stopping to see an elderly man, a former mage who sometimes resisted their attempts to help him. He insisted he could handle himself. Eniri wished he could; it would make her job much easier. After visiting with him a few minutes, she moved on to the other patient, Lady Siratel.

As always, the lights were dim in the Lady's room. Eniri entered softly, not wanting to disturb her if she slept. Lady Siratel might be the oldest Eldani in the city. Her prophetic gift had been shared with multiple generations, always guiding people toward their true purpose. No other Eldani, to Eniri's knowledge, possessed that power.

"Lady Siratel, are you awake?" she asked in a hushed tone.

"The Lady can't speak right now." The voice was harsh, rasping and painful to the ears.

Eniri narrowed her eyes. Ignoring the view of the Starlit Realm, she focused on seeing through the darkness of this room. Lady Siratel sat on the edge of her bed. Behind her, a shadowy figure crouched, holding a short sword across her neck.

"Who are you? What is this?" Eniri took a step backward. She needed help, but would have to leave the room to summon it.

"Don't leave. We're just getting started."

Eniri heard a whisper of something moving through the air, followed by a slicing pain in her left calf. She screamed and collapsed. She fumbled for the injury, trying to stop the blood flow.

"That's better." The shadowy figure moved to be able to see her on the floor. "Now we can talk, but not for long. Talinir is on his way, but he'll sadly be too late to help the two of you."

"Why?" Eniri asked, clenching her teeth against the pain.

"Because, my dear, it will hurt him." The assassin reached around and took hold of one of Lady Siratel's hands. She moaned.

"Why do they call you 'Lady,' anyway?" he asked. "The Eldanim have no nobility. Is it merely a sign of respect for your… gift?"

"Leave her. If you want to hurt Talinir, take me. He barely knows the Lady."

"But she told him his future once, didn't she? Did she tell him of this day?" The assassin lifted the Lady's hand and placed it against his own face. "What do you see in my future, Lady Siratel?"

The old woman moaned again. "Blood…" she whispered. "And death."

"How disappointing. Anyone could have predicted that." He released her hand. "You gave me a much more interesting prediction the last time."

"What did she tell you?" Eniri asked, still trying to stop the blood flowing from the gash in her calf.

"She told me if I entered the primary world, I would never come back." He chuckled. "I guess she doesn't see all."

"You haven't…" the Lady whispered.

"Is this where you're going to justify it by saying I'm not the same person any more? Excuses."

While he talked with the Lady, Eniri scooted back toward the door, leaving a trail of blood.

"Still trying to leave? I suppose our time is up, after all. No sense testing fate." The assassin made a swift motion. Though Eniri couldn't see it clearly, she knew he sliced open Lady Siratel's neck. The body fell from the bed with a disturbing thump.

She scrambled back another foot. Her elbow crossed the door frame.

"That's far enough." The assassin hopped down from the bed. "I killed her quickly so I could have more time with you. I want Talinir to get the full message." Light from the hallway glinted from his bloody sword.

Eniri let go of her wound and rolled back into the hallway. "Emergency shift!" she screamed. "Room eighty-seven!"

The assassin lunged forward, but he was too slow. The entire room dissolved, taking him and Lady Siratel's body into the Starlit Realm. The last thing Eniri saw of the assassin in this world was a sickly green face glaring at her with steel eyes.

She let herself fall back onto the floor, but only for a moment. "Help!" she called weakly, reaching for her calf again. Behind her, she heard footsteps rushing down the hall, and then a familiar face looked down at hers. Talinir.

• • • • •

A grim meeting took place at Harunir and Indala's home a few hours later. High Warden Tiranel joined Talinir and the family to discuss the day's events.

"You should have come to me," Tiranel griped.

"I was trying to save lives," Talinir said. "I did not have time to make reports."

"You did the right thing," Indala assured him. "We're not here to argue that. We need to decide what to do next."

"Unfortunately, the assassin managed to disappear from view right after your daughter sent him into the Starlit Realm," Tiranel said. "I've sent a full squad of wardens to search for him."

"I question whether they have a chance." Talinir placed his head in his hands, leaning on his knees. "Rathri has proven to be remarkably proficient."

"Who is this Rathri?" Harunir asked. Eniri lay snuggled under his arm, her leg bandaged and elevated. "Eniri said he looked human."

"But diseased," she added.

Talinir lifted his head and sighed. "I did not want to believe it at first, but the more I encountered him, the more I had to admit: he has warden training."

"Impossible!" Tiranel protested. "I've never trained a human in our ways, nor did my predecessor. Anything before that, and it would be far outside a human lifespan."

"He's not human." Talinir hesitated, then went on: "From what I can guess, he was one of us who unfolded himself into the primary world. And there, he did something so horrendous that he suffered one of their curses, trapping him in the body that you saw."

The other Eldanim stared at him, horror in their eyes. "Unthinkable," Tiranel whispered.

"Do you have any idea who he might be, High Warden?" Indala asked.

"We have lost wardens before..." he admitted. "We assumed they were lost to the Durunim."

"Surely not very many," Harunir said.

"No, not many. I would have a complete list in my office. We might be able to narrow it down a little, but... what good would it do?"

"Perhaps if we knew who he was, we would have a better idea of his motivations," Indala suggested.

"His motivations are clear," Talinir said. "He hates the humans because of his curse. And because my purpose is to help them, he fights against me. I have faced him three times now."

"He matches your skill?"

"Matches and maybe exceeds it." Talinir did not like to admit it, but he had to be honest.

"That narrows our search greatly," Tiranel said. "You are one of the finest swordsmen we have ever trained, Talinir. There are not many who would equal you."

"Any bit of information might help us," Indala said. "What if he has relatives still within the city? High Warden, take Talinir and see if you can narrow that list down."

"What about speaking to the other Council members?" Talinir asked. "Every day we delay could cost more lives."

"Tomorrow. And I will go with you. No more letters of recommendation. We must make our case and then hold a Council meeting as soon as possible."

(((18)))

Seri ran her hands across the purple fabric of her new robes. It was probably her imagination, but they felt more comfortable than her blue or orange ones. Despite how it had happened, this was the fulfillment of her dreams, she kept reminding herself.

"The ceremony would normally take place in the Inner Sanctum," Master Magnus explained as he led her down the hall. "But we're still repairing the damage and clearing it of debris. In the meantime, we're holding your induction ceremony in the council chambers. I know it's not the best, but we all have to make sacrifices right now."

Seri moved as if in a dream. Putting on the robes made it real. This ceremony would make it official. And yet part of her still struggled to believe. She expected another mage from Arazu to pop around a corner at any moment and demand the position that rightfully belonged to him. She knew of at least four such mages who had been skipped over for her promotion. She would have to visit each one later and try to smooth things over, in case any of them harbored ill feelings about all this.

Magnus paused and leaned closer to speak in a lower tone. "I had to change into my purple robes in front of the other Masters. We, uh, decided to skip that part of the ceremony for you."

Seri's eyes widened. "I should think so!"

The other Master chuckled and resumed walking. Seri, face flaming, hastened to follow. Why had he even told her that? She thought Plecu was the annoying one. Then again, this Master had been appointed by Volraag, after working as a palace mage for Lord Varion. Seri shuddered.

Ixchel did not follow her this time, trusting in the Masters. Seri

116

wanted Dravid to come, but no one else was allowed to view the ceremony, apparently, except the Masters themselves and the Lord of the land in question.

Seri entered the audience chamber and saw Lady Lilitu waiting. Masters Tzoyet, Plecu, and Ganak stood in front of their seats. Magnus took his place as well. Seri stood beside the Lady, facing the Masters, on the platform for those who were addressing or being questioned by the Conclave. The Masters all sat, save Master Tzoyet.

"Lady Lilitu," he began, "as sovereign of the land of Arazu, have you made your selection for the next Master Mage to represent your land and people?"

"I have," the Lady replied. "She stands before you now. Seri-Belit of Arazu."

Seri felt a thrill run down her spine. On instinct, she waved her hand and absorbed a rush of magic.

"Seri-Belit, mage of Arazu," Master Tzoyet intoned, "are you prepared to take on the weight and responsibilities of this station, to become a true Master Mage, to represent your land, your people, and your Lady?"

"I am prepared."

"Are there any objections to the elevation of Seri-Belit to this Conclave?" Master Tzoyet turned and met the eyes of each of the other Masters. One by one, they shook their heads. Seri let out a breath she hadn't realized she was holding. At least none of them would complain here.

"Very well. My Lady, if you would step off the platform, please?" Master Tzoyet gestured and Lady Lilitu nodded. She stepped away, leaving Seri alone.

Master Tzoyet instructed her to stand still and then took his own seat. He placed both hands on the arms of his chair and closed his eyes. Seri watched him, but nothing happened. She looked to the other Masters, who had also closed their eyes. What were they doing?

She felt the movement of magic a second before it reached her. A trickle of vibration entered the platform on which she stood and ran up her legs. "Bonded in service to Antises," Master Tzoyet declared. A moment later, another trickle of magic reached her. "Bonded in service to Antises," Master Ganak repeated.

Intrigued, Seri activated her star-sight. She saw narrow beams of orange magic flowing out from the two Masters' chairs, across the floor and to the platform. Another beam shot out from Master Magnus.

"Bonded in service to Antises," he said. The final beam and declaration, from Master Plecu, took just a second or two longer to come than the others, but at last it did. Seri stood trembling as the four trickles of magic combined into her, circling through her body.

"Can you feel what we are doing?" Master Tzoyet asked.

"Yes, Master." At her answer, the beams faded and stopped.

"Now that the power has flowed through your body, it is time to return it," he instructed. "Send back the same amount to each of us."

The same amount? Exactly? Seri swallowed. She hadn't been paying attention that closely. How could you even measure such a thing? For a moment, she panicked, believing her induction would be cancelled. "It need not be exact," Master Tzoyet added, his eyes still closed.

Seri relaxed. That she could do. She just had to focus on the directions. She closed her eyes, but popped them back open right away. Unlike the other Masters, seeing things helped her. She focused on allowing power to flow out from her feet into the platform. As it moved, she started to guide it. To her surprise, she found it remarkably easy. Within the floor, she could sense some kind of channels which absorbed her magic and directed it to each of the Masters' chairs. It must be similar to the communications device. She sent a trickle back to each Master, hoping she had done enough. Each one, in turn, stiffened briefly as her power reached them.

"From us to you, and from you to us," Master Tzoyet declared. "We are all bonded in service to Antises." He stood and opened his eyes. The other Masters did likewise.

Master Tzoyet pointed to the chair on the Seri's far right. "Come and join us, Master Seri-Belit."

Heart pounding, Seri climbed the steps to the Masters' platform and moved in front of the chair. The other Masters sat. She followed their lead. The hardwood chair's surfaces were smooth from years of use, but still firm and unyielding. It would not be comfortable to sit here for long discussions. No wonder the Masters sometimes grew grumpier the longer meetings went on.

"The ceremony is complete," Master Tzoyet announced. "Welcome to the Conclave."

Lady Lilitu applauded politely. Seri continued to struggle with the reality. She sat on the platform with the Masters, in one of their chairs, as one of them. A Master Mage. It was real.

• • • • •

Kishin pulled the sword free from the body of the Durunim scout. At least he had a sword again, though it didn't compare to the warpsteel blade he'd obtained from Talinir. He wiped the sword on the grass, then worked to take the Durunim's belt and scabbard.

Strange how he felt nothing from killing this enemy. No guilt. No regret. Perhaps it had to do with the "cause" concept Nehesy kept trying to feed him. He killed this man, or whatever he was, to defend Antises. Did that make all the difference?

The Durunim's skin was disturbing. Even dead, it appeared to absorb light and warp Kishin's perceptions. He shook his head to clear it. He considered taking the scout's uniform, but Nehesy didn't seem to be planning anything requiring subterfuge. Then again, Nehesy didn't have a plan at all, at least one he shared with anyone else.

Kishin returned to the current campsite to find Jamana and Adhi listening at Nehesy's feet. No doubt he had been dispensing more of his vague "wisdom."

"Killed a scout," Kishin announced. "He would have found you three in a minute or less."

"Thank you," Nehesy said. He stood up, leaning on his staff. "We must not be far from the enemy army now."

Adhi and Jamana scrambled to their feet as well. "What should we do?" Jamana asked.

"You? Nothing. But I have a task for our friend Kishin here."

Kishin narrowed his eyes. "What do you want now, old man?"

Nehesy fumbled with his bag and brought out a scroll. "I have a message for you to deliver."

"Now I'm a messenger?"

"It's a significant upgrade from assassin, if you ask me."

Kishin shook his head. "Who is the message for?"

"Murdak, king of the gods."

"And I should just walk up to him and hand him this message? Like you had this acolyte deliver a message to me?"

"Wave a flag of parley…" Nehesy pulled a white cloth out of his bag. "Like this one! And you should be just fine."

Kishin took the white flag. "Do you at least know which direction his camp lies?"

Nehesy pointed. "That way. I would guess under two miles."

Kishin turned and started walking.

"I would leave the Durunim belt and sword behind, if I were you,"

Nehesy called. "It might not send the right message."

Kishin growled. He still wasn't sure why he listened to this old man, but running away didn't sound any better. He removed the belt and sword and left them with his pack.

He found the Durunim camp in just under two miles. The old man's selective knowledge grated at him. As he approached, waving the flag, he took stock of the enemy. He couldn't count the Durunim, but there had to be a few thousand, at the least. Moving among them, he spotted a dozen or more of the golden-skinned gods. Beasts of burden and a handful of the fearsome tunaldi were picketed in several locations around the camp's outskirts.

A squad of Durunim came to meet him, curved swords at the ready. He kept the flag and both his hands in the air. "I come with a message for Murdak, king of the gods!" he called.

None of the Durunim spoke, but they indicated which way he should walk. Surrounded by the squad, he entered their camp, aiming for an enormous tent in the center. As they walked, his eyes sought out everything. Everywhere he looked, he saw soldiers, professional, single-minded, ready for battle. Without magical help, none of the armies of Antises would stand a chance against them.

As they drew near the tent, he saw that it was more of a canopy: a roof from the elements, but no walls. The squad stepped away from him and allowed him to enter alone. Nothing much lay beneath the canopy, save some other tent supplies waiting to be erected. Directly ahead, a huge litter rested on the ground. Kishin immediately knew the figure seated there must be Murdak.

He halted and stared, unable to control himself. The king of the gods was enormous, possibly eight feet tall or more, and built like a well-trained athlete. In fact, his body glowed with absolute perfection. On either side of him sat a goddess, both of them with beauty surpassing anything Kishin had seen in all six lands. Though he had not been attracted to a woman since his curse took hold, Kishin felt desire rise up inside.

"Come near, messenger," Murdak called. "Let your eyes be free while here."

Kishin blinked. The strange feelings faded, but did not leave him entirely. He approached the chair, bowed, and offered the scroll.

Murdak gestured. Another god, younger and smaller, stepped out from somewhere and took the scroll from Kishin. He smirked and took it to Murdak.

"What an unusual messenger," Murdak observed, taking the scroll but not opening it. "Your condition: is it the result of disease or a curse?"

"A curse," Kishin answered, surprised at how quickly the words came to his mouth. Some form of compulsion came through Murdak's voice.

Murdak clicked his tongue. "What a shame. We have come to abolish that horrible system, you know. No one else need suffer as you have."

Kishin said nothing. Marshal spoke much the same, but his motivations were different. At least, Kishin thought they were.

"Which of the Lords have sent you to us?" Murdak asked, as he began to unroll the scroll. "Kuktarma? Arazu?"

"No Lord sent me."

Murdak raised an eyebrow. "Really? Curious." Then he looked over the message. His face showed no discernible emotion, but when he looked up again, his eyes drilled into Kishin with new intensity. "The man who sent you. He claims to be… Nehesy?" The two goddesses sat up, suddenly interested.

"That is what he calls himself."

"Hmm. But you are not convinced?"

"I do not know if he is who he claims to be," Kishin admitted. "But if such a man were still alive, he would appear like this man, I believe."

Murdak crushed the message in his hand. "He is near?"

"Near enough," Kishin answered. He struggled not to give away the campsite's exact location.

Murdak studied him, and then stood. "Hear, all ye gods!" he cried aloud. The one who had taken the message re-appeared, along with half a dozen more of the gold-skinned people. One of them in particular stared at Kishin, a strange man with pale hair pulled back at his neck. Despite himself, Kishin trembled. He had no magical senses like the mages and Lords, but the raw power around him made him shiver.

Murdak held up the crumpled message. "I have received a message from a human claiming to be our old friend Nehesy!"

"Ridiculous!" one of the goddesses exclaimed.

"Humans have very limited lifespans," another god said. "It cannot possibly be the same man." A murmur of agreement followed his words.

"He wants to meet with me! This human!"

Laughter erupted. "Ignore him, lord!" one of the other gods called.

"Why?" Kishin asked.

The laughter faded. Murdak looked back at him. "Why?"

"Why refuse to meet with him? Are you afraid?"

"I am Murdak, king of the gods. I defeated your founder, Akhenadom. I defeated your new King, Marshal. When last I saw a puny acolyte called Nehesy, I left him a quivering pile of broken bones. I do not know fear."

"Someone defeated you," Kishin observed. "Or did you choose to spend the past thousand years in the Otherworld?"

Silence fell over the assembly.

"Allow me, lord," said one of the goddesses, getting to her feet. "I will crush his head and throw it in the nearest refuse pit."

Murdak held up his hand, and the goddess sat down again. He did not say anything for a lengthy silence. Kishin knew he had gone too far, but Nehesy sent him on this mission, not one of the acolytes. He may as well be himself.

"Nummotem!" Murdak called. Another god stepped out of the crowd, wearing a strange animal pelt decorated with both spots and jagged stripes. "Since you failed with the Lord of Mandiata, here is a new job for you." Murdak gestured at Kishin. "Go with this... messenger back to where he came from. Find out who this 'Nehesy' really is. Then do what you think should be done."

"With pleasure." Nummotem stepped up beside Kishin. "Lead the way, messenger."

(((19)))

"This was… this was Master Hain's office." Seri stopped in the doorway. She couldn't. Not this office.

Master Tzoyet nodded. "It is the office of the Master Mage of Arazu. It was Hain's. Now it is yours."

"I, I don't know. I still miss him."

"As do we all." Master Tzoyet entered the office and walked to the desk. "Hain was the wisest mage I've ever known. His death was a loss to all of Antises."

Seri swallowed. She hadn't known him for very long, but in those few months, she had worked with Master Hain every single day. Relationships of all kinds grew strong with daily contact. "He taught me so much."

"He saw something special in you." Master Tzoyet turned to look at her. "The rest of us did not understand at the time. Some thought his acceptance of you as his acolyte to be a sign of his deteriorating years." He paused. "Those who thought that were wrong."

Seri joined him at the desk and ran her fingers across the ancient wood surface. Master Hain sat here, worked here, taught from here. And now it was hers. She took a deep breath.

"I can never match up to him. I can never replace him." She lowered her head. "All I can do is try to honor his memory."

Master Tzoyet nodded. "Well said." He walked back to the door. "I will leave you to get settled in. I'm sure you can find an acolyte or lesser mage or two around who can help move your things."

Seri tried not to laugh. Her things? She and Ixchel could move all of their "things" in one trip. When you traveled around two different worlds, you couldn't carry much with you.

"We will see you tomorrow morning at the third hour," Master Tzoyet said, pausing at the door. "While the Masters are not swamped with duties, we do have many ongoing tasks, starting with our morning gathering."

"Of course," Seri answered, her heart sinking a little. That would be the only downside to all of this: she now had even more responsibilities. She would have even less time with the book. And Dravid.

•••••

Kishin led the way back toward Nehesy's camp, casting glances at his new companion. Nummotem stood around seven feet tall, golden-skinned and impressive in all his features. If not for Murdak, Kishin would have thought Nummotem to be the most perfect human male ever seen. His clothes, bright and colorful, clung tightly to his body as he strode along without a worry. A strange animal pelt of yellow-orange fur toppled with both spots and jagged stripes hung from his shoulders.

"Do you hail from Kuktarma or Arazu, little man?" the god asked him.

"Neither. I come from Ch'olan." The words came out of Kishin's mouth before he intended them to. Once again, the vibratory voice of a god compelled his answers.

"Ah, I have little knowledge of your people. Some of your gods are among us, of course, after the failure at the portal in the north. Should you return after this, I can introduce you to them."

"I have no desire to meet any more gods." Kishin shoved a hanging branch out of his way, letting it fall back behind him, hoping it would hit Nummotem.

"You should," Nummotem replied. "Each of us possess different ways of helping our people. In time, we hope to be able to rid this world of its curses, such as the one that torments you."

Kishin gritted his teeth. While he knew the dangers the gods posed, if they spread this message throughout Antises, they might gain an untold number of followers. If he had learned anything in his years as a leper, it had been how many people suffered from curses, and how many more mourned for family members who suffered.

"Until all curses are lifted," he said under his breath.

"What was that?"

"What will you do to Nehesy when we arrive?" Kishin asked out loud.

"It depends on whether I see him as a threat or not."

"What does it take to be a threat to the gods?" Kishin tried not to sound too sarcastic.

"Threats come in many forms," Nummotem said placidly. "Your King possesses significant power, making him a threat to all but the most powerful of us. Fortunately, Murdak has defeated him once already and will do so again. Your Lords have power, but are not a threat to us, save in the unlikely event they unite together. Even then, they would not prevail for long."

The god stopped talking while Kishin led him in a climb up a steep incline. They didn't need to go that way, but Kishin's annoyance with the situation made him seek out more difficult paths.

"But there are other types of threats," Nummotem resumed. "Threats of ideology. Belief. This Nehesy may represent one of those, especially if he is siding with the despicable priests of Theon."

"Is Theon your enemy, then?" Kishin found himself interested in the discussion for the first time.

"Theon is not a god. He is an idea, sold to your people by Akhenadom, in his zeal to lead you away from us."

Kishin glanced back at him. "You're saying Theon doesn't exist?"

"No. I've never seen him. Have you?"

"No." Kishin considered the conundrum, but not for long. "We're here," he announced.

The two of them stepped into the hollow where the campsite waited. Nehesy sat on a piece of a fallen tree Jamana had dragged into place, his staff laid across his knees. The acolytes stood on either side of the old priest.

Nummotem pushed Kishin aside, much to his annoyance, and strode forward. "You are the one claiming to be Nehesy, are you?"

"I am. You are the one claiming to be Nummotem, god of Mandiata?"

"Yes, I..." Nummotem narrowed his eyes. "You know me." Kishin moved to the side to find the sword he'd left behind, watching the god carefully. Nummotem's eyes flickered to Jamana. "Ah, the mage acolyte. We met before, in Tenjkidi. That explains it."

"I did not know you were coming here," Jamana said.

"Regardless." Nummotem studied Nehesy. "You are old, but you cannot possibly be the Nehesy we knew a thousand years ago."

"I am the same. It is by the will of Theon that I sit before you after all these years."

"Preposterous. You have no magic within you, nothing at all to indicate any way that could be true. Still, your words are a dangerous message. You are a minor obstacle to be removed." Nummotem gestured. To Kishin's shock, vines erupted from the trees around them, wrapped around Jamana and Adhi, and pulled them away from Nehesy. Kishin grabbed his sword and ran to cut them loose. He reached out toward Adhi only to have something wrap around his ankle and send him sprawling to the ground. He rolled and saw a tree root encircling his leg.

Nehesy did not move. "No magic within me?" He sighed. "Your senses have grown dull over the years, Nummotem. Allow me to remove the scales from your eyes."

Now Nehesy gestured. Kishin had no magic sense, but he saw how all three of the others reacted. Jamana and Adhi's eyes widened and they sucked in their breaths. Nummotem took a step back, uncertainty filling his eyes.

"This is not... possible," the god said.

"All things are possible." Nehesy stood and lifted his staff. A tremor ran through the ground beneath them. The root holding Kishin's ankle stiffened and then shattered as though made of a brittle substance. Kishin scrambled to his feet. He cut Adhi free from the vines and hurried to do the same for Jamana.

"Everything in Antises has its own vibration," Nehesy said. "While you and your fellow gods wasted your time in the Otherworld waiting for this day, I spent a thousand years studying and learning every single one of them. And once you understand the innate vibration of a thing..." He waved his hand and a nearby sapling bent as if bowing. "Then you gain control over it. That includes the plants you boast of mastering."

"You are still just a small, ancient human," Nummotem growled, stepping forward. "I can—"

"Did you not hear me, Nummotem? I said everything." Nehesy lifted his hand and Nummotem stopped as if frozen. But even as he stood still, his body began to vibrate. "That includes the bodies of men... and gods."

"What... are you doing?" The god's voice sounded like each word strained him to utter, his lips barely moving.

"Your command of the plant life here revolves around channeling the magic of your world through specific conduits within your feet and hands," Nehesy explained. "I am sealing those conduits off."

"No…"

Kishin and the acolytes stared. The assassin couldn't decide if he felt more wonder or horror at the old man's powers. Nehesy made claims, but until this moment, Kishin had never taken them completely serious.

Nehesy clenched his fist and released it. Nummotem stumbled back two steps. The god's face, freed from its paralysis, fell into fury, clenched teeth and a bestial snarl. His perfect beauty transformed into an image of unhinged rage.

"You will suffer like no other, old man!" Nummotem swept his arms together, but nothing happened. His face struggled to express his emotions. His eyes widened and contracted. His mouth opened and shut. His nostrils flared.

Recognizing what was about to happen, Kishin pushed past Jamana and leaped in front of Nehesy, sword aimed at the powerless god right as he started to charge. Almost impaling himself, Nummotem stopped and glared at Kishin.

"Go back to your master," Nehesy said, taking his seat once again. "Tell him who you have seen and what happened to you. And then tell him I still wish to meet, unless he is afraid of a withered, ancient human."

Nummotem stared daggers at Kishin, then spun on his heel and stalked away. Kishin kept an eye on him until he moved out of sight.

"If anyone is afraid, it is that one," Adhi noted. "He may not return to his master at all. From what I have seen, I do not think Murdak takes failure well."

"He will return," Nehesy said, his voice heavy with weariness. "He has nowhere else to go."

"Are you all right, sir?" Jamana asked.

"I am very old, acolyte. Though I possess great power, it is difficult for me to use it." He leaned on his staff. "This is one of the reasons the two of you are here. The longer this lasts, the more I will need to lean on you."

"Of course," Adhi said.

Jamana scratched his head. "At the high place, I was able to channel Volraag's power. Might we do the same with you?"

"It is a possibility. Again, one of the reasons you are here."

Kishin sheathed the Durunim sword. "And it is becoming clearer why you needed me. If I hadn't been here, that might have gone very different, old man."

Nehesy nodded. "I told you that you could make a difference."

Kishin snorted, but maybe, just maybe, he was in the right place.

<h1 style="text-align:center">(((20)))</h1>

Marshal laughed. "Victor told me this morning, but I had to come see for myself."

Seri got up from Master Hain's desk and gave him a mock bow, twirling her new purple robes. "Master Mage Seri of Arazu at your service, Your Highness."

Tich came in behind Marshal. "How's that work? A woman as a 'master'?"

"We may have to change the title," Dravid said from his seat beside the desk. Released by the infirmary, he had brought the book to Seri's new office to study.

"Congratulations," Marshal said, bowing in return. "I'm thrilled for you."

"How did it go with Lord Tyrr?" Seri asked.

"We're about to go back," Marshal said. "We'll leave Raeton at noon with Lord Tyrr to stop the Durunim army. After that, we'll move on to the portal."

Victor and Ixchel entered the room together. "Volraag's secure," Victor reported. "I've got my stuff. Ready to go."

"And so we split up again," Dravid observed. "We just can't stay together, can we?"

"It's necessary," Marshal said.

"Isn't it always?"

Marshal nodded. "Well, I guess we'd better get moving. Wouldn't want to keep Lord Tyrr waiting."

"Or the princess," Tich said. Marshal frowned at her.

"There's a princess?" Victor asked.

"Oh, you'll love her," Tich told him. "You've got the same hair."

130

Victor put a hand to his own hair, then pulled it away when he noticed Ixchel studying him. Marshal almost laughed.

"So this is the young King," said a feminine voice behind him.

Marshal turned to see a new arrival standing in Seri's doorway. Tall and slender, she looked as if she could be Seri's older sister. She moved into the room, her elaborate green gown rustling around her legs. She bowed to Marshal, not expressing any reaction to his ravaged face. Everyone else in the room straightened up. Dravid pulled himself up onto his foot.

"Ah, Lady Lilitu, I presume." It couldn't be anyone else. "My condolences on the recent death of your husband."

"Thank you." The Lady's eyes roved over the assembled friends. "You form quite the interesting group here. And from what I've heard, Antises owes its very existence to all of you. You have my gratitude."

"It was mostly Marshal," Victor said. "The rest of us are pretty much just following him around."

"And yet, without you, he would have fallen to Volraag in the north," she observed. She walked through the room, stopping beside Seri and looking at Dravid. "And without you, Seri and the King would have failed to stop the earthquakes."

Marshal wasn't sure what to think of the Lady knowing all about them. He knew Seri would have told her things, of course, but it still felt odd for this stranger to know so much.

"And Ixchel, my daughter's guardian. I know her well, of course." Her eyes settled on Tich. "You I know the least. Tich, wasn't it?"

"It was. There's not much to tell about me."

Lady Lilitu studied her. "No, there is far more than you will admit." She glanced at Marshal. "Not the least of which is your relationship to our King."

"That hardly matters," Marshal said.

"Doesn't it matter who our King speaks to in confidence? I'm sorry, Marshal, but when you accepted the Kingship, you accepted all that goes with it. Your life is no longer your own. It belongs to all of us."

"That doesn't seem very fair," Victor said.

"Of course it's not," the Lady agreed. "But my life is not my own, either. It belongs to the people of Arazu. Everything I do matters to them. If I should seek to re-marry now, that would be of immense interest to them all, for example."

"That's because we've always been ruled by Lords," Seri pointed out. "They're wondering if there will be another Lord someday."

Lady Lilitu smiled at her. "Of course they are." She looked back to Marshal. "And once the news spreads throughout Antises about the new King—and it is spreading, thanks to you reopening the portals—the people will start wondering if this King… will have a Queen soon. And whether she will bear the next King." Her eyes flicked to Seri, and then Tich.

Marshal swallowed. "Um, this is a topic that I'm sure can wait until we deal with the current crisis."

"Can it?" The Lady took Seri's chair and sat. "You speak about the current crisis as if it will be resolved in a matter of days."

"That is our hope."

"But is it not more likely that things will continue for much longer? You allowed the gods to enter in the east. They have already established a foothold in the west. Their powers equal or surpass ours. I'm afraid the 'current crisis' may last much, much longer."

Marshal's heart sank. Already, the delays with Lord Tyrr had made him wonder about this very thing. If they ran into trouble in Rasna, it might drag things out. But Antises, the land, could not wait for too long. It needed healing.

"Even if we pause long enough to perform a Passing," the Lady went on, "in all likelihood, we will have to immediately return to the issues of war. It could drag on for years. In any case, with these powerful enemies at the doorstep, it becomes all the more urgent that the King have an heir."

Victor stirred. Marshal kicked his foot. "If you say anything, I will hurt you," he whispered. Victor snickered.

"As I entered, you were discussing a princess. Lord Tyrr's daughter, I believe." The Lady paused and Marshal nodded. "Lord Tyrr is no doubt scheming to marry her to you as soon as possible. And he will not be the last. Did you meet Lord Meluhha's daughter?"

Marshal's eyes widened. Kumara had been pleasant and attractive, but he'd been careful in their discussions. Had Lord Meluhha already been trying to manipulate him?

"I see you did. The new Lord Bakari has a younger sister. I will not be surprised if he brings her with him when he arrives soon. Lord Rajwir has no daughters, not since his child was killed, but I believe he has an eligible niece. And, of course, I have a daughter."

Marshal's mouth fell open. Seri's eyes widened and she ducked her head.

"A union of the Kingship, the Lord's house of Arazu, and the

Conclave of Mages would be... greatly beneficial to all," she went on. "But I believe my daughter has interests elsewhere." Her eyes settled on Dravid. "For now."

No one spoke for a moment.

"Listen, I don't care who you are," Tich burst out. "You can't walk in here and take over everyone's lives. Marshal can make up his own mind. So can Seri."

"Can they?" Lady Lilitu's voice was soft, but everyone heard her words. "I told you: our lives are not our own. We have to think of others."

Marshal couldn't deny part of what she said. It did, after all, tie in with all that Talinir told him about being a King and serving the people. He just hadn't considered that his... romantic connections would be a part of it.

"We will... consider your advice," he said. "I do not take your words lightly. Right now, though, I have to focus on the immediate needs. We are leaving for Raeton this very moment."

"I wish you well in your endeavors."

Marshal nodded, then left the room, followed by Tich and Victor.

"Can I say something now?" Victor asked in the hallway.

"No. Let's go find Lord Tyrr."

•••••

Talinir followed Tiranel into his office again. The High Warden went behind his desk and pulled open a drawer. He took out a large, leather-bound book, admired the cover, and placed it on the desktop. Talinir moved closer to see it.

"This is the record of every warden of Intal Eldanir over the past five hundred years," Tiranel said.

"You think we will find Rathri in this record?" Talinir asked.

"If he is a warden as you say, he will be in here." Tiranel opened the book to the first page. A single name was written in a tight but fancy script across the top of the page. Upside down, Talinir could not read much of the rest of the page, but it seemed to be a record of the warden's accomplishments.

"There is one page for each warden?"

The High Warden nodded. "The order is by date. This warden, Ranirtel, began his service five hundred years ago."

"We have no other way to search, then?" Talinir tried not to show his concern. It would take hours, maybe days, to skim through a book of this size.

Tiranel withdrew a much smaller book from his desk. "This is the Book of the Fallen, the list of every warden that has been lost to us, either through death or disappearance." He placed it on the desk beside the larger book. "It does not, however, tell us anything else about them. For that, we will have to look up their entry in the main record."

"So if we look up the record of each missing warden, we can see if any of them match what we know about Rathri," Talinir concluded.

Tiranel nodded. He pushed the smaller book to Talinir. "Read me the names and I'll find them in the main record."

Talinir took a seat and began. The first three wardens in the Book of the Fallen had all been killed and their bodies recovered. The fourth one had disappeared, but when Tiranel looked him up, they discovered an average warden with little to distinguish him. Given Rathri's abilities, Talinir felt certain this could not be the same person.

And so it continued. They compared record after record. Tiranel set aside three of them as possibilities, but none of them felt quite right to Talinir.

"Nirhatal." Talinir read a name from about halfway through the small book.

Tiranel paged through the larger record book until he found it. "Oh. This one."

"What is it?"

Tiranel sighed. "This was a dark day in the history of the wardens," he said. "But I do not think it is he."

"What happened?"

"A couple were murdered in their home. We believed it to be their son, the warden, who killed them, but it could not be proven. He denied it, of course. It was horrendous. His father was one of our greatest smiths. He made most of the warpsteel swords we use today." Tiranel clenched both of his fists with the painful memory.

"Then it could be him, couldn't it?" Murders in Intal Eldanir were rare, but did happen. If Rathri had already been a murderer before getting trapped in the primary world…

He shook his head. "We lost him soon after. He was killed by a tunaldi… or so we believed." He tapped his fingers on the desk. "There were some questions about it, now that I recall."

"Was his body recovered?"

"No." Tiranel scanned over the record page. "I remember being surprised, because he was one of our most promising young wardens... much like you, an exceptional swordsman. But I assumed the murder of his parents upset him enough to allow the creature to catch him by surprise."

"Forgive me, High Warden, but this sounds like Rathri. How long ago was this?"

"Two hundred and sixty-seven years. And you say he's been in the primary world ever since?"

"I cannot be certain when he was cursed." Talinir swallowed. "But does it really matter? It seems we've found him."

Tiranel tossed the book onto the desk and sat back. "It does us no good. I thought perhaps if we found a family member still living, we might learn more, or set a trap for him. But if he truly is Nirhatal, then he has no family remaining."

"No siblings, no grandparents?"

"Not so much as a cousin. Highly unusual."

Talinir's shoulders slumped. "Perhaps... if there is a warden who trained with him...?"

Tiranel nodded. "I'll look through the records of his training period, and ask around. Maybe someone was close to him and can tell us more." He stood up. "In the meantime, you have council members to visit."

Talinir stood and gave the High Warden a short bow before leaving. They might have discovered Rathri's former identity, but were no closer to ending his threat.

<h1 style="text-align:center">(((21)))</h1>

"I'm not going this time," Tich announced at the portal room.

"What? But…" Marshal didn't know how to react. "I need you."

"To keep you grounded? Victor can do that just as well as I can. He's dying to comment on what that Lady had to say."

"I really am," Victor admitted.

"Tich…" Marshal took her hand. He glanced at Victor. "Please," he said a little lower, "don't run."

"I won't. I promise." She squeezed his hand. "I'll be here when you get back. I just… I thought about it off and on all night. If I go along with you on this military mission, I'll just be in the way."

Marshal wanted to argue, but it would be a lot easier to move and attack without having to worry about protecting her.

"Plus, you're taking him." She gestured at Victor. "And that leaves us one short in keeping an eye on that rat Volraag."

"Uh, he's got a Lord's power, you know," Victor said.

"I'm not going to stand around watching him, like you do," she said, rolling her eyes. "I'm not really worried about him blasting his way out. But… I'm worried about what he might do with his words. The man can talk, you know." She let go of Marshal's hand. "You go blow things apart. I'll wait here and watch to make sure things don't fall apart before you get back. They made Seri a Master Mage, so she's preoccupied. Dravid's busy with that book. Ixchel thinks only about fighty stuff."

"So we need someone who'll use her brain," Marshal finished.

"I wasn't going to say that, but I'll take it."

"All right. I'll miss you."

She gave him a push. "Don't get all mushy on me, or Victor will have more to mock you about."

"Oh, I've got plenty."

Marshal smiled. He didn't feel quite right leaving like this, but he didn't want to argue with Tich, either. He nodded and stepped up to the portal. He took one last look at Tich, then stepped through.

On the other side, he found Lord Tyrr waiting for him. "About time. Let's move." He paused as Victor entered. "Who's this?"

"This is my closest friend and advisor, Victor," Marshal said. "He took the cloak from one of the Remavian Guard he killed."

Tyrr grunted. "The fewer of those around, the better." He eyed Victor's red cloak, then turned away.

Marshal and Victor followed him outside the palace. Victor stopped in his tracks at the site of the Pillars. "Sorry," Marshal said. "Wish we had more time to look them over, but duty awaits."

Victor nodded, but his eyes remained on the Pillars. "Remember Nian?"

"Yeah. Wish he was here." Marshal meant it. Nian had been one of the few advisors he trusted implicitly. Everyone else, the Lords and Masters, had their own agendas.

"Are you coming?" Lord Tyrr asked from ten steps ahead. Marshal and Victor hastened to join him.

They followed a road exiting the palace and winding off to the right. As it descended behind another hill, they lost sight of the Pillars. Just ahead, about twenty horses waited, held by servants while a squad of Rasna's best soldiers loaded their equipment and mounted.

Victor nudged Marshal. "Ever ridden a horse?" he whispered.

"Not once."

One of the horses with a rider broke away from the others and came to meet them. To Marshal's surprise, Aluri sat holding the reins. She wore tight riding pants and a bronze breastplate. A circular shield hung on her back and a sword at her side.

"King Marshal." She inclined her head. "Good to see you again."

Marshal introduced Victor, as Lord Tyrr mounted his own enormous warhorse. Servants arrived with two more horses, presumably for the two guests. Victor grinned at Marshal, put his foot in the stirrup and swung up with a smooth motion. His horse, dark brown, snorted and flicked its head. Victor adjusted his position in the saddle and looked down. "Coming?"

Marshal shook his head. His horse, black with a white foreleg, looked much bigger than he'd expected. It also didn't look very friendly. "I'd rather fight a curse-stalker," he muttered.

He started to lift his foot to the stirrup when Aluri rode up beside him. "Based on our earlier conversation, I'm guessing that you haven't had much experience with horses," she said quietly.

"No, I haven't," Marshal admitted.

Aluri motioned to the servant who had brought the horse. "His Highness needs some quick instruction," she told him, continued to keep her voice low. The servant nodded and hurried to Marshal's side. He spoke quickly, explaining the use of the reins, stirrups, and how to sit in the saddle. Marshal tried to absorb it all, but knew no matter how well he listened, he would look like a fool for much of this trip. After his quick lesson, the servant assisted him in mounting his horse.

In the saddle at last, Marshal adjusted to get his feet into the stirrups. Victor trotted his horse up beside him. "So that's the princess you were talking about," he observed. "Devouring fire. Now I understand why Tich was so annoyed. She's impressive."

"Then you marry her," Marshal griped.

"To victory!" Lord Tyrr shouted. He spurred his horse down the road. The soldiers immediately followed him. Aluri and Victor started out as well, but paused when Marshal struggled to get his horse moving. Aluri turned her horse in a circle and came up beside him.

Once they were all moving, Marshal tried to adjust to the horse's motion. His still-healing foot did not like the feel of the stirrup.

"If the constant motion becomes painful, I suggest you post a trot," Aluri said.

"Post a what?"

She smiled. "It means alternate sitting and then standing in the stirrups."

"I can stand?"

"Yes, here, let me show you." As she leaned over and instructed Marshal in proper riding technique, his eyes flickered to Victor. He continued to grin, winked, then set out after the Rasnian soldiers.

Whether he liked it or not, Marshal would be riding beside Aluri the rest of this day. Or at least until he could steer this creature on his own.

• • • • •

If Marshal had known how much soreness he would accumulate from riding a horse, he would have insisted on walking the entire way. Aluri's suggestion of alternating sitting and standing helped somewhat, but not enough to prevent the soreness up and down the inside of his legs. Combined with his perpetually-sore knee, and the still-healing stab wound in his foot, he wondered if he'd even be able to stand up the next day.

Ignoring the camp chair available for him, he collapsed onto the ground next to Victor's chair in front of a large tent. Victor, munching on a slab of pork, chuckled. "Didn't you enjoy being carried by such a noble beast?"

Marshal, lying on his back, pointed at Victor without looking at him. "I'm going to make a law against mocking the King. It will have your name in it."

"As an exception to the rule, I'm sure. Tich had it right. You need someone to mock you."

"That's not what she said."

Victor shrugged. "Close enough. Besides, I'm an expert at the job."

Marshal put his hands on his face and moaned. "I'd rather fight all the Durunim and their gods than get back on that horse tomorrow. How much further do we have to go, do you think?"

"At least a couple of days," Victor replied. "Give it time. Your body will get used to the horse eventually."

"After all the skin on my legs has rubbed off."

"It's not that bad. At least you had pleasant company to ride with."

Marshal lifted himself up on his elbows and looked around to be sure Aluri wasn't in sight. "She almost never stopped talking, Victor," he growled. "I tried not to answer every question, but I didn't want to flat out lie to her, either."

"She's just trying to get to know her future husband."

"I'm not her future husband!"

"Have you told her that?"

"What? I can't just blurt out that I'm not interested in marrying her, can I?"

Victor shrugged again. "Maybe. Or maybe you could tell her that you're already… courting someone."

"Courting? I'm not courting anyone."

"What do you call your relationship with Tich, then?" Victor rolled his eyes.

"I call it complicated."

Victor tossed the pork bone into the grass and wiped his hands on his pants. "Look, Mars, Lady Lilitu was right about some things back there, you know."

"Do we have to talk about this?"

"You've got to face it at some point. Do you like Tich?"

"I do. I'm just not sure if I… love her."

"You're right; that's complicated." Victor leaned toward him. "But you have to decide if you want to pursue it. If not, you have to tell her and move on."

Marshal grimaced.

"No one said being King would be easy."

"I don't think anyone in history has ever said that," Marshal complained.

Victor laughed. "Maybe you should try asking Aluri more questions yourself. Find out about her. Maybe she's not so bad. I mean, she's definitely easy to look at."

"I have no experience in this. First I was the 'Curse Boy,' Then I got these." Marshal pointed to his face. "No girl has ever shown interest in me, and now they all want me?"

"Good thing you've got me."

"Oh, because you're such an expert?"

Victor put a hand over his heart in mock dismay. "Of course I am, Your Highness. When it comes to matters of the heart, I am the closest thing to an expert you will find on this side of Antises."

Aluri's servant approached and bowed. Marshal acknowledged him with a wave. He didn't realize the servant had come along. "What can I do for you?"

"Your pardon, Your Highness." The servant glanced at Victor, then back. "The princess asked me to bring you this." He offered a small vial. "It contains an ointment that is beneficial for those who, ah, are unused to riding."

Marshal took the vial and nodded. "Tell the princess that I am grateful."

The servant bowed again and scurried away.

"Look at that," Victor observed. "She cares about you. She sent—"

"Quiet, you." Marshal pulled himself up and limped into the tent.

"If she comes to check on you herself, should I send her in?" Victor called.

Marshal spun and threw a burst of power into Victor's chair. It fell apart beneath him, landing him in the dirt. He laughed again as Marshal shoved his way into the tent.

(((22)))

"Why have you delayed so long in coming to see me?" Volraag demanded.

Master Magnus folded his arms. "I had very little motivation to come here, after all you have done."

Volraag looked past him. "Holcan, do you mind? I would like to speak with my mage alone."

Ixchel did not answer, but she moved further away from them. Volraag rolled his eyes. His imprisonment was not uncomfortable, but the constant presence of guards reminded him of his status. He glared at Ixchel until she backed further away down the hall.

Volraag turned back to the Master mage and beckoned him into the small room which had become his home on Zes Sivas for now. "You can speak freely now."

"I am speaking freely. Your actions hardly demand my loyalty, Volraag."

Volraag leaned against the wall and stroked his beard. "Who was it that gave you this position, Magnus? Who chose you instead of four other better qualified candidates for this job?"

"I do not deny what you have done for me," the mage acknowledged. "But that pales in comparison to your crimes against Antises itself. And you abandoned Varioch! We are being invaded, even now, by enemies you invited in!"

"I did no such thing. Who told you this?"

Magnus's head moved back and tilted. "Everyone says it. The new King, for one."

"Do you understand who this King is, my friend?"

"What do you mean?"

Volraag sighed. "Marshal is my half-brother. He stole our father's power and led me in a chase across Antises in a futile effort to get it back."

"He has told us of being Varion's son, of course, but—"

"And the enemy? Lord Tyrr let them in. Why do you think we fought against him at the border? I knew of his desire to open the ancient high place. I could have stopped him there, if it hadn't been for the interference of my half-brother. Tell me, where is your precious King now?"

"He has gone to seal the high place," Magnus said.

"And who is he working with?" Before the mage could answer, Volraag did it for him: "It's Lord Tyrr, of course. They have been in league for over a year now. And now, they both will emerge from the crisis looking like heroes." Volraag pushed away from the wall. "Lord Tyrr has a daughter of marrying age, Aluri. As soon as Marshal is recognized as King by all existing Lords, you can be sure that a royal wedding announcement will follow. And Lord Tyrr, Varioch's greatest enemy, will have control over this puppet King through his daughter. The Masters and Lords are playing right into his hands."

"This is… not what I have been told."

"But it fits with what you see happening, does it not?" Volraag pressed.

"How can I trust you?" Magnus's voice sounded accusatory, but Volraag could see it in his eyes: the man wanted to believe. Of course he did.

"Don't you remember our conversations about this? When we discussed my father's reckless abuse of his power? And how the other Masters have been no better?"

"Yes, but… how have you been any better?"

"Everything I have done has been for the good of Antises," Volraag insisted. "When have I taken from the common people? Or abused my power against them? I have ever only fought against those in power, those with too much power, those who abuse their power." He lowered his voice and stepped in closer. "All I have done is to fight against the system, fight against the Lords and those that support them. It is everything we talked about, you and I, when we grew up in the shadow of the monster, Varion."

Magnus stepped back from him. "I'm a Master now. I can't… I have to work with the others."

"The Masters are part of the same system of oppression. They support the Lords, encourage them in their abuse. I chose you to be a Master because you have never been servile, never abased yourself to them, or done less than your conscience demanded. Look at the other Masters. Plecu, for example, is wholly Lord Tyrr's toady. Do you doubt the others are any better?"

"Master Plecu is obnoxious," Magnus admitted. "I was inclined to support the new King entirely because he opposed it."

Volraag reached out and put his hand on the mage's shoulder. "I made you a Master so you could fight them, not go along with them. You are young and growing in power and influence. These old Lords and Masters must be swept aside, so that we can change everything."

"I'm not the youngest any more," he muttered.

"And why is that?" Volraag pointed to the hall. "Why does this Holcan guard me? It's all connected. Lady Lilitu is also scheming to control this so-called King. And so who does she appoint as Master? The King's best friend! Marshal has no closer ally than Seri, I can tell you, though she does not have his best interests at heart. She has been manipulating him since the day they met. She's tried to do the same to me, all on behalf of her mother."

Magnus said nothing, but he continued to listen, and did not pull away.

"It is well known that Lady Lilitu would not give Lord Enuru an heir. She wanted his power for herself, and now she has it. And with her daughter on the Conclave of Mages, she can manipulate the new King and all of Antises on her own behalf. Just like Lord Tyrr is trying to do. You see? They're all alike. This is what I fight against!"

"Seri has no right to be a Master," Magnus admitted. "The Lady forced us to recognize her."

"Of course she did. But we can put a stop to it still."

"How?"

Volraag smiled. He made a show of walking to the door to make sure Ixchel was out of hearing before returning to Magnus and speaking in a quiet whisper. "You do not yet know the full extent of their plans. Tell me, has Marshal spoken to the Masters about a new Passing?"

"Yes, of course. It's one of the first things he insisted on."

"And he has his own mage friends doing research on the founding of Antises, correct?"

Magnus nodded, his eyes widening ever so slightly.

"He's made no secret that he wishes to use this Passing to strip away my Powers. He already possesses the powers of a King and Lord. After the Passing, he will possess at least one more. What is to stop him from stealing all of the Lords' powers and ruling all of Antises without any to stand in his way?"

Magnus's intake of breath indicated his horror at the suggestion. Good.

"Marshal will take all of the power," he repeated. "The Lords will be impotent. And the Masters will fall in line because Seri will support him."

"This is outrageous!" Magnus burst out. "I will speak to the other Masters. I will persuade them. I—"

"Do you think they will listen?"

Magnus slumped. "No. It would be useless to talk with Plecu. Tzoyet and Ganak… I don't know."

Volraag nodded in sympathy. "We are trapped on every side, it seems. But all is not yet lost."

"What else can we do?"

"Our first task can be simply delaying what is happening," Volraag suggested. "And there are two keys to that: these new portals Marshal has opened, and Seri. I think we should deal with both at the same time."

Magnus glanced at the door, as if he expected Ixchel to charge in at the mention of Seri's name. "What do you mean by 'deal with'?"

"We destroy the portals," Volraag said. "And persuade Seri to… step down."

"She'd never do that!"

"Leave it all to me. I can be… persuasive."

Magnus cracked the knuckles on one hand. "Do you want me to tell her you wish to see her, then?"

Volraag shook his head. "No. No matter how we do this, I will have a limited time in which to act. I will need you to deliver multiple messages. If done right, we will trap the King, at least two of the Lords, and perhaps one or two Masters, denying them the use of the portals. But I will need to… confront Seri at the same time."

"What about"—Magnus jerked his head toward the hallway—"her?"

"That's one of the messages you will deliver." Volraag smiled. "If you follow my instructions, not only will we delay and maybe even stop the so-called King's plan, but you will find yourself with much more influence than you have now. Given time and opportunity, we will re-shape Antises forever!"

•••••

Volraag lay back on his bed and relaxed. He had always been able to manipulate Magnus. At least that hadn't changed. And now he could set a plan in motion. No more sitting around waiting.

A chuckle echoed in his room. "That's why I've always liked you, son of Varion," a voice said. "You take action."

Volraag knew the voice. He sat up, clenching his fist and drawing his magic into it. A shimmer appeared in the corner of the room furthest from the door. A moment later, Curasir stepped into view. He gave a mock bow, his white hair slinging around his face.

"Why are you here?" Volraag demanded. "I should blast you back into your world." He lifted his fist.

"Now, now," Curasir said, raising his own hands, palms out. "I'm here to help you."

"Like you helped me at the high place?"

"That was all Murdak. I had nothing to do with that." Curasir placed a hand over his heart. "I had no idea he would not honor the agreement with you."

Volraag glared at him. "You lie more than any… being I've ever met. I cannot trust a single word you say."

"When have I lied to you? Name one!"

Volraag didn't answer. Aside from the betrayal where Murdak stripped power from him, he couldn't think of anything specific. He let the power die down and released his fist.

"You see? I have ever been on your side, son of Varion."

"Then stop calling me that. I need no reminder of my father."

Curasir inclined his head. "Very well, Lord Volraag. Whatever you desire."

"I desire for you to leave me alone."

"But I can help you! I couldn't help but overhear your conversation with the good mage a few minutes ago. Your plan, as it stands, is a good one, but it could be better."

Volraag considered it. Curasir was insufferable, but he could not deny the Eldani's power. "How so?" he asked.

"First, what is it that you plan to do about Seri? You left that rather vague in your discussion with the mage."

"I will persuade her. She will step down from the Conclave."

"And how will you do that?"

"Her weakness is the crippled boy. If I threaten him, she will do whatever I ask."

Curasir shook his head and walked across the room, stopping before he stepped into the sight of anyone who might be watching from the hallway. "She will know your threats are empty. What can you do, after all?"

"If I can escape this room to destroy the portals and speak with her, she will fear that I can escape again and harm him."

Curasir cocked his head and gave him a skeptical look. "She will move him into her own room, or assign other mages to guard him. It will not work."

"What do you propose, then?"

Curasir sighed and walked back toward the corner. He stopped and leaned against the wall, arms folded. "I will admit this saddens me to have to say this. I had hopes for that girl early on. She's basically a demigod, you know."

"What do you mean?"

"Oh, you didn't hear that part? Her mother may be the Lady of Arazu, but her father... is one of the gods. That's why she's advanced so rapidly. It's in the blood, one might say."

Volraag pondered this information, considering how he might use it.

"It's no good threatening her with that, either," Curasir added. "She won't care."

"Are you saying she's immune to threats?"

Curasir shrugged. "Anyone can be threatened, if you have the right leverage. And you did, at first. Threatening those she loves would normally be the way to go. But you cannot back up those threats."

"You could."

"Ah, there we are. That's entirely true. But it's not really what I had in mind. Harming a crippled acolyte is a bit... beneath me, you know."

"So far, all you've done is tell me what won't work. Are you going to get around to telling me what will?"

"Of course. You need to kill her."

Volraag almost laughed out loud. "You can't be serious."

Curasir did not smile. "I am serious. She has become the biggest barrier to your success and that of my masters. Eliminating her solves many problems. Most of all, little Marshal will have no idea what to do without her."

Volraag scowled at him. "You seem to forget the Laws of Cursings and Bindings. And before you argue, I have sworn not to do anything that would bring a curse on any of my offspring!"

"Yes, well, it seems everyone wants to get rid of those pesky Laws, don't they?"

Volraag didn't answer. He wasn't sure about his own position on that. It didn't really matter at the moment, anyway. The Laws existed right now. He could not kill anyone himself, and he no longer had access to a reliable assassin.

Curasir sighed again. "All right, all right. I'll do it. You're luring her to the portal room, correct?"

"That's the plan."

"I'll meet you there. You keep her distracted long enough, and I'll kill her."

"You can't just do it all by yourself?"

"No, see that's the problem. She's grown powerful enough to sense my approach and defend herself. Unless, like I said, you distract her. Smashing those portals should do the trick." Curasir unfolded his arms and rubbed his long hands together.

"What about her bodyguard, the Holcan?" Volraag pointed to the hallway. "With my plan, she'd be distracted, at least briefly. And since I intended no physical harm to her mistress, their Bond would not summon her. But when you show up..."

"She'll come running," Curasir finished. "I am aware. Which is why we will do this quickly, before she can arrive. Even so... the girl is just a human with a short sword. If necessary, I can deal with her with little difficulty."

Curasir stepped away from the wall. The air around him began to shimmer again. "It's all coming full circle, you know. I first met Seri here on the island, intrigued by her heritage. At the same time, I was killing the other Masters and taking their power." He paused. "Now I'll do the same to her." He turned sideways and vanished.

Volraag studied the spot where he had stood for a minute or more. Then he got to his feet and moved to the door. "Holcan! Are you still there?"

Ixchel looked back at him. "I have never left."

When she said nothing more to indicate she knew of Volraag's visitor, he nodded and went back to his bed. Curasir, despite his insistence on wanting to help, still served the gods. However he offered to help, it would benefit them. Still, it might still be something Volraag could use... especially if he found a way to get around all of them: King Marshal, the gods, Lords, Masters... Volraag was surrounded by hostile forces on every hand. Hostile forces that all distrusted or hated each other. It could not be more perfect.

(((23)))

Marshal did not sleep well. The ointment from Aluri helped some, but the soreness on his legs was only one of his many pains. Bouncing along in the saddle for so long made his right knee ache again and exacerbated the wound in his left foot. His many other older injuries continued to trouble him as well. Consequently, he woke up grumpy and agitated at having to get back on the horse.

Victor sympathized with him, losing the teasing from the night before. He could tell when his friend needed encouragement, not jokes.

Only a few minutes after they broke camp, Aluri directed her horse beside Marshal's again. "And how are you this morning, Your Highness?"

"In no mood for that nonsense," Marshal responded.

"I beg your pardon?"

Marshal turned to look at her, trying not to scowl. "I have no idea whether you're using that 'Highness' term seriously or if you're just mocking me. And either way, I don't want to hear it."

She nodded. "Very well. How would you like me to address you, then?"

"My name is Marshal. Not 'King' Marshal, either. Just Marshal."

"All right. And I'm Aluri. Not 'Princess' Aluri, either, despite what the servants and my father keep saying. Just Aluri."

Marshal blinked. He hadn't even considered how she might feel about titles. "Well. I'm glad we got that out of the way."

"Yes. So… why would you think I'm mocking you?"

Marshal gestured at himself. "I can't possibly be what you expected in a King. I'm a scarred-up peasant from a tiny village in Varioch. I have no idea how to behave among Lords and Ladies. I've never even

148

ridden a horse before!" He winced. "And everyone can tell."

Aluri kept her eyes forward and did not answer. Marshal looked to Victor, who shrugged.

"The point is, I have no business in your… society. And honestly, I don't really want it."

"What do you want, then, your—Marshal?"

"I want to save Antises. And I want an end to all curses." He couldn't be sure, but it looked like Aluri trembled a little. "Those are my goals. Beyond that… I don't even dare to think about it."

"What do you know of curses?"

Marshal hesitated. There was something in her voice that hadn't been there before. Her words were clipped, like she wanted to say something more, but didn't.

"I lived under a curse for almost all of my life," he said at last. "You've heard that Lord Varion was my father. He raped my mother. I got the curse for it."

Aluri's brow wrinkled. "But… you bear no curse now?"

"My mother died to free me from it."

Aluri turned to Victor. "Is this true?" she demanded.

"Uh, yeah. I grew up with him," Victor replied. "And I was there when… when his mother died."

Aluri licked her lips. They rode on in silence for a minute or two. Marshal looked at Victor again. Neither one of them knew what to say now.

"When we met, I told you about my family," Aluri burst out. "I did not tell you all."

"I… all right…" Marshal did not know how to respond.

"I said I was the oldest of Lord Tyrr's children. That is true… now." She looked ahead to make sure Lord Tyrr wasn't near. He seemed satisfied to leave his daughter with the future King. All part of the scheme, no doubt.

"I had an older brother. When I was twelve, and he thirteen… my father killed a man. To this day, I don't even know why."

Marshal swallowed. He knew what happened next.

"My brother fell under a curse the same day. His body grew twisted and deformed."

Marshal waited for her to speak again.

"He killed himself two months later."

Marshal felt like someone had punched him in the gut. With the warnings from Tich and Lady Lilitu, he had been thinking of Aluri only in the context of Tyrr's schemes and real or fake romance. Along the way, he forgot to think about her as a person, as another human being of Antises, trapped under the Laws of Cursings and Bindings.

"I… I am sorry for your loss," he said.

Aluri gave a short nod, and wiped at her eye. "Since that day, for the past six years, I have lived in terror of what my father would do next. And what my curse would be." She turned to look at Marshal. "So when you speak of ending the curses… you can imagine what thoughts come to my head."

"It is my life's goal," Marshal said. "I know the pain, the unjustness. It needs to end."

"Do you truly believe such a thing is possible?"

"I do. I don't know exactly yet, but I have the smartest mages I know working on it right now."

"Do you…" Aluri broke off, and put the back of her hand to her mouth. She stared straight ahead for a few moments, then took a deep breath and let her hand fall back to the reins. "You say your mother died to lift your curse. Do you think… could I have died to lift my brother's curse?"

Marshal stared at her, his mouth open. He had not seen that coming.

"He was my best friend," Aluri said in a rush. "My only real friend. I would have done anything to help him. Anything. But I didn't know…"

"I don't know how it works," Marshal told her. "I don't. My mother read about it in, uh, the Law of Theon, I think. Or part of it, anyway. And a priest agreed with her. If she sacrificed herself for me, then my curse would be lifted."

"I could have saved him," Aluri said, almost too quiet to hear.

"I didn't want her to do that!" Marshal insisted. "I don't think your brother would have wanted that either. You were a child, Aluri! I don't have a curse now, but I don't have my mother, either. And she was the only one who loved me as… as a treasure." Remembering Aelia's name for him brought a lump to Marshal's throat. He tried to swallow, and tears welled up in his eyes.

"You, you've given me a lot to think about." Aluri spurred her horse and shot ahead.

Marshal tried to do the same, but his horse wouldn't speed up. He looked to Victor. "How do I make this thing go faster?"

Victor shook his head. "I'd let her go, for now. That was… intense."

Marshal stared after the princess. "I didn't know. I didn't want to hurt her."

"You couldn't have known." Victor let out a long breath. "I hope you really can end the curses. The more we travel and hear, the worse it gets."

Marshal gripped the reins tighter. "We're going to do it, Vic. I don't care what it takes."

•••••

After two more days on the road, the Rasnian expedition finally drew near the invading Durunim army. Marshal had grown increasingly frustrated by the passage of time. In addition, Aluri had not spoken to him directly since the conversation about curses. Prior to that, he would have been happy about the situation. Now… it nagged at him.

Throughout the last day, they caught glimpses of eidola from time to time. None of them remained in view long enough to pursue. Marshal found himself wishing for Talinir's view into the Otherworld.

As he and Victor prepared for the new day, Lord Tyrr rode up to them. "Today is the day," he announced. "We shall engage the enemy and see if you truly have the makings of a King."

"After all this, you still doubt me?" Marshal asked quietly.

"I do not doubt your power." Lord Tyrr wheeled his horse about. "Only the will behind it." He rode back to the head of the column.

"I am so tired of this," Marshal complained as he finished strapping his bedroll to the back of his saddle.

"He'll see the truth today," Victor said.

Two hours into the morning, Lord Tyrr called for a halt. Marshal and Victor joined him at the front of the column. Aluri glanced at them but did not speak. "Our scouts report the enemy is half a mile ahead," Tyrr reported. "They're not even sending out their own scouts. Just marching straight through the countryside without concern."

"They don't fear us," Victor said.

"They will," Marshal growled. He started his horse forward.

"Where are you going?" Lord Tyrr demanded.

"I want to meet their leader." Marshal kept moving. "And give him an opportunity to surrender."

"Are you mad?" Lord Tyrr rode up next to him. "We're here to destroy them!"

"Of course we are, but we need to find out what kind of powers this god possesses. I'll talk to him, he'll brag about who he is, and we'll probably end up fighting. They don't seem big on negotiation. Meanwhile, you can move into position on his flank." Marshal gestured vaguely to his left.

Lord Tyrr shook his finger at Marshal as if he would argue the point, then snorted and turned back. He issued orders to his men, and they began peeling off to the left.

Victor rode up next to Marshal. "This is the plan?"

"It is now."

"You realize they know we're coming. Lord Tyrr said there weren't any scouts, but we've seen eidolons. Isn't that the same thing?"

"Could be. I don't care. It's time to get this over with."

Victor spurred his horse in front of Marshal. "What is going on with you? This is reckless, Marshal!"

"I'm tired of all this." Marshal waved at everything around them. "We came here to deal with this problem and get Lord Tyrr back to Zes Sivas. But it's taking too long. I'm stuck out here in the middle of nowhere with a Lord who's, at best, scheming against me, and his daughter who's bounced from trying to seduce me to hating me. And every minute we spend here is one more minute for Antises to fall apart and Murdak to march through Kuktarma."

"I get it. It's frustrating. But a lot of things still have to happen, don't they? Seri and Dravid have to figure out how to change the Laws. Talinir has to convince the Eldanim. Everything takes time."

"It's time that Antises doesn't have." Marshal kept going.

Victor sighed and followed. In a short time, they topped a hill and could see far down the road. The Durunim army marched toward them, only a few hundred yards ahead.

"You are not welcome here!" Marshal shouted. He dismounted and started walking, letting ripples of power wash out under his feet. Victor caught Marshal's horse and waited.

As Marshal walked down the hill, the Durunim came to a halt. A rider at their head broke free from the others and approached him. His enormous size marked him as one of the gods. He wore golden armor, metal not magical, and carried a spear and shield with a sun-like illustration on it.

"Go back to the Otherworld!" Marshal called. "You will not succeed here."

The horseman stopped and looked down at him. "Who are you to stand in the way of the gods?" he demanded, his voice vibrating with magic.

"You are the invader here. Who are you?"

The god chuckled. He removed his helmet, revealing an almost boyish-looking face. He shook out long, black hair and smiled at Marshal. "Behold your god, human. I am Laran, and I return to the people now known as Rasna. My people."

"The Rasnian people serve Theon now," Marshal replied. "They have no need of other gods, especially those who bring an army with them."

Laran gestured at the Durunim. "But I am the god of war! For me, an army is like clothing to you. I never travel without it. But come! I have told you my name. What is yours, scarred man?"

"I am Marshal, King of Antises. You will return through the portal to the Otherworld, or I will destroy you."

"Ah, the cursed King. I have heard of you." As Laran spoke, an eidolon shimmered into place to the right of his horse. A moment later, another one appeared to his left. "What makes you think you can destroy me?"

"I wield the power of this world," Marshal answered. He allowed it to build up inside him. At this point, nothing would make him feel better than to unleash everything he had at this god and his followers.

"And I," Laran replied as yet another eidolon appeared, "wield the power of boundaries. You should learn yours, little King." He waved his hand in the air. A thin line appeared in the ground in front of his horse, a tiny indentation in the dirt. As if someone were dragging a stick along the ground, the line shot away in both directions, curving back around either side of the waiting army. Laran pointed at it. "This is your boundary for now. My army is protected."

"By a line in the dirt?"

Laran nodded once. "You are welcome to use your power now." Another eidolon appeared, and then another.

Marshal clenched his fist, but he needn't have bothered. At that moment, the ground erupted off to the left side of the army. Lord Tyrr attacked, hurling a massive burst of power at the gathered Durunim. Dirt, grass, and trees went flying into the air… but the Durunim stood still. Nothing touched them.

Marshal released a quick burst of power at Laran. The ground between them was torn apart, as always, but it stopped at the line in the dirt. More eidola appeared around Laran.

"You see?" Laran said. "Boundaries."

Marshal let loose with a much stronger blast. Again, it stopped before reaching its target. Off to the left, Lord Tyrr tried again as well.

"You waste my time, little King." Laran turned to those behind him. "Archers! Rid me of this human!"

Marshal let power wash out of him in a continual flow, creating a barrier around himself. Dozens of arrows flew at him only to shatter as they met his power. Laran waved and the arrows stopped.

"We seem to be at an impasse. What now, King of humans?"

"Stay inside your boundaries," Marshal said. He turned his back on the god and climbed back up the hill to where Victor waited.

"Now what?" Victor asked.

Marshal looked back. "I never expected a power like that. At the very least, we've stopped him for now. He can't move his army without breaking that boundary."

"You hope." Victor eyed the strange god and his entourage. "Your power can't get through it, but can anything else?"

"What do you mean?"

"Can we walk through it?"

Marshal watched Laran speaking with an eidolon. "I don't know."

Victor tied the horses to a tree branch. "If we can walk inside it, maybe your power will work there. Or maybe I can fight him." He let his flail hang loose.

"I'm wondering about those eidola," Marshal admitted. "I'm not sure what to do about them, short of crossing into the Otherworld myself to fight them."

"Do you think his boundary exists in the Otherworld?"

Marshal smiled. "There's only one way to find out." He drew his sword.

(((24)))

The High Council chamber looked no different from the last time Talinir had been there. The sun shone through the domed glass roof, casting varying patterns through the hexagonal panels. For now, Intal Eldanir remained in the primary world. Normally by now, it would have shifted back, but the Council decided to delay the shift while the wardens hunted for Rathri in the Otherworld. Even now, Talinir could see them with his right eye, scouring the land around the city.

Observers packed the chamber today. Word had spread over the topic of debate and everyone wanted to hear the Council discuss it. Aside from Aelia's appeal months ago, nothing as significant as this had been debated in decades.

The high councilors entered and took their places behind the twelve podiums that lined the wall. Talinir had visited each one of them in the past three days. Very few had been willing to outright commit their position during the visits. Most remained undecided or skeptical. The High Warden and High Mage entered as well, finding their newly-created positions below the councilors' podiums.

Once in place, one of the councillors stepped out from behind his podium and stood in the open. The crowd immediately grew quiet. He returned to his spot.

The second councillor, a woman with a voice that echoed from the dome, spoke. "This session of the High Council of Intal Eldanir is called to order. Let those with ears to hear, hear. Let those with minds to reason, reason. Let those with hearts to understand, understand. Let those with wisdom to speak..." She paused. "Speak."

Talinir had heard this opening many times, but they stirred him even so. He would be speaking soon. Did he possess the wisdom necessary for this task? Marshal was counting on him.

A shadow passed in front of the sun for a moment. Talinir glanced, as did a number of others, but saw nothing. A bird, most likely.

The High Warden stood and explained the difficult situation with Rathri and the current efforts to find him. "I requested that the city remain in the primary world until this assassin is found," he concluded, "but I have been overruled. The shift will take place shortly, even while we speak here."

Talinir jerked his head. He had not heard about this. Why would the Council make such a decision? Were they committed to staying out of the primary world as much as possible? He frowned, suspecting another reason. He knew all about addiction to the lights of the Starlit Realm. He also knew he was not the only one to have struggled with it.

Councilor Eltaru, whom Talinir knew opposed involvement in the primary world, stepped forward. "Our primary topic of discussion today is a proposal which comes from the humans of Antises. The High Council has heard this proposal already, but for the sake of the rest of you, I ask Warden Talinir to repeat the request."

Talinir took his place at the thirteenth podium. Though it faced the Council, he would really be speaking to the crowd around and behind him. "I have returned to Intal Eldanir at the request of Marshal, King of Antises. Most of you will remember when he visited us here last year, when his mother Aelia requested our help in lifting his curse." A murmur ran through the crowd. "The Council rejected her request, but since that time, Marshal's curse has been lifted and he now stands as King over all six of the human lands." This brought on a new murmur. Talinir hoped this unusual turn of events would predispose some of them toward his cause.

"A desperate situation is brewing in the primary world," Talinir went on. "Our enemies, the Durunim and their golden masters, together with some human allies, have worked to open the three ancient portals between the two realms."

"Shift in ten," a male voice echoed through the chamber.

Talinir paused, annoyed at the interruption. He could finish his speech in ten minutes and still prepare for the shift, but it would distract everyone else from his words. Some would be ignoring him entirely, preparing themselves for the shift. Someone on the Council must have known this, and planned for it.

"Through the efforts of King Marshal, two of the portals were closed, but not until a Durunim army entered through the easternmost portal. The portal nearest to us remains open, though the King hopes to destroy it soon. In the meantime, a larger army of Durunim continues to amass through it into the primary world.

"The humans, even with the powers of their Lords and the King himself, are ill-equipped to fight against these foes. We all know of the martial prowess of the silent Durunim. And each of their masters, who call themselves gods, possess great power as well, equalling or sometimes exceeding that of the Lords and King. In other words, without aid, the humans will lose this war. The Durunim will sweep across Antises, and their masters will rule over all. With all six lands under their control, as well as the nexus of magic at Zes Sivas, they will have a solid power base to return to fight against us.

"The King therefore makes this request: that the Eldanim enter the war against the Durunim in the primary world, helping the humans against our mutual enemy and ensuring a peaceful future for all of us."

A silence from the councilors followed his speech. The crowd buzzed with their own discussions. At last Eltaru lifted his hand and the crowd grew quiet.

"You have presented the human King's request. Do you wish to speak in support of it, warden Talinir?"

Talinir bowed. "I do, sir. But I will withhold my comments until later in the discussion." It was his right, and he preferred to wait until some negative statements had been made, so he might respond to them.

"Very well." Eltaru looked at the other councilors as Talinir took a seat. "I do not see any reason that we should even consider this particular request. Our word continues to bind us: when the humans bound the magic of Antises, we swore to leave them to their own destruction. They now face that destruction, though from an admittedly unforeseen source."

"Yet we have always wished for a change in the primary world," Indala said, staking her position early. "This may be our chance to enable that change."

"The human Aelia used this argument before," another councilor said. "Regardless of whether we wish to see change, we do not need to be the agents of that change. I agree with Eltaru that our sworn word is binding upon us all."

"Since this is a military matter, perhaps we should hear from our High Warden," suggested Telra, one of the few Talinir knew to be an ally.

High Warden Tiranel stood behind his own podium, much lower than the councilors. "The Durunim continue to harass us on a regular basis, as you all know," he began. "But we have not dealt with a large force of them for months, and now we know why. As Talinir said, they are invading the primary world, seeking easier prey."

"Shift in five," the voice announced. Talinir began his own preparations, knowing everyone else would be doing the same. A few moments of silence passed before anyone else spoke.

"How do you rate our odds against these foes, were we to intervene?" Indala asked.

"Talinir has provided me with numbers from his own scouting of both armies," the High Warden said. "Against the eastern army, we could prevail without significant loss to ourselves… but I am not accounting for the Durunim's masters. Their powers and abilities are unknown to us, and could significantly alter my assumptions."

"And against the western army?" Eltaru asked.

"That army is larger by far," the High Warden admitted. "As it stands now, we would suffer numerous casualties in such a battle. However, I am informed that the human King will be fighting against them himself very shortly. Again, my assumptions do not take into account the Durunim's masters."

"You are saying there is a strong element of risk," another councilor said.

"There is always a strong element of risk in war," the High Warden replied. "Otherwise, it would not be war, but a massacre."

"Shift in two."

By now, everyone should have prepared themselves and would no longer be distracted. At least, Talinir hoped that was the case.

"A massacre is what the humans will be facing," Telra declared, "without our aid."

"Yet the argument remains," Eltaru said calmly. "They are the architects of their own demise. Why should we help them?"

"It seems to me," said Nimruti, a councilor whose opinion Talinir had not been able to discern, "that the heart of this question is the Durunim themselves. Do we consider them, as Eltaru does, the deserved destruction of the humans? Or do we consider them our responsibility, since they were once a part of us?"

"Shift in one."

There it was: the argument that Talinir had made to each of the councilors in turn, and the one he most hoped would sway them. The

Durunim, after all, had once been Eldanim, but were transformed by the gods, stripped of their free will, and enslaved as mindless warrior drones.

"High Mage Harunir," Telra said, "you have attempted to work with the Durunim prisoner from the recent attack. What have you learned from this?"

Talinir perked up. Harunir had not mentioned anything about the prisoner to him. What did this have to do with the topic?

Harunir stood behind his lower podium beside the High Warden. He opened his mouth to respond.

At that moment, Intal Eldanir shifted. The city migrated across the barrier into the Starlit Realm once more. Sunlight vanished, replaced by the light of the everliving stars.

And chaos broke out.

(((25)))

Seri frowned at the note. Master Ganak didn't say why she should meet him in the portal room; he only commanded her to do so. Did Master Mages ordinarily command each other to do things? Being a Master should protect her from this kind of thing.

She stalked down the hall into the Citadel of Kings. She had been about to meet with Dravid about the book again. It seemed like they never got time to discuss it. Being a Master made her even more busy than before.

She descended the stairs. "Master Ganak?" she called as she entered the portal room. "I don't know that I appreciate the tone of—" She stopped and grabbed for any magic she could find.

Volraag stood next to the portal machine. He placed his hand, not on the top of the pedestal, but above one of the metal plates projecting a portal. He unleashed a tremendous burst of power, sheering the plate from the pedestal. The portal crackled and imploded on itself.

"Welcome, Seri. It's time we had a reckoning."

Seri activated her star-sight. The broken pedestal leaked yellow beams of magic. Which portal did he destroy? From this angle, she thought it might be Ch'olan.

"How are you here?" she demanded, gathering more magic.

"Please. You sent away the only ones capable of keeping me contained. None of the people you use as guards have any chance of stopping a Lord." Volraag moved to the next metal plate and lifted his hand.

"Wait!" What about Ixchel? Had he...? No. She would know through their Bond. Ixchel was fine, but... some distance away.

"Why should I?" Volraag blasted a second plate from the side of the pedestal. Another portal, Varioch's, imploded and vanished.

"What are you doing? Why? How does this help you?"

"It's very simple. If I make it difficult for Marshal and the other Lords to get here, I have more time to establish control here. Who will stop me?" He moved toward the next metal plate. Rasna.

"The Masters!" Seri threw a burst of magic at the floor in front of him, tearing up a couple of tiles. Volraag smiled, but stopped.

"The Masters? Magnus will do what I tell him. Plecu is spineless. That leaves only Ganak and Tzoyet to deal with. I can handle them."

"And me."

Volraag shook his head, continuing his maddening smile. "You won't be here."

A shiver ran down Seri's back. Volraag, despite all of his selfish pursuit of power, had never harmed her directly. In fact, he had protected her, from his own father and from Rathri.

Volraag reached for the Rasnian portal generator.

A lasso fell over his head and shoulders and yanked him back. "What is this?" he sputtered.

Volraag released a quick burst that shredded the rope. He spun around… and met a wooden club. Tich stepped out of the shadows as Volraag collapsed to the floor. She looked at the club in her hand. "I wanted to just punch him, because it would have been more satisfying, but… I didn't know if he had some kind of magic protection. Guess he didn't." She paused. "I should have used my fist."

Seri let out a relieved gasp and rushed forward. She grabbed Tich and hugged her. The other girl stiffened. "What… You don't need to do this."

Seri released her. "That was incredible, Tich! How did you know?"

She shrugged. "I told Marshal I'd keep an eye on him. I overheard him making a plan with his mage."

"Magnus?"

"Yeah, that one. He—" She broke off as the sound of slow clapping filled the room.

Seri turned. Curasir stood on the other side of the portal device. The white-haired Eldanim stopped applauding and bowed.

"That was delightful," he announced. "The mighty Volraag, taken down by a girl with a stick. I can't possibly be upset that you thwarted his plan."

"You never seem upset about much of anything," Seri said. "I don't understand you at all."

"He caused us enough problems in the Otherworld," Tich grumbled. "You know him too?"

Seri gathered more magic again. "His name is Curasir. He's an Eldanim… or are you Durunim?"

"The former," he replied. He stepped closer, and swooped up one of the broken panels from the floor. "Fascinating device," he murmured, flipping it over to study it.

"But he works for the gods, I think. He's a liar and a manipulator. He's fought Marshal at least twice that I know of." Seri watched him closely. "But I have to admit: I don't know why he does all this."

Curasir sighed. "It gets so boring when I have to explain it to lesser minds, though."

Tich stepped forward. "Yeah? Well, maybe you can—"

Curasir snapped his fingers together. "Let the adults talk for now, please." Tich's eyes widened, and she crumpled to the floor.

Seri leaped to her side. "What have you done to her?"

"She's asleep. I could kill her, I suppose. Then you wouldn't have any competition for the King's affections."

"What?"

"Oh, that's right. The cripple." Curasir rolled his eyes. "I keep forgetting about him. Ah well, it doesn't matter. Neither of them will be claiming you as their own, anyway." He shook his head. "I'm afraid, my dear, that you have become too much of an impediment to all that needs to happen. And impediments must be removed."

Seri's breathing accelerated. Threats. That should be enough danger to bring Ixchel running. But what could she do against an Eldanim mage? No, Seri needed to handle this one herself. "You said we were going to talk. Explain it to me. What do you hope to gain in all of this?" She pointed at Volraag and the pedestal.

Curasir walked near one of the portals and touched its edge. Then he turned his hand to the side and examined it. Was he… looking at his fingernails in the light of the portal?

"In the beginning, I was only following orders, you know." He turned to look at her. "Murdak and the others wanted Marshal to come into his power, and have his curse removed. It weakened the barriers between the worlds so they could return. Then it was just a matter of opening the high places. Since Marshal turned me down, I went to Volraag." He glanced at the fallen Lord. "He proved much easier to manipulate."

"Why do you serve them? You say you're not a, a Durunim, so…

why?" Seri continued to gather magic into her body. She was certain Curasir knew what she was doing, but he didn't seem to mind.

"Power, my dear. It's all about power. Poor Volraag understood that, but can't see beyond his own limited perspective. I mean, he hasn't even seen the Starlit Realm!" Curasir chuckled. "I, on the other hand, like all good Eldanim, walk between two worlds. And I admire them both. But this one..." He spread his hands and walked around the room. "So much that you all take for granted. And without those pesky stars staring down at you."

"You prefer our world?" Seri tried to follow the rambling. From what she'd heard from Marshal, most of the Eldanim would much rather stay in the Otherworld.

Curasir continued to laugh softly. "Do you know? I told Marshal that humans destroyed the Otherworld and I wanted to restore it, stripping the magic away from Antises and back there. He believed me too, I think."

"You tell a lot of lies."

"I do, don't I?" He pointed at Volraag's still form. "And yet I convinced him I only tell the truth. It's not always intentional, you know. As I said, at first I was following orders. But now..." He turned toward her with a new glint in his eyes. "Both Marshal and Murdak want to end what was done here, releasing the magic of this world from its hereditary owners, undoing your Laws of Cursings and Bindings. I want the opposite."

"What?"

Curasir flipped his hair back over his shoulder with another sigh. "Lesser minds, as I said." He pointed at the pedestal. "You already know that just as this thing is a tiny wellspring, pulling magic inward to run its mechanisms, Zes Sivas itself is a massive wellspring doing much the same."

Seri remembered the vortex of power she could see at the heart of Zes Sivas. Magic erupted here like no other place in the world. "It pulls magic from the Otherworld into ours."

"Yes, of course it does." Curasir held up a finger. "But what if that process were... accelerated? What if we pulled all of the Starlit Realm's power through Zes Sivas?"

"Wouldn't that destroy the Otherworld entirely?"

"Of course it would! But then we'd only have one world, and what a glorious world it would be! The gods could reign here, if they still wanted to, but mages like us would have power beyond theirs. I would be a god myself! And I could enjoy all… that humanity has to offer." He eyed her with a new look. Seri couldn't be sure if it were lust or some kind of greed, but it gave her a sick feeling either way.

"Not you," Curasir said, pointing at the stairs. Ixchel leaped toward him, sword high. She froze in mid-air. Curasir sauntered around her immobile body. He reached past her shield and ran a finger along the scar on her side.

"Leave her alone!" Seri threw a small burst of power at Curasir, just to remind him she could.

He shook his head again. "So limited still. I had hopes for you. I truly did." He pointed at Ixchel. "You see this? I'm using your kind of magic to do this. You could too, if you applied yourself."

"Why me?"

"Why you what?"

"Why the fascination with me? You told me about the star in my eye. You encouraged me to learn more. Why?" As she asked, Seri moved closer to Ixchel. Her star-sight showed beams of cyan energy wrapping themselves around her, holding her motionless. If Seri could analyze it enough, she should be able to disrupt it.

Curasir ran a hand through his hair. "I came here primarily to gather power for my encounter with Marshal, but also to check on you. I knew about your heritage and was curious to see how it would manifest itself. She told me you were here, of course."

"She?" Seri already knew the answer, but didn't want to believe it.

"Your mother. The delightful Lady Lilitu." Curasir rubbed his hands together. "She's even more fun to manipulate than you are, my dear. So much more mature, and yet…"

"You helped her lie to me. Is that it? What is the connection between you two?" Seri stepped closer to Ixchel and released a beam of reddish magic toward her. The cyan beams trembled a little, but didn't change. Not quite the right frequency.

"Oh, the Lady and I are connected in so many ways. Did she tell you who your father was?" He raised his arched eyebrows and grinned.

Seri studied him. "I don't believe you."

He shrugged. "It's not me. I'll admit it. But wouldn't that be fun? I'd make a great father."

Seri tried again to free Ixchel. Nothing happened. "You'd make a horrible father."

"Maybe so. I haven't done such a good job with you, after all."

"You were talking about Lady Lilitu," Seri prompted. The longer she kept him talking, the more magic she could gather on her own, and possibly find a way to defeat him. Fortunately, Curasir loved his own voice.

"Yes, well, she was seeking a way for her dear Lord to have children. Barring that, she wanted to inherit his power herself, thus becoming the first Lady who's a Lord." He cocked his head. "Or however that works. Your language is difficult. Anyway, that seems to have worked out well for her."

"You helped her, then?" Seri sent a burst of magenta into Ixchel's bindings. They shifted, but did not come apart.

Curasir shrugged again. "I promised her many things. I taught her how to use her power. All means to my end, of course. But really, that's enough about me. I'm afraid I have to kill you now." He drew a sword.

Seri examined him. The sword glowed with power, though nothing like the one he'd lost to Marshal. As for Curasir himself…

"You're bluffing!" she exclaimed. "You don't have the power to defeat me."

"Perhaps not." He gestured and the power within him grew. "But I can draw on the magic of both worlds here, while you can draw on only one." He shook his head. "It will take longer than I'd planned, since Volraag failed so spectacularly, but the outcome… is not in question."

(((26)))

Marshal and Victor stepped into the Otherworld. At once, three Durunim attacked them. Marshal dodged the first one's sword and struck back with his own. Victor went into a blur of action, spinning and dodging. His flail struck one of the Durunim's legs at once, taking it down.

Marshal parried another blow from the far taller adversary. He stepped back to draw it toward him. The tactic worked. As the Durunim lunged forward to stab, Marshal sidestepped and brought his sword up under its thrust. He slashed across it chest and let it fall. He finished it off with a stab to the back, then turned to see Victor's progress.

His friend stood alone, both Durunim lying dead beside him. He grinned. "We've come a long way from Talinir's first lesson!"

Marshal agreed and looked around. A cluster of Durunim, perhaps a dozen, stood together not far away. Marshal assumed they surrounded Laran in the primary world. He struggled not to gaze at the stars, but took a quick look anyway.

"Why didn't you use your power?" Victor asked. "Felt the need to get your new sword bloody?"

Marshal looked down at it. "No, I just remembered as we crossed that Talinir warned me against using too much power here. Predators in this world are attracted to it."

"You mean like the tunaldi?"

Marshal nodded and started toward the Durunim. "I'll still use it if I need to, but these don't look like too much of a threat, unless they all come at us at once."

"We can handle them," Victor said with confidence, falling in beside him.

The Durunim stood in a huddle, waiting. When Marshal and Victor came within a dozen yards, they suddenly shifted, half to the left and half to the right. A blinding light appeared between them. Marshal shielded his eyes and took a step back, dropping into a defensive stance. Beside him, Victor did the same. But no attack came.

Instead, the light faded. Between the Durunim stood one of the gods, tall and golden-skinned with long black hair. He wore a silver breastplate with the same sun image Laran's shield boasted. The light decreased into two flaming points of brightness on his outstretched hands, and then vanished altogether.

"Greetings, mortals. I am Cautha. Have you come to worship me?" His voice vibrated with power. For a brief moment, Marshal almost knelt, the compulsion was so strong.

"Not hardly," Victor answered. He began to spin his flail with his left hand.

"As long as you remain in this world, we have no quarrel with you," Marshal said. "We are here because another of your kind is threatening my people."

"You mean my brother Laran," Cautha said. "You could not touch him there, so you thought to get to him through here. Very creative on your part, I must say. But futile, since you did not know about me."

"You believe you can stop me? Do you understand who I am?" Marshal asked.

"I know what you told my brother. And yes, I can stop you." Cautha drew a sword with his left hand and pointed it toward them. To Marshal's eyes, it looked like an ordinary sword, not warpsteel or even Eldani-made.

"I don't know, Mars. He has a sword," Victor said. "Maybe we should surrender."

"I am in no mood for this," Marshal growled. "Let's take him out fast and get back." He took a step forward.

"Durunim, I require your worship!" Cautha declared, pointing at the nearest one of the silent warriors. It immediately dropped its sword and knelt before the god. Cautha reached out his other hand toward it and gestured. The Durunim trembled and collapsed to the ground. Cautha rose a foot taller, gaining height and mass, and his golden skin grew brighter.

Marshal stared. Did the act of worship actually provide Cautha with more strength somehow? As if to emphasize what he did, the god nudged the Durunim's body with his foot. It didn't move. Dead?

"If that's what happens to worshippers, you're going to have a hard time recruiting more," Victor muttered.

"My followers willingly sacrifice themselves for me, though it is only temporary," Cautha said. "I grow with each one of them. And when I no longer need their life force, I return it. Now do you understand?"

"Get him," Marshal said. He and Victor charged.

To their surprise, the Durunim all stepped back and allowed Cautha to face them alone. The god waited until they were almost upon him. He gestured at Victor with his free hand, and a burst of light struck him in the face. With his sword, he parried Marshal's first strike, and used his greater height and strength to push back. Marshal stumbled back two steps. Victor, blinded, swung wildly with both flail and sword, striking nothing.

Cautha also took a step back and snapped his fingers at two more Durunim. Both rushed to kneel before him. Both fell motionless to the ground as he absorbed their life or whatever he did. The god now stood ten feet tall. His clothing and sword grew with him.

"Victor! Are you all right?" Marshal called.

Victor waved with his sword. "Yeah, yeah. He just blinded me for a second. I can see all right now. Mostly." He looked up at the towering figure of the god. "Uh, you might have to use some magic on this one."

Marshal charged forward instead. He channeled more power into his sword. If he needed it, it would be a much more effective method of attack.

Cautha swung his enormous sword down. Marshal dodged it, and swung his blade up, trying to cut the god's forearm. But the giant moved much faster than he expected, pulling his own sword back. He lifted his knee and kicked Marshal with his instep. The kick caught him on his ribs and launched him back five or six feet. He hit the ground and rolled.

He scrambled back to his feet in time to see Victor attempt something similar, but with equally poor results. The kick hurt, but nowhere near as hard as Murdak had hit him. That was his only comfort. Victor stayed engaged longer than Marshal had, and broke off on his own, rather than getting kicked back.

"Maybe if we attack at the same time," Marshal called.

Victor scowled at him. "Think so?"

"I'm sorry," Marshal admitted. "I should have waited for you."

As they spoke, Cautha absorbed another one of the Durunim, growing at least another foot. He laughed, his voice now booming with its vibrations. "Kneel, humans!" he demanded.

Victor gasped and dropped to one knee. "I can't… I didn't want to do that!"

Marshal stayed on his feet, but it was painful to resist the commanding words. Would Cautha's magic power continue to grow as his body did? If so, he would be able to command both of them with only one or two more of the Durunim sacrificed.

Marshal leveled his sword and unleashed a burst of power. Cautha staggered back a step, just as Marshal hoped. He bent and unleashed a wide burst of power around the god, targeting not him, but his Durunim followers. His power tossed them in every direction, scattering them far and wide, and denying their "worship" for Cautha.

"Victor! I need you to stall him!"

Victor struggled to get back to his feet. "Oh, why not? Got anything to cover my ears while you're at it?"

Marshal turned to the side and focused. He honestly didn't know how this worked, but it had become easier over time. He focused a particular vibration through the sword and cut across the air. His blade tore open a gash with sunlight pouring through. He glanced back to see Victor whirling past Cautha, catching him in the ankle with his flail. The god stumbled and cried out.

Marshal cut three more slices through the air, forming a doorway. He turned and yelled, "Victor! Let's go!" As his friend raced back toward him, Marshal lifted his sword high and unleashed as much power as he could, pulsing it over and over into the sky.

Cautha, limping, stared at him. "What are you doing, little human?"

Marshal waited until Victor ducked through the doorway, then lowered the sword. He took a quick look around and saw movement in multiple directions. He looked back at Cautha. "Just calling the wildlife," he answered. He stepped backwards through the doorway into the primary world, with one last reluctant gaze up at the stars.

Cautha's yell of anger followed him. The doorway collapsed in on itself and vanished. Marshal stood back on the hill looking down at Laran and his army.

Victor sheathed his sword and bent over, catching his breath. "Got any other ideas?"

•••••

Something had gone horribly wrong. Talinir grabbed at his head with both hands. Around him, so did everyone else in the Council chambers. A high-pitched shriek filled the air above shouts of dismay and pain. Talinir's vision warped. For a moment, both eyes saw the many-starred sky of the Otherworld, and then sunlight shone through the chamber's domed roof again. Another shriek sounded as everything warped again, revealing the stars in all their majesty once more.

The mechanism for shifting the city between worlds must have malfunctioned... or been sabotaged. Harunir leaped to his feet and raced for the door. The High Mage would determine what went wrong.

But even as Harunir reached for the door, it exploded inward with a burst of vibratory magic, throwing the High Mage back across the room. At the same moment, the city shrieked and plunged back to the Primary World.

His senses reeling, Talinir stopped and took control of himself. Panic would not solve this problem. Whatever the cause, Intal Eldanir was shifting back and forth between the worlds. Without time to prepare themselves, the Eldanim were being unfolded back and forth into each world completely, rather than their normal shifts. Talinir, however, had experienced being fully inside the Otherworld before, when Marshal had yanked him through a portal. Out of everyone here, he might be best equipped to handle the chaos.

He took a quick look around the chamber, even as the city jolted back into the Starlit Realm again. The main doors lay in ruins. Eniri and other medically-trained Eldani tried to assist Harunir and the others injured by the explosion, but their efforts were hampered by the shifts.

Talinir looked up. A shadow stood atop the dome, looking down at them. It could only be Rathri.

Considering what happened to Harunir, would it be safe to use the doors? Talinir had no other choice. He avoided the unused set of doors and made his way through the damaged ones, counting on the explosion to be a one-time event, a trap for the first to try to exit.

Once he made it through safely, he searched around the outside of the building until he found a way to climb. The city shifted four more times before he made it to the top of the dome. Rathri stood there on the flattest part of the dome, an exultant look on his ravaged face.

"Why am I not surprised that you are doing better than all those below?" the assassin asked, gesturing. "I suppose all the time you've spent with humans lately has helped you somehow."

"What have you done?" Talinir demanded.

From within his clothing, Rathri produced a small device and held it up. Spherical in shape, it looked at first as if it were made of glass, yet power vibrated within. Talinir peered closer and saw a spiral of thin metal, a coil of some kind, wrapped around the glass.

"While I traveled with that fool, Volraag, I had him charge up a dozen or more of these," Rathri gloated. "Do you like it, warden of the Eldanim?"

"Warpsteel," Talinir said, realizing it in that moment. "You've used warpsteel. You learned the process from your father and came up with a new use for it."

Rathri nodded. "So you discovered my past. I expected as much. Not that it does you any good." He tossed the device up and caught it again. "Within this glass is a core of pure warpsteel. The coil is attached to it. I have but to flick the end of it with a touch of our very own Eldani magic, and it begins to release its magic, just like one of your swords."

Except once the tiny coil released its power, the core would be next. Judging from the way the device shook, it would be quite the explosion of power. "You used one to sabotage the shifting, and another to trap the doors below." Talinir drew his own warpsteel blade, not sure of his next action. Another shriek and the sun beat down on them again.

"Oh, there are more than that hidden below." Rathri laughed. "The other great thing about these is that I can time them to take as long as I want before that final release. Soon enough, Intal Eldanir will fall, crashing into the ground, as its people lose their minds from the shifting. But by then, the High Council and everyone below us will already be dead."

"Then I have but one course of action." Talinir breathed a quick prayer to the Maker of the Stars and launched forward, sword poised to strike.

Rathri dropped the device, which landed on the dome and rocked, but did not roll away. In the same movement, he swept out his own two blades, crossing them in front to block Talinir's first strike. Talinir whipped his sword back, spinning himself to bring it back up to parry the counterstrike he knew would come. He threw his own body in a twist back, his left hand slapping the glass surface of the dome, as Rathri's second blade extended in a stab where he would have been.

"Why, Nirhatal?" he asked. "I thought you hated the humans, not your own people."

"I warned you." Stars replaced the sun again as Rathri deflected another of Talinir's stabs and used the momentum to flip to the right. "I cannot allow you to help them. The Durunim and their masters will destroy or enslave the humans. And without the Eldanim, nothing will stop me from doing as I wish, killing whoever I wish, whenever I wish."

"There will always be someone to stop you." Talinir dodged and took a step back.

Rathri spread his arms wide, blades extended in either direction. "Who? Gods? No one has stopped me yet. I have killed more humans than anyone in their history, and today… I kill more Eldanim. And no one stops me!" The sun burst into blazing glory behind him as the city shifted.

Another explosion of power echoed from far below. "That would be on the left side, far from the doors. I wonder how many crowded over there to escape the first explosions?" Rathri cocked his head and charged.

Like their battle at the Kuktarma high place, Talinir and Rathri fell silent, letting their swords do the talking. Rathri executed a flurry of blows, driving Talinir back toward steeper parts of the dome. Talinir responded with a feint which allowed him to shift to the right, rolling out of range of flashing blades before leaping back to his feet.

Stars and sun traded places more times. Talinir hoped those below were gaining some semblance of control, even as his own head ached from the shifts. They had to have seen this fight taking place by now.

First blood went to Rathri: a short gash across Talinir's left thigh in the moment the city shifted to the Starlit Realm. Unlike Rathri, Talinir had to deal with his own height changing with each of the shifts. It lent occasional advantages when fighting a shorter opponent, but it made him more vulnerable in the moment of each shift.

"Right about… now," Rathri said. A hideous smile split his corrupted face.

Talinir shot a glance to the top of the dome, now about twenty feet away. The device!

An explosion of magic burst out from it, throwing Talinir and Rathri both off their feet. Three of the huge glass panels at the top of the chamber's dome shattered. Their shards tumbled into the screaming crowd below.

(((27)))

As Curasir moved toward her, Seri released another burst of power at Ixchel, a blend somewhere between red and pure magenta. It shot through the cyan beams surrounding her, disrupting them and setting her free. Ixchel dropped to the floor beside Seri, sword and shield at the ready.

"Very good," Curasir complimented her, "though tiresome, because it prolongs things."

"You will not touch her!" Ixchel growled, lunging forward. At the same time, Seri sent a burst of multi-colored magic at the Eldani.

Curasir took the force of her blast with a grunt and parried Ixchel's attack.

Seri stepped back and let Ixchel engage. She moved fast, keeping Curasir busy, not allowing him time to use his magic. Seri tossed in another blast of power a couple of times, but it didn't seem to help much.

The problem lay in Seri's lack of offensive uses for her magic. She could throw magic at things, and blow things apart, but that was it. No wonder the other Masters doubted her; she knew nothing.

To her credit, Ixchel appeared to be doing well against Curasir. "I've never been all that much of a swordsman," he admitted, taking another step back. "It never appealed to me. All that effort and blood." Another slash from Ixchel almost took off his hand.

"And that's why I do this instead." As Ixchel stepped in toward him again, he swung his sword at her shield. On impact, a burst of magic exploded from his sword. Ixchel flew backward into the air and slammed against the wall. As she fell, the Ch'olan banner fell with her, entangling her. She hit the floor and lay still.

Curasir turned to face Seri. "For you, on the other hand, a sword will do quite well." He took a step toward her, no longer smiling.

Seri unleashed the magic she had been gathering, pouring it out against him in full force. To her surprise, Curasir stepped sideways and disappeared. Her burst of power struck the stone wall next to the steps and blew shards of rock into the air.

She backed against the wall, trying to watch in every direction. Curasir's ability to shift between the worlds made him unpredictable. He could re-emerge anywhere. Seri kept her eyes wide, watching for magic, though it proved difficult in this room. Magic burst from the floor all over the place, and glowed bright and powerful from the pedestal. Her senses were almost useless.

Seri inched along the wall to Ixchel. She couldn't be dead, or the Bond would have broken. Seri knelt and picked up Ixchel's shield. She didn't quite know how to hold it, but it was better than her robes. She held it by the edges in front of her chest.

Should she try to move up the stairs and find more help? If she stayed here long, the first of the three sleepers to wake would probably be Volraag. She couldn't deal with him and Curasir at the same time. Maybe she could find one of the other Masters.

Curasir appeared right in front of her. "Surprise." His sword stabbed forward. Seri tried to lift the shield higher, but wasn't fast enough. A hard impact struck her shoulder. That couldn't be the sword, could it? Then Curasir pulled back and pain erupted. She cried out, both from the pain and from seeing her own blood on his sword.

"Foolish child." Curasir sneered and stabbed again. This time, Seri managed to get the shield in front of it, but the impact of the sword knocked it from her hands. She lost her balance and slid down next to Ixchel.

"Farewell, Seri-Belit. It would have been so much more pleasant to have you on our side, but..." Curasir shrugged and brought his sword down.

Seri lifted her right arm and channeled all her remaining magic into and around it. The vibratory waves deflected Curasir's blow. The sword caught her sleeve and tore it open. She would not be able to repeat that trick. The room was full of magic, but she didn't have time to absorb and use it.

Curasir's sword swept back.

Seri kept her arm up, knowing it would do no good. She closed her eyes.

The sword descended.

Something burst into life inside her, something unlike the magic of Antises, unlike Dravid's magic, unlike anything she had experienced. A tickling shot up through her body. No, not a tickling. A flickering.

Seri opened her palm as the sword approached it. Red and orange flames exploded from her hand, enveloping the sword and rushing along its surface to Curasir's arm.

The Eldani mage dropped the sword and leaped back, cursing, his arm ablaze. He stared at Seri, open-mouthed, for just a moment, then stepped sideways and vanished.

Seri's hand fell to the stone floor, which felt far cooler than it had a moment ago. Only then did she consider how much blood was pouring from her shoulder, soaking her new robes. That couldn't be good. Even as the thought spun into her mind, her head swam and her vision blurred. She slumped beside Ixchel.

"Devouring fire!" Tich's voice penetrated her fading consciousness.

"Literally," she wanted to say.

• • • • •

Rathri regained his feet before Talinir and ran back up the dome's remaining surface toward the hole. Talinir raced after him.

The assassin leaped and landed on one of the hexagonal panels at the edge of the destruction. It tilted under his weight, attached only on one side. He looked back.

"Red, Talinir. Everything will be red." The city shifted; the stars burst into view. Rathri slashed at the connections holding his perch in place.

Seeing his plan, Talinir leaped onto the next nearest panel.

Rathri's panel broke loose and fell, taking him with it. He laughed, balancing on the wildly-tilting pane of glass as it plummeted toward the Eldanim in the chamber.

Talinir dove from the top. He slammed into Rathri, wrapping one arm around his torso, too close for their swords to find purchase. The combatants flipped off the falling panel, which rotated with them. They continued to tumble, head over heels, as did the panel.

Rathri broke free from him at the last moment, shoving Talinir away and flipping backward to land in the ruins of broken glass, chairs, and bodies from the earlier crash. Talinir twisted and landed in a crouch as the panel struck and shattered behind him. The city shifted again, letting sunlight blaze down through the twisted remains of the dome.

Rathri backflipped away from Talinir, and landed next to an Eldani woman staggering with hands over her eyes. In one swift move, he slit her throat. "So many victims. So little time."

Talinir, his body aching from the impact, chased after him. Around him, wounded and confused people crawled, staggered, and moaned. Rathri darted through the crowd, stabbing and slashing as he went. Talinir caught up to him in front of the High Council's dais. He threw himself at the assassin and engaged him, keeping him too busy to attack anyone else.

Catching hold of Rathri's right wrist with his left hand, Talinir slammed his sword against the assassin's left blade as hard as he could. Rathri's sword cut into the wood of the dais and stuck. He released it and shoved Talinir in the chest, pushing him back.

Rathri produced another one of the crystal and warpsteel devices, flicked it with his thumb, and tossed it on the dais. Eltaru, the closest Councillor, stared at it, unable to comprehend what he should do.

Talinir took a step toward the dais, but Rathri jumped in his way and cut at him with his remaining blade. "Oh no. It doesn't work that way, warden of the Eldanim." He stepped back and pointed his sword toward another figure huddled on the floor nearby. "Unless you wish to abandon these people to me."

Talinir hesitated. The explosion might harm or kill a number of people, including Councillors, but if he let Rathri loose, who knew how many bystanders he might kill in their current state of confusion. Emphasizing the point, the city shifted back into the Starlit Realm. The building trembled. The continual shifting couldn't be good for the city's structural integrity.

Someone moved behind Rathri. Talinir lunged forward to keep Rathri's attention on him.

Tiranel crashed into Rathri, wrapping his arms around the assassin and pinning him. "Go, Talinir!" he yelled.

Talinir didn't wait. He leaped onto the dais and grabbed the device. He turned and scanned the room. Dozens of Eldanim remained inside, incapacitated by the shifting, afraid to move through doors because of the traps, or both. He couldn't stop the device, and there was nowhere to throw it… except up. Talinir spun and threw the device as hard as he could toward the open spot in the dome.

It exploded before it reached the top. A wave of vibratory magic impacted almost everyone in the chamber, but for most, it was only a mild shaking. A few people near the center of the room were knocked off their feet.

Talinir turned back and leaped down, but too late. Tiranel lay unmoving on the ground. Rathri stood waiting, bloody sword in hand. "Red, warden. It's all turning red."

Another segment of the dome creaked and bent inward, weakened by the latest blast. "Get out!" Talinir yelled. He pointed toward the door he had already used. "That way!" A few people heard him and scrambled in the right direction. Others either didn't hear, or couldn't comprehend.

The city shifted again. This time, the entire building shook. The weakened part of the dome fell, another three or four hexagons breaking loose and rushing toward the ground. Screams filled the room again as glass shattered and shards struck dozens of people. Rathri spread his arms and laughed.

Talinir gritted his teeth. No matter what he did, Rathri kept killing people. He had to find a way to end this.

The assassin ran and leaped onto the dais. Talinir jumped at the same moment and parried a sword strike aimed at Telra. He found himself staring straight into Rathri's face. His eyes, always so full of life in contrast to his skin, were wider and wilder than ever. "Come, warden of the Eldanim!" he mocked. "How long can we keep this up before the whole city tears itself apart?"

Rathri spun back around and dove toward another huddled Councillor. He managed to stab him once before Talinir tackled him again, knocking him off the dais and rolling into shards of glass and broken chairs. Both of them bounded back to their feet and exchanged blows again. Talinir caught Rathri in a short cut across his left side. Rathri's blade ripped Talinir's shirt open, but barely scored the skin on his stomach.

The building shook even harder as it shifted back into the Starlit Realm. Rathri was right: this couldn't keep happening without severe consequences to the city and its people. But Talinir had no control over that. The only thing he could do was stop the killing here and now.

"Fight me!" Talinir snarled. "Leave these others alone!"

Rathri feinted a stab at his feet, then flicked his blade up. Talinir took a step back to avoid it, but tried to slash at Rathri's sword arm. Rathri took advantage of the step to lunge toward another Eldani man crouched nearby. Talinir dove forward and deflected another blow, leaving himself open. Rathri slashed across his back, cutting deep.

Talinir gasped and stumbled.

"Too soon!" Rathri stepped back, allowing Talinir to regain his footing. "You can't die yet, warden of the Eldanim. You need to witness more of this!"

No. Talinir had to end this, no matter what it cost. "Warden of the Eldanim." Rathri kept mocking him with the title. As a warden, he had one and only one sworn duty.

"A warden… protects."

Rathri lifted his blade to stab down at another innocent. Talinir leaped forward again, but this time he didn't deflect the blow. He took it. Rathri's blade cut straight through the center of his chest. Talinir caught hold of Rathri's hand with his, holding the blade in place.

The assassin's mouth dropped. "Why?"

Talinir's warpsteel sword pierced through Rathri's left side and up through his chest, emerging behind his right shoulder.

Rathri pulled back. Both swords came free. Both combatants fell to their knees.

"Sacrifice." Rathri nodded, dropping his blade.

Talinir did the same, his hands going to the hole in his chest.

Rathri lifted his hands, covered in blood. "See? Red…" He toppled to the floor.

Talinir watched him, staying erect only long enough to be sure his foe would not jump back up. And then he fell.

His last view was of Tiranel's face watching him from several feet away, also lying on the floor bleeding. The High Warden gasped for words:

"Well done… warden."

The floor shook. Stars and sun exchanged places. Another hexagonal panel fell from above. Talinir closed his eyes and let himself go.

(((28)))

"Did your little excursion into the Otherworld accomplish anything?" Lord Tyrr asked.

"We met that guy's brother," Victor said, thumbing at Laran, who still sat astride his horse behind his "boundary."

"And we may have dealt with him," Marshal added. "At the very least, we gave him trouble of his own."

Lord Tyrr snorted. He and Aluri had returned to join them at their vantage point overlooking the Durunim army. "Then what have we accomplished here? This god seems unassailable."

"At least he's stopped here," Victor pointed out. "He hasn't moved since he made that boundary or whatever it is. Maybe it disappears if he leaves it."

"So we wait until he moves and then ambush him?" Lord Tyrr rubbed his beard. "It is a possibility, but one that has no evidence to support it. Nor do we know how well he can resist our powers on his own."

Marshal played with his sword hilt. "I'm tempted to let him stay here and go around. I could deal with the portal and then return."

"Leaving us here, without your power?" Aluri asked.

"I don't know." Marshal stared at Laran. "I don't know what to do."

"I do." Victor snapped the chain on his flail. "We need to try this."

Lord Tyrr laughed. "Of course! When the power of Lords fail, try a rusty old piece of metal! We should have done that first!"

Victor held up the end of the flail. "This thing is infused with Eldanim magic, put together by one of those gods. If anything can get through that boundary, this can."

"It's a possibility," Marshal said. "I'm willing to try it."

180

"So what then?" Lord Tyrr asked. "You walk down there in front of that entire army and start smacking it with your flail?"

Victor looked down at the Durunim. "Maybe?"

"I'll go with him," Marshal said. "If he does crack the boundary, I'll be ready to attack… and I can protect him."

Lord Tyrr looked at Aluri, then nodded. "I will stand ready to join you, if it works."

Victor started down the hill. Marshal joined him. "You sure about this?"

"No. But I need to hit something. Something that can't dodge." Victor's face looked like stone. "I'm tired of these gods avoiding real battle."

"You didn't think that giant was a real battle?"

"You know what I mean."

It did not take long to draw close enough to the army to be spotted. "Ah, the King returns!" Laran called. "I hear you met my brother."

"Yes," Marshal answered. "He's got a few problems of his own now."

"I'm sure he'll be fine. Have you returned to test your power against mine again?" Laran shook his head. "I'm afraid the results will be the same."

"No." Marshal pointed at Victor. "He's going to."

Laran wrinkled his brow. "He is… human. What can he possibly do?"

"This." Victor swung his flail in an overhand arc, making one complete spin before he brought it down where the boundary line traced through the dirt. The flail's head smashed against something invisible, and bounced off. As it did, Marshal caught a glimpse of a shimmering in the air.

"That did something! Do it again!"

Laran frowned. "Archers!"

Again, a rain of arrows descended toward them. Marshal threw out his power, shattering them before they could arrive.

Victor wound up and struck the boundary again. This time, Marshal was sure he saw the shimmering. The line in the dirt shifted, as well.

"What is that thing?" Laran demanded. "What do you have there?"

Victor grinned. "Just a rusty old flail!" He took the handle in both hands and spun it above his head.

Laran pulled his helmet back on and took out his spear.

Victor brought the flail down again in a tremendous blow. This time, the shimmering exploded outward through the air, arcing through a barely-visible dome over the army. Just as quickly as it appeared, it vanished.

"It's much more satisfying to break something when you can see it," Victor complained. "Whoa!" His last exclamation came as Laran spurred his horse forward and stabbed at him with the spear. Victor managed to spin just enough that the spear struck his torso at an angle and glanced off his breastplate. The tip cut a gash across his upper left arm.

Caught by surprise, Marshal whirled and threw a blast of power at the god. Laran flinched, and his horse side-stepped, but nothing else happened. How was that possible?

"Marshal! Arrows!" Victor yelled.

Without turning, Marshal threw out his power, just in time. One arrow got through and embedded itself into the ground right beside his foot.

Keeping the power vibrating around him, Marshal pointed at Laran. "I need you to keep him busy! His armor is absorbing my power or something! I'll deal with the Durunim."

"Right." Victor switched his flail to his left hand and drew his sword. "Keep a god busy. Isn't that what you told me to do in Kuktarma?"

"It worked, didn't it?" Marshal muttered. He turned to find a swarm of Durunim charging toward him, curved swords lifted. He waited until the arrows stopped falling, and then unleashed a wave of power forward. The Durunim went flying in every direction.

Almost as soon as they hit the ground, the arrows started falling again. Where were those archers, anyway? Marshal couldn't keep his shield up and attack at the same time, and the Durunim had figured that out. As more of them charged, the arrows kept coming. They were risking hitting their own people in order to get at him.

It wouldn't work for them, though. While he couldn't unleash a big blast again, he could increase the intensity of the power he used to shield himself. Any Durunim who came near were repelled back, some of them violently. They couldn't hurt him, but he couldn't do as much damage as his first attack.

Victor yelled something behind him, but he couldn't make it out. He hoped his friend was doing better than he was.

A burst of power from the side struck further back in the Durunim army. The arrows ceased. "Thank you, Lord Tyrr," Marshal breathed.

He let loose with everything he had, running forward to meet the Durunim head-on.

For a brief moment, he felt sorry for them. His emotions regarding the Durunim were constantly conflicted. When Marshal used his power to stop a battle between Varioch and Rasna, he had reshaped the earth instead of attacking the opposing army directly. His brief experiences with war made him reluctant to use his power against other human beings. The Durunim were not human, but they were living beings, former Eldanim corrupted by the gods. Could they be restored to their former state? Did they even want to? By all he knew, they appeared almost mindless servants to the gods. He still didn't want to kill them, but... they were invading his world, killing his people. As King, the defense of the people was his responsibility.

Between Lord Tyrr and himself, they soon dispatched the entire force of Durunim. Marshal returned to find Laran sitting astride his horse. Victor faced him, but neither seemed eager to fight.

"All done?" Victor asked.

"Yeah, what happened here?"

"Goldie here put up his boundary again."

Marshal looked up at Laran. The god's eyes glared at him through his helmet's view slit. "What now, oh mighty Laran?" he called. "Your army is gone. What should we do with you?"

Lord Tyrr rode up, along with Aluri and their escort of soldiers. The Lord of Rasna dismounted in a rush and drew his sword, a massive blade. Marshal would have needed to use both hands to wield it. Lord Tyrr held it with one hand as he pointed at the god.

"Break apart his magical shield and let's be done with him!"

Marshal glanced at Victor, who hefted his flail. They could do it. But...

Laran tossed his spear to the ground and pulled off his helmet. "I must admit defeat," he declared. "I appeal to your mercy, King of Antises."

"You cannot stay here," Marshal said.

"You have made that abundantly clear." Laran nodded. "If you will open the door for me, I will return to the Starlit Realm and trouble you no more."

"No!" Lord Tyrr roared. "He must pay for the villages that his army destroyed!"

Marshal winced. It was a fair point. However... "Was the death of his army not enough payment?" he asked Lord Tyrr quietly.

"They but obeyed his orders! He is the true perpetrator behind this! If we had not stopped him, he would have led them to Raeton itself!"

Laran dropped his shield onto the ground beside his spear. "The metal on my shield, along with the spearhead, should more than compensate your land for its losses," he offered.

"What about your armor?" Victor asked.

Laran laughed. His golden armor dissolved around him. Marshal had suspected it was some kind of magical construct.

"Very well." Marshal concentrated and cut open a doorway to the Otherworld, about five feet high and a couple feet wide. No use letting a tunaldi cross over, just in case.

Laran chuckled nervously. "My horse and I cannot fit through such a narrow space," he said.

"Your horse is staying here," Marshal said. "Lord Tyrr? I think you would look magnificent on top of that horse, don't you?"

Lord Tyrr only growled in response.

Marshal gestured at the doorway. "Dismount and leave, never to return. Make your decision quickly. I won't keep this open for long."

Laran glared at them for a few seconds, then snorted. He slid off the horse, gave it a last pat, and approached Marshal's doorway. As he ducked down low to enter, Lord Tyrr struck. With a massive two-handed stroke, his sword came down on the back of the god's neck. Laran's severed head tumbled into the Otherworld. His body fell, halfway in and halfway out.

"He was leaving!" Marshal cried. "Why?"

Lord Tyrr shoved the rest of Laran's body through the doorway. "I told you. He killed my people. As Lord of Rasna, I could not let that stand."

Marshal glanced up at Aluri. She held a hand over her mouth, her face much whiter than normal. Horror at her father's actions, or fear of a curse? War created exceptions to the Laws of Cursings and Bindings, and Laran hadn't been human. Even so, Marshal didn't blame her for her fear. And he couldn't agree with the Lord's actions.

Lord Tyrr wiped his sword clean and put it away, while the others stood in silence. He picked up Laran's shield and hefted it. He gestured and one of his soldiers took the horse's bridle.

"It's been a good day's work," he announced. "Let's make camp here."

• • • • •

Kishin waited in the darkness. How many times had he done just this, waiting for a precise moment, the moment at which he could take someone's life? His mission tonight was far different, though still requiring the same skills he had developed over decades.

These gods were so predictable and audacious. They traveled in luxurious style, forcing their servants to carry all of these nonsensical extras through the portal to this world. Their army could have been twice as big if their leaders had been willing to surrender a few comforts.

But no. The tent Kishin watched proved the opposite. The gods desired their comfort, and nothing else mattered. This god's tent was second only in size to Murdak's. Kishin calculated his entire home back in Ch'olan could almost fit within this one tent. Ridiculous.

And exactly as Nehesy predicted. "You'll find him in the second-largest tent. Of that I have no doubt," the old man said a few hours earlier. "In fact, I suspect it will be as close to Murdak's tent size as possible without exceeding it."

Kishin moved a few inches closer. The damp ground from recent rain made it simple to shift his weight soundlessly. As always, he could take his time. Assassins must have patience. But he was not an assassin any longer. He needed to constantly remind himself of that.

"Murdak needs more persuading to answer my challenge," Nehesy said.

"Do you want me to take another message?"

"No. I want you to speak with his biggest rival."

"The gods have rivals?"

Nehesy nodded. "Murdak, as you might have heard, is the chief god of the people of Kuktarma," he explained. "This particular army is being led by a consortium of gods, including many of his pantheon, but also many from the peoples of Arazu and Mandiata."

"Ah. Rivals."

"Exactly. Namnirnu is the chief of the Arazu pantheon. His power is immense, but Murdak's is greater. Even so, they've never liked each other, and struggle to work together."

Kishin had not expected Nehesy to be so well versed in subterfuge, or to propose a plan like this. Still, if he truly were a thousand years old, he was probably well versed in just about everything. What would that be like? To live for a thousand years? Kishin struggled to imagine it. How skilled could one become in their chosen professions over a thousand years of experience? He reminded himself that these gods they worked against might be far older still. Perhaps he should exercise even more caution than usual.

Over the next two hours, he moved across the open space surrounding Namnirnu's tent. Crouching beside the tent, he took out his dagger. Adhi's dagger, actually. The young lordling had been reluctant to let him use it, but he didn't have much choice. The Durunim sword was too big for this kind of work, and their little band had few other weapons. Kishin had blackened the blade before setting out, making sure it would not reflect any kind of light that might wander near him. He slid the dagger into the side of the tent and cut a foot-long gash. He waited for a full three minutes for any kind of reaction to his actions. Hearing none, he spread the gash apart and crawled into the tent, inch by inch.

He found himself in a dark room, but light shone through a curtain hanging over a doorway. Even the idea of separate rooms in a tent seemed extravagant. What was this one even for?

He stood and stretched his legs, shifting up on the balls of his feet, and then onto his heels. Hearing nothing else, he took a step toward the doorway.

"Come in, human. I've been listening to you approach for the past three hours." The voice vibrated with command.

Kishin saw no reason to pretend any longer. He stepped through the doorway and entered the largest room of the tent.

An enormous god lounged atop a colorful couch among a dozen or more pillows. Unlike most of the gods Kishin had seen so far, he sported a lengthy black beard, curly and oiled. He wore a round metal cap topped with four horns of some ox-like creature.

"Kneel in the presence of your supreme lord, father, creator, and the raging storm himself," the god demanded. "I am Namnirnu. Why do you come before me as a thief in the night?"

Kishin knelt, compelled by the voice, though he maintained enough resistance to convince himself it was part of his act. "I come only to exchange words with the great Namnirnu," he answered.

"Words? What is the point of that? If you are not here to worship me and seek my favor, I should probably kill you." The god looked closer at him. "Ah, you're that messenger who came before Murdak the other day."

"I am. And now I come before you."

Namnirnu chuckled. "What did you do to Nummotem? He came

back terrified and powerless. Murdak threw him out of the camp."

"Nehesy is nothing if not impressive." Kishin shifted on his knee. He tore a strip of dead skin from his forearm.

Namnirnu eyed him. "Your condition is quite unusual. Though Murdak promised to end the system of curses that plagues your people, I doubt he can do anything for you."

"I do not expect him to." Kishin smiled. The god had mentioned Murdak first, making his job so much easier. "I expect him to answer Nehesy's challenge."

"Ha!" Namnirnu stretched. "He will never do that. Accept a challenge from a simple human? Regardless of who this Nehesy claims to be, Murdak won't do it."

"Is he afraid?"

"Murdak knows no fear." The way he said it, immediate and rote, sounded like a common saying, rather than a sincere belief. Interesting.

"Even after what happened to Nummotem?"

Namnirnu wagged a finger at Kishin. "The difference in power between Nummotem and Murdak is enormous. Hardly a comparison at all."

"Much like the difference between Nummotem and… yourself?"

"That much should be self-evident." He cocked an eyebrow and Kishin and waited. "No? Oh, that's right. I often forget humans can't sense the powers of others. How sad it must be to walk around without the most basic of senses."

"I, uh, believe those who use magic can do something like that."

"But you don't. And yet you crept into the tent of one of the most powerful magic wielders in two worlds. Either you're very brave or very stupid."

"One of the most powerful? Not *the* most powerful?"

Namnirnu snorted. "Thousands of people used to worship me, human. You think I don't recognize insincere praise when I hear it?"

"Very well. I will be blunt." Kishin shifted to his other knee.

"Please do." The god waved dismissively.

"Nehesy sent me here to ask you to persuade Murdak to accept the challenge."

"I? I cannot persuade Murdak of anything. He does as he pleases."

"Still, I'm sure you could… point him in that direction."

He snorted again and sat up. "I suppose I could imply cowardice on his part in front of the others, or some such obvious manipulation. But why would I do that?"

"If Murdak wins the challenge, it does not affect you at all." Kishin pulled himself into a crouch. "But if he loses... then all of this is yours."

Namnirnu rolled onto his side. "If this Nehesy is powerful enough to defeat Murdak, what good will that do me? I will be the next target... not that I believe he's so powerful, of course."

"This... may be hard to understand," Kishin suggested. "It is hard for me."

"Are you questioning my almighty wisdom?" Namnirnu asked drily.

"Not at all. It's just..." Kishin hesitated. "Nehesy says that his power is reserved for only one purpose: defeating Murdak. He even implies that once his job is done, he will die. He claims to be empowered by Theon for this one task."

Namnirnu rolled forward, crossing his arms under his chin to stare at Kishin. "Now that is interesting. And far more believable than the idea that a simple human could defeat Murdak on his own. You should have started with that."

Kishin bowed his head. "Alas, I do not possess almighty wisdom."

"Ha! I like you, human. You have wit." He narrowed his eyes. "And you smell of death."

"My curse—"

"No, not that." Namnirnu pulled himself up and got to his feet. He towered over seven feet tall, looming over Kishin's kneeling form. "You have killed, and often. I can smell it. With the magical laws in place here, such an occurrence is rare. Humans who have killed are exceedingly rare. But you... you stand out. How many have you killed?"

"I do not know." Actually, Kishin knew the exact number. But why share it?

"That many? Fascinating." Namnirnu took a step to the side and looked at him from a different angle. "As I said, I like you. I will let you live today." His voice changed. "Give me your arm."

Startled, Kishin lifted his left arm without thinking. Namnirnu took his hand. "You may return to Nehesy and tell him what you will of this conversation." He shifted his grip to Kishin's wrist. "But after all of this, I may have need of someone with your unique skills. Come back to me, and we will talk again." He shifted his grip to Kishin's forearm.

"I... thank you, my lord." Kishin wasn't sure if that would be the proper address, but it sounded right for now.

Namnirnu's grip tightened. "But your impudence and arrogance will not be tolerated." He squeezed. Kishin gasped. "This is for the hole you put in my tent." Both bones in Kishin's forearm snapped. Somehow, he managed not to scream. Namnirnu released him.

"When you have healed from that, you will be wiser, I suspect." He waved him away. "Go. Do not enter my presence again unless Murdak is dead."

Kishin held his broken arm and slipped out of the tent. Escaping the Durunim camp would take almost as long as getting into it, and he would have to do so with one useless arm and unbelievable pain. Curse these gods and everything associated with them!

<h1 style="text-align:center">(((29)))</h1>

"We should just leave," Marshal said. "Head out on our own and destroy the portal."

Victor stirred the coals of their meager fire with a stick and didn't answer. A boisterous laugh came from the direction of the much larger fire a couple dozen yards away. They both instinctively looked to see the shadow of Lord Tyrr waving his arms while talking to his soldiers.

Marshal turned back and set his teeth. Was the Lord bragging about his actions today? Celebrating the murder of a defenseless enemy? "We should leave," he repeated.

"Do you want my opinion?" Victor asked, still watching the coals.

Marshal looked up. "Of course I want your opinion. What's that supposed to mean?"

Victor shrugged. "You didn't really listen to Lord Tyrr's opinion today, so I wasn't sure."

"Because his opinion was wrong!"

"Was it?" Victor lifted his gaze and looked into Marshal's face. "You didn't give him much of a chance to explain. You just ignored him and opened the doorway."

Marshal stared back at him. "We can't murder our enemies!"

"Was it murder, or was it justice?"

"How can you say that? Laran was a prisoner who had surrendered his weapons!"

"Would you consider Lord Tyrr unarmed if he set down his sword?"

"No, but—"

"He was one of the ancient gods, Marshal!" Victor interrupted. "Without weapons or armor, he was still incredibly powerful."

"That doesn't—"

"Who decides justice, Marshal?"

"I don't... I don't know."

Victor pointed his stick at him. "You said it was murder. He called it justice. Who decides?"

Marshal frowned. "If it were anyone else, the Laws would decide. But he's a Lord."

"The Laws still decide, don't they? Wasn't your entire life proof of that?"

Marshal winced. "That's not fair."

"The Laws? Or my point?"

"Both."

"He's right, Marshal." Aluri's voice broke into their argument. She emerged from the shadows and stood beside their fire. Marshal and Victor jumped to their feet, but she waved them back down and sat herself, pulling her skirts around her legs.

"For now, the Laws of Cursings and Bindings decide whether justice is done," she said. "If my father broke those Laws today, then one of my siblings has been cursed, and we will learn of it on our return. If not..." She shrugged. "Then it is justice."

"Either way, it's not right," Marshal said. "It doesn't... feel right."

"You say you wish to end the Laws." Aluri looked at him. "So that magic no longer makes such decisions. If so, then what will replace them? As your friend asked, who decides justice?"

"I don't know," he answered honestly.

"Will you, as King, impose a new set of laws on all Antises? Will you, alone, determine what is right and what is wrong?"

"No." Marshal shook his head. "I can't do that. I'm not... I'm not trying to take Theon's place."

She spread her hands. "Then will you let each of the lands determine their own laws? Their own justice?"

"I... I guess that makes the most sense."

"And what if Rasna decides that murder requires swift justice? A death for a death? But Varioch has a different law, and a murderer flees across the border? What then?"

"I haven't thought about things like that," he admitted.

"These are all things that must be thought of," Aluri pressed. "I applaud your dream, your goal. But you have to think beyond that. What will Antises look like without magic to enforce our laws?"

"People will go crazy when they realize there aren't any consequences," Victor said.

"There will have to be consequences," Marshal said, "but determined by human authorities, with room for mercy, not blindly enforced by uncaring magic."

"An admirable ideal, but one that will not come easy. When the Laws are lifted, there will be chaos." She fixed her eyes on Marshal's. "Antises will require strong and steady leadership to get us through the days that follow. Will that be you, Marshal?"

He didn't answer. How could he answer? He didn't even think of himself as any kind of leader, let alone a strong one.

Aluri nodded. "The fact that you do not immediately answer says much about you. Maybe you are the right one."

"I'm not," he said. "I just… I just want to make sure no one else has to go through what I did. I want everyone to live without curses."

"As do I." She got to her feet. "I… told you of my own fears. I understand your desire. But if you succeed, there will be much work left to do. Goodnight to you both."

Marshal smiled as Victor's eyes watched the princess leave. Victor sighed and looked back at the fire. "I don't think she even remembers my name," he grumbled.

"I thought you were interested in Ixchel."

"That doesn't mean I can't want to be noticed by a beautiful woman."

"I'll put you in charge of justice after we lift the curses. That'll make her notice you."

"Oh no. You're not dumping that on me." Victor shook the stick at him.

Marshal sat in silence for a few moments, also watching the fire. "Everyone keeps bringing up what happens after we lift the curses. I'm just trying to get that done. I don't… I have no idea what happens after that."

Victor lowered his voice. "Were you even planning to live through it?"

Marshal looked up sharply. "I'm not planning on killing myself."

"That's not what I asked. Did you… expect to live through lifting the curses?"

"I don't know." Marshal swallowed. "I… I'm prepared, if that's what it takes. It's my only goal in life, really."

"The only one? There's nothing else in life that makes you want to keep living beyond that?"

"I…" He looked down again. "Sure. I mean, there's Tich. And you.

And Seri. I like… no, I love the friendships we have now. I'll fight for that."

"Then fight for it." Victor jammed the stick into the fire hard, sending sparks cascading. "And realize that not all fighting involves a sword or magic powers." He paused. "Huh. I just thought of that."

"That's it," Marshal said, "you're now chief advisor to the King. Victor the Warrior Sage."

"How much does it pay?"

"You get your own room on Zes Sivas. Beyond that… devouring fire. How *does* a King get money, anyway?"

"Ask Aluri."

"You ask her. You've got a title now. Maybe she'll pay attention to you."

Victor snapped the stick in two and tossed half of it at Marshal.

•••••

Seri woke in her new bedroom, the one once occupied by Master Hain. She wondered if she would ever feel comfortable waking in it. The sharp pain in her shoulder reminded her of the fight with Curasir. She moaned and reached for the shoulder, only to see that her right hand was bandaged. She stared at it a moment, not quite grasping why.

"Is the pain severe?" Lady Lilitu's voice surprised her. She turned to see the Lady sitting beside her bed, hands folded in her lap. The room was empty, otherwise.

"I-it's not too bad. What happened to my hand?" Seri blinked, trying to remember everything.

"When one manifests new magic, it can often have detrimental side effects." The Lady took Seri's bandaged hand and tapped one of her fingers. "Can you feel that? Any pain?"

Seri wrinkled her brow. "No. Just a little pressure."

The Lady sat back. "I was afraid of that." She sighed. "You've damaged the nerves in your fingers, the parts of your skin that can feel. I hope they will fully heal, but you may have a lingering issue there for the rest of your life."

"I remember… Curasir. And fire!" Seri gasped. "I made fire!"

Lady Lilitu nodded. "I have wondered if the ability was within you. Now we know. Another gift from your father."

Seri pulled herself up to sit. Her left arm was in a sling, making things a little difficult. The Lady helped adjust her pillow. "You use magic fire and don't get burned," Seri observed. "Uh, don't you?"

The Lady held up her hand and a brief flicker appeared between her thumb and forefinger. "Yes, but it has taken a number of years' practice. You will do the same one day, but probably sooner than I did, since you have me to teach you."

"You had Curasir."

The Lady hesitated. "Is there an accusation in that statement?"

"He talked about helping you, and you helping him, and manipulating you. And he visited you here. And you used him to lie to me!" Her words came out in a rush, full of emotion and confusion.

Ixchel stuck her head in through the door. "Are you all right, my Lady?"

Seri stared at her. "I'm all right. Are you all right?"

Ixchel nodded. "I'll be outside then." She disappeared.

"Ixchel has been outside your door since we found you," Lilitu explained. "She's watching you carefully, but I think she feels like she failed you, and that's why she stays outside." She shook her head. "There are many powers in this world far beyond her, yet she does not seem to accept that when it comes to your protection."

"I'd better talk to her." Seri started to get up, but the Lady put a hand on her.

"Not yet, my dear. We must get these things out into the open. You wanted to know about Curasir, and the things he no doubt told you during your fight."

Seri sat back.

"Curasir says many things," she continued. "Some of them are outright lies, many of them are a twisted combination of lies and the truth, and some, a few, are true. He says whatever he thinks will serve his own purposes."

"He told me a lot this time." Seri frowned. "But I don't know how much of it to believe."

"Then I will tell you everything I know, and you can compare it. I hope you will trust my words."

Seri didn't answer. She wasn't entirely sure she could.

"I met Curasir three years ago," the Lady began. "It was thrilling for me, at the time. I had never met one of the Eldanim before. He was fascinating to me on so many levels. Lord Enuru and I welcomed him into our court and spent a great deal of time discussing his world and ours together. Now, of course, I don't know how much of what he told us of the Eldanim is true or tales he spun to amuse himself at our expense."

"Talinir could tell you," Seri offered. "Or Marshal. He's been to their city."

Lilitu nodded. "It is well that the King met an honest Eldani. They seem to have a good relationship."

"I haven't been around him very much," Seri admitted. "But he seems completely devoted to Marshal."

"And I hear he's been sent back to seek the help of the Eldanim in our war?"

"Yes, he's been gone since we left the high place." Seri coughed.

The Lady got to her feet and brought a glass of water from the nightstand. Seri drank all of it.

"Over time, Curasir became a confidant," the Lady resumed her story. "He already knew of my… indiscretions somehow. I suppose the gods told him."

"Then he does know my father's identity."

"Almost certainly. But even if he were to tell you, I wouldn't believe him."

"After yesterday, I don't think he'll want to tell me much of anything." Seri gasped. "It was yesterday, wasn't it? I haven't been asleep for days?"

"It was yesterday." The Lady smiled. "To continue, Curasir told me of his interest in our mages and Zes Sivas. I introduced him to Master Hain, who invited him to come visit them from time to time. I believe he came here multiple times before you became an acolyte."

And Master Hain introduced her to Curasir. Seri remembered the moment she found out the Eldanim were real. She had been so naive back then!

"Upon hearing that you would be here, Curasir told me he would visit you. I begged him not to reveal our relationship, but he insisted that you needed to know about your potential. He concocted the story about wild magic, and I agreed to it." She smiled ruefully. "I suspected you would see through it, in time, but it made a compelling lie for someone just starting their training."

"I had no reason not to believe it!"

The Lady toyed with a lock of her hair. "And yet, it was another lie that you should not have been told. I am sorry for all the deception in our relationship."

Seri didn't know what to say. She opened her mouth, but Lady Lilitu continued speaking.

"I have never been allied with Curasir in any way other than what I have now told you. He means nothing to me, and I am distraught at how we were all deceived." She looked up and smiled. "But you handled yourself quite well against him, from what I have heard."

Seri looked at her burned hand again. "I guess so. I don't really understand what happened."

"From what I have learned, each of the gods have a distinct power, besides all of the magic they share individually."

"I've seen some of that now," Seri said. "One of them could control plants."

"My lover, your father, had a relationship with fire. He could do amazing things with it, abilities that I will never have." She cocked her head to look at Seri. "Since you are his daughter, you will probably exceed my abilities in time. I gained them through... proximity, whereas for you, as they told you, it is your heritage."

Seri again didn't know what to say. Part of her thrilled to the idea that she would one day wield this fire power alongside her regular mage abilities, both with great skill. She had the title of "Master" now, but one day, she would be a Master Mage in truth, and with multiple types of magic.

Unless Marshal's work removed magic from Antises. She hoped not, not after all her work to get here. Ouch.

The Lady rose. "I will take my leave, and tell your friends you are awake. Rest a while longer, child. You have been through an ordeal."

Seri still had questions. "What about Volraag? Do we have better guards on him now? And Master Magnus helped him escape!"

"You will have to speak with the other Masters about that. I do not know their specific thoughts on either of those matters."

"And what's to prevent Curasir from just... popping back in here to finish the job?" Seri looked around anxiously, half expecting the Eldani mage to appear beside her bed at that moment.

"Nothing... except that you soundly defeated him. He will not be eager to try that again. I do not think we have seen the last of him, but if he returns, it will likely be with a different plan." The Lady looked thoughtful.

Seri didn't find that very comforting, but she kept her opinion to herself. "Thank you, my Lady."

She gave a nod and left the room. Seri leaned back on her pillow and looked at her hand again. Fire. She had really thrown fire at Curasir. How did that work? Where did it come from? So many questions, and a lifetime to study them.

(((30)))

Marshal intended to announce his own plans to Lord Tyrr the next morning, but the Lord beat him to it. "I think it best we split up now," he declared.

"I think, that is, yes, that works for me," Marshal stammered. "Why were you thinking that?"

"I am concerned about more roving bands of Durunim," Lord Tyrr explained. "I have already sent scouts far and wide. We will see what we can find. And you, I am assuming, want to head straight for the high place."

"Yes, I do."

"Keep the horses." Lord Tyrr gave a dismissive wave of his hand. "I expect to see them—and you—back at Raeton in a few days."

Marshal glanced at Aluri. She only nodded at him. "Very well. I will be there as soon as I have dealt with the portal. And then we must go to Zes Sivas."

"Of course." Lord Tyrr turned to his horse.

Marshal looked at Victor, who shook his head. Marshal motioned for him not to say anything, and they moved away.

"He just dismissed the King of Antises," Victor said, when they had put enough distance between them.

"Let him think that. It's what I wanted, anyway." Marshal made his way back to their own horses.

"Do you even know the way to the high place from here? What about back to Raeton?"

Marshal pulled himself up into the saddle. At least he was getting a little better at that. "I can feel the portal." He pointed northwest. "As for Raeton, it shouldn't be that hard to retrace our steps." Marshal glanced back. "Should it?"

"Let's hope not," Victor said, mounting his horse. "Wouldn't that be something? Time for the Passing, all the Lords assembled... where's the King? Oh, he's lost on the back roads of Rasna somewhere."

"Maybe I should leave you behind."

"And miss the chance to see our old battlefield? And watch you get lost?" Victor pointed down the road. "Onward!"

• • • • •

Lord Meluhha arrived on Zes Sivas through the portal, but only for a few minutes. Seri joined Master Ganak and Lady Lilitu in meeting with him in the portal room. As she entered, her eyes shifted to a stain on the floor near the wall. Her blood. She shivered, the wound in her shoulder throbbing. Dravid tried to heal it for her, but while it improved significantly, it hadn't vanished.

"The King is not here?" Lord Meluhha cried.

"No, my Lord. He is in Rasna," Master Ganak explained. "He is working with Lord Tyrr to close the portal there, before returning for the new Passing."

"Meanwhile, the army of the gods marches across my lands unhindered," Lord Meluhha griped.

"Do we know where they're going yet?" Seri asked. "Have they attacked anywhere?"

"They are moving slowly, but in almost a direct line. They clearly have a specific destination in mind."

"What is it?"

"If they continue on this course, they will reach the shores of Lake Litanu." Lord Meluhha folded his arms. "And from there, their path leads here, to Zes Sivas. That is not the only possibility, but it is a strong one."

A chill ran down Seri's back. "They want to stop us. To stop Marshal."

"They want to strike at the heart of Antises," Lady Lilitu said. "It makes sense. This is the most strategic target."

"They'll have to cross the water, but I don't think that will be much of a problem for them," Lord Meluhha said. "But there is more. If they continue on this path, they will strike the town of Candrama within the next few days. It sits on the river Ramasa, on the border with Arazu. It is there that we will determine their true intentions."

"If I remember aright, Candrama is not a small town," Master Ganak said.

"No. I have dispatched messengers to tell them to evacuate. I hope to bring the residents to Simbala, but they will have to travel along the river. It will be difficult going for so many." He hesitated. "Should the Durunim turn at Candrama, to also follow the river, then their target is Simbala, not Zes Sivas. I must be prepared for that eventuality. Our defense forces stand ready to assist the evacuees, and to fight for them if necessary. Should they come, I will need help. I cannot fight these gods on my own."

"I will come if you call," Lady Lilitu declared. "I am sure the King and the other Lords would join us. We cannot allow one of our capital cities to fall into the enemy's hands."

Seri didn't say anything. Marshal might not like this. It was starting to sound like the Lords would go to war before completing the Passing, or dealing with the Laws of Cursing and Binding. But from their point of view, they might be right.

"I will keep you updated," Lord Meluhha said. "I will send one of my sons if I am unable to come myself." He nodded to each one of them and then stepped back through the portal.

Master Ganak bowed to the two women, then moved to the stairs himself. "I will speak to the other Masters about the possibility of a last defense of the island." He paused. "But let us hope it will not come to that."

• • • • •

Jamana pushed another branch out of the way for Nehesy. After two days of pushing their way through a forest with far too much undergrowth, he was sick of trees. "Are you sure we're going in the right direction?" he asked for the third time that day. Despite the old mage's assurances, everything looked the same out here. Jamana had no idea where in Kuktarma—or Arazu!—they might be.

"What has happened to your faith, acolyte?" Nehesy chided.

"It is not my faith that needs reassuring, old man, but my legs!"

"I am not altogether certain," Adhi said, "but I believe we are nearing the Ramasa River. If so, the town of Candrama cannot be far."

Jamana looked at him in alarm. "A town? In the path of the army?"

"My father's scouts would have determined that already," Adhi said. "And they will be evacuating the city."

"Let us hope they get everyone," Nehesy said. "But I have my doubts."

Adhi wrinkled his brow at that, but didn't say anything.

Jamana glanced back at the fourth member of their party. Kishin had been uncharacteristically quiet since returning from his latest mission. The assassin's left arm, heavily bandaged and splinted, hung in a sling. He had not explained what happened to it, saying only that gods were fickle.

Jamana didn't pretend to understand it all. Nehesy had not steered them wrong so far, even if his actions were often confusing at best.

"I do not tell you everything you wish to hear, do I?" Nehesy said in a quiet voice.

Jamana jerked around. "Do you read my thoughts now?"

"No, not like that. After so many years of observing others, I can tell what they're thinking. No magic involved."

"You tell me what to do, but offer little explanation. It reminds me greatly of my old Master on Zes Sivas," Jamana admitted.

"You miss him, do you not?"

"Master Korda? Yes. But he is gone now. Komadi is the Master Mage of Mandiata."

"Things are not always as they appear, you know."

"The trees come to an end ahead," Adhi interrupted. He picked up his pace. Jamana didn't blame him.

But when Adhi reached the tree line, he came to an abrupt halt. "What is it?" Jamana called. He hurried to catch up and joined his friend in looking ahead.

They stood on a small rise that dropped off in a rocky descent. In the distance, Jamana saw the river Adhi mentioned, reflecting the late afternoon sun like a long, curving mirror. He caught a glimpse of buildings on the far shore, marking the location of Candrama. But what lay at the bottom of the rocky descent drew his attention.

A ramshackle assemblage of rudimentary huts and cabins clustered together. An expansive garden stretched out to the left, and a well-worn path led off in the direction of the river.

"This is not on our maps," Adhi said, perplexed. "Why have a village here, so close to Candrama, yet so separate?"

"It's a curse village," Kishin said behind them. "They never show up on the maps."

Jamana watched several figures moving about the huts. One pointed them out to his companion. "We've been noticed."

"Are you saying everyone down there has a curse?" Adhi asked.

"What's wrong, Lord's son? Has your father sheltered you from sites like these?" Kishin mocked.

"I am not altogether ignorant, assassin. It just... caught me by surprise."

Nehesy joined them. "And my doubts are justified, it seems. I see no sign that these people have been warned to evacuate."

"Then we must warn them." Adhi started to pick his way down the rocky descent.

"I would advise against telling them who you are," Kishin called.

Jamana took Nehesy's arm and helped him find a safe way to climb down. Kishin followed Adhi at a distance. Before they reached the village, a handful of people came out to meet them. By the time Jamana reached the group, Adhi had already begun explaining the situation.

"...knew a lot of people were leaving town over there," a man was saying. Jamana tried not to stare at his strange appearance: the man looked as if half his face had melted. Flaps of skin hung over his left eye and covered half his mouth.

"But we didn't know it were everyone," said his companion, a short man who appeared even shorter because of his hunched stature.

"An army of evil forces are heading this way," Adhi said. "Everyone needs to leave."

"And where would we go?" the hunched man demanded. "They don't let us into the cities."

"They don't let us anywhere," the first man said. "We got nowhere to go."

While they spoke, a woman with a twisted right leg limped over to join them. "An evil army?" She laughed. "Maybe we should see if they'll let us join them!"

"You know not of what you speak!" Jamana exclaimed. "These are invaders from the Otherworld, like the Eldanim, but... evil."

All three of the villagers looked at him skeptically. "Evil Eldanim? Now you're just making things up," the hunched man said. "Why would you do this? Haven't we all lost enough already without you trying to drive us out of our homes?"

"As pathetic as they might be," the woman muttered.

"The threat is real," Adhi insisted. "They will not care about your curses. They will just kill you if you are in their way!"

"What do you know of curses, pretty boy?" asked the man with the melted face. "When have you ever suffered in your life?"

Kishin stepped forward and threw back his hood, revealing his diseased face. "I know all there is to know of curses and suffering. Speak to me when you look worse than this!"

The other three took an involuntary step back. Kishin drew his sword and aimed it at the hunchback. "Tell me your curse!" he demanded.

"I… I hurt someone. In return, I got this twist in my back. I can't never straighten up."

Kishin turned his sword toward the woman. "Tell me your curse!"

"Kishin." Nehesy's voice, though quiet, seemed to fill the air around them. Kishin lowered the sword and stepped back.

"Tell everyone," Adhi said. "There is no hope for those who remain behind."

"We have been without hope for most of our lives," the woman answered. "How can anyone take what we do not have?" She turned back toward the village. The two men hurried after her.

"What do we do now?" Jamana asked.

"I don't know." Adhi looked miserable, watching the cursed people move back to their tiny homes.

"I could chase them out, if necessary," Kishin suggested. "They will not listen to reason, but given the prospect of imminent death, they will cling to life and run."

"What should we do, Nehesy?" Jamana turned. The old man stood leaning on his staff, looking off to the east.

"The challenge will be here," he murmured. "This is where we make our stand."

"Nehesy? What about these people?"

The ancient mage turned back to him with a smile of… contentment, yet sadness. "We will do what we can," he answered. "But it may be too late already." He pointed with his staff to the north. "Murdak comes."

<h1 style="text-align:center">(((31)))</h1>

Kishin scrambled back up the rocky hillside and looked around. The gods and Durunim would not be pushing their way through the trees. They would be following a more open path. He set out on a northeast run. It took him only a few moments to break through the trees on this side. Wide open spaces stretched to the northeast before curving more directly east out of his sight.

And there was the army. Durunim and gods, moving steadily toward him.

Kishin stood still, trying to process all of it. Nehesy intended to face Murdak here. If Namnirnu had done his work, goading Murdak on, maybe he would accept the challenge this time. If he did not... they would all be overrun and killed by the Durunim, unless Nehesy had a way of dealing with them.

All of it seemed secondary somehow to the village. When he first suffered his curse, Kishin had almost gone to one of those curse villages. He would have fallen into despair and died alone, lacking any purpose in life. Instead, he chose to fight back against his curse. He found a reason to live, though it hadn't been a very good one.

These people in this village... They had no reason to live, no purpose to life. He knew it, better than most. Anyone else would have left them to their fate.

But he couldn't. He could not abandon them, not knowing what they were going through. Nehesy wanted to make his stand here? Kishin would make a stand too. A last stand, most likely. But hadn't that annoying old priest said he should find a cause?

"Kishin?"

He turned to see Adhi climbing up to join him.

"Nehesy said… oh." Adhi stared. "I didn't think they were that close just yet."

"We have maybe an hour," Kishin said. "Their path will lead them to the curse village. It is the logical path. It will take them to the best place to cross the river and move on, assuming that is their goal."

"We can't stop them."

"No." Kishin watched the army continue its crawl. "We must get everyone out."

"Oh, um. Nehesy wants you to deliver the challenge to Murdak again."

Kishin nodded. "I assumed he would. You two should get those people evacuated."

"We'll do the best we can," Adhi promised. He ran back toward the village.

Kishin stepped into the open and started walking toward the oncoming army. "I'm trusting you this last time, old man," he muttered. "Don't fail me now."

He walked with slow, deliberate steps. No reason to rush. And perhaps the sight of one person walking toward them would confuse the enemy. He snorted. One person with his arm in a sling. Right.

Ten minutes into the walk he remembered the flag of parley. He had no idea what happened to the original. He looked down. The sling holding his bandaged arm was… mostly white. It would have to do.

It took almost half an hour for him to reach the army. As he drew near, he removed the sling and waved it. He tried to keep his bandaged arm in the same position. Without the sling to support it, the weight of the injured limb gave him continual pain.

As before, a squad of Durunim came to meet him, curved swords at the ready. "I come with a message for Murdak, king of the gods!" he called. "Again." Without speaking, they surrounded him and directed him on to meet the army. They passed through one entire rank of marching soldiers before finding the gods.

Murdak rode on a chariot pulled by a pair of unusual horned creatures. The chariot itself, masterfully crafted, looked to have been built since their arrival in this world. The other gods also rode chariots and wagons of various types. A handful rode atop some of the monstrous tunaldi.

On seeing Kishin, Murdak called a halt. He leaped down from his chariot and approached, followed by several other gods including, Kishin noted, Namnirnu. Murdak held a folded-over whip in his hand.

"The messenger dares to return!" Murdak cried. "What ridiculous word do you bring us now?"

Kishin bowed. "Nehesy awaits you just ahead, ready for your challenge fight."

"This is pointless." Murdak gestured to the Durunim. "Kill the messenger and let us proceed. If this Nehesy waits ahead, we will march over him."

"Great Murdak, might I make a suggestion?" Namnirnu said, raising a hand to the Durunim. "How long are we to suffer these distractions? If you kill this messenger, then this gnat, Nehesy, will find another one, and keep pestering you. Why not finish him off?"

"Isn't that what I just said?" Murdak growled.

"If he sees the army coming, he will not be waiting for us," a goddess spoke up. "He will run and hide, and continue to issue his challenges."

"Then what do you propose?" Murdak smacked the whip against his palm.

"Meet his challenge," Namnirnu said. "Who can stand against the mighty Murdak? The people of this world flee before your face, except this one. He is their only hope. End him and let us move on to the Lords and their King."

Murdak glared at him. "I have no need to do so. We can continue on."

"Leaving the humans with a hope to cling to," the goddess said. "And hope is a powerful thing. Is it well to let them keep that?"

"Now, now," Namnirnu said to her, "the mighty Murdak clearly only wants to complete our conquest as expeditiously as possible. It certainly cannot be that he is afraid of this human."

"I think he is," Kishin announced. "And the longer he refuses the challenge, the more we believe it."

"Dog!" Murdak lashed out with the whip. The end struck Kishin in the chest and knocked him over. The whip itself didn't hurt nearly as much as his arm. He cradled it as he got back to his feet.

"Yes, kill the messenger," Namnirnu said, rolling his eyes. "That's always effective."

Murdak spun on him. "You think I don't see what you are doing? You resent my leadership of this undertaking! Always you seek to undermine me!"

Namnirnu raised his hands. "I am on your side, mighty Murdak. I expect that you will swat this gnat and lead us on to victory. I only tire of the interruptions."

"And he is not alone," the goddess added.

"You all scheme against me!" Murdak thundered. "Very well. I will take my place at the head of this army and deal with this Nehesy when I find him. Enough!"

Ignoring Kishin, he leaped back on his chariot and gestured for the army to move on. Kishin backed away, holding his arm. The Durunim lost interest in him as well, moving back to join their squads. As best as he could, Kishin re-fastened his sling. Once his arm was taken care of, he started running parallel to the army. He had to get back before Murdak did. Nehesy might believe he could defeat the god, but even if he did, Kishin had no faith in what happened next. None of these invaders could be trusted.

•••••

Jamana stood on Nehesy's right and watched in the direction Kishin had gone. The old man sighed and leaned on his staff. "This is it, Jamana. It's the moment I've been waiting for… for almost a thousand years." He closed his eyes. "At last I will see those who have gone before me. So many…"

Jamana didn't answer. What could he say to that?

"You have no idea what it's like, acolyte." Nehesy opened his eyes. "To see friends and family grow and die… and then another generation of friends and family grow and die. I know that Theon had use for me, through it all, but it was not what I would have chosen."

Adhi ran to them from the village. "Most of the cursed villagers have fled," he announced, stopping to catch his breath. "But about a dozen remain." He pointed, and Jamana could see some people gathered on the edge of the village. "Some cannot flee, and others simply refuse to."

"We have done what we could," Nehesy said. "And now comes the end. Adhi, I will need you here, on my left. As I told you, I may need to channel some of my power through the two of you. My body, I am afraid, cannot handle all that I need to do here."

"Whatever you need," Adhi said, looking at Jamana. "We stand ready to defend our people."

Kishin ran down the hillside, moving with surprising swiftness across the difficult terrain. He stopped in front of them and bent over to lean against his knee with his good arm. "He is coming," he announced. "But I do not trust them. He may have other plans in play."

Nehesy tossed his staff forward, and Kishin caught it. "You will have more need of this than I will. Use it well." The old man rubbed his hands together. "Is he coming the same direction you came?"

Kishin nodded, looking at the staff in his hand. "There are only a handful of trees up there before it opens up. The army approaches that way."

"Let's make their path easier." Nehesy gestured Kishin to move aside. The assassin did so, but jerked his head when he noticed the cursed villagers watching.

"Why didn't they leave?" he whispered.

"They would not, or could not," Jamana told him.

Nehesy pointed at the tree line to the northeast and rotated his hand. The ground erupted and half a dozen trees shot into the air, uprooted and tumbling. They crashed back down to either side, leaving a wide open space at the top of the rocky descent. Another burst of power leveled the ground out, making Murdak's approach simpler and out in the open. A dust cloud rose, but dispersed toward the east as the wind picked up.

Kishin watched the dust for a minute, then walked away without a word. "Kishin?" Jamana called.

"Leave him be," Nehesy said, putting a hand on his shoulder. "He has another cause right now."

Jamana didn't understand at first. Then he saw the assassin take his place beside the villagers.

"He comes," Nehesy announced.

Jamana turned back to the now-open hillside. A tall figure stepped into view through the last wisps of the dust cloud. Jamana had seen Murdak before, back at the high place, but not this close. In that moment, looking at the height and musculature of the god, and feeling his power radiating outward, all of Jamana's hopes vanished. Nehesy was nothing before him, a twig to be swept away by the wind.

Murdak surveyed the scene from his vantage point, hands on his hips. His eyes swept over the cursed village and the huddled villagers with Kishin, then his gaze locked on Nehesy and the two acolytes.

"Nehesy, I presume?" he called. "I will admit: you look as if you could actually be my old foe."

"We fought once before," Nehesy answered. "You left me for dead, but Theon had other plans. Now at last, we come to the rematch."

"Yes, your challenge. I thought it was single combat. Who are these other two with you?"

"Considering how old I am, you wouldn't begrudge me two young men to help hold me up, would you?"

Murdak shook his head. "If they are to help you, they will share your fate."

"They are aware of this."

Jamana and Adhi exchanged glances. Being aware of the dangers and staring down the ancient god himself were two entirely different things. Jamana's faith in Nehesy, based on his words and actions so far, was the only thing keeping him from turning and running as fast as he could.

"I have already defeated your King, the most powerful human in this world. Yet you challenge me." Murdak laughed. "What hope do you have?"

"My hope is in the one who kept me alive for this very moment." Nehesy placed a hand on Jamana's shoulder and then did the same to Adhi.

"Then die, little man!" Murdak leaped forward, covering half the distance between them in a single bound.

A tingling feeling swept through Jamana an instant before pure magical power erupted from his body. Adhi grunted at the same time. Murdak flinched as it struck him, and dust erupted from the ground.

"Is that all?" The god took a step forward.

The tingling feeling intensified. More dust flew into the air. This time, Murdak actually staggered a step back. Jamana felt a surge of hope. Maybe this would actually work!

• • • • •

Kishin stood in front of the cursed villagers. At his arrival, they murmured amongst themselves, but none of them dared approach him.

Nehesy's power, channeled through the two acolytes, appeared to be holding Murdak back, at least for the moment. But battles were won over time, not in the first few seconds.

Kishin gripped Nehesy's staff. Whatever happened, he would be ready.

A movement caught his eye. He looked to the hillside where Murdak had stood a moment before. Namnirnu and at least a half dozen other gods stepped into view, watching the conflict. Whatever happened here, it would not end with Murdak or Nehesy. Too many other powers were involved.

•••••

Jamana's teeth chattered, and he clamped them together.

"Is it w-working?" Adhi asked.

"For the moment," Nehesy said. "Silence, please."

Murdak took a step forward, straining against the force pounding him. He did not look pleased.

How did the prophecy go? Nehesy's power "would not wane until his foe was defeated for the last time." Murdak was that foe. But what if this was not the time for his final defeat? What if this was just a setback? Nehesy might escape, if the prophecy held true, but what about the rest of them?

"Never… failed me… yet…" Nehesy whispered. The power flowing through Jamana increased again. Murdak stood still against the raging power. Dirt erupted all around him. He tried to yell something, but Jamana heard nothing.

What now? Holding back the god was one thing. But he needed to be defeated, somehow.

•••••

Kishin scanned the battlefield. The presence of the watching gods disturbed him. He didn't expect them to cheat, not with Namnirnu at the forefront, but… Murdak would cheat. If he thought Nehesy had the slightest chance against him, he would have done everything in his power to prevent it. Unless he was arrogant enough to assume he could overcome anything. Possible, but a thousand years had to temper arrogance with wisdom at least somewhat.

If he were to cheat somehow, what would he do?

Kishin started running even before he saw the movement. Another figure was creeping up behind Nehesy and the acolytes.

Kishin raced between them and found himself face-to-face with the strange god he'd noticed in Murdak's court days before. He still bore the golden skin like all the others, but he was barely taller than Kishin himself, with long, pale hair tied back at his neck. He wore dull robes and carried a mace topped with the head of a feline predator. His empty right hand crackled with black fire.

"Leave them alone," Kishin growled.

The strange god stared at him with lifeless eyes and a morose frown. He took a step forward.

Kishin lunged at him, swinging the staff from the left. To his surprise, the god dodged it with ease, stepping back at the staff came near him. He stepped forward again the instant it passed, but gave no counterstroke.

Kishin tried again, swinging low at the god's legs, then spinning into a follow-up strike from above. The god hopped over the low strike, and raised his mace to parry the overhand blow. The staff smacked against the mace with a crack loud enough to be heard over the magical cacophony behind them.

A few more strikes produced similar results. Kishin could not seem to connect a strike against this opponent, but neither was he losing ground. As long as he kept this one from interfering with Nehesy, he would count it a victory. He kept up his attacks, doing his best while wielding the staff one-handed, and hoped for a swift resolution to the big battle.

(((32)))

Despite his efforts, Jamana made an exclamation of pain. The power pouring through his body shook everything. His left ankle throbbed. Ever since he injured it fleeing from the tunaldi, it had a tendency to cause him trouble now and again. With all this vibrating, it hurt more than usual.

"I am sorry, acolyte," Nehesy said with an effort. "But I cannot… falter now."

"D-do what you must," Jamana answered.

He heard the clash of weapons behind him, but couldn't turn to look.

"Murdak!" Nehesy yelled with sudden strength. "You were given power, power beyond almost any creature that has walked two different worlds! Yet you chose to use that power for yourself, instead of others, as it should have been. You had a glorious purpose, but despised it, choosing instead a life of cruelty and violence. And so I declare to you: it is now over!"

"You cannot judge me!" Murdak roared. He stretched his hands apart, forming an enormous shield out of golden magic. He held it before him and took a step closer. "I am the god of justice!"

"You are no god!" Nehesy cried.

Murdak took another step forward. Now a golden scimitar appeared in his hand.

Jamana wished he had Seri's ability to see magic. What an insane sight all of this must be right now!

Nehesy swept his hands off the acolytes' shoulders for an instant and clapped them together. A painful scream escaped his lips, but a new wave of magic swept at the oncoming god. The golden shield shook, and then dissolved entirely in Murdak's grasp. The scimitar disintegrated as well.

Nehesy would have fallen if Jamana and Adhi had not both caught him. Together, they held him up. Murdak took advantage of the momentary slip to charge forward. He almost reached them before Nehesy poured more power through the acolytes and forced him back a step.

"Your time has come, Murdak." Nehesy's words, though he no longer seemed to be yelling, could be clearly heard above the rumble of vibratory magic unleashed. "Because you have so abused this power, it shall no longer be yours."

"I am the god of power itself!" Murdak snarled. "You are an insect to be swatted!"

Nehesy closed his eyes. Jamana could not see what was happening, but he knew Nehesy had to be doing something like the attack he used on Nummotem.

"No!" Murdak screamed. "You will not do this!" He leaned forward, straining as if against an enormous wind, and took a step, his foot sinking into the ground as it tore apart all around him. His hand reached forward, mere inches from Nehesy's face. He towered above the crouched trio, his skin rippling in waves from his own magic and the power being used against him.

Nehesy, held up by the acolytes, lifted his right hand. To Jamana's eyes, the hand looked twisted and broken, as if his earlier magic use had damaged it. Yet he kept going.

Murdak's scream became a guttural roar. His feet left the ground, but not by his own will. He rose several inches into the air.

Jamana squinted against a rising dust cloud. The dust itself swirled around Murdak. Perhaps this was similar to what Seri could see: the dust formed into rings orbiting around the floating god, angled in all directions.

He risked a glance at Nehesy's face. The old mage still kept his eyes shut. Sweat stood out on his brow. His skin, normally wrinkled, appeared flat and stretched across his features.

"No... more..." Nehesy uttered. He clenched his damaged hand into a fist.

Murdak yanked his own hand back and clutched his head. "You are... only... human!" His voice, ragged and furious, shook, but not with his own power now.

"I am a servant of Theon," Nehesy whispered. He pulled his fist back toward his chest.

Murdak screamed, a bestial roar that threatened to knock them all off their feet with the force of its volume alone. The dust swirling around him exploded in every direction. Jamana closed his eyes in vain attempt to keep the dust out. He blinked rapidly, trying to clear his vision. When he could see again, Murdak hung limp in the air, like a puppet waiting for its strings to be pulled. And as if those strings had been cut, the god collapsed to the ground and lay still.

At the exact same instant, Nehesy sagged in their arms and fell. Jamana, released from the flow of power, collapsed to his knees, as did Adhi.

The battle a thousand years in the making ended in the space of a few minutes.

•••••

The strange god backed away at Murdak's scream. Kishin glanced over his shoulder. Was the battle over? His opponent apparently thought so. He moved away from Kishin and circled around toward the village. Kishin turned with him, keeping him in close range, but also curious to see what happened next. He shifted his broken arm in the sling, grateful to have a moment to keep it still.

Murdak lay on the ground, unmoving. Dust settled everywhere. Nehesy also lay on the ground, but the acolytes were on their knees beside him. They would take care of him.

Namnirnu and those with him descended to view the battle's results. He stood beside Murdak and looked down at him, playing with some of his golden magic in his hands.

Kishin split his attention between the unfolding scene and the strange god with the black fiery hand. Tension filled the air. He caught a glimpse of the acolytes lifting Nehesy and retreating back into the trees.

"It appears you have been defeated, Murdak," Namnirnu said placidly. "Have you anything at all to say for yourself?"

Murdak put his hands out to either side and struggled to lift his body a few inches off the ground. He couldn't keep it up and slumped back down. He said nothing.

The magic in Namnirnu's hands formed into a blade. "You have no power, and you have lost everything to a human. You are no longer worthy to be our leader." He looked to the other gods and goddesses, whose number had only grown as the battle raged. "Will the rest of you follow me now?"

"We do!" one of the goddesses proclaimed loudly. One by one, the others assented.

"You have heard them, god of justice," he said to Murdak. "In your condition, you are not only unworthy to lead, you are unworthy to even be among us."

He stabbed down with the magic blade. Murdak's body jerked once and fell still. Namnirnu released the blade and let it stand for a moment before dismissing it. As the magic dissolved, he turned back to his followers, never once looking at any of the humans.

"Our purpose and our goals remain the same. No one remains to stop us, or even delay us now." He pointed through the cursed village. "Bring the army on. We will cross the river and continue toward the island center of this land." Namnirnu glanced at the strange god Kishin had been fighting. "Ne'gal, please rid us of the ones remaining in our way."

Kishin spun as the strange god, Ne'gal, sped up, moving toward the huddled group of cursed villagers. "No!" he shouted and chased after him, staff in the air. His broken arm slapped against his chest, jarring him with pain with every stride, while the Durunim sword hung loosely on his right.

Ne'gal reached the first villager before Kishin could arrive. A young man who looked normal, save for the crutches he used to get around, couldn't move fast enough to escape. Ne'gal touched him with the black hand. Kishin, close enough to see it happen, watched the young man stiffen and then collapse to the ground, unmoving. From only a touch!

"While you still live, you can make a difference in the lives of others." Nehesy's words echoed in his head. Ne'gal reached for the woman with the twisted leg, who scrambled desperately to get away from him. Kishin spun the staff, striking Ne'gal in the wrist and driving his hand into the air. He slid to a stop between Ne'gal and the woman.

"If you must fight, let it be for a cause greater than yourself." Also Nehesy's words.

"I am the defender of these people!" Kishin shouted. "To get to them, you must go through me!" In a lower voice, he added, "Let this be my cause."

Ne'gal continued to move with his uncanny speed, striking at

Kishin with his mace. Before, he had seemed almost content to let Kishin prevent him from interfering in Murdak's battle. Now, given the prospect to go after these defenseless humans, he appeared eager. He had a taste of death and wanted more.

Kishin blocked him with the staff, but the impact nearly knocked it out of his hand. A staff was not a one-handed weapon. But Ne'gal's attacks now came so quickly, he couldn't drop it and get to the sword on his belt. He parried and dodged, doing the best he could, but driven back step by step. All of the movement pulled his sling loose and his broken arm lost its support. He held it tight against his chest, gritting his teeth against the pain.

The villagers must have fled. He could no longer hear them behind him. Even so, he couldn't let this twisted god pursue them. From what he could tell with quick glances, the other gods and Durunim seemed completely uninterested in his fight, moving on about their own business. The acolytes and Nehesy were out of sight.

Ne'gal abruptly changed tactics and leaped forward, black hand outstretched. Kishin had no choice but to slap at the god's forearm to keep from getting touched by those fingers. But as he did, Ne'gal swept in from the left with his mace. Kishin twisted, but a glancing blow still struck his hip. Something might have broken, but he couldn't be sure. Regardless, his right leg buckled, and he struggled to stay upright.

In another moment, Ne'gal would bypass him and chase after the villagers. They would all die.

"Theon, give me the strength," Kishin hissed through clenched teeth.

He swung the staff as Ne'gal started to turn. Seeing it, the god casually threw up his mace to block it.

Kishin's left hand grasped the hilt of the sword on his belt.

The staff slammed against the mace. Ne'gal reached toward him with the hand crackling black fire.

The sword, held by Kishin's broken left arm, swept up.

Kishin screamed at the pain.

The Durunim sword struck Ne'gal right at the wrist and sliced through skin, ligaments and bone. The hand, severed entirely, tumbled away.

Kishin dropped the sword, unable to keep his grip any longer. He leaned on the staff, panting. Another strike from the mace would finish him off, but at least he'd removed the god's hand of death, or whatever it was.

Instead, Ne'gal dropped the mace and clutched at the bloody stump of his wrist. His mouth opened in a silent scream and he fell to his knees.

Not sure what else to do, Kishin lifted the staff, swung it in a loop to build momentum, and cracked Ne'gal on the side of the head. The god slumped to the ground.

"You did it," said a voice behind him.

Kishin looked over his shoulder and saw the woman with the twisted leg about a dozen yards back. He nodded. "Go," he said, gesturing with his chin. She turned and limped away.

Kishin breathed hard. The Durunim army approached, but would bypass his position as they entered the village and continued on their way. If any of them broke ranks to come after him, he would accept that death. He didn't know if he could move at all now. At least, if he died now, he died having fought for a true cause, saving the lives of those who could not defend themselves.

•••••

Jamana's body still ached from the aftereffects of Nehesy's power flowing through him. But he and Adhi kept going, carrying Nehesy away from the battlefield. Just before they moved out of sight, Jamana saw Namnirnu stab Murdak.

"What happened?" Adhi gasped. "Did you see Kishin?"

"No, but Murdak is dead, for certain." Jamana explained what he had seen.

Nehesy stirred. "He's alive," Adhi said. "We're far enough away. Let's set him down."

They laid the old man gently onto a patch of grass in a wide gap between trees. Sunbeams, visible in the bits of dust still hanging in the air, filled the narrow patch with light. Relieved of their burden, they both sank down as well. Though Jamana felt like he had done very little, his exhaustion threatened to pull him down into sleep. But he couldn't do that now.

Nehesy coughed. Adhi pulled a waterskin from his belt and poured a little between his lips. His hands shook, spilling water all around the old mage's mouth. Nehesy swallowed, but did not react.

"His task is finished," Jamana said. "His power wanes, I am thinking."

Adhi nodded, but did not answer.

Nehesy opened his eyes a fraction. "Ready to… get rid of me, are you?" His voice was strained, but they could understand every word.

"You did it, Master," Jamana said. "You finished. Your foe is defeated."

Nehesy gave a weak nod. "And I… I can depart in peace. I would like to see how things go with your friend Marshal, but… I can wait."

"Do you need anything?" Adhi asked. "More water?"

"I will soon be beyond… all need, young Adhi. I go to join my mother and father… my uncle Akhenadom, who started all this… and so many others in the years since." He fell silent for a moment, then continued: "What a reunion it will be… I will be spending days just saying hello again."

Jamana swallowed. Such incredible faith, to believe so strongly about the afterlife. Yet who was he to question it? What was his twenty years of knowledge compared with this man's thousand?

Nehesy's eyes flicked to him. "Have faith, Jamana," he said, as if reading his thoughts. "All will be as Theon wills it." He closed his eyes and let out a deep sigh.

For a moment, Jamana thought he had died. But then Nehesy's eyes flew open again. "Ah. He comes. I see it. And I see… what is to come for you here, acolytes. Your friend Marshal… and the stars…"

Jamana bent over him. "What about the stars, Master Nehesy?"

There was no answer. Nehesy's eyes stared upward, unmoving. Jamana sat back, surprised at the lump which rose in his throat. He hadn't known the old man for very long, but this death seemed like a blessing for him, and a tragedy for the rest of the world.

Adhi reached over and closed Nehesy's eyes. "When we have rested, we will bury him," he said quietly.

Jamana nodded, not trusting himself to speak.

They sat beside the body for an hour or more. Not far away, they heard the tramp of the Durunim feet as the army marched by. Eventually, that faded as well. No other sounds remained, save the occasional bird whistle. Jamana dozed a bit.

His head jerked, and he blinked. A shadow obscured some of the sunbeams. His vision cleared and he looked up at Kishin, leaning hard on the staff. He looked worse than usual, somehow.

"He is dead, then," Kishin said.

"Yes." Jamana's throat was dry. He looked to Adhi, but his friend lay asleep beside Nehesy's body.

Kishin awkwardly lowered himself to the ground, using the staff for support. He seemed to be favoring his right side, in addition to the left arm in its sling.

"The gods are gone?" Jamana asked.

"They are continuing west. They're heading toward Zes Sivas."

Kishin reached toward Nehesy's body, then pulled his hand back. "Did he… did he say anything at the end?"

"A few things." Jamana tried to recite Nehesy's last words.

Kishin lowered his face. "Nothing about me, then. Ah, well. I didn't need his interfering in my life any more."

"I do not think you believe that."

"No? Maybe not." Kishin stretched out on the ground, letting the staff fall. "Let us all rest while we can."

"We'll bury him later," Jamana said. "After that… I do not know."

"After that," Kishin said without opening his eyes, "we go on to Zes Sivas."

(((33)))

Marshal stared at the former battlefield, the disputed land between Rasna and Varioch. Memories flooded him of their time with the curse squad. In his effort to separate the two armies, he had thrown up a dirt barrier and trench. Some of it still existed, but most had been torn up in a massive excavation, unearthing the portal to the Otherworld. A wide road of stone now led down to the shimmering circle. At the top of the road stood a fortress.

Talinir's message had described it, but Marshal couldn't help being impressed. The fortress was huge, built primarily of heavy stone blocks. Even with his power at full, it would take Marshal some time to blast that thing apart.

"I don't see anyone," Victor observed.

Marshal agreed. "Didn't Talinir say there were soldiers camped both outside and inside the fortress? Have they all moved inside now?"

"Maybe they knew you were coming."

"Something doesn't feel right."

Victor looked at him. "You mean magically?"

"No, no." He shook his head. "I can feel the power of the portal itself. And I feel... some power from the fortress? Huh. Nowhere near as much as I would expect if there were as many gods as the Kuktarma portal. That can't be right." He narrowed his eyes, trying to see further. "But I was going to say it just doesn't feel right in general."

"A trap, maybe?"

"Maybe."

They rode out onto the former battlefield. The Durunim had dammed the river, creating a shallow lake on the west end. Victor pointed it out. "Should we destroy that too?"

"On our way out, I guess. I don't see any good use for it."

They continued to ride, out in the open. The only sound came from their horses' hooves. Nothing else moved: not on the road, not around the fortress, or on its walls.

"This is… creepy," Victor said.

The horses stepped onto the road from portal to fortress. Marshal reined to a halt and looked back and forth between them. "Should I bury it before we check out the fortress?"

"Maybe that's what triggers the trap?" Victor shrugged. "I don't know. This is too weird."

"Wait…" Marshal held up his hand and tilted his head. "Do you hear… music?"

Victor turned his head from left to right. "I think… maybe? Coming from the fortress?"

If Marshal strained, he could hear some high, short notes, somewhat breathy, not unpleasant. He slid off the horse. "Let's leave the animals. Just in case."

Victor followed suit. "Whatever you say."

They walked up the road toward the fortress. As they drew nearer, Marshal could hear the music more distinctly. The notes came fast, cascading over each other and forming a distinct melody that attracted him in ways he couldn't describe. He found it beautiful, but he didn't have a lot of experience with music.

"Yeah, that's part of the trap," Victor muttered.

The road curved to the right, giving them a full view of the massive gates to the fortress, solid wood banded with iron. To Marshal's shock, the gates stood ajar, leaving a gap large enough for several horses to ride through abreast.

"Trap, trap, trap, trap, trap," Victor kept going.

"Then let's spring it." Marshal picked up his pace.

The music grew louder as they approached the gates. Marshal tried to see inside, but the angle of the gates kept him from getting any kind of view. When they finally reached it, he and Victor stopped and stared.

They looked out onto an enormous courtyard, fully the size of a small village in itself. Everywhere they looked, they saw evidence of a massive camp now vanished. Scuffed earth, cold firepits, worn paths. But not a soul to be seen.

The music drew their attention off to the right. Not far from the gates, a set of stairs ran up to the massive walls above. A curious figure sat on the stairs, playing on an instrument that looked to Marshal like a set of hollow sticks of varying length bound together. His golden skin marked him as one of the gods, but he didn't look over six feet tall. He continued to play his music with total concentration, either ignoring them or not noticing their presence.

Marshal walked toward him, followed by Victor. Neither of them spoke. The bizarre nature of this entire scene left Marshal speechless. Out of all the possibilities he anticipated, nothing like this had come to mind.

As they drew closer, the god finally took notice of them. He stopped playing and tucked his instrument into a satchel at his side. He slapped a leather hat with a broad, floppy brim on his head. Standing, he greeted them with a cheerful wave and smile.

"Hello! You must be King Marshal! I've been waiting for you!"

Marshal kept his hand on his sword hilt, but didn't draw it. "And who are you?"

The god removed his hat and bowed with a flourish. "I am Term, one of the many gods of your people. I am here with a message for you." He tossed the hat into the air, and it came down perfectly onto his head.

"All right. What's the message?"

Term spread his arms to indicate the fortress. "As you can see, no one is here. All of my compatriots and their troops have departed from this location."

"Where did they go?" Victor asked.

"Ah, that's the real message, isn't it?" Term held up a finger and wagged it at them. "Let me see…" He looked up at the sky, turned to see the location of the sun, put a hand over his eye, and rotated back to them. "Got it." He pointed to the northeast. "The largest group, perhaps half, went that way." He pointed southeast, the direction from which they had come. "The second group went that way, but I'm guessing you already met them. Laran, I believe?"

Marshal nodded.

"As I thought." He let his head hang for a moment in feigned sadness, then looked back up. "But we also sent smaller bands that way, that way, that way, and that way." He pointed in multiple directions, one after the other, ranging from due north to due south.

"So everywhere in Varioch and Rasna," Victor said.

"Everywhere that has a human population, at least." Term bowed again. "That was my message. I'll be off now."

"I'm going to bury that portal," Marshal said. "That doesn't bother you?"

Term pursed his lips and raised one eyebrow, then shrugged. "Not really. Everyone is here now. We have no more use for it."

He hopped off the stairs. Victor aimed a sword at him. "Wait a minute! We don't—"

Term ran. In the blink of an eye, he was past them and at the gates. He gave a jaunty wave and disappeared from view. Marshal hurried after him and looked around outside the fortress. There was no sign of him.

"Fast," Victor observed, joining him.

"Yeah." Marshal looked back at the empty courtyard. "How big was Laran's army, do you think?"

"Some thousands. I don't know. Five?"

"I was thinking that. Maybe a little more. But..." Marshal swallowed. "Talinir estimated fifty thousand Durunim here. And they're now scattered all over the place."

"And if half went that way..." Victor pointed northeast. "Isn't that the direction for Reman?"

"Yes." Another thought came to Marshal: "Or Zes Sivas."

"So we might have two armies coming at us from either side, if they can cross the lake."

Marshal continued to stare toward the northeast. The gods knew what they were doing. By spreading their forces out and threatening people all over the West of Antises, they challenged him. Did he go after them, or stick to the plan? How many would die without his help?

As if to answer his question, a tremor ran through the ground beneath their feet.

"Was that you?" Victor asked.

"No."

"Then it's already starting to come apart again. I thought we'd have more time after you repaired things in Kuktarma."

Marshal took a deep breath. "I'm going to bury that portal. And then we're riding for Raeton as fast as we can. Then back to Zes Sivas. We've been away too long."

• • • • •

Talinir had not expected to wake up. When he did, he found himself under Eniri's care. The city stood firmly stabilized in the Starlit Realm, where his healing could be accelerated. In two days, he was able to get up and about, and the Council requested his presence.

With the Chambers in ruins, the Council met in a much smaller room. Only ten councilors, seated instead of standing, remained to debate the topic, along with High Mage Harunir, himself in a wheelchair. Before resuming the previous debate, Indala reported on the devastation caused by Rathri:

"Forty-seven died in the Chamber, with another two dozen injured. Around the city, seventeen more died, mostly elderly, who were unable to handle the rapid shifts between worlds." She glanced at the other councilors. "The High Warden may or may not survive. His life is still in question. Were it not for Warden Talinir, the toll would have been far higher. In fact, none of us may have survived." She fixed her gaze on Talinir. "We owe you an enormous debt. Eldanim always pay their debts."

Eltaru raised a finger. "I trust you are not implying that we should grant the warden's request in payment of his services. That would hardly seem appropriate. We will reward him properly, but not like this."

"And why not?" Telra asked. "His actions were nothing less than heroic, and deserve to be rewarded."

"At the cost of more lives?" another councilor asked. "Because that is what you are proposing. If we go to war, more deaths will follow."

Talinir stood, though even that simple action pained him. "Honored councilors," he said. "I do not ask you to help the humans because I fought against a madman, but because it is the right thing to do."

"Perhaps we should pick up the debate where we left off," suggested Indala. "I believe we were about to hear from the High Mage."

Harunir's injuries prevented him from standing, but he straightened in his chair. "Thank you, councilors," he said. "As you know, I have spent a good deal of time with our Durunim prisoner, seeking to understand his condition. From what we have been able to determine, as most of you know, these so-called gods are the ones responsible. They take from our people, either by force or… those who go to them seeking power, though it pains me to admit it. And then they… transform them."

Talinir felt for the spot on his arm where one of the gods had seized him. He had come so close to becoming one of their servants, and hadn't even realized his danger at the time.

"The transformation is more than just the outward appearance, though, isn't it?" Nimruti asked.

Harunir nodded. "From what I can tell, these Durunim appear almost mindless. They do not speak. Our prisoner does not even acknowledge when I speak to him. He doesn't even seem to understand when we attempt to communicate via hand signals. They follow only their masters' commands. In short, they have no will of their own."

"Is their condition reversible?" Telra asked.

"I do not know. If it is, I have found nothing to indicate even a direction for proper research."

"This fate awaits all of us, humans and Eldanim, if these gods are allowed to succeed in their aims," Indala declared.

"That is a blatant exaggeration, based on scant evidence," Eltaru argued.

"In my opinion," observed another councilor, "the humans are not far from that state now. The so-called laws they enacted restrict their free will, making them little better."

"Exactly!" Talinir seized on the statement. "And that is what King Marshal wants to change! He wishes to undo the Laws of Cursings and Bindings and restore magic to the land instead of only its leaders."

"Regardless, it does not change our word, spoken a thousand years ago," Eltaru insisted. "We must leave the humans to their own destruction."

"No." Indala stood. "This is not the same. As you keep repeating, we swore to leave them to their own destruction. Their *own* destruction, the consequences of their own actions. This sequence of events is not the consequences envisioned. In fact, it is an outside enemy, formed in part from our own people. Our oath does not bind us in this regard."

"You argue semantics."

"No, I argue the truth. Words matter. Our specific words matter. Talinir, did you not promise to protect Marshal?"

Talinir jerked at the sudden switch in conversation to him. "I… yes, I did. But why…?"

"So regardless of our decision here, you will be returning to continue that duty, will you not?"

"I will. Yes."

"Talinir is bound by his word. As are we," Indala went on. "But it is the specific words that matter. This is not the humans' own destruction, as we swore. So despite this new King's plan to undo the Laws, that should have no bearing on our debate. Whatever happens there, happens, and we will not interfere. But the Durunim and their masters are another matter. They are our responsibility as well."

"Are they?" Nimruti asked.

"Yes," Telra said. "They came from us. They came from the Starlit Realm. We have a duty to stop them. And… to help them, if possible."

"I call for a statement of intent," Indala said. "Were we to vote now, what would your ruling be? All those in favor of granting the human King's request, stand and be counted."

Telra stood immediately. Harunir lifted a hand instead of standing. Three other councilors also stood. Five remained seated.

"I remain undecided," Nimruti stated.

"We are at an impasse," Eltaru observed.

Telra pointed at Harunir. "We possess a majority."

"With all due respect, the High Mage's vote does not count. He, together with the High Warden and High Champion, possess a single vote. But all three must be united."

"If I may," Harunir said, "I know that High Warden Tiranel was in favor of this action."

"Be that as it may, we do not have a High Champion any longer, and —"

"We are bound by our word!" Indala interrupted. "Given only a few moments ago!"

"What are you talking about?"

Indala pointed at Talinir. "We promised to reward him appropriately. What is the most appropriate reward for one who was willing to sacrifice his very life to protect this city, who fought on our behalf when no one else could or would?"

"It is not even a reward, but a recognition," Telra realized. "Talinir… is our High Champion."

Talinir's eyes widened. The High Champion? Surely he did not deserve that honor. To even be considered was beyond his highest ambitions and expectations. "I, I never thought of—"

"Of course you didn't," Indala cut him off. "Which is one of the reasons you deserve it."

"He is very young," another councilor observed.

"But who better to take the position?" Telra asked. "Does anyone dispute this?"

After a few minutes' discussion, the councilors voted. By a vote of 8-2, Talinir became High Champion of Intal Eldanir. His mind struggled to keep up with this sudden shift in his status.

Eltaru stood. "While I do not dispute young Talinir's valor, I must protest the reasoning for this appointment. Those of you in support of the humans' proposal are attempting to force the vote through by adding another voter. This is hardly appropriate."

"It is a fair point," Telra admitted.

"It is no longer an issue." Nimruti stood as well. "I am decided now. I will vote in favor of the proposal."

"Even without the vote of the defenders, we now have a majority," Indala said. "I suggest we cast that final vote now."

Eltaru sat down. Those who had voted in favor before, joined now by Nimruti, all stood.

"It is decided," Telra declared. "Intal Eldanir will go to war with the Durunim in the primary world."

"I bow to the will of the council," Eltaru said.

"But what now?" another councilor asked. "Saying we will go to war and actually doing it are vastly different things."

"Indeed." Indala turned to Talinir. "High Champion Talinir. I charge you to seek out the remaining wardens of high rank and discuss with them our best course of action. Should the High Warden recover sufficiently to be involved, please seek his input as well. The wardens are the closest thing we have to a standing army."

"If I may," Harunir interjected, "I will hold a gathering of mages to discuss our involvement as well. I have a few ideas that may serve us well and minimize potential casualties."

"I suspect we all may be taking part to some degree," Telra said. "If there is no other pressing business...?"

No one responded.

"Then let this meeting be adjourned."

One by one, the councilors left the room, leaving only Harunir and Talinir behind. They looked at each other in silence for a moment.

"I did not think it would happen," Talinir confessed. "I told Marshal as much."

Harunir nodded. "If the assassin's attack had not occurred, I think the debate would have been much more difficult. In effect, he accomplished the opposite of his intentions."

"Wouldn't he hate to know that?" Talinir smiled, but only for a few seconds. The import of the moment still weighed heavily on him. "I'm not sure what happens next."

"A lot." Harunir sighed. "Just because the council has agreed does not mean it will happen any time soon. It may be weeks before the Eldanim can venture into the primary world in enough numbers to be effective."

Talinir got to his feet, wincing at the pain. "Then we must do what we must to accelerate the process. I do not think Marshal has weeks to wait."

(((34)))

Seri entered her office to find Dravid sitting at her desk, poring over the book again. At least he could move about again, no longer restricted to a bed. After another day of dealing with endless minor issues with the Lords and Masters, she needed to see his smile. He turned to greet her. There it was. She couldn't help but smile in return.

"Rough times?" he asked.

Seri collapsed into the reading chair, as she called it, an overlarge chair with enormous cushions. Why on earth did Master Hain have this, anyway? "You have no idea," she told Dravid. "And I had no idea how much work the Masters have to do every day. I thought they just studied and wandered around this place."

"And gave us work to do," Dravid added. "You know, without Jamana around, I wonder who does all the cleaning in the kitchen now?"

Seri giggled. "Just the regular staff, I guess. The Masters need some new acolytes to boss around." She looked up at Dravid. "Speaking of which…"

He shook his head. "I told you. I'm not interested in continuing my magic studies. If anything, I need to keep studying my own power. I'm sure there's much more I can do with it, if I just work at it."

"And probably even more when we combine our powers," Seri said. "So maybe you won't be an acolyte again. We'll come up with another title for you. Scholar of Otherworldly Magic, maybe."

"Ha! What my father would think of that!"

"You never talk about your parents," Seri noted. "We didn't even know how to find them while we were in Kuktarma."

"Just as well. They would have seen me sleeping. It would only have given them reason to worry."

"Have you… written to them lately? With the portals, we can always send stuff now."

"Let me deal with my family. You've got enough concerns with yours."

Seri winced. That much was true. Having manipulated the Masters into accepting Seri into their number, Lady Lilitu now wanted to be kept informed about everything they did. Seri could not go a day without having to spend an hour or so reporting to her and analyzing their current situation. She also wanted to know about their research into the book and the Laws. She was about to ask Dravid about it when he looked back at her with a curious expression on his face.

"Are the Masters allowed to get married?" he asked.

"Huh. I don't know. I guess I never thought about it." Seri frowned and looked up at the ceiling. "None of the current Masters are married, of course. And I don't think any of the ones I've heard about before them were, either. But I don't know if it's a rule or anything. I know some of the other mages who are married. Hm. I'll have to ask Master Tzoyet sometime."

"Maybe sometime soon," he suggested.

"All right, I'll try to remember, but it doesn't seem all that important with all the other stuff we're dealing with right now and—" She broke off at his stare. "What?"

"Seri, I love you, but are you really that naive?"

"What do you mean?"

He laughed. "I can't believe I'm having to clarify this. I wasn't asking as an intellectual exercise." He leaned in and looked her in the eyes. "I'm asking because I want to know if *you* can get married."

Seri stared at him. "Oh."

"Yeah. 'Oh.'"

"I, um, I'll ask him soon, then."

"I'm not actually proposing," Dravid said in a rush. "I mean, not at this moment. But I need to know if it's even possible, right?"

Seri nodded, not sure what else to say. She swallowed and looked around the room. "Ah, so… find anything new in the book?"

Dravid looked back at it. "I've made it all the way through, and I've made a lot of notes, trying to figure out the proper order of the different chapters or sections. It's all such a mess."

"But…?"

Dravid shrugged. "I really don't know. I told you what I discovered at first, about their plans and such. I did find a full page in which Aharu describes the Heart of Fire. She starts to say something about stars at the end of it, but then the next page is missing."

"Stars… I wonder." She shook her head. "Everything is so out of our reach, even after all this time. We know so little."

"Well, we know the greatest power is bound to the King's bloodline, and great power is also bound to the Lords' bloodlines, right?"

"That part I can almost comprehend," Seri said. "The Masters bind magic into things all the time. Marshal channels magic into his sword. I've experimented with it a little myself, but haven't gotten very far. But I'm sure it's possible."

Dravid picked up a dagger from Seri's desk. "I can see binding magic into an object, like this." He frowned. "I don't remember you having a dagger."

"It was Master Hain's. I think he used it for opening mail."

Dravid looked it over. "Like I said, binding magic into something like this? I can understand that. But binding magic into a bloodline? How do you make it continue? How does it pass down?"

"I have no idea." Seri ran her hands through her hair. A couple of strands got caught in her bandages. "But at least that one makes some sense. It's the Laws that make no sense at all."

"I know what you mean." Dravid pointed at the floor. "It's like they bound magic to the land itself, but… how does it detect crimes? How does it choose the punishment?"

"Detect. Choose. You're attributing intelligence to the magic."

"How else could it work? I can't imagine a blind force controlling it. That makes even less sense!"

"I know, I know." Seri pulled on her hair in frustration. "All right. Let's step back and list the things we know for sure."

Dravid lifted a finger. "We know Akhenadom and Aharu are the ones who did almost everything." He added another finger. "We also know they had the help of all the other mages at the time."

"Nehesy said I would have to guide Marshal *into* the Heart of Fire," Seri said. Dravid added another finger.

"You said there's a binding between the worlds, and that's what gave them the idea for bindings between people?"

Seri shook her head. "I believe that's true, but it's just a theory. What do we actually *know*?"

Dravid shrugged. "Most of what we have are theories. There's very little we actually know, besides these three things."

"Oh, Evander, Marshal's grandfather, said Marshal and I together would end the curses, and that you and Volraag would help."

"Me?" Dravid blinked.

"Yes, he said you were the channel, whatever that means. I didn't tell you that?"

"Uh... no."

"Oh, right. That happened right before you ran away from me." Seri played with her robe's sleeve.

"What? I was taken as a slave!"

Seri laughed. "I'm teasing, you idiot. But... I guess it shows that we still haven't told each other everything that happened while we were apart."

"A channel," Dravid repeated, looking off into the distance. "What do you suppose that means?"

"I don't know. You were more of an anchor when we worked together in Kuktarma. And that nearly killed you."

"But I was a channel!" Dravid looked back at her. "Marshal's power was flowing through me the whole time. Looping through my entire body and back out again."

"Really? I didn't know that part. Maybe we should do something similar here."

"Maybe. But how? You and Marshal will end the curses somehow, and you have to enter the Heart of Fire, and I'm a channel, and Volraag... what part does he play?"

"I don't know. I assumed it was just his Lord's power being needed for the Passing." Seri sat up. "But what if it's something else?"

"How so? He's no different from the rest of the Lords."

"No, no, no. He's very different." Seri got to her feet and walked across the room. "Volraag did not come by his powers naturally, remember? He stole them."

"But if the Lords' magic is tied to the bloodlines, then..."

"That would explain why he was able to keep the power without it destroying him, right?"

"I suppose." Dravid frowned.

"There's something else here. I know it!" Seri paced back and forth. "Volraag got his power from Tezan, a wild mage who could take power from one person and give it to another."

"Very convenient."

"Of course it was. But remember: Lord Tyrr rounded up dozens of wild mages until he found that one."

"So he stole Lord Sundinka's power… and then he stole power from Calu! Could that be it? Because he has a god's power?"

"No, they took that back from him. That's why he's not so… you know… big any more." Seri flexed her arms and pointed to where muscles would be if she were that kind of person.

Dravid wrinkled his brow and looked down. "Then I don't see how his being here will make any difference. When we do the Passing, he'll lose the power of Mandiata, and it will go back to that bloodline. And he'll be left with nothing."

Seri stopped. "Or will he? You know… he seemed different in Ch'olan, even before he took power from Calu. Something else happened before then. Something we don't know about."

"How can we find out?"

Seri headed for the door. "By talking with Volraag himself, of course."

•••••

Seri walked at a steady pace so Dravid could keep up. "You're not going near Volraag without me around! Not again!" he argued. It was sweet, so she allowed it.

"Try not to rant at him," she warned.

"Rant? I never rant." Dravid scowled. "So where are they keeping him now, anyway?"

Seri smiled and glanced at him. "Master Tzoyet found some actual cells in the lowest level of the Citadel of Kings. Everyone forgot that's what they were. They've been used to store grain and other supplies."

"Did they clean out the grain before tossing Volraag inside? Wouldn't want to ruin good grain."

"I wouldn't know. It's my first time going there."

Dravid followed her around a bend in the hallway. "Then, uh, how do you know where you're going?"

"Two reasons: one, Ixchel is on guard, and my Bond to her gives me a general idea of where she is. And two, Master Tzoyet told me how to get there."

Dravid chuckled. "And you understood his directions? You've come a long way from that acolyte who couldn't ever find her way around this place."

Seri stopped. "And that was less than a year ago. Now look at us." She shook her head. "It's so weird."

"You're telling me."

Seri resumed walking. She led the way from the Citadel of Mages into the Citadel of Kings. Everywhere they walked, they saw evidence of earthquake damage, much of which had been at least partially repaired. Seri pointed out some awkward spots for Dravid to avoid.

Within the Citadel of Kings, she took a couple of turns until she found stairs descending into the dark. No windows or lamps lit the way here. She reached for an oil lamp to take with them when Dravid said, "Wait. Allow me."

She watched as he shaped a ball with his golden magic and tossed it to her. She looked at it and turned it around in her hands. "Does it glow enough to light our way?"

"Put some of your power in it," he suggested.

Seri channeled a small burst of vibrational power into the ball with her unbandaged hand. To her delight, it shook and threw a wide-reaching glow in every direction. "When did you discover that?" She held it up and spun it around. "It's beautiful!"

Dravid shrugged. "I noticed it from time to time in the Otherworld. The gods always seemed to have lights made of this stuff, and I couldn't figure out how they did it. Then when Marshal's power was flowing through me in Kuktarma, I noticed the construct I made around our hands was glowing."

"Brilliant." Seri descended the stairs, now with plenty of illumination for both of them. At the end of the flight, they walked down a short hall and descended another set. This one ended in a small room already lit by an oil lamp. Ixchel stood waiting for them.

"My Lady. What are you doing here?" she asked at once.

Seri tossed the ball to Dravid, who dissolved it in his hands. "We've come to speak with Volraag."

"That is not a good idea," Ixchel said.

"Maybe not. But it's necessary," Seri argued. "He has information we still need."

"Then I will be at your side the entire time."

"Of course you will." Seri grabbed her hand. "I wouldn't have it any other way."

Ixchel pulled her hand loose and picked up her shield. She opened a heavy oak door and led the way into another hall, this one lined by more oak doors. Each one had a tiny open window at eye level. Light streamed out from the third one on the right.

"What is it now?" Volraag's voice called as they approached. "Is there any more indignity you can visit upon one of the Lords of Antises?"

"Oh, please," Seri said. "You're not a Lord and you know it."

Volraag's face appeared at the window. His hair and beard were a mess and his eyes had dark rings beneath them. "I have the power of a Lord, and I am the son of a Lord. What more does it take? Ah, how pleasant to see you up and about again, dear Seri."

"You're the reason she got hurt in the first place!" Dravid exclaimed.

"Oh, the cripple is here too. Wonderful. To what do I owe this double honor?"

"I need to know all that you've done with magic," Seri said. "We know Tezan gave you Lord Sundinka's magic, and then some from Calu at the Ch'olan portal. But did anything else happen between that?"

"And why would I tell you anything about my power?" Volraag leaned against the door and his head moved out of sight. "Aren't you planning to take what I have left from me, anyway?"

"The only thing you'll lose is what you have stolen!" Dravid snapped.

Seri put her bandaged hand on Dravid's chest. "You have an opportunity to help here, Volraag," she said to the door.

"Help who? My jailers? Pardon me if I'm not inclined to assist you."

"To help Antises. You want to overthrow the system, don't you? That's what we're trying to do: to end the Laws of Cursing and Bindings."

"Oh, yes. That's what my half-brother claims, isn't it?" Volraag's face reappeared in the window. "Very convenient for one who is claiming to be King. Promise to help the people... just as soon as we can figure it out. Oh, it may take some years while I rule over all of you, but eventually, maybe, we'll help you out."

"We're trying to figure it out right now!" Dravid insisted.

"We want to do it as soon as Marshal gets back," Seri explained. "At the same time as the Passing."

"At which point, you take my power, and Varioch no longer has a Lord. I suppose King Marshal will rule over it as well. Lord and King!"

"Pointless," Dravid muttered.

"Volraag, I need to tell you something," Seri persisted. "Remember when we were at the high place in Ch'olan? I went through the portal into the Otherworld. While there, I met Evander, Marshal's grandfather."

"If so, then he would be the real King, now wouldn't he?"

"You're right, except he died."

Volraag snorted.

"But before he died, he told me some things, trying to help us to end the curses. And he said that you were a key to it all."

Volraag did not answer.

"Did you hear me? We need you."

"I heard you."

Seri looked at Dravid. He rolled his eyes. No one said anything. Ixchel walked into a darker area of the hallway, then came back.

At last, Seri tried again: "Please, Volraag. We're trying to figure out how to lift all the curses. I know you want that. Can't you just tell me what has happened to you?"

"You won't like it."

"That's kind of irrelevant, isn't it? I don't like much of what you've done over the past year."

"Very well." Volraag fell silent for a moment. Then: "It happened when I opened the portal in Varioch."

Seri looked at Dravid and raised her eyebrows. Now they were getting somewhere.

"Curasir was there. He had promised me a new source of power if I opened the portal. I took Tezan with me." He moved away from the window again.

Seri bit her lip to keep herself from saying anything. Volraag was speaking so slow!

"He had those dark Eldanim with him."

"Durunim," Seri said without thinking.

"Whatever you want to call them. They brought a… prisoner, one of the Eldanim. I was confused at first." He paused again. "Curasir reminded me that the Eldanim are beings of magic. Tezan didn't want to do it, but Curasir forced him. And then once he started, neither of us wanted to stop."

Seri and Dravid exchanged horrified looks. Did that mean…?

"His name was Ruitel. He died for my cause."

"You—" Dravid cut himself off, but his face turned red. Seri didn't blame him.

"The power is very different. It permeates all of me. I keep expecting my skin to glow."

"So you still have that power?" Seri asked.

"Apparently. I thought it gone when the gods took back their power, but… the effects returned a few days later."

"What are the effects?"

"Warmth. Strength. And salt."

"Salt?"

"I have a perpetual salty taste in my mouth. It makes me crave something sweet." His face appeared in the window again. "Since I'm being so cooperative, perhaps you could help with that." He smiled.

Dravid smacked the cell door with his crutch. Volraag laughed in response.

Seri walked a few steps away. "I'm not sure how this helps us," she said. "It certainly wasn't what I expected."

"Do you still think I'm some kind of key to Marshal's success?" Volraag called, mockery in his voice.

"Evander said you were, so there must be something to it. I just don't know what." She sighed.

"If you want my help, there will be a cost. I'll not help you if you turn me over to the other Lords for judgment."

"You'll do whatever you're told!" Dravid growled.

"Why should I? You've already threatened me with the loss of everything. What more can you do?"

"Don't bother," Seri said to Dravid. "When the time comes, we'll do what we have to." She frowned again. "If the time comes. I can't figure out how this would fit into the plan at all. The original Masters didn't have the help of the Eldanim. Did they?"

"I don't remember it being mentioned in the book," Dravid said.

"What a surprise. Volraag doesn't give you what you want." Tich emerged from the shadows down the hall.

"Tich! Have you been there this whole time?" Seri glanced at Ixchel, who didn't look at all surprised.

"I told Marshal I'd keep an eye on Bumrag here until he got back." She shrugged. "He's not back yet."

Seri glanced at Ixchel. "I think he's guarded well now, though."

"Physically, yeah. I wouldn't want to fight Ixchel; that's for sure." She tapped her head. "But someone's gotta listen when he talks, someone who doesn't believe a word he says."

"We don't believe him either," Dravid said.

"Of course you don't, Dravy. But he's good with his voice. He deceives people out of habit. I'm just here to watch out for that."

"And if you hadn't been watching before, he would have destroyed all the portals," Seri pointed out. "You might have saved my life too.

Thank you."

"No big deal. Sounds like you got the information you wanted from him this time, if you can trust it. What are you going to do now?"

Seri looked at Dravid. "I have no idea."

(((35)))

Marshal stepped through the portal, feeling the now-familiar sensation of motion flowing over his body. And then he emerged in the portal room of Zes Sivas. Victor followed right behind him. They both stopped after a couple of steps and looked around.

"What happened here?" Victor turned his head to look at the pedestal. He whistled. "Somebody smashed this thing."

"Varioch and Ch'olan," Marshal said, identifying the two missing portals.

"It was Volraag." Seri descended the stairs into the portal room. Marshal's eyes locked on to her bandaged hand.

"You're hurt. Did he do that?" His power shook the room in his agitation.

"Volraag wanted to destroy all of these. Tich stopped him. She was amazing, Marshal!"

"But your hand…"

"Curasir tried to kill me," she said. She held up the hand. "This, however, I did to myself. What about Lord Tyrr? Is he coming?"

"He'll be here," Marshal said. "I buried the portal, but the Durunim are all over Varioch and Rasna. It's not good."

Victor pointed to the broken parts of the pedestal. "Is this going to be a problem?"

"We're not waiting on anyone from Varioch, and Lord Rajwir is already here," Seri assured them. "He's disturbed that he can't get back to his land as quick as he'd like, but he understands." She grinned. "He's also sad that now his niece won't get to meet you this visit."

Marshal groaned. "I just got back. Can't we avoid that topic?"

"You can try." Seri giggled. "The female population of this island is increasing. And it's all your fault."

Victor put a hand over his eyes and shook his head. "When we left Drusa's Crossing last year, you could have told me anything. You could have told me we'd fight monsters and visit another world and see all kinds of amazing things. I might have believed you." He pulled the hand away. "But if you told me that women would be throwing themselves at Marshal and ignoring me... I'd call you a dirty liar."

Marshal glared at him, then turned back to Seri. "We need to get cleaned up and eat something." He started toward the stairs. "After a good night's sleep, we can start setting things up for the Passing."

"I'll tell Tich you're back. She's still keeping an eye on Volraag."

"You know what? I'll do that myself. I have some words for my brother."

•••••

Marshal glared through the tiny window at Volraag. "You tried to kill Seri."

Volraag sat on the edge of his cot and returned Marshal's stare with a lopsided smile. "No, I did not. That would create a curse, as you well know, and that is not something I will ever do."

"You conspired with Curasir to kill her. Close enough."

Volraag pointed at him. "You've met Curasir. Has he ever been honest with you? I had no idea he would take things that far."

"They're both liars," Tich said, coming up behind Marshal. "I heard them planning it. Volraag knew exactly what was going to happen."

Marshal spun around. "Tich!" He took a step toward her, but didn't know what to do next. Should he hug her? Kiss her?

Before he could make up his mind, she moved beside him, bumped him with her hip, and then tapped on the window's edge of Volraag's cell. "Good thing I was listening."

"Oh, you're still here?" Volraag got to his feet and approached the door. "I should be angry with you, but if you saved Seri, I suppose that's good."

"Stop it," Marshal insisted. "Stop trying to convince me of something we both know isn't true."

Volraag spread his hands. "We are on opposite sides here, brother."

"But we shouldn't be! Why don't you get that?" Marshal stepped up and put his face next to the window. "We both want an end to the system, to the curses!"

"You want to end it one way. I want to end it another."

"How? I just don't understand."

Volraag sighed. "You want to end the curses because you had one. An unjust one, in fact. But the curses are just a symptom, a small part of the whole thing." He moved closer to the door. "I want to end all of it. Curses. Bindings. Lords. Masters. Kings. Everything. Burn the whole thing down." He gestured around him. "Raze this island down to the water. Whatever it takes to get the power out of their hands."

"We could have been allies," Marshal said softly. "We should have been allies."

Volraag shook his head. "You're part of the system now. King and Lord. I'll take you down too, if I can."

Marshal closed his eyes and let out a breath. It was pointless. And so sad. He turned away from the cell and put his arm around Tich. It felt a little awkward, but he kept it there. "I'm hungry. Want to come eat with me?"

"Sure. Now that you're back, I don't have to keep watching this guy any more." She sauntered toward the exit. Marshal followed, letting his arm slide off her shoulders. She grabbed his hand with hers.

"Oh, please," Volraag mumbled behind them.

• • • • •

While eating lunch, Marshal discovered the truth of Seri's words. Lord Bakari approached their table, followed by a girl Marshal didn't recognize.

"King Marshal!" the young Lord cried, bowing as he drew near. "I am delighted to see you return to us. I hope your visit to Rasna was successful?"

"It was," Marshal said.

"Excellent. May I present my sister, Tatiska. She has been dying to meet you."

The girl stepped forward and also bowed. Marshal smiled at her, but as usual, didn't know what to say. She was pretty enough, and he could see the family resemblance to Bakari. But she couldn't be more than fifteen years old!

"It is… good to meet you," he said at last. "Welcome to Zes Sivas."

"I, I…" Tatiska stammered, with a quick glance at her brother, "I hope to get to know you better in the days to come, Your Majesty."

Tich leaned in. "Have you met the young Lady Kumara? She's Lord Meluhha's daughter." She pointed across the dining hall. "They're right over there. I'm sure the two of you would get along very well."

"Oh!" Tatiska brightened. "Yes, we've met before." She turned to look.

"She needs more girl friends," Tich added. "She's got seven brothers, you know."

Marshal stifled a laugh.

"If your, Your Majesty will excuse me," Tatiska said, with another bow. She hurried across the room.

Lord Bakari frowned, but followed her, after another bow to Marshal.

"Good job," Marshal said. "I had no idea what to say there."

"Yeah, I could tell."

Marshal sighed. "I just… I don't want to deal with this. We have world-changing stuff going on. Why is everyone concerned about my love life?"

Tich smacked him on the back of the head. "Did you not hear anything Lady Lilitu said to you?"

"Ow!" Marshal rubbed his head. "As I recall, you griped at her for telling people how to live their lives."

"I gripe at everyone. Doesn't mean she wasn't right. You accepted the Kingship." Tich straightened in an attempt to imitate Lady Lilitu's posture. "Your life is not your own," she quoted in a snooty voice.

"You sound nothing like her."

"Kumara over there is trying to get your attention."

Marshal resisted the urge to roll his eyes. He glanced toward Lord Meluhha's table. Kumara smiled and waved. Marshal nodded and smiled in return, then turned back to Tich. "Let's go somewhere more private." He got to his feet.

"Oooo, that'll make people talk."

He held out his hand to her. "I don't care."

• • • • •

"He ran across the water, I tell you!"

Marshal followed Tich out of the Citadel of Kings. He had a good idea who she had seen, even before he saw the golden-skinned figure standing on the ruined quay.

"Term?" Victor joined them.

"Looks like it," Marshal said. "Let's see what he wants now."

"Should I go get Seri?" Tich asked.

"No, I think this message is for me." Marshal stopped on the grass. He hadn't been to this side of the island since the time he first met the Masters and opened a portal to the Otherworld.

"Term!" he called. "What are you doing here?"

The god touched his hat and gave a short bow. "Greetings, King Marshal. Can't say I'm very impressed with what you've done with this place. Needs some work."

"He's kind of short for a god, isn't he?" Tich observed.

"And yet here I am." Term spread his arms. "Term, god of messages, at your service."

"Deliver your message, then," Marshal said, putting his hand on his sword hilt.

"Very well. I come from Zeyus, ruler of the gods of Varioch and Rasna. He wishes to know your intentions. Will you be solving these annoying earthquakes?"

"I do not owe him answers any more than I do Murdak. You're all alike."

Term held up a finger. "Ah, haven't heard the latest then, I see. Murdak is no longer a factor. The eastern armies are now commanded by Namnirnu. I've spoken to him, and he has much the same questions."

Marshal digested that bit of news. Did it mean Nehesy and those with him had succeeded? Without Murdak, he felt a lot more confident of their chances. But he had no understanding of the powers of either of the gods Term named.

"Regardless of your answer, I am also instructed to suggest that surrender would be your best option now," Term announced. "I am, of course, empowered to accept such a surrender." He removed his hat and held it over his heart.

"Why would I surrender?" Marshal almost smiled.

"You cannot hope to stand against all of us. Namnirnu to the east. Zeyus to the west. What hope have you here on your tiny little island?"

"This tiny little island now holds almost all of the power of Antises." Marshal took a step closer. "Between myself, the Lords, and the Masters, we do not fear you."

"And how long will the Lords remain with you when we begin to sack their cities?" Term asked. "How long will you yourself stay here when we march on Reman?"

"We are here to alter the future of Antises itself," Marshal answered. "When we are done, we will deal with all of you."

"You want to end the curses. So do we. Let us work together on this great cause."

"We'll handle that on our own. Thanks all the same."

"Is it not a difficult prospect?" Term waved his hat toward the west. "We have some among us who know exactly how the magics must be altered to change this. Why not wait for us, so we can help you?"

"Uh, because you want us to call you gods and worship you," Victor said.

"How about this?" Term suggested, taking another step closer. "We will send two advisors, alone. They can guide you on this task, and then we can negotiate what happens after that."

Marshal didn't answer. Something felt strange, but he couldn't figure it out.

"While your troops sack our cities, right?" Victor asked.

"We could arrange for an immediate halt to that activity while we work on the curses," Term offered.

"Mighty convenient," Tich muttered. "They're offering an awful lot, all of a sudden."

Marshal agreed. "Why would you help us?"

"I told you: we want to end those foolish laws with their curses and bindings just as much as you do."

"And you know how this can be done?"

"We can't trust them," Victor whispered.

"Some of us do," Term answered. "Those who are wise in the ways of magic, both of Antises and the Otherworld. They can help to shape things so that no one suffers an unjust curse ever again."

It clicked then. "Shape things. You don't want to end the Laws completely," Marshal said. "You just want to re-shape them."

"We want an end to curses, just like you."

"No, you don't." Marshal allowed a trickle of power to flow out of his feet, making the ground tremble. "You'll just replace the Laws with ones that benefit you." Nian's words from long ago came to mind. "The Laws of Cursings and Bindings are based on Theon's laws, but they were made by men. You gods will make new laws, designed by you, to work for you."

Term put his hat back on. "Anything we do is only for the good of humanity."

"Just like you've done things for the good of the Eldanim?" Marshal clenched his fists, understanding it all now. "You've turned them into mindless servants with no free will at all! The Durunim can't choose whether to follow you or not! That's the fate you have in mind for us too!"

"I see that you are not interested in negotiation after all," Term observed. "In that case, I'll leave you to await our arrival."

"Let me speed you on your way!" Marshal growled, unleashing power at the ruined quay. Rocks exploded, but Term raced away, running across the water.

"That is not natural," Tich said. "If Theon meant for us to walk on water, he'd… eh, never mind."

"I don't know," Victor said. "Looks kind of fun to me."

Marshal turned back to the Citadel. "He may have come to frighten us, but I finally understand now. Let's assemble everyone. It's time to end this."

(((36)))

Seri took charge of arranging the gathering, consulting with Master Tzoyet.

"Aside from the inner sanctum, do we have a good meeting place?" she wondered. "I don't think the Lords would like us looking down on them in the council chamber."

The older Master nodded. "Yes, we have such a place. It's in the Citadel of Kings."

"Let's see it then."

He led the way. Seri now knew about half of the second Citadel's layout, but Master Tzoyet soon diverted into a section she hadn't explored yet. He came to a pair of double doors and pushed them open. Seri stepped into the room and stopped short.

"Why have we been meeting in that crowded council chamber when we have this?" she demanded.

The room formed an enormous rectangle. Running down each of the longer sides were elevated seating areas that could easily hold several times the population of Zes Sivas. Tall windows lined the walls behind the seating areas, letting in plenty of sunlight, no matter the time of day. In the center of the room, a large elevated platform held two intricate tables. Seri walked closer to get a better look.

Each table formed a long arc, making up a half circle. But while they faced each other, the tables did not form a complete circle. Instead, they intersected on either end, one crossing over the other. A narrow gap allowed someone to slip in between the tables. In the very center sat a chair, presumably for the King. Six other chairs lined each table, one for Lords and one for Masters. Each chair had the symbol for its land carved into the back.

"It's in the Citadel of Kings," Master Tzoyet said, as if that explained it.

"It's perfect!" Seri said. "We should meet here more often!" She ran a finger along one of the table tops. "We might want to dust, though."

• • • • •

Marshal looked at the King's chair. Like the other chairs in the gathering room, it had a symbol carved into its back. This one had been worn down over the centuries. He traced one of the lines with a finger. "It's… like the symbol on my sword," he said. "But what is it?"

Victor leaned down to peer at the design. "Some kind of flying creature? I don't know."

Seri hurried over to them. "The others are on their way. Take your seat, Marshal," she instructed. "Victor, you'll have to—"

"He stands beside me," Marshal interrupted.

"I do?"

"I made you chief advisor, remember? Also King's champion. And whatever other title we think of."

"Um, all right," Seri said. "But you'll be moving around a lot."

"Why?"

She grinned. "Sit down, Marshal. Figure it out."

Marshal raised his eyebrows, but sat down in the chair. Only then did he discover that it rotated. He could turn to face anywhere else on the tables, so as to pay attention to individual speakers. "Interesting."

"Yeah, I'll, uh, stand over there," Victor said, pointing to one of the table intersections. "I'm not going to walk in circles beside your chair the entire time."

Marshal looked around the rest of the room. In the nearest audience section, he noticed Tich and Dravid among many of the other residents of Zes Sivas. Tich waved. He smiled and returned the gesture.

"Here they come," Seri said. She left them to find her seat at the Masters' table.

Masters Tzoyet, Plecu, Ganak, Komadi, and Magnus entered and joined her. Six Masters on six chairs. Master Komadi, the replacement for Master Korda, had only arrived the day before.

Lady Lilitu entered next, followed by Lords Meluhha, Rajwir, Bakari, and Tyrr. They took their places at the Lords' table, each admiring the symbols on the chairs. The seat for Varioch remained empty, but Volraag entered a moment later, escorted by Ixchel and several other mages and soldiers. They led him to another chair, some distance from the tables.

"Why is he here?" Lord Tyrr demanded.

"What we decide today will affect him," Marshal said. "There may come a reason to seek his opinion. It's not likely, but I wanted him here, anyway."

"And he still possesses a Lord's power," Magnus pointed out.

"That he stole from my father!" Lord Bakari snapped.

Marshal turned the chair back and forth as they spoke. Hmm. Maybe he shouldn't try to face every speaker. He might get dizzy.

Master Tzoyet stood. "I call this gathering of Lords and Mages to order," he announced. "King Marshal is now presiding."

All eyes turned to him. Marshal wanted to make himself smaller. He resisted the urge to straighten his clothing.

"Have we all acknowledged him as King?" Lord Meluhha asked, with a look at Lord Tyrr.

"It is not in question any longer," Master Ganak interceded. "He is recognized as such, though we have yet to plan an official ceremony."

A ceremony? What would that involve? A crown? Marshal's head itched at the thought.

"We are gathered here for multiple purposes," he announced in as loud a voice as he thought necessary. "We must discuss the invasion of Antises by the Durunim, a new Passing ceremony, and the proposed end to the Laws of Cursings and Bindings."

"What about him?" Lord Bakari demanded, pointing at Volraag. "You promised he would be judged here by the Lords!"

"And he will be," Marshal answered, "once we hold the Passing and his stolen power leaves him."

"Will that indeed happen?" Lord Rajwir asked.

"The power of each land is bound to the bloodline," Master Ganak said. "Once Volraag surrenders the power, it will return to its rightful place, the ruling bloodline of Mandiata. Thus it has always been." He hesitated and glanced at Lady Lilitu. "With a few notable exceptions."

"Because of this, the issue of the Passing is foremost," Marshal declared. "I propose we waste no time and hold it tomorrow."

"What is the rush?" Lord Meluhha asked. "Since the great shaking, we have only had tiny tremblings. Can this not wait until we deal with the invaders?"

"We cannot afford to wait," Marshal said. "Antises must be healed, and my power alone will not do it. In Kuktarma, I managed to slow things down, patch it up. But it will not hold. Without all of our power, it will continue to come apart."

"But not for some time, surely," Master Ganak said. "Perhaps Lord Meluhha is right. The invaders do take precedence."

"If we all spread out again to fight the invaders, it will be difficult to bring us all back," Lady Lilitu said. "We are all here. The Passing, despite its pageantry, is a relatively short and simple process. I agree that it can be held tomorrow without difficulty."

"The Masters are in agreement with this as well," Master Tzoyet announced. "We have prepared the inner sanctum. All it awaits are the Lords."

"Good," Marshal said. "Now I'd like to turn to—"

"And then we will have the judgment on Volraag?" Lord Bakari interrupted.

"Oh, he'll be judged all right," Lord Tyrr grumbled.

"Volraag will be dealt with. I have promised you this." Marshal clenched the arms of the chair in frustration. "But we must discuss the issue of the Laws."

"Why? This seems to me the least pressing issue," Master Komadi said. "We have danger to Antises from within, and from invaders. Those must be dealt with, and now."

"The Laws of Cursings and Bindings have served Antises well for a thousand years," Lord Rajwir pointed out. "Why seek to overturn them now?"

"But they do not serve us well!" Marshal countered. "My own life is proof of this."

"An occasional aberration is the price to pay for the peace and security the Laws bring us," Master Plecu said.

Marshal stared at him, open-mouthed. Plecu lowered his gaze. What was happening? All of them knew what Marshal wanted. Why were they suddenly opposed to it?

"Even if we knew how to end the Laws," Master Ganak said, "most of those here are not sure it should happen."

"To be quite honest," Lord Bakari said, "the whole issue seems more of a desire on your part, Your Majesty, than of an actual problem."

"An actual problem?" Marshal jumped out of the chair and walked to face Lord Bakari across the Lords' table. "Have you seen my face, Lord Bakari? Perhaps you need a closer look?" He leaned across the table. "I was attacked by a curse-stalker. I lived all of my life until recently, unable to speak or communicate in any way. And all because of someone else's crimes!"

"As he said," Lord Tyrr spoke up. "It seems like a personal issue to you."

Marshal whirled to face him. "Of course it's a personal issue! I don't want anyone else to suffer like I did. Does that make it wrong?"

"Perhaps."

"Your own daughter told me of the fear she lives in, on a daily basis!" Marshal leveled a finger at Lord Tyrr. "The fact that your actions might one day bring a curse down on her terrifies her!"

"He's not wrong," Volraag said from his chair.

"Oh, well, if Varion's boy agrees with it..." Lord Tyrr muttered.

"I must ask the obvious question," Lord Rajwir said. "If we were to end the Laws, what would happen to us?" He gestured at the other Lords. "Would we lose our power forever? Would you lose the King's power?"

"I don't know," Marshal said. "We're trying to figure it out."

"I won't sacrifice the very thing that makes me a Lord, just to fulfill your personal vendetta against our system!" Lord Tyrr slammed his fist on the table. "You are a complete fool if you think we will agree to that!"

"We don't know that will happen," Seri argued. "The two things are not necessarily connected."

"Of course they are!" Master Magnus replied. "Otherwise, how would the Lords be immune?"

"Perhaps only that part of the Laws could be removed?" Lord Bakari suggested.

"It's called the Lords' Betrayal for a reason!" Seri snapped, rising to her feet. "Everyone in all of Antises knows that what the Lords did is wrong!"

"But we do not have the skill here and now to do such a thing," Master Ganak said. "I wish indeed that we did."

Marshal moved back toward the middle as Seri sat back down. "If I am to be your King," he began.

"If," Master Magnus said, just loud enough to be heard.

"If I am to be your King," Marshal repeated, "then this is my purpose." He pointed toward the windows. "A messenger of the gods came here yesterday, and made it clear what their purpose is: they will re-shape the Laws to their own desires. Curses will fall on anyone who displeases them. Is that what you want?"

Lord Meluhha steepled his fingers together. "Forgive me, King

Marshal, but you set up a false choice: to eliminate the Laws or have the gods remake them. We also have the option to leave them as they are. It would take our power to change the Laws, and the gods cannot force us to do so."

"We've seen their power!" Seri burst out. "Would you oppose their will when they hold the lives of all your people in their hands? Maybe they'll just kill you and manipulate your children instead!"

"They are welcome to try," Lord Tyrr growled. "They will not find us easy prey."

Volraag erupted in laughter. Everyone turned to look at him. He almost fell out of his chair with the convulsions, real or contrived. Lord Tyrr started to rise to his feet, but Lady Lilitu put a hand on his. He settled back, still glaring at Volraag.

At last Volraag stopped, wiping his eyes. "I am sorry for the breach in decorum," he declared. "It's simply all too amusing. I've seen the power of these gods. So have several of you. While the power gathered here is quite impressive, the gods are greater." He held an arm up in the air and flicked his wrist to point at Marshal. "I'm told their leader beat our little King here within an inch of his life." His face turned serious. "I've tasted their power. Tasted it, I tell you. It is nothing like what we wield." He shook his head. "We do not stand a chance."

Silence fell across the gathering. Marshal closed his eyes. Volraag's interruption might sway the discussion, but would it go in the direction he wanted? He considered telling them about sending Talinir to the Eldanim, but decided against it. Hope in something that might not occur would not be a proper motivation.

"If we do not stand a chance, then we should negotiate," Master Plecu said. "We should send an embassy to them, seek to find a way to co-exist."

"The only way we'll co-exist with them is as their slaves!" Marshal insisted. "Many of you have seen the Durunim, their warriors." He turned to lock eyes with Lords Tyrr and Bakari. "They are mindless drones. But they used to be Eldanim, free people like us. Their free will has been stripped away, taken from them. They have no choice but to serve. Is that the future you want for our people?"

Master Magnus made a sound as if to begin speaking, but said nothing.

"I, for one, value my free will," Lady Lilitu spoke up. "I will fight for it. And my people."

"As will I," Lord Meluhha said. "I will not yield to these creatures, be they gods or not."

A few murmurs came from the other Lords and Masters. It sounded like agreement, but no one else spoke loud enough to be heard.

"And it is for this same reason that we must end the Laws of Cursings and Bindings," Marshal said. "They take our free will from us in much the same way."

"I appreciate what you are trying to do," Master Tzoyet said. "I am eldest here, and I can attest to the unjustness of the Laws." He shook his head. "I have seen too much." He lifted his eyes to Marshal. "Now you are here, and you were freed from a curse yourself. We have a prophecy that such a thing will lead to the ending of all curses. It is an admirable thing. A good cause for which to fight." He paused. "But now is not the time, I am afraid. We must deal with the immediate threats. We hold the Passing tomorrow, and then we find a way to stop these invaders."

Marshal's heart sank. He needed them, all of them, to end the Laws. But if they refused to do it now, when could he hope to bring them all together again?

"It has to be now," he said aloud.

"Why?" Master Tzoyet looked at him with a dull stare. "You have spoken of the power of the gods coming toward us even now. And this procedure, if it succeeds, would possibly weaken us, perhaps even strip the Lords of their power, right when it is needed most. If we are to survive, we need as much as power as we can bring to bear against the enemy."

"I cannot argue with this logic," Master Ganak agreed.

Another murmur swept the group. Marshal closed his eyes and bowed his head. He clenched and unclenched his fist. "I will never stop fighting for this," he said without looking up. "I—"

A loud boom echoed through the room. All eyes turned to the main doors. Something had struck them.

"Are they locked?" Seri whispered to Master Ganak, but loud enough that Marshal heard her.

"No, someone just wants our attention." Master Ganak stood and was about to say something, but the doors flew open, pushed aside by two young men in acolyte robes.

"Jamana. Adhi." Seri stood too, ready to rush to greet them.

Then Kishin walked in, stumbling toward the tables with a heavy limp. He leaned on a staff, his left arm in a sling.

"Assassin!" Lord Meluhha leaped to his feet. "How did you escape my dungeon?"

"I released him, father," Adhi said, hurrying up beside the limping Kishin. "I will explain that later. First, you need to hear what we have to say."

"Nehesy, son of Aharu, has fulfilled his final task," Kishin declared, his voice strained. "Murdak is dead."

Many voices responded at once: "Who is Nehesy?" "Who is Murdak?" "What are you talking about?" "Why is he even here?" And so on. Marshal sat down in his chair and considered the news while questions and debates flew back and forth. Murdak, most powerful of the gods, was dead. Term's news had been accurate in that regard. With Murdak out of the way, Marshal felt a little more hopeful about their chances.

"Who leads the gods now?" he asked in a loud voice, overriding everyone else.

"It is Namnirnu," Kishin answered. "Be warned. He may not have the same kind of power as Murdak, but he is frightening in his abilities."

"How so?"

Kishin staggered and almost fell. Jamana caught his good arm and helped him remain up. The assassin had seen better days.

"He controls wind and water," Adhi said. "We got here as fast as we could by boat, but…" He glanced at the other two.

"Namnirnu forms a path through the lake," Kishin said. "Even now, his army marches toward you on dry ground, in a path he creates through the waters!"

"How much time do we have?" Marshal asked.

"At their current rate…" Kishin's head bowed, then he pulled it back up and took a deep breath. "I would say they will be here tomorrow afternoon at the earliest, tomorrow's sunset at the latest."

The gathering erupted in commotion. Lords and Masters alike talked over each other, insisting that all other concerns be put aside, calling for a defense of the island, suggesting an evacuation through the portals, and so on. Marshal let them debate. He hadn't expected this at all. It appeared that despite his best efforts, everything might fall apart.

The earth trembled. Everyone fell silent as even the stones beneath their feet shifted. One of the enormous windows buckled and fell inward, shattering. The trembling lasted for only about half a minute, but felt much longer.

"If we hold the Passing first thing in the morning, how long does it take us all to recover?" Marshal asked the Masters.

"A… a couple of hours, at most, your majesty," Master Tzoyet answered.

"Then this is what we will do: we will hold the Passing at dawn," Marshal declared. "We will heal Antises, to preserve our lands and people, even if we fail in what comes next. Then we will face this so-called god and his army together. He will regret ever leaving his world for ours!"

(((37)))

Seri closed the door to her office and sighed. "That could have gone better," she admitted.

"No kidding," Tich said. She leaned on Marshal's shoulder as he sat at Seri's desk, a pensive look on his scarred face.

"At least they agreed to the Passing," Victor said. He leaned against the wall and toyed with his flail.

"Even that took some doing." Seri shook her head. "I don't know what to think, Marshal. I can't believe how many of them want to keep the Laws."

"Where are the others?" Tich asked. "Everyone took off in different directions."

"Master Komadi went somewhere with Jamana. He said he had big news for him." Seri had to admit her curiosity almost made her follow them. "And Dravid went with Kishin to the infirmary. The assassin is in bad shape. It's a miracle he made it here as it is. Dravid is going to try to heal him."

"Did Ixchel go with them?" Victor asked.

"No, she was escorting Volraag back to his cell."

"Why would Ixchel go with them?" Tich wanted to know.

"Kishin is her father."

Tich straightened and folded her arms across her chest. "Does anyone have a normal family?"

"I do," Victor said. "But I haven't seen them in almost a year now."

"We can't wait," Marshal said suddenly.

"Wait for what?" Tich asked.

Marshal looked up. "Tomorrow, during the Passing. If the opportunity presents itself, Seri, we do it. We end the Laws."

"We don't even know how!" Seri protested. "And the Lords and Masters aren't on our side."

"We don't need them." Marshal clenched his fists. "We do it alone."

"I don't see—"

"You said we had to enter the Heart of Fire, right? The only time the Heart of Fire manifests itself is during the Passing. We do it then. We enter the Heart and see if we can do it."

Seri rubbed her hands together. "I want to do it, you know. But I just don't see how."

"It's your vision that's the key to all of it," Marshal said. "I know it."

"What?"

Marshal got up. "Your vision. Your star-sight. You were able to figure out that portal generator because of it. Once we're inside the Heart, maybe you'll be able to see the Laws and how to remove them."

"Maybe." Seri frowned. It didn't sound quite right. "If Dravid anchors us again..."

"Yes, that's got to be part of it."

"But what about Volraag? We haven't figured out how he ties in."

Marshal shrugged. "We have to try. We may not get another chance."

"Uh, are you sure about this?" Victor asked. "I mean, I'm all for defying those power-hungry Lords, but... we already said we don't know what will happen when the Laws are gone. What if the Lords lose their power completely, right when that enemy army is about to arrive?"

"Even with all our power, we're not guaranteed to win that fight," Marshal said. "And if the gods win, they will twist the Laws. We have to remove even that possibility from them."

"What's to stop them from creating their own laws all over again?"

"Me." Marshal tapped his chest. "If it looks like they'll win, you'll have to kill me. It's my power that's the key to everything. If I die, the power vanishes. I have no relatives, no bloodline. It goes back to Antises."

"We don't know that!" Seri exclaimed.

"No one's killing you while I'm around," Tich added.

"Least of all me," Victor agreed. "That's not a plan, Marshal."

"We need to be prepared for this possibility," Marshal argued. "No matter what, the gods cannot coerce the King's power to their will."

"You think you're that weak?" Tich demanded. "You think they'll torture you or something?"

Marshal looked at her. "They kept me in a box in the Otherworld, because I thought you and the others were prisoners. If they have any of you prisoners and threaten you, how can I refuse them?" He looked from her to Seri and Victor. "You three—and Talinir—are the closest friends I have. I couldn't let them hurt you."

"It's not going to come to that," Victor said. "You'll be the last one standing, anyway."

"We can't take that risk."

"Then kill yourself!" Victor said savagely. "I'm not going to do it for you!"

Marshal nodded slowly. "All right." He looked back to Seri. "Tomorrow morning?"

She shook her head. "I don't know what to say. There's so much we don't know. But..." She let out a long breath. "I suppose we'll take it one step at a time and see what happens. Maybe... maybe we'll get lucky."

"And maybe Theon will show up and guide you," Tich said. "With all the other crazy stuff happening, I'm not ruling anything out."

• • • • •

Marshal lay in his bed awake, long after everyone had gone to bed. So much depended on tomorrow morning. He couldn't possibly sleep. In only a few hours, either his dream would come true, or everything would fall apart, and there might not be any way to ever solve it.

The power of Zes Sivas pulled at him, as it had from the moment he set foot on the island. Most of the day, he could ignore it, but when he lay still on his bed, the presence of the island's power threatened to overwhelm him. His own power wanted to reach out to it, embrace it.

And so, the few nights he had spent here, he had let part of his power flow out, trickling down through the floor and cascading through the walls of the citadel. The power of Zes Sivas rushed to meet his, entwining around it, as if delighted to make its acquaintance. To his own delight, he found he could sense the surroundings of his power. Was this something deliberately built into the citadel for the King? Some kind of special channels in the walls for the King's power? He would have to ask Seri to look that over if they had time when all of this was over.

He couldn't identify people, but he could sense those with power, like the Lords and Masters. Through this, he could gain a fairly good idea of which room's walls he explored. On the previous night, he identified the rooms belonging to the Masters. With a careful twist of vibration, he managed to open one of the doors. He hoped it wasn't Seri's. Fascinated, he continued to explore, discovering the dungeon, the gathering room, the portal room, and more.

Tonight, he resumed the practice. Anything to occupy his mind, take it away from the stress of the next day. He let his power roam through the walls of the citadel, exploring until his thoughts grew fuzzy. His eyes closed.

"Sleep is such a human thing, don't you think?" A voice intruded on his semi-consciousness. "It reveals your true… vulnerability."

Marshal's eyes flew open. In the darkness of his room, he had difficulty making out the shapes around him, but he knew the voice: Curasir.

"I wouldn't move very fast if I were you," the Eldani said. "It might hurt."

Something pressed against Marshal's neck. He turned his head slowly until he could see: an eidolon stood beside his bed, shadowy sword at his neck.

"Yes, I'm aware this isn't much of a threat to you," Curasir went on. "I'm sure you've thought of two or three different ways to use your power to get out of this."

Marshal had, actually.

"You needn't bother. This wasn't a threat against you. Merely making a point." Curasir gestured and the eidolon pulled his sword away.

Marshal sat up. "If you aren't threatening me, why are you here?"

"Oh, I am threatening you, just not like that. After all, I cannot hope to match you in raw power, not any longer, anyway."

Marshal's eyes darted around the room. Two other eidola flanked Curasir.

"I must thank you, actually," Curasir went on. "You explained exactly how to do it a few hours ago."

"What do you mean?" Marshal asked.

"You said"—Curasir's voice changed to sound exactly like Marshal's—"'If they have any of you prisoners and threaten you, how can I refuse them?'"

"What have you done?" Marshal threw back his covers and started to get out of the bed.

Curasir held up a hand. "Stay right there, King of scars. You need to understand the situation before you act. Haven't those Lords been trying to teach you that lately?"

Marshal sat still.

"As I told you, the sword at your neck was an illustration… of what is happening elsewhere in this citadel right now."

Marshal's blood went cold. "Who?"

Curasir stepped up next to his bed and leaned in closer. "All of them," he whispered, then straightened. "Well, anyone who matters to you, anyway." He began ticking off his fingers. "Seri, of course. Victor. The cripple. The other two acolytes. Oh, and the crazy girl with the sword." He frowned. "I do hope she, out of all of them, doesn't do anything rash. Is that everyone?"

With every identification, Marshal's heart sank further. All of them with swords to their necks? But wait… he hadn't mentioned…

"Oh, and your girlfriend. The short one who likes to run her mouth. Never can remember her name."

Tich also. Curasir really was threatening all of them. "What do you want?" he growled.

"For starters, I'll take this sword back." Curasir walked to the where the sword leaned against the wall and picked it up. "I'd gotten rather attached to it. I suppose, by birthright, it does belong to you. But I can make so much more use of it."

"Birthright?"

"You haven't figured that out yet? I'm disappointed. I'll have to re-evaluate my estimation of your intelligence." Curasir paused. "Then again, you do seem set upon that girl. Should have been my first clue."

"Was that Akhenadom's sword?" Marshal had figured that much out, or at least suspected it.

"Oh, very good. Yes. Yes, it was. The Eldanim forged it for him." Curasir drew the sword halfway out of its scabbard and admired it. "Warpsteel, of course, but… perhaps better. This may have been the finest sword they ever crafted."

Marshal calculated that as long as he could keep Curasir talking, the better. Plus, he had an idea now. A crazy one, to be sure, but when things got desperate…

"You keep saying 'they.' Does that mean you no longer think of yourself as Eldanim?" he asked. At the same time, he reached out with his power again, into the walls of the citadel.

"What an interesting question!" Curasir waved the sword at Marshal. "It's probably an unconscious thing on my part, to be honest."

Marshal twisted the power and prayed to Theon that his gambit worked.

•••••

Volraag tossed and turned on his cot. The Eldanim power he had absorbed lowered his sleep requirements, but even so, he despised the situation. With all the power at hand on this island, why couldn't someone find a better mattress? He'd made the request three times now. Were they doing it just to spite him? He wouldn't put it past that bastard brother of his...

The lock on his cell door popped open and the door creaked open a couple of inches.

Volraag sat up and stared. This was new. Some convoluted mind game? But no, his brother didn't think that way. Nor did any of the Masters. Most of the Lords were more direct in their schemes... except Lady Lilitu. She knew the beauty of a long-term, twisted plot if any of them did.

He got up and approached the door. No sound came from beyond it. Where was his guard? That annoying Holcan with the scant clothing?

"Hello?" No response came to his call. He pushed the door open further. No magic explosions. No swords. Strange.

He stepped out of the cell and looked around. In the dim light, he saw no one. Who could have unlocked his door? Magic, perhaps? But if so, why?

He walked to the doorway at the end of the dungeon (such as it was), and peered out. He chuckled at the sight. Ixchel sat on a stool just outside the doorway. An eidolon stood beside her, sword held against her neck. Ixchel's eyes, full of fury, shifted from the eidolon to Volraag.

He held up his hands. "This is not my doing," he said, then wondered why he bothered to defend himself. He admired the view a moment longer, then headed up the stairs. He had no doubt Ixchel's eyes were burning a hole in his back as he left.

If an eidolon were here, then someone from the Otherworld was behind this, probably the one who unlocked his door. Curasir seemed the most likely suspect, but just the thought of him made Volraag grind his teeth. The Eldanim had deceived him until Murdak could steal his power and toss him aside. Freeing him would not make things even.

He bounded up both flights of stairs, then stopped. Where should he go from here? A very strong part of his mind suggested heading to the dock, finding a rowboat, and setting out alone. It might take days to cross the lake, but it would be worth it to escape from these people, power intact.

But no. They would pursue him. Marshal was too dead set on this Passing, and he needed Volraag's power for that. Besides, the unlocked door and the eidolon piqued his curiosity. Something was happening on this island, and he wanted to know what it might be.

He took a step, then paused. How could he even find his way around this place? The Citadel of Mages had been confusing enough when he had come the last time. Now he was in the Citadel of Kings. Which way should he go?

He closed his eyes and focused on his magical senses. The power of Zes Sivas itself pulsed from below, making it difficult to tell anything else. But one large concentration of power seemed to come from his right. Marshal, most likely. He put a hand against the wall as he focused, then opened his eyes in surprise. A small vibration of power flowed through the wall. He put both hands on the wall and felt around. Sure enough, it was like a flow of magic, descending back down toward the dungeon. But where was it coming from? That's what he needed to find out.

Keeping one hand on the wall, Volraag made his way down the hallway. At the next intersection, he felt around until he found the flow again. A right turn. He took it and soon found another set of stairs going up. The flow ascended, so he did as well. In short order, he found himself looking at a door, engraved with that same winged creature that seemed to dominate the decor in this citadel. The King's bedroom, no doubt. He leaned in and listened.

"…the creature on the pommel?" That was Marshal's voice.

"Oh, that." Curasir. Volraag ground his teeth. "It lived here once. The creature, I mean. Zes Sivas was its home before you humans arrived. Akhenadom killed it, and then slapped its image on everything as his own symbol. A bit ostentatious, if you ask me. But we're getting off the point here."

"The point of how you're threatening all of my friends? I'll find a way to stop you."

Curasir laughed. "Even you can't use your power in seven different places."

"I don't have to. I just have to cross into the Otherworld and blast all of your helpers at once. No rooms there."

"A fine strategy, if you were free to cross over. But for that, you would need this sword… not to mention that if I let you do something like that, it would sort of defeat the whole purpose of threatening you. Rest assured, at the first indication of you using any power whatsoever, at least one of your friends dies. And even if you were free to do something, telling me your strategy isn't the brightest thing. I keep overestimating your intelligence."

Volraag agreed. Why would Marshal be telling Curasir the strategy to defeat him? It guaranteed he couldn't use it, unless… oh. Marshal was talking to him. Volraag almost laughed. Marshal wanted him to help. He was the one who opened the cell door, because he couldn't rely on any of his friends.

His first inclination was to blast the door open and attack Curasir. What did he care if Marshal's friends died?

"Let them go, Curasir. I'll be in debt to you. Then we can negotiate. Isn't that enough?" Volraag almost rolled his eyes. Marshal was making himself sound like a complete idiot in order to communicate to the person behind the door.

Still, he made his point. If he helped, then Marshal would be in debt to him and be willing to negotiate. It wasn't a promise of freedom, but it was the best he might expect to gain. Three choices, then. First, try to escape the island. The plan had little chance of success, and leaving Marshal in Curasir's clutches might have very bad results overall. Second, barge in now and deal with Curasir himself. He liked that choice the best, but Marshal would never forgive him for killing his friends. He would end up in a worse situation than now, with little reward… other than the satisfaction of crushing Curasir's head. Still tempting. And finally… he muffled a sigh. Putting Marshal in debt to him at least gave him something out of all of this.

He moved away from the door. He would have to cross over into the Otherworld, as Marshal suggested, and he knew only one other person who could do that. He smiled. At least he might be able to have a little fun with all this.

•••••

Marshal sensed Volraag leave the door. He could only hope his half-brother had understood the implied offer in his words. Now he had to stall Curasir for as long as it took.

"Enough of this," Curasir said. "As you yourself said, you are trapped. You will do as I ask. Now."

"What is it you want?"

"I explained all this before, but that was to Seri. Don't you people tell each other anything?" Curasir gave an exaggerated sigh. "We're going to make this island draw magic faster than it does now."

"What will that accomplish?"

"It will... no. Enough. My servants can only hold their swords at ready for so long before they get bored and start cutting throats." Curasir gestured to the door. "Let's go. To the inner sanctum, as you call it."

Marshal got to his feet and walked slowly toward the door.

"As I just said, they can only hold those swords for so long. You might want to walk a little faster."

Marshal opened the door and picked up his pace. His only hope now was Volraag.

(((38)))

After a few wrong turns, Volraag made his way into the Citadel of Mages. Once there, he knew where to go: the quarters belonging to the Masters. His time spent here last year helped him negotiate the twisting halls to his destination.

Fortunately, each of the Masters' doors were engraved with the symbol of their land. He located the sheaves of grain representing Arazu. The door was locked, which baffled him. Why even bother with a lock on an island full of mages? A trickle of magic opened it with ease.

The Masters had respectable quarters. The outer room of the suite was an office and meeting place for guests. Seri had yet to modify it much from the previous elderly inhabitant. Volraag couldn't remember his name. The decor spoke of old age. From the desk, he picked up a thin dagger. The previous Master must have used it as a letter opener. Seri didn't seem the type to use any kind of blade. He moved on past the desk to the bedroom door and paused to listen. No sound came from within.

This door, at least, was unlocked. Volraag eased it open and looked into the bedroom. As anticipated, an eidolon stood beside the bed, sword outstretched. At least Seri had altered the bed from its previous owner. The canopy's scalloped curves held a distinctive feminine allure, as did the pale purple bedclothes. Volraag could see little of Seri herself from the door. She might still be asleep.

He considered for a moment. Once he started this course of action, everything would have to happen very rapidly. The problem was that Seri would argue with him, as she always did. The dagger would have to be his persuasion, though she would hate him even more afterwards.

He slipped through the door and rushed the eidolon. It barely had time to turn its head to see him before he reached it. He stabbed up through the chest, adding a burst of magic. The creature flew back against the wall beside the bed and slumped down. It began to fade from view.

"Ow!" Seri sat up in bed, a hand to her neck. The eidolon's sword must have nicked her. "What was—Volraag!"

He swung the dagger to her neck himself, replacing the sword. "Get up. Now. Don't argue."

Seri's eyes widened, noticing the eidolon fading away, and scrambled out of the bed. Only then did she realize that she stood in her nightgown with a man in her bedroom. She folded her arms across her chest. "What are you doing?"

"Take me to the Otherworld. Now!" He pressed the dagger, moving closer beside her. He put the other hand on her shoulder. She trembled.

"Why? What good will that do?"

"The lives of all of your friends literally depend on it!" he hissed. "Do it now!"

Either his intensity or the dagger convinced her. She reached out with her hands and seemed to take hold of something he couldn't see. Purple fire and darkness enveloped both of them. For an instant, incredible pain permeated every inch of Volraag's body, and then they were through.

He and Seri stood in the midst of a pile of ruins in a strange half-light. Above them stretched a dark sky filled with the most enormous stars imaginable, twinkling in dozens of colors. Volraag stared in awe, forgetting the dagger.

Seri leaped a step away from him in her bare feet. "Ha! Just the passage filled me with as much power as a Lord, at least. We're on equal footing now!" She whirled back to face him, her nightgown shimmering in the starlight.

"Glad to hear it. Now duck!"

• • • • •

Marshal reached the stairs descending to the inner sanctum and paused. Curasir seemed distracted by something, speaking in a low voice to the nearest eidolon. Maybe Volraag was up to something?

"Keep going," Curasir ordered.

"What's happening?"

"We're about to transform the worlds," Curasir answered. "Nothing else matters."

As he started down the stairs, Marshal realized one problem with his plan. Until someone else showed up, he had no idea whether his friends remained in danger.

•••••

Seri could not believe Volraag's gall. Showing up in her bedroom and ordering her about while she was still in her nightgown! She had a mind to throw every bit of magic she could absorb at him.

But something in his voice made her obey his command this time. She ducked, but kept her eyes on him, star-sight active.

Volraag unleashed a wave of power in all directions at chest-height. From her point of view, it looked like he was using everything at his disposal in as powerful a burst as he could make it. The mixture of colors dazzled her. It wasn't on Marshal's level, but still impressive nonetheless.

She turned and saw Durunim falling from his attack in every direction. At least a half dozen had been scattered across the island. The nearest ones were cut in half by the force of Volraag's attack, while those further away were tossed into the air. None of them survived.

"There." Volraag dusted off his hands. "I've saved everyone. Marshal owes me now."

Seri straightened up. "What are you talking about?"

"And I saved you directly. In our world." He chuckled. "Guess that means you're Bonded to me."

Seri almost screamed in frustration, but she could feel it. He was right! "What is this? What happened?"

Volraag explained what he had seen and heard thus far. "And now I've removed the threats to all your friends," he concluded.

Seri considered. "But Curasir is still with Marshal." She looked down at her feet and frowned at the dust settling on them. Then she realized her feet were completely bare. And that she was wearing only a nightgown. And that Volraag's eyes were watching her. Could this be any more humiliating?

The ground shook. Seri wobbled, and Volraag caught her arm. "Earthquakes here too?" he grumbled.

"No! That's not normal..." Seri yanked her arm away from him and turned toward the heart of Zes Sivas. Her star-sight confirmed her worst fears: the swirling maelstrom of power at the center of the island… was shrinking, pulling in on itself.

"Marshal, what are you doing?" she moaned. She gathered up her power and whirled back to Volraag. "Hang on! I'm taking us back!"

"Wait, I—"

Purple flame and blackness enveloped them.

●●●●●

Marshal stood in the center of the inner sanctum, wearing only the loose pants he slept in. "You want me to do what?"

"All I ask is that you pull on the power of Zes Sivas," Curasir said. "Nothing more."

Marshal frowned. He reached out, both with his arms and his magical senses. He could feel the pulsing, enormous power of the heart of Zes Sivas, its magic pouring into this world. Tentatively, he grasped some of it and pulled toward himself, but it slipped from his hold.

"Try again," Curasir ordered.

Marshal wrapped his own magic around the incoming magic and pulled, but nowhere near as hard as he knew he could. Curasir's instructions didn't make a lot of sense. He could stall it, make it look like he was complying, while only doing the bare minimum.

"Yes, keep going," Curasir urged. "More!"

Marshal glanced at the Eldani mage. Surrounded by his three eidola, his face stood out pale in the shadows. His grin stretched from ear to ear, looking so out of place among all the angles on an Eldani face.

"What do you hope to accomplish with this?" Marshal asked, giving the magic another slight tug.

"All it takes is a little pull," Curasir said. "You've started the process. It won't take long before it reaches a point of no return."

Marshal dropped his hands and let the power fade. "No return for what?"

"The merging of the worlds," Curasir proclaimed. He lifted both arms into the air. "Think of it! One world! But with all the magic!"

"People live in the Otherworld!" Marshal took a step back from the center of the platform. "What will happen to them?"

"No one important remains there now," Curasir said, lowering his arms. "It doesn't matter."

"Doesn't matter?" Marshal clenched his fists. "You're asking me to kill thousands for the sake of my friends!"

"Hm, yes. I suppose I am. Are they that important to you, or not?" Curasir raised a hand. "I can give the order right now."

"No!" Marshal raised his own hands. "I don't—I mean, I'm not—How could such a simple action destroy an entire world?"

"Welcome to real power, Your Majesty. The King of Antises can move mountains. And in this case… destroy worlds."

"No. I can't." Marshal shook his head. He hadn't even expended that much power. How could this be true?

Curasir drew the King's sword and leveled it at him. He walked forward until the tip touched Marshal's bare chest. "You know what this sword is capable of," he whispered. "Should any of your friends somehow escape my soldiers, I will use this on them."

"If they escape, you have to deal with me," Marshal answered.

Curasir cocked his head. "Bold words. All it would take right now is a little push on my part." The pressure from the sword tip made Marshal take another step back, but Curasir followed him.

"I haven't been completely honest with you, oh King." He gestured back to his eidola. Two of them took position on either side of the sanctum's entrance, swords at ready. The third moved around behind Marshal.

"You see, one of your friends did escape, and I suspect will be rushing to your rescue here shortly." Curasir licked his thumb and rubbed at a spot on the sword's blade. "Except the moment anyone comes through that entrance, they're attacked and I… push."

"And then we all fight, and you don't get what you want," Marshal said. "What good is that?"

"You've started the process already." Curasir smiled again. "All I have to do now is wait."

A tremble rolled through the ground beneath them. Marshal's magical senses were going wild, not just from the proximity of the heart of Zes Sivas, but from its growth. Maybe he should have called Curasir's bluff sooner.

"Then why not leave now?" Marshal asked. "If you've already got what you want."

"Because I owe your little friend a debt." Curasir raised his right hand and for the first time, Marshal noticed the damaged skin all over it. "She burned me. I intend to burn her back."

At that exact moment, Volraag leaped into the room and landed in a crouch. He threw both hands outward to either side and power blasted out. He caught both eidola in mid-charge, throwing them back across the room and against opposite walls. Seri appeared behind him, clad only in her nightgown. She made a gesture with her hand, and Marshal heard a grunt behind him. The third eidolon. That left only Curasir for him.

At the first sound, Curasir stabbed forward. The tip of the sword pierced Marshal's skin, but stopped there, vibrating. Marshal glared at the Eldani mage. "You taught me yourself that my power doesn't have to come through my hands."

"Very clever, but I also taught you that the sword absorbs your power indefinitely. We are at an impasse, human."

"Are we?"

A blast of power struck Curasir from the side, knocking him away from Marshal. He managed to stay on his feet and held the sword up. Seri advanced from one direction, Volraag from another. Marshal took position in a third direction. Together, they stepped forward.

"I can absorb all of your magical attacks," Curasir said. "You know it, Marshal. And my ultimate victory still comes, even now!"

As if in answer, the ground shook again.

"Whatever you did, undo it!" Seri shouted. "It's more important than him!"

Marshal stepped back onto the central platform and concentrated. How to reverse the flow of power? Pushing didn't seem right. How could one push against a fountain exploding upward? "I need to get to the other side! Cross over and pull the power back!"

"I'll clear the way for you," Curasir called. He waved and started to turn, about to shift to the Otherworld, like he always did.

In that moment, Volraag struck. Rather than blasting at the Eldani with his power, he used it to blast himself across the room. He stabbed the dagger into Curasir's neck. "Absorb this!" he snarled, his hand shaking with power.

Curasir's head exploded in a bloody mess. The King's sword clattered to the ground, followed a moment late by Curasir's headless body.

Seri stared, her mouth open in shock. Spatters of blood decorated the front of her nightgown. "You... you..."

Volraag picked up the King's sword and looked at it. For a moment, Marshal thought the battle would start up again, but with a different opponent. Instead, Volraag held the sword out toward Marshal. "I believe this is yours."

Marshal took it and nodded. No time for words. He focused and cut a new portal to the Starlit Realm. He stepped through into a trembling world. Everything was shaking.

He could solve this. He had to. He reached out for the magic, calling it to himself.

Seri came through the portal, followed by Volraag. "You can't just run off on your own!" she scolded. "I can help you!"

"Then do it!" Marshal said through gritted teeth. It wasn't working as easily as it had on the other side. When he thought he had a hold on the magic, it slid out of his grasp and vanished into the primary world.

"Give me your hand!" Seri grabbed his and began gesturing with her other hand. As before, their powers merged, allowing him to see as she did, a spinning cacophony of light and color surrounding them. Her gestures absorbed beam after beam of multi-colored light. And beyond that, he saw the maelstrom of Zes Sivas, appearing as thought it collapsed in on itself.

"How do we stop it?"

"Dravid's power would come in really handy right now," Seri muttered. "All right. Together, draw the power toward us. Pull it in."

Marshal knew that Seri and the other mages did this kind of thing all the time. With his power amplifying hers, maybe it would work. He focused on working in unison. His power alone wasn't enough.

"It's working!" Seri cried. "But not enough. Keep trying!"

Marshal wasn't sure how she could even tell. To him, it all still looked like a huge mess of light and color.

"Give me your other hand," Volraag growled on Seri's other side. They both looked toward him. "I'm a Lord, you know. Use my power too."

Seri grabbed his hand. Immediately, the light and color spinning around the two of them embraced him as well. All three of them focused on Zes Sivas, trying to pull its power toward them. Ever so slowly, the appearance of collapse began to change. Marshal couldn't be sure, but it looked like it might be all right.

"Is that it?" he asked.

"It's looking normal again," Seri said. "But keep going a moment longer to be sure."

To Marshal, the maelstrom of power looked like it was unraveling. Was that "normal"? When last in the Otherworld here, he hadn't paid much attention to the island's power. Tich had distracted him by diving through his portal.

"That should do it!" Seri released both of their hands and stepped back.

The vision of color faded from Marshal's view. Worn out, he put both hands on his knees and took several deep breaths.

"Was the danger really that great?" he asked after a moment of rest.

"I don't know for sure," Seri answered, "but it looked really bad. Curasir wanted to merge the worlds."

"And it was that easy?"

She looked at him. "For you, maybe it was. I keep telling you that your power is unbelievable."

Marshal closed his eyes, partly from weariness, and partly to keep from looking at Seri in her blood-spattered nightgown. He wondered if she realized how she appeared.

"The salt is gone," Volraag said.

Marshal turned. His half-brother stood several feet away, staring up at the stars. "What do you mean?" Seri asked.

Volraag rotated slowly. "Ever since I absorbed the Eldanim power, I've had this... salty taste in my mouth. When we crossed over here, it vanished."

"Fascinating." Seri rubbed her face with one hand. "I wonder if Eldanim have the same sensation in our world. I'll have to ask Talinir sometime."

Volraag looked at her. "I envy you," he said. "You're the child of both worlds. You must feel at home in either one." He looked around at the devastation and the stars. "I don't feel at home in either."

Marshal wrinkled his brow. Why was Volraag being so... vulnerable? It wasn't like him at all. Unless combining his power with theirs made him absorb some of Seri's personality, at least temporarily? He had to admit he always felt... different, after they did that.

"We can't stay here," he announced, picking up the sword again. "All of this power will draw predators, and probably very soon." He started to create a new doorway. "And I'm sure Seri wants to change clothes."

Her expression as her eyes widened was completely worth it.

•••••

Seri couldn't believe Marshal had said that. Change clothes indeed! He should talk. He wasn't even wearing a shirt. And it showed off all his muscles… and more scars. The fresh one across his back still looked horrible. Strange to think it had been inflicted by the sword he now used.

Stepping through Marshal's doorways provided a much more pleasant experience than her own travels between the worlds. She breathed a sigh of relief at the simplicity of it all… and lack of excruciating pain.

No sooner did they re-appear in the inner sanctum of Zes Sivas than Ixchel came bounding down the stairs into the room. She rushed toward Volraag, sword raised, face clenched in fury.

"Ixchel, wait!" Seri shouted.

Her bodyguard came to a halt, sword only a few inches from Volraag's chest. He looked at it with a mild expression. "As hard as this may be to believe, Holcan," he said, "I'm the one who just saved all of you."

"He did," Marshal agreed. "And I am immensely grateful."

Volraag turned his head toward the King. "How grateful?" His voice sounded tired. His face was devoid of its usual arrogance.

"When your case comes before the Lords, I will do everything in my power to preserve your life," Marshal promised.

Volraag gave a short nod. He licked his lips. "The salt is back," he muttered.

Tich burst into the room a moment later. Seri frowned. Why was she fully dressed? Did she sleep in those clothes? Tich came to a halt and looked over everyone in the room.

"Are we having some kind of bed clothes party? Am I overdressed?"

Marshal laughed. "Come here!" He ran to her and pulled her to him. Seri felt a twinge of something. Not jealousy, surely. Maybe envy? "I am so happy to see you alive!" Marshal kept laughing.

"Oh. Are you referring to that shadow thing with the sword? I had just figured out how to escape it when it shot through the wall like something threw it."

"That was me," Volraag offered with a wave. He sat down on the edge of the central platform. Ixchel stood above him, refusing to take her eyes from him.

"Really? Huh."

Dravid stumbled in next, followed by Adhi.

"Are you all right?" Dravid demanded, hurrying toward Seri.

"I, I'm fine," she said, then shivered. His eyes wandered over her. How she must look to him!

"Here." Adhi removed his own shirt and threw it over her shoulders. She smiled and pulled it across her chest with folded arms.

Marshal looked around. "Has anyone seen Victor? Or Jamana?"

"Jamana is still sound asleep," Adhi reported. "I woke up with a bhoot standing over me with a sword. And then it was gone."

"Same here," Dravid said.

"Bhoot?" Tich repeated. "You call them bhoots?"

"I would greatly appreciate it if you would check on Victor," Marshal said to Adhi. The acolyte nodded and ran back up the stairs.

"What happened?" Dravid asked. "There's clearly a… story here." He looked at Curasir's headless body, Volraag, and then back at Seri. She ducked her head, cheeks flaming, and pulled Adhi's shirt tighter.

"Curasir had one more scheme to force me to do his bidding," Marshal explained. "Thanks to Volraag, he failed." He glanced at the body. "And he'll never trouble us again."

"I guess not," Tich muttered. "Did you do that?"

"That was me again," Volraag called without looking up.

"Now that I believe."

Seri looked up and saw Tich running her hand across Marshal's bare chest. He took it and turned to face everyone else. "I think it's best if we all go back to bed," he said. "We have an enormous day ahead of us tomorrow. Volraag, I'm sorry, but I'll need you to return to your cell for now. Ixchel?"

"Get up," she told him. He complied without saying anything. Together, they left the sanctum.

Seri shivered again. So strange to see Volraag behave like that. Almost like seeing the Otherworld had broken something in him. And what had he called her? "Child of both worlds"? She hadn't thought about it that way, but it sort of made sense. If the gods were meant to live in the Otherworld, and humans in the primary world, she was both. But the Eldanim lived in both: a third race. She had no connection to them. They were the true children of both worlds, weren't they?

She looked up to see Dravid watching her anxiously. He looked like he wanted to hug her, but was afraid to, probably because of her clothes. And the blood. "I'll be all right, Dravid," she told him again. "Really. It was just… intense."

Adhi returned. "Victor is snoring," he said.

Marshal smiled and nodded. "Time for the rest of us to join him. Dravid, please make sure Seri gets to her room."

"And I'll make sure you get to yours," Tich added.

Marshal didn't argue.

As they moved up the stairs out of the sanctum, Seri recalled Volraag's words about the salt. If he did have Eldanim power within him, perhaps seeing the Otherworld had awakened something in that power, or pulled at it somehow. That would explain his sudden melancholy. As if... he saw a possibility of something amazing... and instantly understood it could never be his.

Seri almost felt like crying.

<h1 style="text-align:center">(((39)))</h1>

Marshal would have been preferred to skip all the pomp and formality of the Passing and just do the job. But that was apparently too much to ask of the Lords and Masters. This was the way it had been done for centuries; it must be done this way now.

On the six platforms representing each of the lands, the Masters knelt, waiting and meditating. Dravid waited back behind Seri. Marshal and Seri insisted on his presence, but the other Masters protested strongly. Marshal himself waited in the central platform.

Master Ganak rose and joined him. He spread his arms and looked up. "The hour has come!" he proclaimed. "Beneath Theon's light, let the power of Antises return to its home and heal our land!"

The other Masters murmured their agreement.

"Let the Lords of Antises come forward!"

The door to the sanctum opened to reveal Lord Tyrr, reflecting the light in a shining uniform of gold and bronze. Marshal stifled a laugh. The costume was so different to the Lord's usual pragmatism.

"From the land of Rasna, we welcome Lord Tyrr!" Master Ganak proceeded with the introductions as each Lord entered the room and took his place at the platform for his land.

"From the land of Ch'olan, we welcome Lord Rajwir!"

Lord Rajwir, complete in his feather headdress and endless jewels, walked past the empty platform for Varioch and took his place.

"From the land of Mandiata, we welcome Lord Bakari!"

Marshal shifted his stance and watched the young, powerless Lord enter. His father's tiger pelt was too large for him, but he insisted on wearing it. Ixchel escorted Volraag in behind Lord Bakari. Once he was in position, she left the room. The other Lords might be nervous about

Volraag being loose, but after the previous night's adventure, Marshal trusted him to keep the peace this once.

"From the land of Arazu, we welcome Lady Lilitu!"

"Lady" had always been the title for the wife of a Lord. How did they distinguish that from the power Lilitu truly held now? Marshal suspected the Masters simply didn't care. He hadn't heard any of them refer to Seri as a "Master" yet, come to think of it.

Though all eyes in the room were already fixed on the door, Lady Lilitu drew extra attention. She glided into the sanctum wearing a shimmering yellow gown which left only her right arm and shoulder bare. Her long dark hair had been braided with gold beneath an oval frontlet of thin gold plate. A single white crystal shone from the center of the frontlet. Her ears, neck and wrists gleamed with more gold. Marshal couldn't help thinking she might be the most beautiful woman in the world.

Master Ganak swallowed, and continued: "From the land of Kuktarma, we welcome Lord Meluhha!"

Marshal had seen Lord Meluhha's finery multiple times now, but he couldn't help raising his eyebrows at the size of the crown the Lord wore.

"Finally, we recognize the Lord of Varioch and presumed King of all Antises, Marshal!"

Presumed?

"Most here have acknowledged you as King," Ganak said quietly. "Today, you dispel all doubt and truly claim the title." He left the center and took his place on Kuktarma's platform. Master Tzoyet took his place beside Marshal.

"As the most senior Master of the Conclave, it falls on me to facilitate this occasion. Our time is precious. Lord Tyrr, if you will begin the process?"

Lord Tyrr stepped to the edge of his platform. After a glare in Volraag's direction and a brief glance at Marshal, he raised his hands and closed his eyes. On the central dais, in front of Marshal and Master Tzoyet, golden light pooled. It spread outward in a slow growth. Marshal watched, his impatience increasing with every moment. He glanced toward Seri. She returned his look. The process had begun. There was no turning back now.

●●●●●

Victor tried to skip a stone across the lake, but the gentle waves kept him from getting more than two skips. He twisted his neck with an audible pop.

"Ouch," Adhi said. "Didn't that hurt?"

"Nah, I do it all the time." He glanced at the Citadel of Mages. "Do you suppose they've started by now?"

"I am certain," Jamana answered. "But it will take quite some time."

The three young men stood outside, near the southern dock of Zes Sivas. Victor had suggested going outside, and Jamana had recommended this spot.

Tich and Ixchel emerged from the citadel and walked down to join them. "It has begun," Ixchel confirmed.

No one said anything. Tich wandered off to look at the cypress trees. Jamana took a seat on the ground, gazing out over the water. Adhi stood near him, arms folded, a pensive look on his face.

Ixchel came to stand beside Victor. He watched her for a minute.

"Have you spoken with him?" he asked at last.

"I have not," Ixchel answered. "Why do you keep asking?"

"Because he's your father," Victor said. Her attitude perplexed him. "Why don't you want to get to know him?"

"I've told you. He abandoned me as a child. He is a murderer. Cursed twice over. I do not wish to speak with such a one."

"You know…" Victor bent and picked up another stone. "If Marshal is successful, Kishin will lose his curse again."

"And then he will murder again. Without consequence."

"I don't know about that." Victor threw the stone as hard as he could and watched it arc out over the water. "I think he's really changed now. Did those two tell you what he did?" He gestured to Adhi and Jamana.

"They did."

"And that didn't change your mind?"

"No."

Victor felt like throwing up his hands. "What do you want from him? What can he do to get your attention?"

Ixchel didn't answer at first. At last, she turned her eyes on his. "I do not know how to answer that."

"I don't—" Victor broke off, then tried again: "I can't begin to understand what it was like to, to be abandoned by your father like that. I can't. But… I also can't understand not having mercy on him when he wants to be different."

"That is what this is all about," Jamana said softly. Victor hadn't realized the acolyte could hear them. "Mercy, not compulsion."

"That may be true," Ixchel said. "But I do not know how to change what I feel."

Tich strolled back toward them. "Hey, do you notice the wind is picking up?"

Victor frowned at the interruption. But now that she said it, he could feel the force of the wind against his face. In fact, it seemed to be growing by the second.

"An east wind," Adhi noted.

Jamana got to his feet. "They're coming."

• • • • •

Seri watched Lord Tyrr finish letting his power flow out. When he lowered his hands, he stepped back and almost fell. Master Plecu caught him, though not without effort. Just like the last Passing. Except this time, Lord Tyrr shook Master Plecu off and regained his balance. He glared in the direction of Volraag.

Marshal and Master Tzoyet stepped further back to make room for the image of Lord Tyrr's power: a square-shaped floor of glowing, pulsing liquid light, each side a dozen feet in length.

At a call from Master Tzoyet, Lord Rajwir raised his hands and began the process. As he focused, the light grew straight up from one edge of Lord Tyrr's square. When he finished, a vertical wall of light formed the second section of the growing cube.

"Volraag. It is time," Master Tzoyet said.

Marshal's half-brother looked around the room. Then with a resigned slump of his shoulders, he stepped forward and raised his hands. Seri found it curious how even the newest Lords knew instinctively how to perform this process. Perhaps the magic itself informed them.

Lord Bakari stood a few steps behind Volraag on Mandiata's platform, a satisfied smile on his face. When this was done, the power would flow to him. Or so they all believed, anyway.

When he finished, Volraag staggered back. Master Magnus crossed over to assist him, and Volraag followed him back to Varioch's platform.

Lady Lilitu was next, and performed exactly as the others. When she was done, she fell back. Seri caught her, as was her duty, surprised at how light she felt. She considered the oddity of herself here as Master, helping out the Lady, her own mother. She wondered if such a relationship had ever existed at the Passing before. Well, not mother-daughter at any rate. Perhaps father-son.

Lord Meluhha released his power next. The cube of light lacked only a roof now.

As it had the last time, the power radiating from the cube filled Seri's body and mind, overwhelming her senses. And Marshal hadn't even gone yet! She helped Lady Lilitu take a seat on the edge of her platform, and then turned to watch the next stage.

"The Passing awaits the Heart of Fire," Master Tzoyet announced. "And the power of Varioch."

Marshal stood only inches away from the light. He lifted his left hand and closed his eyes. In moments, the roof of the cube formed, spreading more rapidly than any of the previous Lords' work. It now stood complete, a solid cube of pure light, six sides of radiant magical energy.

Marshal lowered his left hand and raised his right. This time, his scarred face took on a firmer look. His jaw set and his closed eyes clenched tighter. Within the cube of light, another light burst into existence. Like Tezan's false attempt last year, this light shone red, a sparkling, growing heart of red flame. It appeared to fold in on itself every few seconds, even as it grew, slowly filling the interior of the cube.

Seri gasped as the process changed from Tezan's. The cube itself lifted from the platform and began to rotate in the air. The Heart of Fire filled it completely, pulsing, glowing, spinning, folding, and radiating such a massive amount of power everyone else in the room fell to their knees.

Marshal stumbled back a step and lowered his arm, but did not kneel. He opened his eyes and stared at the Heart of Fire. Seri didn't blame him. With or without her star-sight, it was the most beautiful thing she had ever seen. She lost track of how long she knelt in place, gazing at it in awe.

Marshal turned to look at her. With a start, she remembered their goal. She got to her feet and looked back at Dravid. He nodded, and pulled himself up as well. She turned to look at Volraag. She still didn't know what his role would be, but Evander said they needed him.

She locked eyes with Volraag. The Bond screamed inside her head and yanked her toward him. And Lord Tyrr plunged a dagger into his back.

<h1 style="text-align:center">(((40)))</h1>

Talinir, High Champion of Intal Eldanir, counted the wardens assembled in the city's largest open area. Harunir told him at least five thousand Eldanim were trained as either wardens, mages, or warriors. Less than half that many gathered before him now. He wondered about the rest, but had no time to worry over it.

"Every Eldani fighter is worth several humans," he told himself. But they weren't fighting humans; they were fighting Durunim, former Eldanim themselves. But with their free will removed, their fighting prowess couldn't equal that of trained Eldanim wardens. In addition, a dozen wardens, the front line of their army, had been equipped with Stars of Indalanim, all that could be found. They would be shielded from Durunim blades, but not the magic of the gods.

Talinir didn't know how powerful Harunir's mages were, but he doubted they were on the same level as the gods. But maybe combined with Marshal and the Lords, they had a chance.

Now they needed to get from Intal Eldanir all the way to Zes Sivas. He only hoped Marshal could hold out until they arrived.

• • • • •

Victor shielded his eyes against the wind. "What do you mean? 'They're coming'?"

"This wind is from Namnirnu," Jamana explained. "He's clearing the way for their army."

"How—" Victor broke off as he saw what it all meant.

The most powerful wind concentrated in a narrow zone, perhaps a hundred feet wide. Victor and the others moved outside of it, right up against the citadel's outer wall. Even there, the wind's force felt stronger than any storm he had endured.

But where the strongest wind blew, the water of Lake Litanu shifted. As they watched, the waves stopped lapping against the shore and began flowing in opposite directions to either side. The water level receded, forming a trough that grew steadily deeper.

"What are you doing here?" Ixchel's voice demanded to his right.

Victor turned and saw Kishin hobbling toward them. He leaned on his staff, buffeted by the wind. He paused and pointed at the trough in the water. "The gods are coming. We all must be prepared to fight."

"You are in no condition to fight," Ixchel said. "You should go back inside."

Kishin shook his head. "I will not wait within stone walls for death to come to me. I will face it here."

Ixchel flinched and spun away from him.

Victor turned back and saw that the trough had deepened, already exposing the earth nearest to the island. And then it grew wider, and wider. He couldn't imagine the amount of power it took to do something like this. Could Marshal do this? He had torn the earth itself apart multiple times. But water? Somehow that seemed... harder.

"This is insane," Tich said. No one responded. They all felt the same way.

Victor blinked and snapped out of his awe. "Tich, go tell Marshal and the Lords. I don't care if you have to interrupt their Passing thing. They need to know. Adhi, you and Jamana—"

"The Lords will be unable to help us," Adhi interrupted. "They have released their power now and will not regain it for another hour or two. Even then, they will be exhausted."

"What about the Masters?"

"They should be all right."

"Then tell them, Tich. Just go. And you two, gather the rest of the mages. Anyone with power. We have to be ready to take a stand."

The three of them dashed away, leaving Victor with Ixchel and Kishin. The trough in the water was now several dozen feet wide. Victor could see more and more of the ground. Very soon, there would be a complete path to the island, wide enough for an army to march through.

"What can we do?" Ixchel asked.

"I don't know."

•••••

Seri opened her mouth to scream, but no sound came out. Lord Tyrr twisted the dagger with a brutal grin, wrenching Volraag up and then dropping him to Varioch's platform. Master Magnus scrambled to Volraag's side as Tyrr stepped back.

"What have you done?" Marshal whispered in the silence that followed.

Still holding the dripping dagger, Lord Tyrr returned to his own platform. "Justice is served!" he announced. "The rest of you wanted to debate over it. I took action." He pointed around the room at each of the other Lords. "Don't pretend any of you didn't want to do the same!"

"That wasn't justice! That was murder!" Seri shouted. She circled the Heart of Fire and ran to Volraag's side. Was he still breathing? Maybe Dravid could save him.

But when she saw him up close, she knew. It was too late. Volraag lay on his side, left arm sprawled out, right arm held against his chest. As Seri fell to her knees beside him, he coughed. Blood spattered from his mouth.

"I, I'm sorry," she said. "We didn't anticipate…"

"S-seri," he choked. "Take it."

Take it? Take what?

He lifted his bloody hand up toward her. It shook as he managed to whisper: "The… power. Eldanim."

"I'm not Tezan," she protested. "I can't…" But maybe she could.

Pushing down her gag reflex, she took hold of his hand, holding it in spite of the blood. He coughed again and more blood erupted from his mouth. An exclamation escaped Seri's lips.

She blinked to activate her star-sight, and focused on his hand. His body, usually glowing with the Lord's power, appeared dark and empty now, except… a purple glow, very faint, that permeated his bloodstream. Purple, like the fire between the worlds.

"T-take," Volraag repeated.

It couldn't be as easy as her usual method, could it? She grasped his hand tighter, feeling the slickness of his blood. Taking a deep breath, she twisted her fingers, trying to pull. At first, nothing happened. And then a trickle of… something began to flow into her.

For an instant, Seri felt stronger, almost invincible. A warm glow spread throughout her body. She stared at her own skin. Her star-sight gave it a soft glow. A salty taste filled her mouth. She licked her lips, craving something sweet.

Her star-sight shifted strangely. The world looked... off. As if the light wasn't hitting everything right. And then she saw the Starlit Realm overlapping their own. Like one of the Eldanim, she saw both worlds at once. The confusion of imagery overwhelmed her mind and she slammed her eyes closed. How could the Eldanim bear it? Even with her eyes closed, she saw the stars. One in particular moved out of its position.

And then it was over. She opened her eyes and everything looked normal again. Volraag looked up at her. "End it," he whispered. And his head fell back. His hand went limp in hers and slipped out. It fell to the floor. He didn't move again.

Volraag was dead.

"The curse," Marshal murmured.

Seri's eyes widened. "The Bond!"

•••••

Aluri, daughter of Lord Tyrr, sat before her mirror, brushing her hair. The latest reports from the generals lay on her desk beside her hair ribbons. In the Lord's absence, she had many responsibilities, and the location of the Durunim armies was pre-eminent. At dawn, she had received report of an attack on a town about twenty miles west of Raeton itself. She had dispatched new scouts to locate the enemy. If they came any closer, she would have to summon her father back from Zes Sivas at once. Without his power, the army did not stand much of a chance against the dark warriors and their god masters.

Satisfied with her hair's appearance, she set her brush aside and reached for the powders she used on her face. The generals wouldn't care much about her face, of course, but the rest of the palace staff would take immediate notice if she neglected any of her usual preparation. She needed to appear above the problems, as well as maintain her reputation of beauty.

She dipped her brush in the specially-prepared powder for whitening her face's complexion. Some women used enormous amounts of this powder, but Aluri preferred just a touch. She raised the brush to her forehead and stopped.

A blemish had appeared on her forehead, a very large one, in fact. She frowned. How had she missed that? She leaned in toward the mirror to get a closer look.

The blemish doubled in size.

Aluri gasped and recoiled from the mirror. What was happening? She looked again and a second blemish appeared on her cheek. Both of them grew, even as she watched, turning an ugly purple and red, expanding into grotesque bubble-looking deformities.

"No," she whispered.

She yanked up the sleeve of her gown, revealing three more of the deformities. At the same moment, the pain began. Everywhere one of the deformities appeared, a throbbing pain erupted: not agonizing, but sensitive and searing, not unlike light burns.

"What have you done?" she moaned, putting her face in her hands.

She grabbed her hairbrush and threw it at the mirror. "Father, what have you done?" she screamed.

•••••

"We need more time," Victor muttered, glaring against the wind. He and Ixchel walked to the edge of the island and looked down the newly formed path through the water.

To his surprise, the surface appeared mostly smooth. A few rocks protruded from the ground here and there, but they lacked any sharp edges. Most were covered in some kind of moss or other plant life. Trickles ran here and there, settling into small puddles, depending on the angles of the surface.

Directly in front of them, the ground sloped down about five feet, and then plunged off an abrupt incline before resuming a slow sloping. The water of the lake formed two walls, growing higher and higher as the path descended. Victor could only imagine how deep Lake Litanu reached.

"It looks dry enough to walk on," Ixchel observed.

"Yeah." Victor peered ahead. "And that's what they're doing. I can't quite tell, but I think I can see the beginnings of the army there."

Ixchel nodded. "They are coming."

Victor ran a hand along his facial hair. "Once they get here, it'll be too late. If the gods and Durunim are unleashed on this island..."

"Without the power of the Lords, it will be a slaughter," Ixchel finished.

Victor took a deep breath. He knew what needed to be done. If he had learned anything from Marshal over this past year, it was that one man could make a difference.

He looked over his shoulder. "Tich is taking too long. Maybe you should go after her and make sure the Lords listen."

"Marshal will listen to her."

"I know, but I'm thinking he's pretty busy right now. I should have sent Adhi instead of Tich."

Ixchel hesitated. She looked out toward the approaching army, then back at Victor. "Do you want me to go?"

"Yes." The answer came too fast. "I mean, I'm worried, so you should go. And you can be back quicker too."

"What are you going to do?" She looked at him with narrowed eyebrows.

Before she could react, Victor reached out, pulled her head to him and kissed her. Her eyes widened and she yanked herself free.

"We might not get a chance later," Victor said before she could ask. He turned back to watch, hoping she wouldn't say anything else.

He breathed a sigh of relief when he heard her footsteps padding away. He looked back until she disappeared into the citadel.

"What *are* you going to do?" asked Kishin. Victor had almost forgotten he was there.

"Something stupid, no doubt."

Kishin nodded. "I would come with you, if I thought..."

"You stay here," Victor warned him. "Someone needs to explain to Ixchel when she comes back."

"I know my opinion matters little to my daughter, but..." Kishin looked down and winced as he shifted his stance. "I would welcome a union between the two of you. You have proven yourself an honorable man."

"That... thank you." Victor took a deep breath. "Honorable and stupid."

"The two often go together."

Victor laughed. He walked forward to the edge of the incline. He sat down on the dirt and slid forward. His descent lasted about a dozen feet. The ground gave way under his boots, but not by much. The magical wind seemed to be drying it.

Victor stood and dusted himself off. He unhooked his flail and held it in his left hand, then drew his sword with the right. With a deep breath, he began walking.

He could see the army now, in the distance. If he could get close enough, he might be able to do some damage to their front lines at least. Slow them down just enough for Marshal and the Lords to regain their powers.

"For Antises."

(((41)))

Seri's head exploded in violent pain. This time, she knew the cause: her Bond to Volraag.

Amid the excruciating horror in her mind, her chest heaved. Her heart felt drawn, pulled toward Volraag's body on the floor. The pull became as unbearable as the pain in her head, and then… it snapped.

Seri fell back. She had experienced all of this when Master Hain died, but it didn't make it any easier. Her chest felt like every rib inside had shattered. Masters Plecu and Magnus stood over her, trying to speak to her, but she couldn't hear them.

Her mind filled with memories of Volraag: her first sight of him when he arrived on Zes Sivas with his father, his subsequent rescue of her from Varion's attempted rape, confiding in him about Tezan, fighting against him so many times, arguing with him on the ship, and his final moments of giving her the Eldanim power. Yet even as these memories flooded her, they became twisted with new, more devastating outcomes: Volraag laughed as Varion assaulted her, his own father turned and killed him, Rathri the assassin cut off his head, and most disturbing of all… an image of Marshal blowing his half-brother apart with magic.

"No," she whispered, knowing what came next. Something came for her, something deadly and unbelievably powerful. She lifted her head and stared with her star-sight.

The creature of flame and magic incarnate stood beside the Heart of Fire. It ignored Marshal and reached toward her.

"I'm innocent!" Seri cried. "I tried to save him!"

The being paused, but did not fade away as it had the last time she resisted. The pain in her head and chest lessened, but the being continued to stand there. It had no eyes she could see, but she got the distinct impression it was studying her.

In her first encounter with this thing, she thought it similar to the stars of the Otherworld. Now that she had the chance to see it again, it confirmed her thoughts.

She glanced around. Everyone else, Marshal included, appeared almost insubstantial. She hadn't crossed into the Otherworld, but neither did she seem to be fully in the primary world.

"Are you one of the stars?" she asked, staring up at the majestic being of light.

For a long time, she received no answer. Then: "You possess all three." Its voice did not reach her ears, but appeared inside her mind with a burst of vibration that shook her skull.

Three? What did she possess… oh! "You mean all three powers!"

The being did not respond.

"Is that important? Do I need to do something for you?"

The light began to fade. As it did, the rest of the room grew more solid.

"Wait!" Seri cried. "We need your help!"

The light seemed to flicker, then shone directly in her face. Did that mean something? Was it…?

And suddenly she knew.

The being faded completely from view. The inner sanctum and everyone within looked solid and normal again. The Masters of Varioch and Rasna stood over her, concern on their faces. Marshal stood before the Heart of Fire, mesmerized.

And Seri knew. She *knew* what they needed to do.

•••••

Marshal looked at the body of his half-brother. Somehow, it didn't seem real. He felt loss, but… muted, for some reason. Seri struggled with something beyond his view, but it didn't seem all that important right now.

Volraag had been his last known living relative. Did he have other siblings? Other children of Varion somewhere? Perhaps he should seek them out someday. The thoughts flowed through his mind in a turbulent rush.

Such a waste. Volraag had held such potential. If he had waited, used his considerable abilities and intellect against his own father, in support of the people, he might have gone far. Marshal thought he caught a glimpse of the man Volraag could have been last night, fighting against Curasir.

And Lord Tyrr. He had no concern that his actions would curse one of his children. If he lost all his power because of Marshal's actions, all the better.

He turned back to the Heart of Fire. This was all that mattered now.

When he had formed the Heart in Kuktarma, or rather, between the worlds as Seri described it, it appeared pure, bright, a living thing, an extension of himself. All of those things held true now, but somehow even more. Beautiful, awesome, thrilling. He couldn't think of enough words to describe it. Back then, he had wanted to merge himself into it, become one with the power. Now, that desire filled him. He could think of nothing he wanted more.

"Sorry to interrupt, everyone!" Tich's voice intruded on his reverie. "But there's an army walking through the water toward us right now!"

• • • • •

Victor didn't feel much like a hero. In fact, he felt mostly like an idiot. What could he do, alone, against an army of Durunim and gods? Sure, he carried the only weapon they knew that could harm one of the gods, but he had to hit one first. And to do that, he'd have to get up close, past the Durunim. Could he do that, without getting killed first?

"I'm an idiot," he said aloud.

"No argument there."

Victor almost jumped into the wall of water. "Ixchel! How—what—" She walked at his side like she'd been there all along.

"You're an idiot," she repeated. "You thought you could get rid of me and do this alone."

"I, I wanted you safe."

"Got that. Not your job." She spoke without looking at him, her eyes fixed on the army in the distance.

"Maybe I want it to be my job."

She finally turned to look at him. "You're a good man, Victor."

For perhaps the first time in his life, Victor blushed.

"But it's not your job. Not now. Maybe not ever." She tapped her shield with her sword. "I do have a job. I have to keep Seri safe. That puts me in danger. You can't keep me safe while I'm doing that."

Victor pointed at the army with his sword. "Is this part of keeping

Seri safe?"

"They're her enemies, aren't they?"

He grinned. "You're justifying it. You would be in a better position to stay by her side and protect her until the end."

Ixchel snorted. "Maybe I'm just being pre-emptive."

"Maybe… or maybe you didn't like seeing me walk off to my death."

She kept walking. "I don't know what you're talking about."

Victor kept the grin on his face and picked up his pace to keep up with her.

•••••

Tich's words created chaos in the inner sanctum. The Lords shouted at each other and the Masters. The Masters called for calm, but ran around the room talking to each other.

Through it all, Marshal kept staring at the Heart of Fire. He lifted his right hand and reached for it. He touched the outer wall of the cube… actually, "diamond" would be a more accurate description now that it had rotated. A tremor ran through his arm. It felt not unlike his earliest experiences with magic.

In fact, Marshal realized, his whole body felt like the day they left Drusa's Crossing. Tingles spread through his fingers, like thousands of tiny needles pricking his skin, just like those early days. Back when life was simple, when he knew nothing about his ancestry except his mother Aelia, before he ever met one of the Eldanim, or fought a curse-stalker, or channeled unbelievable power through his body.

Back when he was cursed. When he lived his life in silence, unable to communicate, because his father had committed horrible crimes.

Marshal's face hardened. It had to end. No matter what was happening now with the Lords, the Masters, even the gods… he had to end the curses. He pressed his hand harder against the outer wall of the Heart. It pressed back against him, shaking his arm.

"What's he doing?" Tich's voice again.

"He's about to change the world," Seri said. "Marshal, wait. I know what to do."

Seri's voice continued to go on, talking to Dravid and Tich. Had the others all left the room? He didn't turn to see. His eyes, his entire focus, remained on the Heart of Fire.

"You have a purpose in this world," Aelia always told him. This was it. This was his purpose.

Seri stepped up on his left. "Got us, Dravid? All right. Here we go. Marshal, give me your hand." When he didn't move, she took his left hand in her right. Then she reached up and grasped his right wrist. "Ready? Just a moment…"

Their powers merged again, or at least Seri's merged with him. All of his power now resided outside his body. The rest of the room faded even further, while the Heart of Fire grew brighter, if that were possible.

"Here!" Seri thrust his hand forward. This time, it pushed through the outer wall of light with only a tingling. His fingers brushed against the Heart itself.

Power flowed back into his body, rushed through every bit of his existence, then rushed back out. It continued, forming a loop of power from the Heart, into him, and back.

"We need to hurry!" Seri urged. "Just push!"

He needed no more encouragement. Marshal shoved his hand into the Heart, stepping forward as he did. This time, the power, the red folding flames, reached back for him, enveloped him completely, and pulled him in.

Marshal stepped into the Heart of Fire.

•••••

Otioch, leader of Varioch's Remavian Guard, took the tower steps two at a time in his haste to reach the top. After ensuring the safety of the Lord's family, the Guard was charged with protecting the palace itself. With all the enemies about, he had no time for a mysterious summons to the top of the palace's highest tower.

He burst out onto the roof of the tower. A single figure stood at the wall, facing southwest. Otioch recognized him at once.

"General Cassian! What is the meaning of this? Why did you send for me?"

"Because you needed to see it for yourself," the general answered, stepping back.

"See what?"

General Cassian made a broad gesture. Otioch stepped to the wall and looked down. He gripped the stone wall and stared, unable to believe what he saw. An army stood less than a mile from the city of Reman. Half of them lined up in ranks, ready to attack. The rest spread out in either direction, moving to flank and surround the city.

"Who are they? It can't be Rasna! Not a force of this size!" Otioch tried to calculate it from his position, but the distance kept him from an accurate count. Thousands, at the very least.

"They are the ones Master Magnus warned us about before he left," General Cassian said. "The dark Eldanim, led by one or more of the ancient gods."

"We must send a message to Zes Sivas at once, tell the Lords. Surely, they will…" Otioch trailed off as Cassian shook his head.

"The mages say the message system is broken. They don't know why. Something happened in Zes Sivas. We are without a Lord, without a Master mage, or any other truly powerful help here."

"You… I… I assume you have soldiers taking position at the city walls?"

General Cassian nodded. "We are doing everything we can do. But it is pointless. The walls will not stand against the likes of that." He pointed toward the army. "When they decide to attack, the city will fall."

"Then we have no hope?"

Cassian took a step closer and spoke quietly, though the chance of anyone else hearing them was impossible. "I brought you here so that you can make a decision. If I were you, I would take what is left of the Lord's family and leave as soon as possible."

Otioch watched the enemy moving around the city. "And where would we go? You say Zes Sivas may be in trouble itself. We could flee toward Ch'olan, but I am not certain that any relatives of Lord Volraag would be welcome in any other land now."

"Volraag abandoned his land," Cassian declared. "He may be dead, for all we know."

"No," Otioch decided. "The Guard will secure the family here within the palace, however we can. We will defend them with our lives at the last. And we will hope. And pray."

"Pray for what?"

Otioch turned back to the stairs. "A miracle."

(((42)))

Namnirnu, supreme leader of the pantheon of Arazu, stood tall on his chariot, his arms outstretched. Each arm was held in place by golden magical constructs extending from the chariot walls. A third construct encircled his chest and helped him remain steady in position. Wielding the power of the wind to create the path through the lake exhausted him, but it was well worth the results.

"The path to the island is now clear," one of the lesser gods reported. "It should come within view soon."

"Excellent. Then we shall end all resistance to our rule, once and for all." He paused as something caught his eye. "What is that?"

"What is what, great one?"

Namnirnu glared at him. "I can't point, you fool! Look ahead of us! What do you see?"

The god stared down the path between the water. "I don't... oh. It appears someone comes to meet us."

"Two someones, it seems."

"Is it the King?" asked a goddess from the next chariot. "I didn't get to see him last time. Is he really as scarred as they said?"

Namnirnu reached out with his perception. "I sense... almost no power at all from them. Strange."

"Messengers?" the lesser god suggested. "Oh, no. They carry weapons."

Namnirnu studied the two approaching figures. "It must be a trap of some kind. Dispatch a squad to deal with them."

"As you command."

•••••

Dravid stared up at the Heart of Fire. Within its flames, he could make out the dim outlines of two people: Seri and Marshal. He tightened his grip on the magical cord in his hands.

Tich walked around beside him and examined it. "So this is like a magic rope?"

Dravid nodded. "The other end is with Seri," he explained, his voice hoarse. "I'm her anchor. I can't talk… any more."

"Anchor. Got it." Tich looked back up at the Heart. "You can do it, Marshal. Don't worry about that big army marching toward us right now. Just get the job done and come back."

Dravid wanted to reassure her, but he really couldn't talk any more. He could already feel the strain of maintaining his magic. Heat rose up in his throat. He had no idea how long Seri and Marshal would need in there. And maybe they could even make it back without his help. But maybe not. It might depend on him.

His cord shook. Power rushed down it and into his left hand. He gasped as magic flowed through his body and down through his feet.

"What's going on?" Tich asked.

He couldn't answer. Now he had to deal with vibrations in addition to heat. What did it mean? The power flowed through him into… Zes Sivas?

He had become the channel. Whatever that meant.

●●●●●

"We have movement," Victor said.

"I see them." Ixchel moved further away from him, toward the right wall of water. It made sense, tactically, but he wished she could stay closer.

Durunim. At least a dozen. They spread out to block the pathway, but maintained a staggered line as they hurried forward, well ahead of the main army.

"Can you handle half of them?"

"Can you?"

Victor chuckled. To be honest, he didn't know. He had fought multiple enemies before, and here, with plenty of room, he could let loose with his flail. Even so… six was a lot. Both hands began to shake as his slight magic made itself known.

He picked up speed and spun his flail. He decided to target the two

Durunim closest to the water, but not to make it obvious. He sped toward the third and fourth enemies, keeping his focus in that direction. Only a few feet away, he shifted to the left and spun on his forward foot. Sword outstretched in one hand and flail spinning in the other, he whirled through the line of Durunim. The one closest to the wall dove into the water to avoid Victor's flail. The next one dodged his sword, but the flail caught him in the stomach and sent him rolling across the ground. Ribs shattered from the impact.

Four paces past the line, Victor stopped spinning and turned back. He got the flail going again and rushed toward the third and fourth enemy warriors. His speed now seemed even faster than back in Kuktarma. Apparently, his body continued to absorb magic from his proximity to Marshal. At some point, he should warn Tich about that... if any of them survived today.

His second assault into the line produced similar results. Although the Durunim were all taller than him, with longer reach, none of them wanted to risk getting into range of the whirling flail and sword combination. When he reached them, Victor made sure to dodge to the right a step. Seeing an opportunity, he stabbed one of them through the chest. Unfortunately, his own motion ripped the sword out of his hand. Two down, but he lost one weapon.

He spared a glance for Ixchel, but at the rate he was moving, her motions appeared sluggish, like the Durunim warriors she fought. He knew how fast she could fight. How fast was he moving if Ixchel looked slow?

One of the Durunim wanted to chase him down. He could see its feet hitting the soft lakebed soil one at a time. It felt like child's play to pivot on his left foot, duck his head, and swing the flail at shin level. The chain wrapped around the oncoming warrior's leg and yanked him off his feet. Victor pulled the flail loose, now grasping the handle with both hands.

A throwing dagger struck his breastplate at an oblique angle and ricocheted off. Victor released the flail with his left hand and caught the dagger before it flew too far away. For a moment, he couldn't believe he had done that.

The next moment, he realized his pause had lost him the initiative. Two more Durunim rushed at him, swords lifted. He considered throwing the dagger back, but he had never been very precise with thrown objects. Instead he retreated, but only far enough away to turn back and go into his spin again. This time was more dangerous for him. Without the sword, his enemies had more of an opportunity to dart in between the arcs and attack him. In fact, he was counting on one of them doing just that.

When it came, Victor did throw the dagger: from only a few inches away. He couldn't miss. He didn't take time to watch the dagger hit the Durunim's face, as the same opponent struck him in the chest with a slashing blade. It cut deep into his breastplate, but not deep enough to reach his skin. Victor grabbed at the sword, but missed.

He had to lift the arc of his flail so as not to catch it on the falling body. Another opponent made a stab and managed to catch him on the edge of his back, right where the breastplate ended. Victor let out a grunt of pain. The stab hadn't been deep, but it hurt nonetheless.

The Durunim on the ground was trying to get up. Victor took advantage of the high arc of his spinning flail to come up under its head, just as it lifted. That one would not be getting up again. Four down.

Multiple swords lay on the ground now, but he couldn't take the time to pick one up. His own blade protruded from a body at least a dozen feet away, and two Durunim stood between it and him. He gestured toward them, inviting them to charge him. They advanced together, slowly. Or maybe they were moving fast, and it appeared slow to him. Either way, he could handle this.

He completed the current swing of the flail and let it hit the ground to his right. The Durunim charged in unison. Victor threw himself back, falling to the ground as they attacked. True to his expectation, one swung low and the other high, from alternate directions, hoping to catch him regardless of moves. They hadn't expected him to just fall.

Taking the flail in both hands, he whipped it up and over, smashing into both swords in mid-air. The Ranir stone-enhanced flail shattered both blades. Using the momentum of the swing, Victor rolled to his left and bounded back on to his feet.

His opponents held only broken remnants of their swords, still deadly weapons in close quarters. But Victor had a huge reach advantage now, and he was moving faster than ever. His two-handed flail swing swept in a figure eight, knocking both of them off their feet. He snatched up one of the broken swords and finished the job.

He stood and looked to Ixchel, just in time to see her cut the throat of her only remaining opponent. As fast as he had been moving, and she still did that well! Amazing.

"Got my six!" he called. "You?"

The sound of a splash behind him alerted him almost too late. He had forgotten the Durunim who went into the water! He threw himself forward, trying to rotate in time to see what was happening.

Ixchel threw her short sword, end-over-end. It thudded into the chest of the leaping Durunim right above Victor. The dead warrior fell on top of him.

He scrambled out and got to his feet. Everything seemed to be returning to normal speed now. Ixchel ran over and yanked her sword back. "Now it's six."

Victor nodded, then looked back at the army. "And here come the rest."

● ● ● ● ●

Seri stared in wonder. When Marshal stepped into the Heart, he pulled her along with him. Now they stood—no, they floated—within it. Even when Marshal repaired the Heart between the worlds, it had not appeared like this.

Surrounding her, Seri saw nothing but... her mind groped for a word. Glory. Majesty. She and Marshal, hand-in-hand, floated in the midst of pure glory. Light, wondrous light of every color in the spectrum, swirled around them in a never-ceasing pattern. Red-tinted flames folded in on themselves in every direction, over and over. For several minutes, Seri lost herself wholly and completely. She knew only the majesty of her surroundings, the joy of existence, and the glory of the light itself. Time passed, and she had no conscious recognition of it.

A pressure around Seri's waist brought her to her senses. She glanced down at the golden belt she wore, attached to a cord of the same golden magic that stretched out behind her. Dravid's anchor.

"Marshal," she called. "Marshal!" He finally turned to look at her. "We need to take the next step."

"Such... beauty," he said. "I never dreamed..."

"Yes, but we're running out of time. We need to move into the Otherworld."

"And leave this?" Marshal gave a slow wave.

"We'll come back. But we need help."

He didn't answer.

"The curses, Marshal! To lift the curses!"

He sniffed in a breath. "Yes. Lead the way."

Seri pulled on his hand, focused her attention, and stepped forward…

She and Marshal stepped out into the Starlit Realm. They stood beside the Heart of Fire, appearing exactly the same as it did on the other side. To her dismay, Dravid's cord vanished. Apparently, his magic couldn't stretch through into yet another world.

Seri looked up toward the stars, those immense, multi-colored points of light filling the sky. "We're here!" she shouted. "We need your help!"

"Who are you talking to?" Marshal looked up and then around.

Seri held her breath. Would it work? A hint of movement caught her eye. She focused on a blue star, not the largest in the sky, but significant. It wobbled. "There!" She pointed at it.

Marshal looked up. "The stars?" The blue star shifted position. "Whoa."

And then it fell.

Straight toward them.

●●●●●

Coming down from the magical speed, Victor's muscles ached. Tiredness threatened to sap what strength he had left. And dozens of Durunim, perhaps a hundred or more, now charged toward them.

"Can you handle half of them?" Ixchel asked, glancing at him with a smile.

Victor laughed and retrieved his sword. His entire goal had been to get past the first line of warriors and try to attack the gods directly. It didn't look like he would get a chance at that. The mass of enemy warriors coming their way would overwhelm him.

He spun the flail. "I wish I could think of the right thing to say."

"Die well, Victor." Ixchel raised her shield and charged to meet the foe.

"That works, I guess." He followed after her.

Two against an army.

(((43)))

Kishin slid down the incline, using his staff to keep from sliding too fast. Even so, the impact at the bottom created an eruption of pain in his hip that brought tears to his eyes. He lurched forward to follow Victor and Ixchel.

He had no idea what he was doing. He could barely walk, let alone fight. If Ixchel even saw him, she would be more concerned about his welfare than anything else.

Yet he couldn't let her walk into certain death without pursuing her. Even if he arrived only in time to die with her, at least she would see his resolve. But only if he arrived before she died.

Grimacing from the pain, he tried to pick up his pace.

•••••

"What's happening? Where did they go?" Tich demanded.

Dravid didn't know how to answer. One moment, they were watching the dim images of Seri and Marshal inside the Heart of Fire. The next moment, they vanished.

The power continued to flow through him and back into the Heart. In fact, the negative effects diminished. The heat within his chest faded. Maybe one type of magic was canceling the other out? He breathed a sigh of relief. His own part in this might be easier than he'd expected after all.

Except… if his cord no longer connected to Seri, what was holding it in place?

•••••

Victor entered his magically-enhanced speed, racing to meet the Durunim army. To him, it didn't feel like he grew faster, but like everyone else grew slower. Ixchel fell back behind him. The enemy warriors charging him moved with glacial steps, as if they only walked in long, slow strides.

When many of them came to an abrupt stop, he almost didn't notice. Then some of them pointed up, up and behind him. He would have assumed a trick if it weren't so many.

Only a few dozen yards separated Victor from the army now. More than enough time to take a quick look over his shoulder and…

Victor stopped. His flail stopped spinning.

The air above him, right at the surface of the lake itself, shimmered. The image of something enormous materialized, then faded. The air shimmered again.

He knew what it meant. He'd seen this exact thing once before.

Victor began to yell. He wasn't even sure what he yelled, but his excitement could not be contained.

The city of Intal Eldanir reappeared and became solid. The sound of a horn reverberated through its white stone walls.

And the Eldanim descended, armed for war.

●●●●●

Seri squeezed Marshal's hand as the star fell. The blue light grew brighter and brighter. When it neared the ground, it shifted its appearance, becoming the same figure of flame and magic incarnate she had seen in the inner sanctum. Or maybe not the same, since this one maintained a blue glow.

"The stars are… alive?" Marshal said. Then he nodded. "I guess I always knew that, somehow."

"I didn't," Seri said. She stepped closer to the light. "I represent all three races," she announced. If she understood correctly, it was the only way she could even speak to these creatures. "I come to petition for your help." She pointed at Marshal. "This is the King of Antises. Together, we wish to remove what was done before."

"We wish to end the Laws of Cursing and Binding!" Marshal cried, before she could get to it.

For a very long time, the glowing being did not respond. The power it radiated pulled at Seri's senses. Almost, she wanted to reach out and try to absorb some. But she knew that would be a fatal mistake. When trying to gain help from a friend, you did not try to steal the friend's very essence.

"Do you wish to end them, or revise them?" The voice again echoed through her head without reaching her ears. The way Marshal bent his head and winced, she knew he felt it too.

"To end them!" Marshal said. "I want nothing left!"

A long silence followed his words.

"Then you are the one we have been waiting for."

Seri didn't have time to process the response before she saw it. Another star descended toward them. And then another. And another.

● ● ● ● ●

An Eldanim warrior flew over Victor's head and landed in a crouch a few yards beyond him. Three more followed him. And then more, and more.

Ixchel came to stand by Victor. Together, they watched an entire army of Eldanim descend, charging into the ranks of the Durunim.

"I guess Talinir got through to them," Victor said.

Another one landed behind them. "I did my best," Talinir announced, rising up.

Victor spun to look at his friend. "You did great! Devouring fire! I never expected to see the entire city!"

Talinir looked much the same as always, with the annoying feature that made him look taller than his physical height. But his outfit had altered considerably. He wore a type of light armor in multiple segments across his entire body, topped by a green cape that flowed from his shoulders.

Victor pointed at it. "Nice touch with the cape. Green is really your color."

"Where's Marshal?" Talinir asked. "And the Lords?"

"Back on the island," Ixchel said. "The Passing just happened."

"Then we're on our own." Talinir surveyed the water-encased battlefield.

"What are you talking about?" Victor laughed. "I think we just won!"

As if in response to his claim, something erupted in the midst of the fight. A dozen or more warriors from both sides flew into the air, many of them splashing into the water.

"This battle is far from won. We have gods to deal with. I think—" Talinir broke off. He turned in a slow circle and faced Zes Sivas. He stared up at it, as if suddenly mesmerized.

"Talinir?" Victor waved at him. "Hello?"

"He's not the only one," Ixchel said.

Victor turned around and took an involuntary step backward. All of them, Eldanim and Durunim alike, had stopped their fighting and were staring up at Zes Sivas. In the distance, Victor heard the gods yelling at their soldiers.

"What's going on?"

Ixchel cocked her head and watched Talinir. "I think it's something in the Otherworld that has their attention."

"Talinir?" Victor pushed at him. "What's happening over there, Talinir?"

Talinir didn't move from his pose, but answered in a slow voice: "The stars fall."

(((44)))

The stars fell.

A tear trickled down Marshal's face, pooling in one of his scars. Ever since his first glimpse of the Otherworld, the stars had called to him. Their beauty pulled him, almost to the point of wanting to abandon everything else. And now…

Now they descended from the heavens and surrounded him. He and Seri stood in the midst of burning figures of ethereal fire. Colors like he'd never imagined encompassed them, shining with the brightness of the sun itself. Yet somehow, he could still look at them. Perhaps Seri's star-sight allowed it, protecting their eyes from the power of the light.

Voices filled his head. Some he could understand. Others spoke in a language he'd never heard. But every one of them vibrated with power, with magic beyond anything he could do at his most powerful.

"End the Laws, not reform them."

"Waiting so long."

"Akhenadom's blood."

"Power of all three."

"Maker."

"Wise to keep the power flowing in place."

"Delays reunion."

His head ached with the power. He turned to Seri, trying to understand.

"What is happening? Did, did the stars make the Laws?"

"They enforce them!" Seri exclaimed, turning her face back and forth, delight in her eyes. "Dravid was right. I should have seen it so much sooner!" She finally looked at him, light reflecting from her own face. Did his look anything like that? "When Master Hain died, one of them came to punish us for the breaking of the Bond. The same thing happened a few minutes ago when Volraag died. The stars enforce the Laws of Cursing and Binding!"

"But… why? This is what Akhenadom and the mages did? How?"

"Know this." One of the stars stepped closer, a massive figure of purple-red tint. It inclined its head toward the two of them and its voice crowded out the murmurs of all the others.

"Three representatives of the races came to us, a thousand years ago. The human you knew as Akhenadom."

"Representatives of all three races? That's not in the histories!" Seri interrupted. "So the Eldanim were here? And even one of the gods?"

"Know this. The three of them proposed an alliance with us, with our power. Akhenadom said to enforce rules of the One Above. We serve, so we agreed."

"The one above? Do you mean Theon?" Marshal asked.

"Know this. We doubted, at first, because of the presence of…" It paused. "You call gods. They tried to steal power for themselves before. Waged war, we did. Devastated this land. And yours. Know this."

"The Great Cataclysm!" Seri cried. "You're saying the gods did all that?"

"Know this. Reached too high, they did. But this one, he knew the evil. And repented. Together, sought us out. Mages of your world summoned magic. Bound it to blood, they did. Summoned more magic. Bound it to the land, we did. Our job, our task, to watch for violations."

"Dravid said a blind chance couldn't be behind the Laws," Seri said. "Something had to guide them. And it was you. All along, it was you!"

"Know this. Saddened by the results, we are. You come to end the Laws? We will help."

"If you're the ones enforcing the Laws, why can't you just… stop?" Marshal asked. "If there's no enforcement, there's no Law."

Could a star shake its head? Marshal thought he saw movement where a head might be. Or maybe he was just projecting human characteristics onto these beings to try to understand them.

"Know this. Bound to the land is the magic. Bound to the magic are we. It must be released."

"Then let's do it. Tell us how."

The star lifted an arm and pointed toward the Heart of Fire. "In there. You, as King, must do this. She, as representative, must guide you. It is well that you have kept the power flowing so that it does not return."

Kept it flowing? Marshal looked at Seri. "What does that mean?"

Her eyes widened. "Dravid! He's the channel! Somehow, he's keeping the Heart of Fire from finishing its work and returning to you and the Lords!"

"Know this." The star's voice echoed in Marshal's head again. "You must do this. But sacrifice required."

"I am here to do whatever it takes."

"Your name?"

"Uh, Marshal. My name is Marshal."

"Remembered, you will be. Marshal. With Akhenadom. We will remember."

• • • • •

Kishin moved as fast as his injured hip allowed. The fighting wasn't far now. He was almost there.

Yet what would he do when he arrived? His primary weapon now, this staff, had limitations. When he used it, he risked losing his balance. Since arriving at Zes Sivas, he managed to find a decent short sword from a forgotten armory, but wielding it while leaning on a staff might not be much of an option either.

He thought he had found a cause back in Kuktarma: defending the helpless. No one here was helpless. His own daughter, Ixchel, was a magnificent warrior. He couldn't be prouder of her. Yet even with the arrival of the Eldanim, he worried for her safety. The Eldanim, for all their power, were not gods. The gods were here, and their power could not be questioned. Evidence stood in walls of water to either side.

Even so, he couldn't stop himself. He was a father. He would act like one, even if it was the last thing he did.

Reality warped around him. The walls of water, Eldanim city, and both armies vanished. The lighting shifted dramatically and the sky exploded in a vast array of multi-colored stars. Though he had never seen it before, he knew he stood now in the Otherworld. Even as the thought registered and he lifted his eyes in wonder to the stars, he noticed something else: they were falling.

But not "falling" exactly. More like flying down... toward Zes Sivas, which appeared in this world as a ruin. And one of them, a dark red star, appeared to be flying down straight toward him.

He cowered, suddenly more frightened than at any moment in his life. The star drew near at a rapid pace, eclipsing anything else, filling his vision. It stopped before him, becoming a flaming figure of judgment and wrath.

A voice filled his head, shaking his skull with its vibrations. "Know this. I have brought you here, human, to give you a final choice."

"Wh-who are you?"

"Know this. I am the one responsible for your curse. Both of them."

Kishin felt he should be outraged at this, but instead he merely nodded. In this place and in this situation, it seemed the only appropriate response.

"Your King lifts curses soon." Though the fiery figure made no perceptible move, Kishin felt pointed toward Zes Sivas. Marshal must be there now.

"Know this. Only one to ever be cursed, cured, and cursed again."

Kishin didn't see that as news. Of course no one else had ever done what he did.

"Choice you now face. Self or others."

"What do you mean?"

"Do nothing, and curse will be lifted."

Then it was true. Marshal would lift the curses. But that didn't give him a choice to make. "What is the choice?"

"You can fight."

He almost laughed. "I want to fight. But I am in no condition to do so."

"For this purpose I brought you here. To heal you for one final battle."

"Final?"

"Know this. If you accept this gift, you may not survive."

"Isn't that true of all fights?"

"You may fight for them." The air wavered before his eyes. Kishin saw faces: Ixchel, Victor, Marshal. "Those you have wronged."

"And if I… choose to do so, I will die?"

"Unknown."

Kishin shifted his weight against the staff. If he did nothing, his curse would be lifted. No one expected anything more of him, anyway. And he could reconcile with Ixchel after it was all over. She would be more inclined to listen to him without this ravaged skin, wouldn't she? But that depended on her surviving the battle. The other choice meant he could help her. And the others. He bowed his head.

"If I must fight, if I must kill… it must be for a cause. This… is a cause worth fighting for."

"You have chosen then?"

"I choose."

"You have chosen well. Know this: my gift is temporary. And there will be pain."

Reality warped around Kishin again. The primary world shifted into view, complete with walls of water, battling armies, and floating city. But he barely noticed. Intense pain wracked his body. He dropped the staff and fell to his knees. Fire flooded through his veins, burning, searing, purifying. His broken arm straightened, ripping free from its sling. His hip flared and grew strong again. And then it was over.

Kishin stood to his feet, strength radiating through his body. He drew the sword and picked up the staff. Now he could fight. He sprinted toward the battle.

• • • • •

One by one, the stars rose toward the sky again. Marshal watched them, reluctant to turn his eyes away. "I could live a thousand years and never see anything that… glorious… ever again," he said softly.

"That makes two of us." Seri sighed and turned to face the Heart of Fire, pulling him around with her. "We shouldn't waste any time. Dravid is holding this in place, but there has to be a limit."

Marshal discovered wetness on his face, more than he expected. He didn't remember shedding so many tears, but it didn't surprise him. "What do we do?"

"I guide you into there." Seri pointed at the Heart. "And then you… find the binding magic and release it."

Marshal sniffed and tried to wipe his face. "I don't know how to do that."

"We'll have to go on instinct, then." She took another look at the ascending stars. "They didn't seem all that worried."

"They didn't—" Marshal broke off, not entirely sure of what he meant to say.

"Right. Let's go." Seri reached forward with her free hand. Her hand penetrated the outer barrier of the Heart and grew faint. She took a deep breath and plunged forward. Still holding her hand, Marshal followed.

If he had to lose the vision of the stars, at least he had this. If not for the stars, this would be the greatest view of all time. Once again, they floated in pure majesty and glorious light.

"Reach out!" Seri called. "Find the magic!"

Reach out? For a moment, the concept eluded him. Then he remembered the past few nights of extending his magic through the walls of the citadel. Perhaps something like that? He closed his eyes against the beauty, not without an ache of regret, and reached out with his other senses. That included the ill-defined magic sense he used to detect other sources of power. He strained it as far as he could.

And then understanding exploded over him. His own magic, the magic of the King of Antises, floated before him. Around it, he could sense the individual powers of each of the Lords, one of which also belonged to him. Beyond that, he could feel the vast cauldron of magic belonging to Zes Sivas itself. Multiple bursts of power here and there must be the various mages throughout the island.

Beyond that, he felt an enormous web of magic stretching out in all directions from the island. Was this what the star had talked about?

"Anything?" Seri asked.

In response, Marshal released her hand. She had done her part. The rest was up to him.

"Marshal?"

He extended both hands now, his senses expanding every moment that passed. The web of magic was indeed bound to the land itself. In a thousand places, he sensed spots where it broke free in fits and bursts. Wild magic? And then he discovered the web's connections to the Otherworld… and the stars. Such a vast, interconnected system. It defied understanding. He couldn't fathom the power it took to maintain the web, let alone establish it in the first place.

His senses continued to expand, and he found he could sense people. In fact, he could sense… all the people. Every citizen of Antises was connected to this system. The magic pulled at each of them, binding them to itself, to the land, to specific places, to each other. He only thought the system was vast before; now it went beyond even his wildest imagination.

How to release the bound magic? The star said it would require sacrifice. But what?

Marshal opened his eyes and considered his surroundings. He and Seri floated inside the Heart of Fire, but it wasn't quite like the experience in Kuktarma when Seri took them between the worlds.

Since this power was bound to Antises, but also connected to the stars of the Otherworld, it only made sense that the place to release it was in between both worlds. To get there, he would have to end the Passing, to get rid of this temporary… location. Shelter. Diamond structure. Whatever.

But if the Passing ended, all of the Lords' power would flow back to them. What if he needed it? And then there was Seri. She said she endured enormous pain when traveling between the worlds. He turned back to her.

"What is it?" she asked. "Have you figured it out?"

"Tell Dravid to release the power," he said. And then, with the gentlest of whispers, he gave her a magical push.

Seri flailed her arms and fell backwards. "Marshal? Wait! Wait!" Her body passed through the outer barrier of the Heart of Fire and disappeared from his view.

<h1 style="text-align:center">(((45)))</h1>

Seri landed beside Dravid on her behind. "Ouch!"

Tich appeared beside her at once and helped her get to her feet. Dravid, holding on to his cord, stared at her, but didn't say anything. His look radiated concern.

"What's happening? Where's Marshal?" Tich demanded.

"He's going to do it," Seri said, gasping for air. "He knows what to do now." She took a deep breath. "Dravid… let go."

"Are you… sure?" he asked, his voice ragged.

"Marshal said it. I have to trust him."

Dravid looked down at the golden cord of magic in his hands. His fingers came loose, letting go all at once.

Seri expected the cord to shoot into the Heart of Fire. Instead, it simply dissolved in the air and vanished. Dravid fell back, but caught himself on his elbows. Seri knelt by his side and took hold of one of his arms.

All three of them looked up at the Heart of Fire. Seri could see Marshal's vague silhouette within.

"He can still get back, right?" Tich asked. "Even without you or Dravid?"

Seri had no answer.

•••••

"What do you mean the stars are falling?" Victor looked at the sky. "You mean in the Otherworld?"

"Yes." Talinir shook himself and tore his eyes back toward Victor and Ixchel. "It is… disconcerting."

"It's affected all of you," Ixchel noted.

Victor and Talinir surveyed the battlefield. Many of the Eldanim and Durunim continued to gaze upwards, but more were breaking out of the spell. Those that did turned on their mesmerized opponents and struck them down. Dozens fell. It was impossible to tell which side gained any advantage.

Talinir looked back at Victor, his eyes darting over the young man's appearance and weaponry. "Victor... how would you like to fly?"

"What did you have in mind?" Victor asked, grinning.

Talinir took another quick look at the fighting ahead of them. "I'm thinking we can end this battle all at once." He pointed with his sword. "If we can get you to the god that's pushing back the water, and you can take him down..."

"Wouldn't we all drown?"

"Harunir and the mages will get us out," Talinir answered, pointing up over his shoulder.

Victor saw a second group of Eldanim descending from the floating city. This group held no swords, but he couldn't help feeling a thrill as they touched down. Several dozen Eldani mages! What a difference they could make!

"Let's try it."

"While you two talk, there are enemies coming," Ixchel noted. She ran past them to meet a Durunim warrior.

Victor spared a brief anxious thought for her, but with all the help they now had, she would be all right.

"Harunir!" Talinir called, running to meet one of the mages. Victor followed, keeping an eye out for any Durunim that might break through the Eldanim lines.

"Hello again, Victor," the mage said. Only then did Victor recognize him as the one whose home they'd visited so long ago. Before he could answer, Talinir spoke quickly, explaining his plan and pointing to Victor's flail.

Harunir took a look at it. "That is a strange use of a Ranir stone. I wish I had time to study it."

"It can do the job," Victor said. "Can you get me over there?"

Harunir smiled. "I'll do it myself. Come!" He grabbed Victor and spun him to face away. Then he took hold of Victor's cloak at the shoulders.

"Don't tear my cloak!"

"I'm only holding you for guidance," Harunir assured him. "Here we go."

Without so much as a jerk, Victor found himself in the air, soaring high above the battling Eldanim and Durunim. He stared down at the battlefield, picking out Ixchel fighting with her usual intensity, and Talinir running to join her. Somehow, the experience of flying wasn't quite as spectacular as he'd imagined.

"There he is," Harunir said. "Do you see?"

"Yeah. The guy in the chariot." He was central, holding his arms out like he was doing something magical. Had to be him. Victor grasped his flail with both hands.

"In a moment, they'll notice us," the Eldani mage went on. "I can shield us from the arrows briefly. How are you at falling?"

• • • • •

Kishin flew into the battle near the last place he had seen Ixchel. He didn't know if he could trust his eyes now. It looked as if one of the Eldani had picked Victor up and flown away with him. Then Ixchel and the others charged into the fight. They couldn't be very far ahead.

Sure enough, he spotted Ixchel in the fray a few seconds later. Despite being shorter than everyone else in the fight, she stood out, her distinctive outfit bright against the dull clothing of the Durunim.

Kishin spun, striking one of the Durunim in the chin with his staff. Its head snapped back and it staggered. He stepped in and ended it with a quick stab of his sword. He moved to the next opponent, dispatching it in similar fashion. He felt stronger and faster than he had in years, perhaps ever. Nothing could stand in his way.

In another moment, he reached Ixchel. Before she noticed his presence, he killed another Durunim as it came at her from the side.

"What are you doing here?" She blocked a downward strike from an enemy with her shield. "How are you even here?"

"Would you believe a star sent me?" Kishin planted himself at her side and fought.

"A star. Sent you to fight beside me."

"To help all of you, yes." He deflected another strike with his staff and counterattacked.

"Then go help Victor. He will need it more than I do."

"Where is he?"

Ixchel waited until she had a momentary breather, then pointed toward where the fighting was thickest. "That way. He fights the gods."

"Then that is where I am needed." Kishin bashed another Durunim down with an overhand blow from the staff, then finished him off with a stab into his back.

"Wait."

He paused, looking at Ixchel. Even now, drenched in sweat, spattered with blood (most of it her enemies'), she was beautiful. His daughter. Perhaps the greatest part of his life, though he'd missed most of hers.

"Thank you," she said. In those two words, he heard far more. She might not be overly expressive with her words, but then, neither was he. "Thank you" was all he needed.

"You're welcome."

Kishin sheathed his sword, then broke into a run through an open space. He planted the staff with both hands and vaulted over two of the enemy soldiers. In the air, he drew the sword again and slashed at the back of their heads. His foot passed through the wall of water along the way. He came down beyond them and kept moving. He didn't know how long this "gift" from the star would last, but he would take advantage of every moment.

• • • • •

Marshal floated alone in the Heart of Fire. The temptation to do nothing, to just enjoy the moment, strengthened the more he waited. By now, Dravid would have released his tether. Marshal needed to act.

He let his senses expand again, and pulled. The power of the King flowed back into his body, filling every part of his being. The sensation felt almost like the first time, when his grandfather died, and he experienced the full power of his bloodline. This time, he felt no need to expend any of the power, which was just as well. It would defeat the whole purpose.

Next, he sought out the power of Varioch and drew it within also. It flowed eagerly back into his body, joining the power already there. He felt whole, restored. His hands vibrated to different rhythms, reminding him of the first time he'd unleashed the power. One hand shook with the power of a King; the other with the power of a Lord. Then his body shook, but soon abated. This was his natural state.

But he needed more. He couldn't let the rest of the magic go back just yet. He reached out and pulled at the other five Lord powers. They resisted him, much like Zes Sivas had resisted his pull the night before. Maybe he had sent Seri back too soon. But if she remained with him after Dravid disconnected, she might not be able to return. He wasn't sure he would make it himself.

"Come on, I need you," he whispered, though he heard no sound from his own voice. For a moment, he panicked, wondering if his curse had returned. He had heard Seri's voice earlier. But no, she heard his as well. This was temporary. Had to be.

He continued to pull. The five Lord powers stretched both toward him and away from him. He had a hold on them, but they wanted to return to where they belonged. He pulled against their very nature.

With a sudden rush, all five powers snapped and flowed into him. He sensed that small portions of each had split off and returned to the Lords, but most of the power surged into his body, joining the power already there.

He felt ready to explode. Though he couldn't see or sense it in any specific way, it seemed like power was leaking from him, from his eyes, his mouth, anywhere the magic could find a way to escape this prison of flesh.

Now that he held all the power, the framework of the Heart of Fire disappeared. Once again, he floated between the worlds. The purple fire surrounded him. But this time, he knew what to look for.

He let his magical senses expand, reaching out in every direction just as he had done a few minutes earlier. It didn't take long to locate the magic that connected to both the lands of Antises and the stars of the Otherworld. He could sense all of it, and… he understood how to release it. He spread magic in every direction. He had to do all of it at once, not just one spot.

This was it. His whole body trembled, but not from magic. He could do it. He could end the Laws of Cursings and Bindings. Lift all of the curses. Break all of the bonds. Exactly what he had been wanting, what he had been striving toward for the past year.

To do it would take almost everything he had. As the magic spread out from him, he knew he would not be able to pull it back. The Lords' powers would return to them, perhaps. Or maybe not. He couldn't really tell. He had no idea what would happen. Would any power come back to him? Would he be able to return? To be with his friends again?

It would be easy to open a quick doorway back to his world. Step out and be with Tich, Seri, Victor… Stop the gods and their armies with all of this power.

Or he could change the world.

Marshal clenched his fists, drew magic inward… and then released.

(((46)))

Seri gasped. Magic rushed outward from Marshal and the Heart of Fire, expanding like ripples in the water. As quickly as it came, it was gone.

"What was that?" Dravid asked. "Did he do it?"

Seri put a hand to her chest, her mouth still agape. "I... I can't feel the Bond to Ixchel." She lifted her face to stare at Dravid and Tich. Tears filled her eyes.

"I think he did it."

•••••

Near the border of Kuktarma and Arazu, the woman with the twisted leg paused to wait for her hunchbacked friend to catch up. Somehow, his curse made him even slower than her.

A sudden vibration swept over her, like the shivers that accompanied a fever. But it came and went all at once.

She turned to look at the hunchback. "Did you feel—" She stopped when she realized she had pivoted on her twisted leg.

She looked down. Two legs. Straight and true. No sign of any twist.

She looked up. Her hunchbacked friend stood tall and straight before her, his mouth open, eyes wide.

She grabbed his hands. He squeezed hers back. Slowly, tentatively, they each shifted their feet to the right. Then to the left. She jumped. He leaped.

And then they danced together. The ground vibrated beneath their feet.

•••••

On the beach in Mandiata, the beggar with no hands stood in the shallow water. He watched minnows darting around his feet. Simple entertainment, but he had little else. His stomach growled, and he sighed. He would have to go back near the city to beg from travelers again. He hated it. But what else could a man with no hands do? Even if there was a work he could do, no one would hire a man with a curse.

A gentle wave disrupted the minnows. At the same time, a wave of some kind swept through his body. He crossed his arms and embraced himself, suddenly cold. Except at the ends of his arms. They were warm. They…

He pulled his arms away from his body and stared. Hands. He had hands. Five fingers on each one. He wiggled them.

The beggar fell to his knees in the surf. He plunged his new hands into the water, feeling its cool wetness on new skin. He splashed water into his face, convinced this must be a dream. The shock told him he was awake. He dug his fingers into the cool, wet sand beneath the water, and lifted up two handfuls of it. The sand dripped out between his fingers.

He began to laugh. His hands shook and the sand erupted out from them.

He laughed harder.

•••••

Chimon the priest made his way down the narrow path that led to the cursed village outside of Woqan. As he did every other day, he carried a large basket of bread. It was the least he could do for those suffering out here. Some of them could hunt and find meat. Some worked a garden. But they had no bread and no means of buying any, since they weren't allowed back in the city.

The ground trembled ever so slightly beneath his feet. No one was a stranger to the shaking earth any more, but this one felt… different. "Antises is full of strange wonders," he told himself and continued on his way.

As he drew near the village, he heard shouting. He quickened his pace, fearing some new disaster had fallen on these unfortunate souls. They were unprotected, outcasts from society. Anything could happen.

He turned a bend in the path and saw three young people running toward him. "Priest Chimon!" they called. "It's a miracle!"

"What do you mean, children?" He set the basket down and waited for them to reach him. He knew these three well. They… He gasped as he understood. All three were running. Yet two of them had been unable to walk for as long as they had been here. The third… the third carried horrible skin blemishes which kept her from living among "ordinary" people. But all three ran to him, elated smiles on their faces, clear skin, full of health.

"It's everyone!" one of them cried. "All of us!"

Chimon trembled and sank to his knees. "Truly? All of you?"

A young man who hadn't walked in four years pulled Chimon back to his feet and embraced him. "The curses are lifted! Come and see!"

●●●●●

"Merish!" Gnaeus yelled at the top of his voice. "They're comin' back!"

Merish, sword in hand, came bounding to his friend's side. The two of them stood at the entrance to Forerunner's refuge. A squad of dark, magical beings assembled below them. Any moment now, they would charge up the hill. Only Merish stood between them and the many refugees who had come to call this place home.

Gnaeus held a shield in his one good hand, hoping to do some good. But the last time he had done this for a swordsman, that man had died. He looked at Merish, his only friend. He couldn't die. Not Merish. He looked back at Gnaeus with that huge smile he always wore when holding a sword.

A vibration swept over Gnaeus. For a moment, he wondered if Marshal had returned. But no. He was long gone, taking Topleb home. He'd probably stayed in Ch'olan, if he had any sense.

"We will not die today," Merish said.

Gnaeus nodded, then gasped. "Merish! You spoke!"

Merish cocked his head. "I suppose I did. How about that?"

Instinctively, Gnaeus reached toward his friend with his free hand, his right hand. He grasped Merish by the shoulder before he realized his hand could grasp things. He pulled it back and stared at it. His hand, no longer withered and twisted. How? How could this be?

"No curses," Merish said. He drew a second sword from its sheath at his side and offered it to Gnaeus.

He took the sword and swung it, amazed at every motion. "No curses," he repeated.

Merish pointed at the enemy warriors now ascending the hill. "No curses!" he cried and charged.

Gnaeus was right behind him.

Merish was already amazing with a sword. And with his intelligence restored? The enemy didn't stand a chance.

Even so, Gnaeus worried as his friend cut into the first two creatures. A third one charged at him. His hands shaking, he held up his shield to block the sword that swung toward him.

Power erupted from the shield and threw the enemy warrior through the air.

Gnaeus stared in amazement, then whooped.

"Merish! I got magic!"

Merish, spinning and cutting through the enemy almost faster than he could see, called back: "We both do!"

• • • • •

At the gates of Reman, screams filled the air. The boy who sat by the gate listened to them all, trying to figure out what was happening. Someone said something about enemies. A woman moaned that they were all going to die. If only he could see! His master hadn't come for him on schedule. Without him, he couldn't find his way back to their home. He banged his wooden bowl against the road. Three coins inside it clinked together.

And then they clinked again as a tremor shook the bowl. The boy frowned. The tremor wasn't like the ones that shook the city so bad last month. It was a tiny thing, and it seemed to have come from… inside him?

He blinked.

Light exploded in his mind. His wooden bowl. It was a darker brown than he thought. It was…

He could see! He lifted his head and spun it in every direction, scrambling to his feet. He could see! Just like before the curse. Before the darkness. Before the cruel master. He could see!

But he could see even more than before! Everywhere he looked, he saw colorful beams of light shooting out from the ground and waving like grass in the wind. He laughed and grabbed at a red one. The beam of light shot into his hand and vanished. At the same time, he felt something settle inside him, something that vibrated ever so slightly. He ran around, grabbing more and more of the light beams, letting them fill him up inside, filling him with something he couldn't understand, but felt oh so good.

Then he noticed everyone else also running, but not in circles. They all ran inward, away from the city gates and walls. A red-cloaked soldier stumbled and fell beside him.

The gates of Reman, never intended to resist an actual army, burst open. The boy stared at an army of sinister-looking warriors. Dark lightning crackled around their faces, grim faces that somehow reminded him of the master he'd never seen.

He scowled. These were not good men. They would mistreat people, like his master. He would not allow that.

He strode in front of them and held up his hand. "Stop!" he commanded.

The warriors paid no attention to him, marching forward into the city.

"I said stop!" the boy screamed, raising his other hand.

Power exploded from him, smashing into the Durunim army, throwing dozens of them back, ripping the gates from their hinges and tossing them for miles.

The red-cloaked warrior scrambled to his feet beside the boy and looked down at him. "Can you do that again?" he asked.

The boy shrugged and grabbed for some more beams of light. "Sure."

●●●●●

The little girl cowered in her usual hiding spot behind the inn of Efesun. Only this time, she didn't hide from mocking children, but three terrifying creatures who stalked the town's main road. They appeared in shape like men, but their skin absorbed the light. They carried dark blades and killed everyone they found.

She held her malformed right arm against her chest. Monsters. Monsters had come to Efesun. Were they looking for her? Were they hunting the cursed, like other monsters she'd heard tales of?

She shivered, though the weather was still quite warm, even for her ragged clothes. She'd never shivered in fear before. But she'd never seen monsters before, either.

A warmth spread through her arm, and she looked down. The shadows in the alley made it difficult to see, but she could feel the truth of what happened. Her arm stretched out straight and whole. She ran her left hand up and down it, and then lifted the arm into the air as she stood. She made a fist, then released it, spreading her fingers wide.

Her curse was gone! Lifted, just as she'd always dreamed would happen! Praise Theon!

A scream came from the road out front. The monsters! They hadn't vanished. But what could anyone do against creatures like that?

Even as she thought it, a new feeling spread through her body. Something vibrated in her throat. A confidence she'd never known swept through her. She ran around the inn, and emerged in the road. The three monsters stood over their latest kill. One pulled his sword free, dripping blood.

"No more!" she cried. Her throat and mouth vibrated as she spoke. All three of the monsters stopped what they were doing. In slow motion, they turned to look at her. One took a step toward her, raising his sword.

"Stop!" she shouted. The monster froze.

The men of the village peeked out of windows, wondering what this meant. Seeing them, the girl called, "Come on out!"

When they all stepped out of the buildings, it shocked her more than the monsters obeying her. As long as this vibration continued in her throat she could tell people what to do!

She pointed at the three invaders. "Slay the monsters!"

•••••

Aluri positioned the dagger against her chest. Her father valued her so little, he would sacrifice her well-being for whatever selfish crime he wanted. Better to let him return to find her dead than cursed. Maybe it would have enough impact on him to stop risking his other children. Besides, she couldn't face a life with this pain and deformity. Not a daughter of Lords.

She took a last look in her mirror. The blemishes covered almost all of her face now. Her maidservant had been unable to look her in the eye. Aluri didn't blame her. She looked horrible.

She closed her eyes, took a deep breath, and steadied her hand. One thrust. All it would take.

A ripple passed through her body. A new symptom? She opened her eyes.

A clear face stared back at her from the mirror. The blemishes were gone. The pain was gone.

She reached out a trembling hand and touched the mirror. To her shock, it shattered around her fingers and flew in every direction.

"No!"

At her shriek, the shards stopped. They stood still, vibrating in mid-air in a brilliant display all around her desk. She drew her hand back. The dagger fell from her other hand. At the same moment, the broken mirror shards all fell as well, dropping straight down from their hovering positions.

How was this possible? A curse could not be reversed. It could…

She breathed out the name in a whisper: "Marshal."

<h1 style="text-align:center">(((47)))</h1>

"Falling?" Victor asked

"Can you land well from a fall?"

"Uh, I've never thought about it before. I... guess so?"

Arrows arched through the air toward them. Harunir said something Victor couldn't make out. The arrows all stopped and tumbled down, as if they had been dropped. They swooped in closer toward the army.

"Close your eyes," Harunir warned.

Victor snapped his eyes shut at once. *"i hatel nirhatal!"* the mage cried. Even behind his closed lids, Victor's eyes burned as an incredibly bright light exploded in front of them. He tried to squeeze his eyes tighter, but it didn't help.

"Open them! Here we go!"

Victor opened his eyes and blinked five or six times before he could see anything at all. Far closer than he'd anticipated, dozens of Durunim stood dazed or wandering, holding their hands to their eyes.

"Now!"

Harunir released him. The momentum of the flight carried him directly toward one of the staggering enemy warriors. Victor twisted to get his feet in front of him. He struck the Durunim in the chest and bore him to the ground. He attempted to leap forward on the impact, but stumbled and tripped instead. He rolled forward, nearly smacking himself in the face with his flail.

Victor scrambled to his feet and drew his sword at once. The god in the chariot wasn't far, but three Durunim and another god stood in his way. All of them appeared blinded for the moment. Victor charged forward, dodging past the Durunim. But before he could move past the god, a pair of unblinded eyes focused on him. A golden sword appeared in the god's hands and then burst into flame. Victor dropped into a defensive stance and spun his flail.

"Interesting choice," the god noted. In his other hand, a flail made of golden magic appeared. Like all of the gods, he stood at least a foot taller than Victor, with impressive proportions. His clothes reminded Victor of Seri's father, but with brighter tones.

"Who are you supposed to be?" Victor asked.

"I am one of the seven Sebittun, war gods, defenders of Namnirnu. Should you overcome me, by some miracle, you will face my six brothers." He spun the flail and it also ignited in flames.

"Wonderful."

The god attacked at once with a sword stroke. Victor instinctively parried it with his own. Sparks flew when the swords collided. The heat of the flames brushed against his face. With the swords together, Victor tried to sweep his flail up underneath the god's sword arm, but his opponent danced backward to dodge it.

The vibrations in Victor's hands sped up, making him grip his weapons tighter. His movements became faster and smoother. Unfortunately, this war god matched him speed for speed and blow for blow.

"You're fast for a human," the god observed.

"And you're slow for a god." Victor dodged the flaming flail, and got his own moving again. "And I'll admit: that wasn't my best insult. I'm distracted."

"Distracted?" The god's eyebrows narrowed and a scowl split his face, as if he felt insulted.

"Sorry, man. You're just not my primary target." Victor turned into a full spin again, whirling with sword outstretched in one hand and flail in the other.

The god took one step back, then slung his own flail in a wide arc to collide with Victor's. If Victor's flail had been ordinary, this would have been a great strategy. At the very least, it would tangle the two flails together and put a stop to Victor's motion.

But Victor's flail wasn't ordinary. His Ranir stone-enhanced ball struck the flaming magic flail straight on, and plowed right through it. The god's flail exploded in a shower of golden magic and fire. Victor continued his spin and cut a gash across the god's chest. As he fell to his knees with a scream, he threw his flaming sword at Victor.

The sword skimmed past his left forearm, cutting a short gash, and then bounced off his breastplate. The heat from the flames burned his arm and singed his beard.

It didn't matter now. The chariot was within reach. He lunged forward, but the chariot lurched into movement, rolling away from him. A couple of nearby Durunim also seemed to be recovering from the blindness and started in his direction.

"Is this how you use my gift, Victor?"

He whirled at the voice, far too close behind him, and stared up at another god. But he knew this one.

"Wolf?"

Once part of the Curse Squad in Varioch, Wolf—or Calu—looked much the same as the last time Victor had seen him, leaving through the portal in Ch'olan. Tall and strong like the other gods, his hair hung almost to his waist, a cascading mix of brown, gray, and white.

"You know my name." A flaming sword appeared in Calu's hand. "I gave you that flail to fight against your own people, not us."

"You fight against my people," Victor answered, glancing at the chariot moving away. "I'll use whatever I have to stop you. And thanks, by the way. The flail is great."

Calu roared at him and lunged forward. Victor managed to get his sword up in time to parry the blow, but the force of it drove him back. He almost fell to his knees. The chariot kept moving.

Calu attacked again, and again, keeping up the pressure. Forced to defend, Victor couldn't get his flail moving. He tried swinging it, but couldn't gain enough momentum while dodging and blocking.

"We were friends, Calu! We cared for you!"

"I told you when last we parted: all debts are paid. We are friends no longer!"

Victor grunted as he dodged another blow. He managed to get a short strike in with his own sword, but not enough to get past Calu's own breastplate.

"What are you the god of, anyway?" he asked, trying to find some kind of advantage. "Wolves? Hair?"

Calu laughed, a deep, boisterous laugh. For some reason, it intimidated Victor more than all the magic he'd seen so far. Something about the laugh awoke primal fears within him, fears of the dark, fears of what lurked in the dark... Calu pulled back his arms, displaying his muscles. His gold skin turned black, as black as coal, and then began to glow. Red patches of lava-like fire appeared on his face, arms, and legs. His hair crackled but did not burn, its lighter color providing a sharp contrast to the black-and-red of the skin.

Yet even in his fear, Victor recognized a brief moment of opportunity. He broke away from Calu, chased down the chariot and smashed his flail into its wheel. Like the other god's flail, the chariot was also made from their golden magic. And like the flail, it shattered when Victor's weapon hit it.

Calu seized Victor by the back of his neck and threw him to the ground. Where his hand touched Victor's neck, the flesh burned. "You fool! He's the one holding back the waters!" The dark god raised his flaming sword.

• • • • •

Kishin danced and fought his way through the Durunim. He caught a glimpse of Namnirnu atop the chariot and aimed for it. Of course. He would be the one holding back the water. Victor would be there.

One moment before he reached the chariot, it collapsed and Namnirnu fell. Kishin's first impulse was to chase after him, but then he saw Victor on the ground and a flaming, molten god poised to kill him.

His last leap carried him almost to them. He landed on his knees and slid. He spun the staff over his head and brought it in to strike at the back of the molten god's knees. The blow knocked the god off his balance and his strike went wild. Victor glanced at Kishin, but kept his focus on his opponent. He scrambled to his feet and spun his sword and flail in a dual whirlwind.

Kishin kept moving. When his slide ended, he came to his feet and rushed past Victor toward Namnirnu. The leader of the gods recovered from the chariot wreck and climbed to his feet. He spotted Kishin and snarled. "You again! We have no time for this! Get out of my way and let me protect us all!"

His voice vibrated against Kishin's ears, and for a moment, he felt compelled to obey. He lowered his sword. At that moment, a twinge of pain sparked from his hip. His healing gift must be wearing off. He raised the sword and took a step forward.

Namnirnu threw out his arms to either side, as if he were holding up the walls of water around them by his very will. The wind of his power pushed at Kishin, almost knocking him off his feet, even though he wasn't in the direct path. He took a step forward instead.

"You can't!" Namnirnu bellowed. "Do you want everyone here to die? Does your own life mean so little?"

"My life?" Kishin took another step against the wind. "If it takes my life to put an end to your army, then it's well worth it." He took another step, though this one was only a few inches. "Aren't you gods all about sacrifice?"

Another god rushed at him from the side with a spear. "I am one of the seven Sebittun, war gods, defenders of Namnirnu!" he bellowed. "Should you—"

"I didn't ask." Kishin stepped back and brought his staff up, deflecting the spear. He stabbed the war god in the chest. He yanked his sword free before his opponent fell, and turned back to Namnirnu.

The wind struck him again, almost knocking him off his feet. Pain erupted in his hip and left arm. He wouldn't be able to keep going for much longer. He sank to one knee.

"That's more like it," Namnirnu thundered. "On your knees!"

A ripple passed over Kishin, a gentle feeling of vibration. He gasped, seeing pure, undefiled skin on his arms. He raised his face and smiled.

"No!" Namnirnu shouted at the sight. "It cannot be!" His eyes glared at Kishin, as if refusing to believe what he saw.

"You've lost," Kishin said. "In so many, many ways." He lunged back up, holding the war god's fallen spear, leaving the staff on the ground. He threw the spear, catching Namnirnu in the thigh. The impact was just enough to force him to a knee instead.

The wind stopped. Kishin leaped forward.

Namnirnu manifested a golden shield at the last moment, but Kishin shoved it aside, his arm screaming in pain. He stabbed down with his sword into Namnirnu's chest.

Namnirnu choked, his mouth moving, but no words coming out. Kishin leaned in close, pushing the sword deeper. "...curse!" the god gasped.

"Let me tell you my curse." Kishin released the sword and spread his arms wide, knowing what was coming. "It's gone. I am free forever."

A wall of water swept him off his feet and plunged him into darkness.

(((48)))

Marshal floated between the worlds, almost unconscious. Had it worked? It must have worked. He had expended every bit of magic he possessed, and he'd felt the bindings falling apart. If the curses hadn't been lifted, at the very least they would never happen again.

He smiled. He'd done it. Now he could rest. His entire body ached. His old injuries hurt even more: his left foot, where the assassin stabbed him; his right knee he'd twisted in Kuktarma; the long scar across his back from Curasir and the sword; his broken rib and whatever damage it had done within him, all from Murdak; and the scars across his face from the curse-stalker so long ago now. He could feel all of them now, and he suspected it would get worse. Without his magic to shield him, this was a dangerous place. And he had no way out of it.

He drifted. His eyes saw purple flames and nothing more. He blinked. Had he fallen unconscious? He had no concept of time here. How much had passed? Were the others all right? "I did my job. Now it's up to them," he whispered, but still couldn't hear his voice.

Tich would be broken-hearted when he didn't come back. He regretted that most of all. She'd suffered enough; he hated to add to it. But she was strong. He hoped she would be all right.

Seri and Dravid would comfort each other. He smiled at the thought, no longer envious. That was as it should be.

Victor. Victor would understand. He knew all along the price that might be required. He would rage for a while, but he'd be all right. Maybe he would find happiness with Ixchel. Marshal hoped so, not just for Vic, but for Ixchel as well. She needed love in her life, more than just her service to Seri.

"You are greatly loved."

This voice reverberated through his head. At first he thought the voice might be Aelia. They were her words: the truths she'd always tried to ingrain in him. This time, he knew them for truth. He was greatly loved, and not just by his mother. Victor, Seri, Tich... all of them. But it wasn't Aelia speaking. Or at least, it wasn't just her. He thought he heard two voices: his mother's, and one other—deeper, stronger, powerful.

"You are valuable."

He was the King of all Antises; of course he was valuable! He almost laughed. But beyond that, he knew: every life is valuable. That's why he had fought so hard to get here and do this, no matter what it cost. Even those who deserved their curses, like Kishin, still held value, solely by being human.

"You have a purpose in these worlds."

That was different. Aelia always told him he had a purpose in this world. But the voice said "these worlds." He supposed it was true, though. He had changed both worlds. He'd made a difference.

He tried to turn, to see where the voice came from. Purple flames surrounded him. He couldn't even tell if he turned. Everywhere he looked, he saw only the space between worlds. No speaker. No one else, nothing else as far as his eyes could see. Who spoke to him? Maybe it was one of the stars. Or... beyond them.

"Who are you?" he called out, but again could not hear his own voice.

He floated in silence, though he couldn't tell how long. And then the voice spoke once more:

"Well done."

• • • • •

Victor couldn't believe his eyes. Kishin, moving and attacking like his old self. If anyone could stop the big god, it was the assassin. For now though, Victor still faced Calu, and Durunim warriors had noticed them.

"This is pointless, Victor," Calu growled. "You cannot win here, even with the Eldanim. Our power is too great."

Victor spun into his whirlwind, sword and flail outstretched. No breath left for arguing. He only had to keep Calu distracted long enough for Kishin to get to the one that mattered.

Calu smacked down on Victor's sword with his own flaming weapon. The impact made Victor stumble. In that instant, Calu caught his flail by the chain with one burning hand. Victor's stumble turned into a fall as the flail was yanked from his grasp. He fell into a roll and rose up with sword aimed at Calu. His left hand burned where the skin had been torn from his palm.

The god smiled and tossed the flail away. "No more. You fall here. Your scarred King falls here. Your mages fall here. It's over."

Victor heard a shout from the direction of Kishin and Namnirnu. "Yeah, I think it just about is."

"What do you—" Calu looked in that direction and his glowing eyes widened. "Sebittun! Your master is—"

Victor stabbed at him, catching the god in the right hip. Calu grabbed the blade of his sword and squeezed. Flames rushed up the blade to Victor's hand. He let it go and stumbled backward, both hands burning now.

Calu screamed at the top of his lungs. Victor instinctively lifted his hands to stop the next blow, but it didn't matter.

A wall of water smashed into him.

• • • • •

Seri wiped the tears from her face. It worked. It really worked. The Laws of Cursings and Bindings were no more. She couldn't even grasp how much the world would change.

"Why isn't he coming back?" Tich asked.

"I don't know." Seri reached toward the Heart of Fire, then pulled back as something changed.

Five of the six sides of the diamond dissolved and dispersed in every direction. Power returning to the Lords? The sixth side fragmented into dozens of shards of light that melted into the red glow of the Heart itself. Marshal's silhouette within grew dimmer.

Seri tried to touch it, to pull the magic toward herself, as she always did, but it resisted. The Heart floated unchanged in the air. In fact, she couldn't touch it at all. She waved, and her hand passed right through the lowest part of the Heart of Fire. Nothing happened.

"Get him back!" Tich demanded, stepping up beside her.

"Let me try," Dravid offered. Seri turned and watched him shape a long pole out of his golden magic. On one end, he put a circular handle for grasping.

Dravid moved closer and extended his pole toward Marshal's silhouette within the Heart. For a long time, Marshal did not react at all.

"Come on, come on," Dravid muttered.

Marshal stirred and his shadowy hand reached out toward the pole. His fingers wrapped around the handle.

"Pull him out!" Seri urged.

Dravid gave a gentle pull on the pole. The handle came out of Marshal's hand at once. Dravid frowned and extended it again. With slow movements, Marshal took hold of it, this time with both hands.

"Take it slow," Seri suggested.

"I know," Dravid growled. He pulled about an inch. Marshal's hands stayed on the handle. He pulled another inch… and Marshal's hands came free again.

"What's happening?" Tich tried to grasp at the Heart of Fire herself, with no result.

"I don't know." Dravid let the pole dissolve. "He doesn't seem to be able to hold on."

"The magic won't let him," Seri said. "It won't let him go."

"Why not?" Tich spun to face her. Seri's heart broke at the desperate look in her eyes. "Why would it keep him there?"

"The stars said that sacrifice would be required to end the Laws." Seri continued to stare at Marshal's silhouette. "Maybe… maybe he's the sacrifice."

"No." Tich shook her head. "No. That can't be right. We have to get him out!"

Dravid staggered and collapsed, sitting on the edge of the platform. Seri tore herself away from watching Marshal and knelt beside him. "Are you all right?" She put a hand on his arm.

"I'll be fine. Just… took a lot." Dravid patted her hand.

Tich uncoiled her rope and threw one end into the Heart. It fell straight through. She pulled it back, formed a lasso, and threw again, aiming higher. The lasso reached Marshal's silhouette, fell over his still outstretched arm, and fell straight through it.

"Why won't it work?"

Seri stood back up. "I'm guessing stuff from our world doesn't reach into that region without magic involved," she said. "Let me try something."

She took a deep breath. She could do this. She'd crossed into the space between worlds twice now, and she passed through it on her way to the Otherworld. Surely, she could do it again.

A pressure touched her ankle. She looked down to see Dravid wrapping his magic around it. "You need an anchor," he reminded her.

She nodded, then reached out with both hands. The magic didn't feel the same as it usually did. She tried to grab it and pull it open. But nothing happened. She frowned and tried again. Still nothing. She could feel the life of Zes Sivas, the life of Antises itself, but it would not yield to her as it had done before.

"What's happening? What are you doing?" Tich's repeated questions started to annoy her, but she couldn't blame the girl.

"I don't know. It won't work."

"Try again!"

"I am!"

She did try. Again and again. But nothing changed. At last, she stepped back, exhausted. Dravid let the magic around her ankle fade away. "I can't do it. I don't understand it."

"No, I can't accept this." Tich threw her rope at Marshal again. "There must be a way to get him back!"

Dravid pulled himself up on his crutch and moved beside her. He put a hand on her shoulder. "We will get him back, Tich. We'll get all the Masters in here working on it together. At least some of the Lords will be willing to help. And maybe the Eldanim too. Marshal has enough friends with power and, and knowledge that someone will figure something out."

Tich bowed her head. She gave a weak gesture toward the door. "In case you've missed it, we have an army of gods and Durunim about to destroy us all. Without Marshal... I don't think we stand a chance."

Seri swallowed. She had forgotten the external threat. What had happened here while she and Marshal had been in the Otherworld?

<h1 style="text-align:center">(((49)))</h1>

Marshal couldn't understand it. Though he couldn't see the primary world, he had recognized Dravid's magic when the pole came into view. Yet every time he tried to grab it, it slipped from his hands. The magic held him in place and would not let him go.

The pain from all of his injuries spread outward. Bit by bit, it enveloped his entire body. Seri talked about how humans did not belong in this place, and how much pain she experienced coming here. When he had been here before, he felt like he belonged, because his power belonged here, connected to here. But he had no power now. He was an ordinary human, trapped between worlds, with no protection.

This place did not like him. Neither would it let him go.

•••••

Victor swallowed a huge drought of lake water before even realizing he'd gone under. The force of the water tumbled him one way and then another. He slammed into something or someone and saw stars. Something seized him and he swept up into the air, gasping for breath.

"My apologies," Harunir said above him. "You were the furthest away and hardest to reach."

Victor nodded, spitting water and gasping over and over. Below him, the lake smashed together in colliding waves. He glimpsed bodies being thrown about beneath the water, some flailing about, some still already. The horror of the moment took away any thought of celebration.

"Congratulations," the mage said. "You did it."

"No. No, I didn't." Victor spit out more water. "I helped, but Kishin did it. Kishin! Did you find him?"

"The assassin? He was here?"

"Yes! He's down there somewhere! You've got to find him."

"We will do all that we can."

Victor wiggled his fingers, both palms red and bleeding. The injuries reminded him. "My flail!"

He stared down at the water, growing even sicker. He'd owned that flail for so many years. And now he'd never see it again. There was no way he could swim that deep, even if he knew where to look.

"A Ranir Stone cannot be lost," Harunir said. "When everything is settled, I will find it in the Starlit Realm, open a portal, and snatch it from this side for you. A weapon that turns the tide of such a momentous battle should not be left to rust away."

"Turn the tide?" Victor tried to turn his head to look up. "Was that a joke?"

"You're not the only race with a sense of humor, you know."

Victor wanted to chuckle, but everything else felt so wrong. He gasped again as they turned toward Intal Eldanir. The city shone white and beautiful, just as he remembered it, except now it floated a few feet above the level of the water. The sun reflected from both, gleaming with a pure light almost as impressive as the stars of the Otherworld.

An even more impressive sight appeared between them and the city. Dozens of Eldanim mages flew, carrying warriors back to the city, sometimes levitating five or six at a time.

"Did... did you get everyone else?" Victor asked, searching for Ixchel.

"Besides those we had already lost in combat, yes," Harunir said. "I am fairly certain."

A tall warden in a green cape waved to them as they approached the open entrance to the city's streets. "The High Champion awaits us," Harunir said.

"The high what?"

Victor didn't get an answer as Harunir let him drop gently to the street next to Talinir. To his surprise, the Eldani warden grabbed him in a powerful hug. Victor stared to return it, but remembered his torn up hands in time.

"Sorry, man. Wet and bleeding here. Don't want to mess up your new colors."

Talinir laughed. "You did it, Victor. It was all you."

"And Kishin."

"Kishin? The assassin?"

"He's the one who finished it. Can you find him?"

Talinir pointed down at the water. "Even the so-called gods couldn't survive that."

"Most of them, anyway," Harunir said, alighting beside them. "There are some who probably found a way to escape. We may never know for sure."

"Where's Ixchel?" Victor tried to see through the crowd.

"She is here. She—"

Talinir did not finish the sentence as Ixchel barreled past him and seized Victor in a sopping wet bear hug. She let him go and punched his shoulder. "Not bad."

Victor winced and rolled his shoulder. "Do you always have to be so violent?"

"Maybe. Something to look forward to."

"What?"

Ixchel looked past him. "Where is my—Kishin?"

"We are searching," Harunir said, "but so far, there is no sign of him."

"He did it," Victor said. "He saved me, and then killed the leader of the gods. Without him, I never would have made it."

Ixchel stepped to the edge of the city and looked down into the water. Victor moved beside her. He reached for her shoulder, then stopped. "Awkward bloody hands," he mumbled.

The water roiled beneath them, waves still bashing back and forth against each other. Many more bodies floated on the surface, but they all looked like Durunim.

Victor watched Ixchel. She stood stiff, staring at the water. Blood trickled from a number of cuts on her arms and legs, but none of them looked deep. She'd made out far better than he had. Maybe there was something to using a shield.

"What are you thinking?" he asked.

"I don't know." She continued to stare down. "For so long, I hated him. I hated that he left me. When I found out what he did, I hated him for that. Then he came back. He talked about changing. He helped us."

"He saved everything," Victor said. "We're lucky he was here."

"Perhaps."

Victor looked over his shoulder. "Well, I suspect Marshal did something too. How about those stars, Talinir?"

"They have returned to their rightful place," the warden answered.

"About time we did too." Victor looked back at Ixchel. "Let's see about some bandages, shall we?"

Ixchel nodded and started to turn away. "I need to get back to my Lady." She paused and took one last look at the water. She bowed her head, nodded once, then turned to join Victor. "We have more work to do."

(((50)))

Seri stood back and let the other Masters examine the fading Heart of Fire with Marshal within it. Harunir the Eldani mage stood with them, making observations and exchanging suggestions.

"They'll figure it out," Seri told Tich again. The other girl had hardly left the inner sanctum since the Passing ended the day before. She worked with her rope and watched Marshal's silhouette.

"Yeah," she said. Nothing more. Seri watched her out of the corner of her eye. Tich's movements as she played with the end of her rope were crisp and jerky. She hadn't said anything sarcastic in all this time, either.

"Do you even understand this concept of a… place between the worlds?" Master Ganak's booming voice asked.

Harunir waved his hand through the insubstantial corner of the Heart. "It is not… unheard of. By that I mean some Eldani mages have mentioned the theoretical possibility of such a place. But we have never entered it ourselves."

"It makes little sense to me," Master Magnus grumbled.

"I don't get it at all," Victor said, coming up beside Seri and Tich. He gestured with one of his bandaged hands. "I had a hard enough time with another world."

"Shh. I want to hear what they say," Seri told him.

"We have little experience with trying to pull something with magic," Master Tzoyet noted. "Pushing, yes. Imbuing, yes. And many other applications. But not… pulling."

Seri tried to follow the discussion as it went on, but the other Masters ventured into areas she didn't fully understand. She still had so much to learn.

Lord Tyrr burst into the sanctum, eyes wild. "Let him rot!" he bellowed. "Devouring fire is too good for him!"

"Lord Tyrr," Master Plecu began, "if I may—"

"No, you may not!" The Lord leveled a finger at Plecu. "You should have told me he was going to do this. Do you realize everything that's happened now?"

"No more curses," Seri said.

Lord Tyrr glared at her. "You're part of this, just as much as him! You don't understand what this means!"

"It is the fulfillment of prophecy," Master Tzoyet said. "We've been expecting it. Though… not this soon, to be honest."

"I spent years tracking down all of the wild mages in Rasna," Lord Tyrr ranted. "And now dozens more of them are popping up everywhere! Everyone who was under a curse or had a binding seems to have magic now!"

"Of course!" Seri exclaimed. "Their bodies were already attuned to magic, so when it began to flow more freely through the lands, they absorbed it." She put her hands together and brought them near her mouth. "I expect we'll see a lot more wild mages from here on out, with all the free magic available now!"

"You're missing the point, girl, not that I'm surprised. Think about it, all of you! Cursed people with power. There's a reason those people were cursed!"

"You mean like murderers?" Tich muttered.

"Most of them, anyway," Master Plecu acknowledged. "But you raise a good point. There will be some truly evil people with more power than they should have now. We will—"

"If that weren't bad enough, my power is diminished!" Lord Tyrr released a burst aimed at Marshal's silhouette, but only rattled the wall behind it. "I doubt I have half the power I did before! And he stole it!"

"Lord Tyrr." Master Ganak stepped up, drawing himself to his full height and looking down at the Lord. "You have already been asked to leave the island. We have not forgotten how you profaned this sacred place with murder. If you do not leave today, we will force you."

Master Tzoyet stood beside him. "And we have not lost any of our power," he added.

Lord Tyrr's eyes blazed as he looked from the Masters to Seri and then at Marshal's silhouette again. "I'm leaving, because Rasna needs me." He pointed at Marshal. "And let the cords of death take that one where he'll never see the light of day again." He spun on his heel and stormed out.

"Ha! Mages and Lords in real life!" Victor laughed.

"I apologize for that," Master Plecu said to Harunir. "He—all of us, really—is under a lot of stress right now."

"Your entire society's foundations have shifted," Harunir said. "Everyone is going to react to it in different ways."

"Have the other Lords already gone?" Seri asked, stepping away from Tich. She'd been busy with Marshal and Ixchel and so many other things that she hadn't kept track of everything happening on the island.

"Most of them," Master Ganak said. "I thought Tyrr had gone as well, but I suppose he came back to share his thoughts with us."

"Are we any closer?" Seri gestured toward Marshal. "To figuring that out, I mean."

Master Tzoyet answered: "I do not know if there is a solution."

"We can't abandon him!"

"We don't want to," Harunir said. "But neither have we uncovered a way to rescue him just yet. I am not giving up."

"Have you looked at the problem from the other side?" Seri asked.

Harunir nodded. "He appears exactly the same from the Starlit Realm."

"Dravid's power could reach him, but he couldn't hold on to it," Seri said, repeating what everyone in the room already knew. "Why is that?"

"Your friend's power can penetrate the veil between the worlds, it seems," Harunir answered. "But perhaps in doing so, it is changed itself. We simply don't have enough facts." He gestured at Marshal. "It is plain that people and things from this world can exist there, but can't come back on their own. And that your friend's magic can penetrate, but can't connect. Perhaps some union of the two might work better?"

Seri considered that. Maybe combine Dravid's magic with something more solid, from the primary world. Her eyes strayed to the girl beside her.

"Tich! What about your rope?"

"What about it? It goes right through him."

"But if we could weave it together with Dravid's magic, maybe it could get through!"

Tich shook her head. "Do you know how hard it is to weave rope? I apprenticed with a rope maker in Raeton for a few weeks once, before I started sailing. It's not something we can just throw together."

"All right, maybe not weave it, but attach it somehow. Let's find Dravid!"

"You find him. I'm not leaving this room."

"I'll go," Victor volunteered. He ran up the stairs.

Seri smiled, gave Tich a quick hug, and turned back to listen to the mages some more.

• • • • •

Seri tapped her foot with impatience, watching Dravid and Tich discuss how to integrate her rope with his magic. She glanced up at Marshal's silhouette. He hadn't moved in a very long time. That worried her.

A small crowd gathered in the inner sanctum, despite Master Plecu's attempts to restrict it to only those necessary. The Masters were all here, along with Lady Lilitu and Harunir. Talinir stood with Victor, flanked by Ixchel, Jamana and Adhi. All of them waited in silence. This had to work. It had to.

Dravid pulled himself up on his crutch. "All right, we're going to try this," he announced. "My creations aren't very flexible, but I'll make it as thin as I can. I'll make a loop at the end and we'll tie Tich's rope to it. The hope is that even though Marshal couldn't grab my magic, maybe he can grab the rope."

"And then we pull him out," Seri said. "Let's do it."

Dravid smiled. "As you command, Master Mage."

He took a breath and began to shape the magic. The mages in the room watched intently. For most of them, this was the first time they had seen his ability. With glances at Marshal, he made a long, thin pole with a loop at the end. Tich tied her rope to the loop and stepped back.

Dravid moved as close to the Heart of Fire as he could and started to extend the pole. It wavered only a little bit, illustrating how stiff the magical constructs could be, even as thin as he'd made it. Tich fed the rope out as the pole extended, keeping her eyes on Marshal. As the rope entered the Heart of Fire, it became shadowy and indistinct, like Marshal himself.

Seri held her breath. The pole reached Marshal's silhouette, but he didn't reach toward it. Dravid pushed a little more and touched Marshal in the chest to get his attention. He didn't react or move at all.

A couple of the spectators murmured. She knew what they were thinking. The awful thought crossed her mind too. But he couldn't be dead. Not like this. Not now.

"Pull it back," she said. "Let's try something different."

Dravid obeyed. "What did you have in mind?"

"Can you make the loop big enough to—I don't know—grab hold of him? Without him having to grab it?"

Dravid let the pole dissolve. "I'll try. Tich?"

She nodded, but didn't say anything.

Dravid went back to work. Tich formed a lasso of the right size first, and he worked around that. His loop didn't need to be exact; its only purpose was to take the rope to Marshal.

"Suppose he dissolves the magic part once it's in place," Master Tzoyet suggested, "and then the rope can be tightened."

"But without the magic to make the connection, would the rope maintain its presence there?" Master Ganak wondered.

"We'll experiment," Seri said. "Whatever it takes."

The design completed, Dravid struggled to get it into position. Talinir, the tallest of them, stepped up and took it from him. "Allow me."

The process proceeded as before. This time, Talinir moved the loop over Marshal's head and then lowered it. He positioned one side on Marshal's shoulder and let the other drop down onto his arm. "Pull, Tich," he instructed, "but slowly." She obeyed, drawing the rope toward her. With Dravid's magic stabilizing it, the rope did not pass through Marshal. But neither did he move. Tich pulled harder.

Victor moved next to her and grabbed the rope too, in spite of his bandaged hands. Together they pulled, increasing the pressure bit by bit. "It's like something's pulling against us," Victor said.

"I agree." Talinir stayed next to the Heart, a hand on the rope, but also watching Marshal. Seri wondered if his dual vision showed anything different.

She checked on Dravid. So far, he didn't show any strain from holding the construct in place, but she knew he couldn't maintain it forever.

"We will do this," Jamana said. He and Adhi joined Victor and Tich. All four of them strained at the rope, pulling as hard as they could. After a moment, Ixchel joined them as well.

"He moved," Talinir said. "Keep at it."

Seri's eyes darted up to the shadowy image of Marshal. He moved? The five friends continued to pull. Yes! She could see it now: Marshal's body definitely shifted. His torso and arm moved forward, while his head, legs, and other arm hung back. It looked as if he were being pulled through water, except the pace was so much slower. With a full minute of the five of them straining, Marshal moved what appeared to be an inch or two.

Dravid was showing signs of discomfort. He lowered himself to the floor, breathing hard. Could he maintain this long enough? "You can do it," she whispered to him.

"How many can we fit here?" Master Ganak asked. He crossed the room and took hold of the end of the rope, anchoring the others with his weight. He gestured for others to join him. Harunir, Master Tzoyet and Master Plecu added their strength. There wasn't much room for anyone else. As it was, Master Ganak ended up almost at the stairs. "Pull!" he ordered.

Now with nine people on the rope, Marshal's movement became more obvious, yet still excruciatingly slow. Seri found herself reaching out with her hands, as if she could pull him herself.

"Almost…" Lady Lilitu's voice came from behind her. Seri looked back. The Lady's eyes were also fixed on Marshal. She held a fist near her chest. A tiny flicker of flame bounced around her clasped fingers. Seri stared at it a moment, before breaking off and turning back to Marshal.

More and more of the rope and Dravid's construct emerged from the Heart of Fire. Dravid's agitation grew. "Can you dissolve just the parts that are outside the Heart?" Seri asked. He shook his head.

"Victor! Let go now!" Ixchel ordered.

Victor gasped and released the rope. The bandages had torn from his hands, leaving them bloody and messy. "Sorry."

"Your blood makes the rope slippery," Ixchel griped. Victor stepped out of the way and stared up at Marshal.

Seri squeezed her own bandaged hand. It would probably do the same if she tried to pull on the rough rope.

Part of Marshal's chest emerged from the Heart, gaining color and solidity as it did. "Here he comes!" Seri cried.

"The pull against us has gotten worse," Adhi observed. He strained with the rest of them, sweat dripping down his forehead.

"Here he comes…" Talinir stepped closer. He took hold of the rope around Marshal's chest with one hand.

Marshal's face, chin first, emerged through the wall of the Heart. His head lolled forward. In that moment, several things happened at once.

The Heart of Fire vanished.

Dravid screamed and his construct dissolved.

Marshal tumbled forward into Talinir's arms.

Without the pressure against them, those on the rope stumbled backward, releasing it. Most of them fell, except Ixchel and Harunir. Tich scrambled to her feet, pushing off Jamana, and rushed to Talinir's side as he lowered Marshal to the floor. Victor was right behind her.

Seri checked on Dravid. He sat taking rapid breaths, but waved her away. She joined the others around Marshal.

"He lives," Talinir said. "I'm not sure what's wrong with him, but… he lives."

Seri put her hands on Tich's shoulders as she knelt beside Marshal. She looked up at Victor, whose face looked grim. He saw it too. They all did.

Marshal's scars looked worse. It almost appeared as if each scar had a thousand additional tiny scars radiating out from it. The effect made her shiver. What could cause that? A thought occurred. "Check his back," she suggested.

Talinir gently rolled Marshal to the side in his arms and pulled up his shirt. The large gash left by Curasir showed the same effect as the scars on his face. Seri suspected the same would hold true for the foot where he'd been stabbed, and maybe other injuries as well. The flames of the binding between worlds must have done this, focusing on places where he'd already been hurt, amplifying the problems. If it had been anything like what she'd experienced when she'd gone there unshielded, she could barely imagine what he must have been through over the past day and a half.

Jamana, Adhi and Ixchel all gathered around with them. The Masters and others drew closer, but stayed a respectful distance from the cluster of friends.

"He's moving!" Victor exclaimed.

Talinir shifted Marshal onto his back again, holding his head up. His arm twitched. Marshal coughed, and his head shook. Talinir kept him from flopping around too much. At last, his eyes opened.

Tich leaned in. "Marshal?"

He gave her a weak smile and tried to lift a hand. She grabbed it.

Marshal opened his mouth. His lips moved.

But no sound came out.

(((51)))

Seri entered Marshal's bedroom with quiet steps, in case he slept. She found Tich pacing the room, while an Eldani woman stood by the bed, examining Marshal. After yesterday's excitement of freeing Marshal, he'd been examined by the best doctors on Zes Sivas, and now someone from Intal Eldanir as well.

Seri still hadn't wrapped her head around that yet. The city of the Eldanim, which Marshal and Victor had visited on the far side of Varioch, now floated just off-shore from Zes Sivas. She couldn't imagine the magical forces involved in moving an entire city, let alone keeping it floating! And shifting it between worlds! She also couldn't wait to visit it herself, when the opportunity presented itself.

"Oh, good. You're here," Tich muttered. She snagged her coil of rope from a chair and headed toward the door. "I need to do something else." She pushed out of the bedroom door before Seri could say anything.

The Eldani woman looked up. "She loves him, doesn't she?" Her voice and appearance seemed young, but Seri had no reference for understanding Eldanim ages.

"Yes, I'm pretty sure she does. I'm Seri, by the way." She moved up next to the bed, keeping her voice quiet. Marshal looked much the same as he had the day before, though his eyes were closed now in sleep.

"And I am Eniri. I have heard of you from Talinir."

"Can you do anything to help him?" Seri put her hand out to touch Marshal's, but pulled back for fear of waking him.

Eniri straightened and took a deep breath, eyes fixed on Marshal's face. "I do not know. His experience goes beyond what we know of magic, both of this world and the Starlit Realm. You were with him for part of it, weren't you?"

"Yes, but he was fine when he pushed me back into world." She studied Eniri's face. She must be young. She had to be. "I know that the space between the worlds can cause great pain. I've experienced it. But when we went there before, Marshal didn't have that problem. He said it felt like he belonged there."

"But that was when he still held all of his power, wasn't it?"

"Yes. You think using his power to undo the Laws made him vulnerable?"

"I don't know. I just don't know enough about the magic involved. He does hold power within him now, though I suspect it's nowhere as strong as it was."

Seri reached out with her magical senses and studied Marshal. She did feel power radiating from him, but Eniri was right: it was nothing like he used to wield. Maybe not even to the level of a Lord.

"What about his voice?"

Eniri placed two of her fingers against Marshal's forehead and closed her eyes. She held it there for about half a minute, then pulled away with a sigh.

"His thoughts are chaotic, jumbled," she said, "but I detect nothing like his old curse, nothing magical to prevent him from speaking. I suspect it is more of a physical injury within his throat this time."

"Then it may heal."

"It is certainly possible, and hopeful."

Ixchel entered the room and approached. "My Lady, I thought you should know..."

Seri motioned for her to keep her voice down.

Ixchel glanced at Marshal. "My apologies. But you should know. I believe Tich is trying to leave the island."

• • • • •

Seri hurried, as fast as her robes would allow, all the way across Zes Sivas to the dock. Ixchel trailed behind her. They found Tich in the act of climbing into a rowboat. Seri thought it might be the same boat she'd arrived on the island so long ago.

"Tich! Where are you going?" she called, hurrying out onto the dock.

"Away. Anywhere but here." Tich began to untie the rope holding the rowboat in place.

"But why?" Seri bent down and grabbed at the rope with her good hand. "Why would you leave now?"

Tich lifted her face and stared into Seri's with narrowed eyebrows. "Let me go, Seri."

"Marshal will recover. I know he will. That, that Eldani woman just now said it's only physical injuries. He'll get better."

"I believe you."

Seri stared at her. "Then… why leave?"

Tich let go of the rope and sat down in the rowboat. "This is who I am. I told Marshal that. I run away."

"But you don't have to. We're all your friends here. We want you to stay."

Tich looked away. "I'm not a princess, Seri. I'm not a Lady. I'm not the kind to sit by my man's side and nurse him back to health. That's just… not me."

"Of course it's not," Ixchel said, surprising both of them. "You are Tich."

She looked up. "What's that supposed to mean?"

"I think what Ixchel is saying is that no one expects you to be something that you're not," Seri suggested.

"Yes, they are. Everyone is. I can't do it."

Seri sat down on the dock and hung her legs over the side. "You're right. You can't be what other people expect you to be. But you can be what Marshal needs right now."

"What's that?"

"Someone who cares about him. Someone who loves him."

Tich snorted. "He wants me to be his reason to go on living. I'm not good enough for that. I'll only disappoint him."

Seri pushed herself off and landed in the rowboat in a tangle of robes.

"What are you doing?" Tich exclaimed, leaning forward.

Seri straightened herself. "I arrived on this island in this boat. Did you know that? The man who rowed it, named Hauk, asked if they would let a woman become a mage." She spread her arms, and almost lost her balance. "Here I am."

"So?"

"So you can't listen to other people's expectations! Look at Ixchel. She's a crazy warrior woman. Oh, and you should hear her music. But does she care what other people think about her?"

"I do not," Ixchel said. "Except you, my Lady."

"And Victor, even though you won't admit it." Seri turned back to Tich. "See? You be who you are, who you're meant to be, and don't worry about the people that want you to be something different."

Tich sat back and lowered her eyes. "But what if you don't know who you're meant to be?"

Seri gestured back at the island. "Then what better place to find out than surrounded by people who care about you? Near a man who loves you?"

"But—"

"No, you can't be his reason to go on living. And if he asked you to be that, he's an idiot."

"I told him that."

"Good. He needs someone to call him an idiot every once in a while." Seri leaned in closer. "And to show him what love is, because with the life he's led, I'm pretty sure he doesn't know."

Tich looked up, her eyes rimmed in red. "Then maybe you should show him. That's what your Lady suggested, isn't it? A union of the Kingship, the Lord's house of Arazu, and the Conclave of Mages, wasn't it?"

Seri's mouth dropped open. "That's not what I want!"

"It's not? Haven't you been all about learning and gaining power as fast as you can? You're already a Master Mage. Why not queen too?"

"I'm in love with Dravid!" Seri snapped. "Not Marshal!"

Tich smiled, but her eyes still looked hurt. "Maybe so. But are you going to be able to resist all of them telling you that's the way it has to be?" She pointed back at the citadel. "While I was spying on Volraag, I overheard a lot of other talk too. They're going to pressure you into being queen whether you want it or not. The other Masters are practically giddy over the thought."

"They can't tell me what to do!"

"Can't they? They don't want me around. They want you."

Seri narrowed her eyes now. "And you're going to bow to their wishes? Let them have the final say?"

"I didn't say that."

"No, but you're leaving, which is exactly what they want." Seri put out her hand. "Stay. We'll fight them together."

Tich studied her hand for a few moments. "If you start to crack, I'm gone."

"My Lady does not crack," Ixchel said.

Seri giggled. Tich snorted and broke into a chuckle. She took Seri's hand. "We don't have to shake hands like it's some kind of treaty or anything."

"That's not why I reached out," Seri admitted. "I'm going to need help getting out of here."

This time, Tich really laughed.

(((52)))

Marshal wandered far in dreams. Rarely did any of them make any sense. Stars whirled across the sky. Magic exploded from him in every direction. Aelia visited him, sometimes proud, sometimes sad. Friends, both dead and alive, came and went. At one point, he argued with Volraag for what seemed hours, yet he could never remember what they argued over.

When consciousness returned, he didn't recognize it. His eyes opened and saw Eniri, the Eldani girl who took care of him last year in Intal Eldanir. She couldn't be here. Nice smile, though. He closed his eyes and drifted away again. This time, he slept without dreaming, a deep sleep of rest, recuperation and healing.

When he woke again, he saw only the canopy of his bed. The whole thing was far too fancy for his tastes. Why did he need a canopy, anyway? Did it keep things from falling from the ceiling? Did that happen in a castle?

He blinked a few times, and started to shift position. His body protested in numerous locations, from his face to his back all the way down to his foot: everywhere he'd been wounded over the past year. Everything hurt, but… not too bad. Not like before. With a shudder, he remembered his time in the purple flames. The pain had been so great his mind shut down. At least, that was the only way he could think to describe it.

But here he lay in his bed. Seri and the others must have found a way to rescue him. But what about the gods and the Durunim? He sat up, despite the aches, and then stopped.

Tich sat in a chair beside his bed, but she leaned forward onto the bed itself, her head cradled in her arms, sound asleep. He watched her for a while. She must have been there for quite some time to have fallen asleep. He swallowed. She did care. Somehow, despite all his faults and failings, despite all his scars and brokenness, this girl—this woman—stuck around. She saw past all of that. She liked him, not because he was King, like all those relatives of the Lords, but because of who he was. Him. Marshal. He felt a different ache inside at the thought, but it was a good ache.

He didn't want to disturb her, but he was wide awake now. He couldn't get out of the bed without waking her. He sat back and watched her sleep. She was no great beauty herself, by most standards. Her dirty blonde hair was short and unevenly cut. Even in sleep, her face seemed locked in a perpetual smirk, darkly tanned from constant sun exposure. She looked nothing like Aluri, for example, with her perfect hair, complexion, and poise. And yet... Marshal would choose her over any of them. In his eyes, she was beautiful. He needed to tell her that.

She stirred and blinked. Then she lifted her head and gave a long, slow blink. "Y're awake," she mumbled.

Marshal opened his mouth to answer her, but stopped. He remembered. When he first gained consciousness back in the inner sanctum, he'd been unable to speak. Had his curse returned? Was that part of the price he had to pay for ending the rest of the curses? His hands twisted the bedclothes. He looked down and found himself breathing far too rapidly.

"Hey, hey." Tich got up and moved to his side. "It's all right. You did it. No more curses or bindings."

He heard her words, and knew her intent. He also knew that if he'd known this was the price he'd have to pay, he would have done it. It was worth it. He knew that... in his mind. But his heart panicked. He struggled to breathe. His throat constricted. The thought of not being able to communicate with all of these friends—with Tich!—consumed him and filled him with terror.

Tich looked frightened herself. "I, I don't know what's happening. Do I need to get a doctor?"

Marshal shook his head.

And then he realized: he shook his head. He didn't have to think about it. Nod means yes. Shake means no. He knew that, and didn't struggle over it. No curse. He breathed in deeper. No curse.

He looked up with a smile and found her green eyes.

"Tich," he said.

•••••

Seri braced herself when she heard the knock on her door. She'd been anticipating this meeting for the past several hours, and still didn't know what to think. She opened the door and gave a short bow. "My Lady."

Lady Lilitu swept into her office. Today, she wore a blue gown with yellow trim, somewhat muted compared to her typical clothes. She took Seri in her arms and gave her a hug. "No need for formality between us, daughter."

Seri smiled in return and offered her the reading chair. The Lady accepted, relaxing in its cushions, while Seri herself sat at the desk and waited.

"I will be leaving for Arazu in a few hours," the Lady began. "After this time, I won't be coming back here very often. I know the portals make it easy, but I must focus on our land now. So much has changed. So much needs doing."

Seri agreed. With dozens of new wild mages, Durunim raiding parties still at large, and no magical control over unlawful actions, the Lords were all hard pressed now to gain control over their lands and institute changes. Seri didn't envy them.

"I wanted to be sure that all was right between us before I leave." Lady Lilitu gazed at Seri, her eyes looking for… something.

"What do you mean, my Lady?"

"Our relationship has been strained by lies and mistakes, mostly on my part. I want everything open now. No deception. Nothing hidden. You may ask me anything."

Seri hesitated. One question came right to her mind, but she didn't know whether she wanted the answer. "I… that is, in all that I've heard now, about the gods, that is, in the last few months… they're all different, aren't they? I mean, some of them want absolute power, some want worship, some want fear. Was… was my father like that? Or was he different?"

The Lady sat in silence, rubbing her hands together. At last, she answered: "I would like to say that he was different. That he actually cared about me, as a person." She shook her head. "But I can't say it, because I don't know. In our times alone together, he swore that he loved me, and he behaved…" She paused and cocked her head. "He behaved like a human, like a man. He told me many things, promised me many things. But in the end, he abandoned me." She looked up. "He abandoned you."

Seri winced. All of the gods they had met thus far did not seem like people she would want to get to know, but one of them had impressed Lady Lilitu enough. Had he merely hidden his darker desires and nature from her? Or had he genuinely been different?

"He left because he'd gotten all he wanted from me," Lilitu went on. "He had no reason to stay."

It was the most likely explanation. Yet still Seri hoped, somehow, that it wasn't true. Maybe somewhere out there, a lone "god" had turned against the rest of his race and sought to understand humans without lording over them. After all, the star had told of a god who'd done that at the beginning. Maybe someday…

"Is there anything else?" the Lady asked after another silence.

Seri didn't want to bring it up, but as long as the opportunity existed, she should take advantage of it. "Back in Kuktarma, you wanted me to steal Marshal's power for myself."

Lady Lilitu nodded. "I did."

"Why?"

"With the information I had on Marshal, I did not think he could succeed." She sighed. "I am glad I was wrong, and I am honestly amazed at what he has accomplished. But at the time, I worried. And…" She gave a half-smile. "I'll admit that I wanted my daughter to have the glory, to be the one who saved Antises. Selfishness. Pride. I am susceptible to these sins as well."

"Do you think he'll make a good King now?"

"I do not know." She looked down. "We still do not know all that he experienced, and what effect that had on him. We must keep a careful eye on him in the days to come." She looked back up. "I am also troubled that you and he conspired together to end the Laws after the Lords and Masters agreed that should wait."

"We had to," Seri protested.

"Did you?" The Lady raised an eyebrow.

"I… I don't know. But we went in, knowing that if the opportunity presented itself, we would do it. And it did. When Volraag was killed and gave me his power—"

"Do you still possess that, by the way?"

Seri blinked. "I don't entirely know. Volraag said it always gave him a salty taste in his mouth. Since I came back, I keep thinking I taste it, but I can never be sure."

"Perhaps that will be revealed in time. But speaking of your powers, do not think that because I must take care of Arazu, that I have forgotten my promise to train you in your other power."

"Oh, yes, my Lady. I'm looking forward to it!"

"Good. You were saying?"

"I was? Oh, yes. When Volraag gave me his power, I met the star who enforced our Bond. And he recognized that I had all three powers, and then I knew what Evander's prophecy meant, and it was time. I took Marshal into the Heart of Fire, and, and… that's when it all happened."

"I see." The Lady rubbed her hands together again. "I am still troubled by it. And the reaction of the other Lords ranges from annoyance to outrage. If Marshal recovers enough to take his role as King, it will be a difficult reign." She got to her feet. "And that is why it is good that he has you as an ally. Your position within the Masters makes you powerful in more than just magic. He will need your support, in many ways."

"Of course, my Lady."

"Do you have any messages for your parents?"

Seri took an envelope from her desk and handed it to Lady Lilitu. "Thank you."

"It is the least I can do." She smiled, though Seri thought she saw pain in it. "After all I have put you through since you were born, it amazes me that we can still have a relationship at all."

"I think… I think Jamana would call that… grace."

"Your friend is wise. All of your friends did their part in the great victory won here. They deserve honor. Tell them I said so." She sighed and glanced out the window where Intal Eldanir could still be seen, floating above the waves. "I would dearly love to spend more time getting to know the Eldanim. But, as I told the King, my life belongs to Arazu now."

"I think we all live for others, in some ways," Seri said.

"We do." She held out her arms. "One last hug?"

Seri embraced the Lady without reservation. She still had many confusing questions in her mind, but they could wait. When things settled down, they could train together, learn more about each other… and possibly even her father.

• • • • •

Marshal turned the mirror back and forth, examining his face. "And you thought I was ugly before now," he observed.

"You're not ugly," Tich protested. "You're scarred. There's a difference."

Marshal lowered the mirror and stared at her. "What's the difference?"

She struggled for a moment, then sighed. "All right, you're ugly. What do you want me to say?"

"Say only what you think. You and I don't need to watch our words around each other."

"Do you really want that? Total honesty?"

He nodded.

"Then I suppose I should mention that some of the stories I've told you weren't altogether… true."

Marshal laughed a little, but it hurt. His body ached, especially in all the places where he'd apparently "grown" new scars. The places inside, where Murdak had broken his ribs and the other damage, troubled him with each deep breath he took.

"Tell me everything that happened here, while I was… while I was gone, and then unconscious."

"All right." Tich sat back. "That's a tall order. Let me see… Oh yeah. The gods opened up the lake and walked their army through it to get here. Did you know that much?"

"I knew they were coming. Kishin told us."

"Right. Well, they got here faster. The lake opened up while you were just starting the Passing, I think." From there, Tich went on to describe the appearance of Intal Eldanir, and all that happened with Victor, Ixchel, and Kishin.

"Then I wasn't imagining Eniri," Marshal said. "The Eldanim are still here?"

"If you walk over to your window, you can see the city." Tich pointed. "It's still floating out there, which is absolutely crazy, if you ask me. Ships float. Not cities."

"They are magic, you know."

She shook her head. "I don't think I can get used to that."

"You said the curses and bindings were over," Marshal said. "Were you telling the truth then? Is it really over?"

"You have succeeded beyond all expectations!" a voice from the door answered.

Marshal looked around Tich. "Talinir!"

The Eldani warden crossed the room in a hurry and knelt on the other side of Marshal's bed. "I accomplished the task you set to me," he said. "I hope it meets with your satisfaction."

"You brought the whole city." Marshal reached out and Talinir grasped his hand.

"It was the most efficient way to get here."

Talinir pulled up a chair. For the next hour or more, Marshal listened to his story, the description of the battle, and its aftermath. He thought of few questions, but he didn't have to say much. For once, Talinir seemed delighted to talk at length.

When Talinir finished, Marshal allowed himself to sink back on his pillow. "I'm just glad it's all done," he said. "At last."

"Done?" Talinir chuckled. "Your quest may be completed, but the work is far from done."

"What work?"

"The work of being King. You will be needed more than ever now."

"They won't need me now. What can I do?"

"Leadership. Stability. Strength. In time, everyone will know what you have done," Talinir explained. "As the word spreads among those who have now been set free, they will look to you. The days ahead will be difficult ones. You can't change the world and expect it to keep moving without trouble."

Marshal closed his eyes. "I am so tired. I don't think I can show any kind of strength to anyone."

"At the very least, you've earned your rest. I do not think anything will be required of you for a week or more." Talinir got to his feet. "But Antises is not done with you yet, Marshal, son of Aelia."

"She would be happy," Marshal said. "Wouldn't she?"

"She would be the proudest one of all of us. And we couldn't be more proud than we are." He moved to the door. "We will talk more when you are feeling better."

"Thank you," Marshal said with an effort.

Talinir nodded. "I promised." He left the room.

"And I'm back to having vision problems with him around," Tich complained. "And it's not just him. There are Eldanim all over the place. We're all going to end up cross-eyed trying to look at them."

Marshal wanted to laugh, but again: it hurt.

"You can do this King thing, you know," she added. "You're the strongest person I've ever met."

"Didn't I say the same thing to you?"

"Yeah, but you were delusional. I'm being rational here. If anyone I've ever met can handle this, it's you."

"I can't do it alone."

"Then it's a good thing you aren't alone, isn't it?" Tich leaned back over the bed. "You've got Victor. And Seri, who's one of the Masters now. And Talinir brought the whole Eldanim nation."

Marshal finally opened his eyes again and looked at her. "What about you?"

"Yeah, I guess I'm here too."

"I'm glad. I—"

"I almost left," she interrupted.

Marshal blinked.

"You wanted honesty. I almost ran away from you. I was in the boat, ready to go."

"Why didn't you?"

Tich looked away. "Seri talked me out of it. I think."

"Oh." He didn't know what else to say.

"She's got a way with words, you know."

"What did she tell you?"

"To call you an idiot." Tich looked back into his eyes. "So. You're an idiot."

Marshal laughed, which turned into a cough. Tich offered him some water. After he drank, he relaxed and asked, "Was that the only reason you stayed? To tell me I'm an idiot?"

"No. There are other things to tell you."

"Like?"

"I'll get there. Give me time."

Marshal nodded and closed his eyes. "I think we've got a little bit of that now."

"A little bit. Sure." Tich got up and stretched. "Now that you're awake and getting better, I don't have to spend every waking minute in this chair. I need to go stretch my legs a while."

"As long as you don't leave. I need to hear those other things."

Tich smiled. "You'll hear them. I'm not going anywhere now."

(((53)))

Marshal approached the King's chair again, the time with a limp. His foot still hurt, as did so many other places. Still, he needed to be here for this. Everyone wanted to see him, to speak with him. The Lords demanded accountability for his actions. Today, he would face them all. He stood beside the chair and looked around the room.

This time around, the audience stands were full. In addition to the usual residents of Zes Sivas, mages and workers, he saw many relatives of the Lords, along with other representatives of each land. He noticed Otioch, Volraag's former right-hand man. Despite his associations, the leader of the Remavian Guard had proven his worth in the chaos of the past few weeks, fighting the Durunim alongside his men and the new wild mages. Marshal was seriously considering appointing him Lord of Varioch, even though he had no magical power. He wondered what the other Lords would think of that.

The High Council of the Eldanim sat in the front row, here to observe how the humans conducted their governmental affairs. Marshal hoped he and the Lords wouldn't embarrass humanity too much today. Talinir gave him a smile and a nod.

Ixchel stood at the door. As each group entered, she observed them for threats against her Lady and her King (or so Marshal hoped, anyway).

The six Masters entered the room and took their seats. No, there were only five. That was strange. Master Komadi of Mandiata was missing. Seri gave him a big smile, but the others remained stone-faced. He hadn't yet heard what they thought of his actions at the Passing. He was sure to get an earful today.

Victor hurried in next, joining him in the center. "Sorry I'm late," he said, but offered no other excuse. Marshal only nodded.

He looked toward the doors. The Lords would be coming next. He was not looking forward to facing them, especially Lord Tyrr. The death of Volraag still hurt, in a way that other deaths hadn't. Such wasted potential. So many things that could have been between them.

To his surprise, the first ones to enter the room were Aluri and a young man who must be her brother. They moved to the Rasnian chair and faced him.

"If it pleases the King," Aluri announced, "may I present my brother Ziv, the new Lord of Rasna."

"It is an honor, Your Majesty," Ziv said, bowing.

Marshal gave an awkward bow in return. "And your father?"

"He is no longer Lord," Aluri said. "That is all I will say on the matter right now."

Victor looked like he wanted to say something, but shut his mouth.

"If it is acceptable to you, Your Majesty," Lord Ziv said, "I would like my sister to remain here, as my advisor in this gathering."

Marshal nodded. "That is perfectly acceptable. I am sure her wisdom will be of great value to you." Aluri gave him a gentle smile in return. The other Lords might raise eyebrows over it, but what difference did it make? Everything was changing from the old ways now.

Lord Rajwir entered next. He acknowledged Marshal with a slight nod, but didn't say anything. They had a respectful relationship prior to the Passing; Marshal wasn't sure how damaged that would be now.

Lord Bakari entered with a smile. Out of all the Lords, he was probably Marshal's best ally. His father's power had restored to him (diminished though it was) after Volraag's death. Despite the chaos of the past few weeks, he still credited Marshal with his own solidified position as Lord of Mandiata.

Lady Lilitu followed him, resplendent in a glittering silver gown that left both shoulders bare. Marshal tried not to stare too much. He still wasn't sure what to think of the Lady ever since her marriage advice.

Lord Meluhha came last, a scowl on his face. Marshal regretted that most of all. He had spent more time with Adhi's father than any of the other Lords, and thought they had become, if not friends, at least allies. But Lord Meluhha had not appreciated Marshal's decision to end the Laws, and he suspected Marshal had a role in the release and subsequent disappearance of Kishin. Marshal tried to heal the relationship by offering Adhi a position as advisor to the King, but he declined in order to continue his mage studies.

"Everyone's here," he whispered to Victor, taking his own seat. "Start it up."

"Really? I still have to do that?" Victor sighed, then announced in a loud voice: "The council is assembled. All present and accounted for. As chief advisor to King Marshal the First, I declare this meeting begun."

The First? Victor must have thought it would be funny, but it probably grated on some of those present, appearing too arrogant. Marshal tried not to cringe.

Master Tzoyet stood first. "Your Majesty, I would like—"

"Why do you call him that?" Lord Meluhha interrupted. "He is not our King. Not yet."

Master Tzoyet exchanged looks with Master Ganak. "All that remains is a formal coronation," he said. "It is but a formality, Lord. Marshal was recognized as King in this very chamber the last time we met here."

"He is right," Lord Rajwir agreed. "As much as we may dislike his first actions as King, we did recognize him. And he formed the Heart of Fire during the Passing. There is no dispute there."

"Then what does it take to remove a King?" Lord Meluhha asked.

"That is beyond the purview of this gathering," Master Tzoyet said. "We—"

"Then how is it done? We have all the existing Lords and Masters here. If not this group, then who?"

"This is not a necessary or worthwhile use of our time," Lady Lilitu chimed in. "If we were to remove the King, it would have to be unanimous."

"And that will not happen," Lord Bakari declared.

Lord Meluhha grumbled something under his breath, but did not continue the argument.

"As I was saying," Master Tzoyet began again, "I believe our primary order of business will address the problems that have caused Lord Meluhha to have such strong feelings. We must discuss Your Majesty's decision to end the Laws of Cursings and Bindings."

"Against the will of this council," Master Plecu added.

"I will be happy to address the issue," Marshal said. He rose to his feet and looked around them all. Some stared back at him. Some looked away, though he couldn't tell whether it was from their feelings about him or general disgust at his scarred visage. "I want to begin by explaining to all of you exactly who I am, and how I came to be here. Some of you know the story because you were a part of it. Some of you know only parts of it. But you need to know all.

"I was born in a tiny village in the mountains of Varioch called Drusa's Crossing…" Over the next few minutes, he told them his life story, from growing up with Aelia to the quest that led him eventually to Zes Sivas. He spent a great deal of time emphasizing what his life had been like under the curse, describing his mistreatment by the other villagers, his struggles to communicate simple thoughts to his own mother, and the seizures he experienced from the magic growing with him.

From there, he went on to summarize the journey he had taken over the past year, in and out of the Otherworld. He made sure to mention Lady Siratel's prophecies to himself and his grandfather. He concluded with an account of what happened when he entered the Heart of Fire.

"So you see, from the very beginning, my path was laid out before me," he explained. "I knew from the beginning that my purpose was to lift all the curses. The system was unjust and it needed to end." A memory of Nian the priest came to his mind. "And to be honest, I believe Theon wanted it that way. A wise priest once told me that for us to truly follow Theon, or any god, I suppose, it must be our choice. Not a compulsion. I can't force anyone to believe what I believe, and I shouldn't be able to." He looked around the room again. "I shouldn't be able to."

After a long pause, Lord Rajwir stood. "Your story is… compelling. And yet it does not address the main issue: what gave you the right to do this against the will of this council?"

Marshal spread his hands. "Did you not hear me?"

"Yes, we heard. It was your destiny or purpose. But you took action that affected every single person in all six lands of Antises!" He slammed his fist on the table. "You, and you alone, made this decision. You acted, not as a King, but as a tyrant."

"A tyrant," Marshal repeated. "How would you define a King then, Lord Rajwir?"

He spread his arms in return. "We all know what a King is."

"Do we?" Marshal looked toward Talinir. "A friend told me that a King and his land are one. He holds its destiny in his hand. He must love it, guard it, and care for it beyond his own needs and desires. He must be selfless, putting their needs above his own." He glanced at

Lady Lilitu. "A King does not belong to himself. He belongs to his people.

"How could I claim to be King of all Antises, if I did not do what was right and best for all the people of Antises? The Laws of Cursings and Bindings were unjust. We all know that. I have—" He paused and gritted his teeth. "I have been broken for Antises. My body is... not whole. I have experienced more pain in the past year than any of you know. And none of it was for me. I could have quit at any time. I could have."

"Yet you have stated that it was your desire to end the curses," Master Magnus pointed out. "How then can you say you were not pursuing your own desires?"

Marshal took a deep breath before answering. "Was it my desire to end the curses? Yes, of course. But it was a desire born of injustice. Beyond that, what are my desires? For my entire life, I had but one: to live a normal life like everyone else. To be able to talk with the people I care about. To walk around without people staring at me and whispering." His eyes sought out Tich in the audience. "To find a woman I could spend the rest of my life with." He swallowed. "To be loved. To be valued. To have a purpose."

"Sentimental drivel," Master Plecu muttered.

"Master Plecu!" Lord Ziv said in a loud voice.

Plecu jumped. "Yes, my Lord?"

"As I am now Lord of Rasna, I would appreciate you reflecting my will in these type of proceedings." The young Lord pointed across the tables. "In that spirit, you will refrain from negative comments directed against the King of Antises. Is that clear?"

Master Plecu sputtered.

"Such respect for my wishes is not an absolute requisite for your continuance in this position,"—Ziv glanced at his sister, who smiled—"but it is highly recommended."

Marshal tried not to let his eyes go too wide. Aluri's influence on her brother was stronger than he'd anticipated.

Victor leaned in and whispered, "Who would have thought that our best ally among the Lords would be Rasna?"

"We have listened to your story and your explanation," Lord Meluhha spoke up. "But it does not address the central question any more than before. Master Ganak, a question for you."

"Yes, my Lord?"

"Are the duties, responsibilities, and abilities of the King laid out in the Law?"

"They are."

Lord Meluhha fixed his gaze on Marshal again. "Have you read these relevant portions of the Law, young man?"

"As a matter of fact, I have," Marshal answered. Jamana had brought them to him the day before and he'd read through as quickly as he could. "Nothing I have done violates any of the Law as written."

Lord Meluhha snorted. He'd apparently been expecting to trap Marshal with that line of questioning. If not for Jamana, it might have worked. Marshal looked toward the audience, but couldn't find Jamana. Odd. He saw Dravid and Adhi together, but Jamana wasn't with them.

Lady Lilitu stood. "I would have to differ with you, Lord Meluhha. I believe the King has thoroughly answered the central question. Whether we like his answer is a different matter, and not one that is worth debating. The question now is whether we support him under the Law, as you mentioned, and move on with governing our lands, or... not."

"What alternative is there?" Lord Bakari wondered.

"It may be time to go our separate ways," Lord Rajwir said slowly. All eyes turned to him, and an audible whisper ran through the audience.

"What do you mean, Lord?" Lady Lilitu asked.

Lord Rajwir gestured around the tables. "Look at us. Each of us rule a land, a separate land with distinct cultures and people. We were united by Akhenadom and brought here. Our union was formed on the basis of loyalty to his house and a shared worship of Theon. The Laws of Cursings and Bindings guaranteed that our people would not, could not stray too far from that worship, or from their homelands. With the Laws destroyed... what binds us together?" He pointed to Marshal. "We know that he is of the house of Akhenadom, but he is also of Varioch's bloodline. Do we truly owe him any allegiance? What is left to keep us from forming our own individual nations? We could all of us... be Kings."

Silence followed his words. Marshal felt a great dread building up inside him. Out of all the possibilities for this meeting, he had never even conceived this one. How could he even respond to it?

"We are already in the process of establishing our own systems of justice," Lord Rajwir continued a moment later. "Our own laws for dealing with the rise of crime. Why not take it all the way? Why should we have anything to do with a high King over all, or Zes Sivas itself?"

"Zes Sivas is the heart of Antises!" Master Tzoyet protested.

"What does that even mean?" Lord Rajwir shot back. "What is Antises?"

"This is absurd," Lord Bakari said. "Yes, we negotiate with each other as separate lands, but we are one people. Our people cross borders freely, do business with each other, marry each other. We have our differences, but there's no need to throw out a thousand years of tradition."

Lord Rajwir pointed at Marshal. "He threw out a thousand years of our Laws! He tore us apart!"

Lord Meluhha leaped to his feet. Several other Lords and Masters followed, as the conversation grew louder and everyone talked over one another, interrupted and shouting. Marshal looked from one to the other, unable to answer any of them. His eyes sought out Seri. She sat in her chair, trembling. She met his gaze and shook her head, mouth ajar in despair.

Marshal had saved Antises. But Antises was tearing itself apart.

(((54)))

Jamana hurried through the hallway to the gathering room. He could barely contain his excitement. So many wonderful things had been happening. The latest might just be the best.

He glanced behind him at the figure following. "We're almost there," he said, "but I'm sure you know that."

"You've done well, acolyte. Now to see how the others react."

Indeed. This would be fun.

• • • • •

Marshal stood up. He had to find some way of regaining control of this meeting, some way of restoring what was swiftly falling apart. Only one thought came to him.

"My Lords!" he cried. "My Lords! Let me suggest something!"

Either because his voice was loud enough, or because they were getting nowhere with their arguing, the council grew quiet. One by one, the Lords and Masters took their seats again, all ten of them… because Master Komadi remained missing. Curious, but a puzzle for another time.

"My hope was to save Antises," Marshal declared. "I will not see it torn apart now."

"How will you stop it?" Lord Meluhha asked. "You have no leverage against any of us." Several others murmured in response.

"If my Kingship is the breaking point for Antises, then I should not be King."

Marshal's statement brought complete silence to the room.

"What do you mean?" Seri asked.

"Antises must be united," he said. "Choose another King, someone who you all can agree on. Someone worthy of the title. Because that is not me."

"What are you doing?" Victor hissed.

"Whatever I have to do," Marshal whispered back.

"But we have already recognized you as our King!" Lord Bakari protested.

"Then I will step down. Whatever it takes to keep you all together."

"Who else would be King?" Lord Ziv asked.

"Perhaps… perhaps one of you Lords," Master Magnus suggested. "Can you all agree on one of you?"

The Lords looked at each other. Lord Meluhha actually laughed.

"I do not see that as likely," Lady Lilitu said drily.

"May I say something?"

Everyone turned to see who had spoken. One of the Eldani councilors stood. Marshal recognized her as Indala, the one who supported he and his mother last year.

"We, we would be honored to hear from a member of the Eldanim High Council," Master Tzoyet stammered.

Indala surveyed the Lords and Masters, then spoke without emotion or inflection in her voice. "I have consulted with the other members of the High Council you see here before you, including our High Mage and High Champion. We are all in agreement." With little effort, she vaulted over the audience chamber railing and walked toward the council tables.

"Over the past few weeks, we have done what we can to aid you in the transition of your world. We are also in negotiation with many of you for new agreements between our two peoples, trade deals between Intal Eldanir and Antises." Several of the Lords nodded. "We have entered into these negotiations with the understanding that this man, Marshal, is King over all Antises." She paused for effect. "If this is not to be the case, we will be withdrawing our aid and ceasing all negotiation. We have no desire to deal with the petty bickering I see before me now."

"Ouch," Victor muttered.

"Lady Indala!" Seri burst out. "If I may, why do you hold the King in such high regard?"

Indala gave her a brief glance, then pointed at Marshal. "The Starlit Realm blooms again," she announced. "This man brought healing, not to your world alone, but to two worlds. And if the stars themselves honor him, how can we not do likewise?"

Marshal almost gasped. The Otherworld was growing again? He had to see that. He made a mental note to visit as soon as possible.

A disturbance at the door drew his attention for a moment. Ixchel was discussing something with someone outside the door. She looked confused, but she hadn't drawn her sword.

"Let me be sure that I understand this," Lord Rajwir said. "You are saying that you will not do business with us unless we accept the King that you support."

"Essentially," Indala answered.

"You would come here and tell us how to govern our lands? This is outrageous!" Lord Meluhha pounded the table.

"You do not seem to be doing much of an impressive job on your own," Indala said calmly. Marshal winced. He wished she hadn't said that.

"My Lords," Lady Lilitu implored, "let us consider exactly what we would be throwing away by defying the Eldanim on this matter."

"It would be a grave loss," Master Ganak said.

"But is it one we are willing to pay?" Lord Rajwir asked. "What is the price of our independence?"

Ixchel stood aside and Jamana entered at the door. His grin looked even larger than usual. Irritated by the disturbance, Marshal turned back to the Lords, in time to hear Indala say, "Did all of you not hear me? The stars honored King Marshal. They told him his name would be remembered alongside that of Akhenadom."

"That's a bit much," Master Magnus muttered.

"Forgive me, lady Indala," Master Tzoyet said, "but we do not have the same understanding. To you, what is the significance of these stars?"

The seated Eldanim murmured. Indala raised a hand to silence them. "To those who have not seen the Starlit Realm, it is an understandable question. The stars of your world are not the same." She hesitated. "Suppose the sun and moon came down and did homage before one of you. It is a poor analogy, but it begins to point toward the significance. We hold the stars of our world with utmost reverence and awe. That they would honor this man"—she pointed at Marshal—"tells us all we need to know of his character and his accomplishments."

Marshal was glad he wasn't expected to say anything in response. He licked his lips, utterly speechless.

Indala beckoned, and Talinir rose, impressive in his High Champion's armor and green cape. He descended from the crowd and joined her. "For those who have not met him, this is Talinir, High Champion of Intal Eldanir. Should Marshal remain as King, Talinir has requested to stay as well. He will be our ambassador to Antises, and protector of the King, should he agree."

"Gladly," Marshal exclaimed. Talinir smiled and gave a short bow.

"This is most impressive," Lord Meluhha admitted. "But even so, I am not certain that anything else binds Antises together any longer."

"Then you are a fool." The voice came from the door. Marshal turned back in that direction and gaped, along with everyone else. Jamana and Ixchel stood aside to allow another large figure in purple robes to enter the chamber. Marshal had never met the man, but he felt certain he knew him.

"Who dares?" demanded Lord Meluhha, unable to see past the other Lords, who had risen to their feet.

The tall figure strode into the chamber. "I dare. I am Master Korda of Mandiata, and I have much to say on this topic."

All of the Masters had leaped to their feet at his entrance. Seri almost danced for joy in her spot.

Marshal tried to grasp what this meant. Everyone thought Master Korda to be dead, slain by Nummotem while Seri escaped from the god's pursuit. Lord Bakari had appointed Komadi to his place, yet Komadi was nowhere to be seen now. Marshal glanced at Lord Bakari. Unlike everyone else, he remained seated, a knowing smile on his face. He had planned this! Marshal shook his head. Lords and Mages alike truly loved their drama.

"I didn't see that coming," Victor said.

"Nor I," Marshal replied.

Master Korda strode to his seat at the mages' table and bowed to Marshal. "Your Majesty, I apologize for my tardiness. There was some dispute about my… life."

"It is good to see you alive and well, Master Korda," Marshal answered.

Korda nodded and addressed the room: "Before I speak, let me quickly assure you all that I am indeed alive. I understand that most of you considered me dead. As you can see, such is not the case."

• • • • •

Seri couldn't help herself. "But how?" she burst out, then covered her mouth, eyes wide.

Master Korda chuckled. "It is a fair question, but one even you should understand, Master Seri-Belit. Did you not describe for me the method in which you crossed from our world to the other? I will admit that I was unable to duplicate it at first, but when Nummotem was about to kill me, I found the... desperation necessary to accomplish the task. Unfortunately, I was badly injured already and fell unconscious upon my arrival in the Otherworld." He gestured to the Eldanim. "An Eldani warden found me and restored me to full health."

Seri couldn't believe it. In her brief journey to the Otherworld with Ixchel and Ekur, they had been only a few yards from Master Korda. If only they had known!

"Fascinating," Master Ganak said. "Why have you not returned to us before now? That was, if I am thinking correctly, over two months ago."

"The warden who rescued me was on a mission to the outmost borders of our lands to the east. I was unable to repeat the journey back to our world at first, and he could not leave me alone, so I traveled with him."

"Forgive me, Master Korda," Lord Rajwir said. "I am sure your story is fascinating, but we are at a crux point in our debate here. You said you wished to speak on that topic?"

"I did." Korda glared at him. "My story is relevant to the discussion. Listen well. When the warden and I reached the end of our journey, an outpost of the Eldanim in the far East, I was at last strong enough to return to our world. I found myself near a city, where I was able to obtain passage back to Antises."

He held up a finger. "But the ship would only take me to the very edge of Kuktarma, where I had to disembark and find new transport that could bring me here." He began to walk around the tables. "You see, there are other nations out there, as we all know, at least vaguely. But they rarely do any business with us here. The Laws of Cursings and Bindings frighten them, you see." He stopped and looked at Marshal. "That is, they were frightened. Word is already spreading that the magical laws have been lifted. Unless I am greatly wrong, we will soon be flooded with visitors from other lands, seeking to do business, or... seeking to do harm. Not all lands are ruled with justice."

"What are you saying?" Marshal asked, eyes wide.

"When these visitors arrive, what will they find?" Master Korda asked. "Will they find six weak and fragmented lands, struggling to survive, easy prey for a powerful warlord? Or will they find Antises united under a King and allied with powerful friends from another world? Think carefully, my Lords. How would you want them to find us?"

Master Korda let his words sink in as he returned to his seat. Before sitting down, he paused and added, "I, for one, am more than happy to support this King. You have my full support, Your Majesty."

"Thank you, Master Korda."

Seri admired Marshal for keeping calm. She was about to explode. Keeping her mouth shut right now was the right thing to do, but she could barely contain herself.

Lord Bakari stood. "Indeed. Thank you, Master Korda. It is good to see you in your rightful place again. Now." He looked to each of the other Lords. "With this information, what say you, my friends? Shall we voice our confidence in our King and in our union?"

Lord Ziv stood. "I stand confident," he announced.

"As do I." Lady Lilitu joined them.

Lord Meluhha got to his feet slowly. "It appears I have little choice. I remain disturbed by the actions of the King and his allies during the Passing, and I fear it sets a grave precedent. However…" He gave an elaborate sigh. "I cannot deny the character I saw in this young man while in my land. If he holds true to that behavior rather than the former, I stand confident in his leadership."

All eyes turned to Lord Rajwir. He did not move.

"My Lord," Master Tzoyet said. "It is the prudent move."

Lord Rajwir gave an exaggerated sigh. "Were we all to split into individual lands, I would prefer it. But it seems that if I refuse now, Ch'olan would stand alone. And while we do not fear our neighbors, there is strength to be found in unity." He stared at Marshal. "Even if I do not approve of the leader of the united." He stood.

"Antises stands together!" Master Korda's voice boomed. "Let those who would seek to prey on us rue this day. Master Tzoyet, have we any other business to deal with?"

Master Tzoyet jumped, surprised to be addressed. He got to his feet. "I, uh, I do not believe that we have anything else that is pressing right now. I am sure there will be many small meetings among us to discuss current conditions."

"And I would hope to speak with each of you in turn," Marshal declared, "to see if there is any way that Zes Sivas can help you in our current struggles."

"Of course, we must schedule the formal coronation," Master Tzoyet continued. "I am sure it will be an event like no other in… well, in centuries. With that being said, I rule this gathering adjourned."

Seri jumped to her feet and applauded. Many in the audience did the same. Then she rushed to embrace Master Korda. The big man laughed.

"Well, little Seri. When I sent you to seek for the lost King, I'm sure neither of us imagined it would lead to this." He gestured broadly.

"No!" Seri laughed too. "I am so happy to see you right now. You can't imagine."

Jamana came up behind them. Seri scolded him. "If you knew about this, you…"

"I?" Jamana pointed at his chest dramatically. "I knew nothing."

Master Korda put his hand on Seri's shoulder. "If Master Hain could see you now, he would be proud indeed."

Seri swallowed against the lump that rose in her throat. "Thank you," she whispered.

"Seri!" Marshal called. She turned to see him speaking with the new Lord Ziv and his sister. "I need your input on this."

"Go," Master Korda said. "Serve the King. We will speak more later."

Seri nodded and hurried to Marshal's side.

(((55)))

Over the next few weeks, Marshal watched the transformation of Zes Sivas in absolute awe. The Masters insisted that the coronation take place in the traditional throne room, but that part of the citadel had been destroyed, thanks to Volraag's attack and subsequent earthquakes. But now workers from Rasna, Arazu, and Mandiata joined with Eldanim engineers to reconstruct it far quicker than Marshal would have thought possible.

Marshal did not sit around, however. One-by-one, he visited the four lands accessible through the portal room. With the advice of the Masters and Adhi, he strengthened the ties that already existed, and worked to mend fences with Lord Meluhha and Kuktarma. He regretted being unable to visit Ch'olan. Volraag's destruction of the portals worked even more detriment than he'd planned. At the very least, Marshal sent multiple messages and gifts to Lord Rajwir and Lady Ajaw, hoping to bring reconciliation. He received no answers.

As for Varioch, Marshal had to lean heavily on Volraag's former staff. His half-brother may have been a power-hungry zealot, but he knew how to surround himself with strong leaders. Marshal appointed Otioch as Magistrate, a concession to the other Lords in name, but effectively the same rank. He governed Varioch under Marshal's approval, along with help from General Cassian and others. The Masters speculated greatly on whether Marshal's King powers and Lord powers would eventually separate in future children, or if his first-born would inherit both. This led to even more interest in Marshal's marital possibilities.

After multiple battles, especially in Varioch and Rasna, the Durunim and the remaining gods retreated, disappearing to parts unknown. It troubled Marshal that so many of them still remained in the primary world. The Eldanim wardens joined the hunt, but there was a limit to what even their skills could uncover. The gods hid their paths well.

The proliferation of wild mages, the most unexpected aspect of ending the Laws, continued to expand. While it seemed almost everyone whose curse had been removed developed an affinity for wild magic, many who had not been cursed were now manifesting abilities. Seri and the Masters theorized it to be a natural outcome of one simple fact: more magic was now available, instead of bound up in the Lords and King.

Marshal could feel his own power within him. He couldn't be sure, of course, since he had no way of measuring it, but he thought his power level now matched what he had possessed before the death of his grandfather. In other words, his power equaled one of the Lords, or the power the Lords used to have. By all accounts, it still made him the most powerful magic wielder in Antises, just… nowhere near as powerful as before.

He climbed the stairs to the outer wall of the island to get a better view of the ongoing construction. There he found Harunir, the mage, and his daughter Eniri.

"Greetings, Your Highness," Eniri said.

"Please." He waved his hand. "You knew me when I was a dying, frightened curse boy on the run. You don't have to talk that way now."

"If you insist." She smiled, and he suddenly felt embarrassed. He turned to look at the construction.

The wind had a strong bite to it on the wall. Winter held the island in its grip, but it wasn't too bad. It hadn't gotten as cold as the previous winter, at least from Marshal's point of view. But then again, he had grown up in the mountains.

"It's going so fast," he observed.

"The men work hard," Harunir replied. "We show them what to do, and they do it."

"You're doing so much for us." Marshal shook his head. "I don't see how we can repay you."

"You already have," Eniri said. "You healed the Starlit Realm."

"I didn't even know that would happen," Marshal protested. He had slipped away and taken a look for himself. Indala's claim that the Starlit Realm "bloomed" seemed a little exaggerated to him. He'd seen water flowing, and a few bursts of plant life here and there. Different, but not as dramatic as the Eldanim proclaimed.

"It doesn't matter. You still did it. And then there are the stars."

Marshal leaned against the nearest battlement. "I still don't understand that part. Until that happened, I had no idea the stars were living beings of some kind. Did you know that all along?"

Harunir and Eniri exchanged glances.

"And why are you Eldanim so reluctant to share any of this with us? Talinir was the same way!"

"You have to understand," Harunir said. "Hundreds of years ago, the Eldanim had their own… religious disagreements. We split into two factions. Anger fueled the conflict. A few blows were exchanged. And one of the factions, a very large group, left us. We have never heard from them since, though we suspect they became the first of the Durunim."

"And this… disagreement was about the stars?"

Harunir nodded. "Ever since, we have been hesitant to say much on such topics, over the fear that we would create more conflict."

"I see." Marshal thought for a minute. "No, I don't see. Do you think you know the truth about the stars?"

"We do."

"Then why keep it to yourself? What good is truth if it is kept a secret?"

"If the truth could bring harm, it may be well to keep it secret."

"Truth is truth," Marshal argued. "Truth should be shared, proclaimed for all to know."

"You may have a point," Harunir conceded. "But it has not been our way."

Marshal laughed. "Ways change, Harunir. Look around. Everything in my world is changing."

"Has Talinir told you about the third world?" Eniri asked. Harunir shot her a look, but didn't say anything.

"When he was training us, he said something about it," Marshal recalled. "Something about a war beyond our understanding."

"The stars are the ones who fight that war."

Marshal pulled his coat tighter against the wind. "I don't understand." He gestured toward the sky. "I haven't seen the stars move, except when they came down to speak to me. How are they in your sky, and yet also fighting a battle? And they were also enforcing our Laws. All that at once?"

"It is why we revere them," Eniri explained. "Just as we Eldanim are beings of two worlds, the stars bridge the gap between the Starlit

Realm and the third world. They are beings above our comprehension… for now. We study them, try to understand them better. And someday, we will join them."

"Yet they spoke to you," Harunir said. "They spoke directly to you. Can you understand how that affects us? You have been granted an honor we all dream about."

Marshal looked back at the construction. "I didn't know. There's so much I still don't know."

"I will tell you what I can," Eniri offered. "Not all at once, though. Give me time to… work past my inhibitions."

"Sure," Marshal said. "Just… not in front of Tich. I think she gets jealous when I pay too much attention to other women."

"Is she to be your queen, then?"

Marshal glanced at her. "I don't know. Maybe. We're still working on it."

"Then may the stars guide you."

Marshal nodded, then thought of something else. "Who guides the stars? Talinir talked about their Maker a little."

"He is the One Above All."

"Is he Theon?"

"How can we answer that?" Harunir asked. "It may be so. From what I have read from your Akhenadom, they sound remarkably similar. But for me to say they are the same? I just do not know."

"I think he spoke to me too," Marshal said in a quiet voice.

Eniri caught his arm. "What did you say?"

Marshal looked back at her. "I think the Maker, or Theon, or whoever it is beyond it all, spoke to me. After I ended the Laws. I thought it was Aelia, my mother, at first, but then the voice changed."

Eniri let her hand slide loose from his arm. "If you are right, then the honor paid to you is beyond even what we thought." She shook her head. "I believe I will go back to being formal with you, King Marshal. You deserve it."

"Please don't. It's hard enough around here. I want my friends to treat me like a friend, not a ruler."

Her eyes widen, and she looked at her father. "Do you consider us your friends?"

"Of course. You sheltered us, sided with us in Intal Eldanir. You were kind to my mother. Of course you're friends." He straightened. "In fact, have you met my other friends?"

"Only the girl, Seri," Eniri said. "And Victor, of course."

"Come on, then." Marshal gestured toward the stairs. "It's time you met them. I want all of my friends to know each other. In fact, I need all of you."

Eniri looked at Harunir. "Go ahead, daughter. I have work to do here. And I believe Marshal's friends will be more… your age."

Marshal laughed. "Most of them, anyway," he admitted. "Come on."

Eniri followed him down the stairs. Marshal glanced back and smiled. Last winter, he'd been alone with only his mother and not a single friend in the world. Today? He couldn't believe how many people he could call friend. Forget the kingship. This was what really mattered.

(((56)))

"Wake up, Curse Boy. It's time to get crowned!"

Marshal opened his eyes and rolled over. He sat up and only then realized who woke him. "Tich! What are you doing in my bedroom?"

"Please. I was in your bedroom for days, remember?" She opened his wardrobe and looked through its contents. To Marshal's surprise, she wore a green gown that left her shoulders bare. Her hair had been done up in a bun, and thin gold chains hung from it. She looked incredible.

"That was when I was… recovering."

"So you're recovered. What are you wearing to this big deal, anyway?"

"They've, uh, laid something out for me over there." He pointed at the couch next to the wall.

Tich wandered over it and examined the clothes. "I suppose these will do. The newest acolytes had to draw you a bath next door, by the way. Should be ready by now."

Most of the Masters were now taking on new acolytes, another change in the way Zes Sivas did things. With the proliferation of wild mages, the Masters believed the newly magic-sensitive citizens should be trained as much as possible.

"Tich… thank you. I wish you could be a part of the ceremony today."

"I don't do ceremonies."

He chuckled. "Sure. But you'll be watching, right?"

"Of course."

"And you're… all right with who I've chosen to participate?"

"Why wouldn't I be?"

"I just want to be sure."

"Of course I'm all right with it, you idiot. It makes perfect sense."

"You look beautiful, by the way."

"I'll wear this thing for today only. And maybe your funeral. Now go take your bath."

"All right. I'll do that… once you leave the room."

Tich looked back with her usual snarky look: lowered eyebrow, elevated half-smile. "I'm not stopping you."

"I'm serious, Tich. I don't… I don't wear much while I'm in bed."

"All right, all right. I'm leaving." She paused at the door. "I'll see you later."

Marshal waited a few moments after she shut the door to be sure she was really gone. He climbed out of the far-too-large bed and made his way to the side room where his bath awaited. Steam rose from the water as he climbed into the tub. Over the past few weeks, he had come to enjoy these baths. Aside from very brief times during their journeys, he hadn't had this kind of opportunity, especially not with hot water.

"Maybe I could get used to being King," he admitted to himself.

After the bath, he confronted the clothing. At least this time, he understood the various pieces. The outfit had been chosen with his upbringing and culture in mind. At the same time, the material used in his trousers and shirt were fancier by far than anything he'd ever worn, even compared to his fine clothes from Kuktarma. He struggled a little bit with the vest, made as it was of stiff leather, but it had been tailored to fit his body. Once in place, he examined himself in the mirror. The vest, while strong enough to stop a hidden knife, appeared as if made of some other fine material. He turned back and forth, watching the movement of the colors. The primary theme appeared to be metallic, with gold, silver, and bronze. Some of the trim stood out in red and green. At least none of the colors were overly bright.

A quick knock at the door signaled Victor's arrival. He slipped inside and whistled. "Nice outfit. You almost look like a King."

"I guess that's good." Marshal looked over Victor's outfit. He looked every inch the soldier. His tattered Remavian Guard cloak had been repaired and cleaned. Along with his leather breastplate, now engraved with the King's insignia, he appeared both regal and ready for action. "You're going to be turning heads much more than I will."

"Well, I've always been better looking than you. Everyone knows that. Even your mother." Victor leaned in closer. "I never told you, but after she asked me to watch out for you, she also begged me not to overshadow you too much. 'I know you're more handsome, Victor,' she said, 'but let him think he's a little bit attractive, if you can.'"

Marshal laughed. He picked up his sword belt and buckled it on. "I really wish she were here, Vic."

"I know. I do too. She'd be thrilled, and super proud of you."

Marshal nodded. He looked in the mirror one more time and took a deep breath. "I guess I'm ready."

Victor looked him over again. "Yeah, that'll work. Talinir is waiting for us. Let's go."

•••••

Seri surveyed every angle of the throne room. Everything had to be perfect, completely perfect. After all, this kind of event hadn't happened in four generations.

The throne room itself was spectacular. The Eldanim's contribution to its re-design and re-build was evident in some of the sharp angles, but also in the domed roof made of enormous glass panels. Seri couldn't imagine the craftsmanship it would take to create even a single one of those panels. The dome perfectly covered the oval-shaped throne room, built as it was above the inner sanctum where the Passing took place. The marble floors gleamed as though freshly polished (they had been), a red carpet leading from the doors to the throne rippled as though someone had conjured a breeze to blow across it (someone had), and the walls were covered in carved intricate patterns Seri had yet to decipher.

Seri had expected the throne itself to be something elaborate and eye-catching. However, the Masters managed to find the original throne in the ruins months ago and insisted on keeping it. It was large and strong, solid oak covered in brass highlights. The workers restored it to its original sheen, polishing the brass and staining the oak. It stood in the direct center of the room, on top of a short platform of red marble inlaid with gold.

Six smaller thrones faced the King's, three on either side of the red carpet. The Lords (and Magistrate Otioch) took their places in the thrones, waiting for the ceremony to begin. The Masters, including Seri, each took their places standing behind each Lord. Lady Lilitu, dazzling in a purple and gold gown, glanced up at Seri and smiled. She returned the smile, then took a quick look at the rest of the audience. Master Korda whispered a few words to Lord Bakari, and then moved to stand in front of the throne, along with the high priest of Varioch, an elderly man in white robes.

All of the families of the Lords were here, of course, along with many other nobles, government officials, and prominent citizens. Seri's parents, Ekur and Ninsha, waved at her from the Arazu section. She spotted Adhi, along with his brothers and sister, at the head of Kuktarma's delegation. Tich stood with the delegation from Rasna, next to Aluri, to Seri's surprise. All of the mages of Zes Sivas stood together in their various colored robes, including the new acolytes in that orange color Seri disliked so much. Jamana grinned at her. He now wore green robes, an indication of his promotion from Master Korda. A large contingent of Eldanim, led by their High Council, stood in a place of honor near the throne.

Her eyes at last fell on Dravid, who stood with the Eldanim. He stood unsupported by a crutch. To those who didn't know, he looked like everyone else. But only yesterday, Talinir had presented him with an artificial leg, powered in part by Dravid's own magic. The mages of Intal Eldanir delighted in creating magical devices, it turned out, and had jumped at the chance to tackle this project. Dravid's walk was still unsteady, but he walked. It was more than he or Seri had ever expected. Her heart skipped a beat when he smiled at her. He'd also been gone for a few days before the new leg, traveling back home. She'd missed him more than she'd expected to.

A haunting melody floated out into the air, and the crowds grew quiet to listen. Seri craned her neck to see beyond the throne. She spied Ixchel, sitting on another platform. For the first time since Seri had known her, she had consented to wearing a different outfit, a simple dress of blue. Her hair hung loose, but she kept the green feather attached to a ribbon that pulled it back from her face. She concentrated on playing her instrument, the flute-like device she'd somehow kept safe through all their journeys. Beside her, an Eldani man Seri didn't recognize played a tall stringed instrument which produced surprisingly low bass tones to compliment Ixchel's melody. The combination of the tones made a lump rise in Seri's throat. She swallowed hard. She couldn't start crying. How would that look for a Master of Zes Sivas?

The doors of the throne room swung open. First to enter were Talinir, High Champion of Intal Eldanir and ambassador of the Starlit Realm, and Victor, Defender of Zes Sivas and chief advisor to the King.

They strode in together, their red and green capes flaring behind them. Four steps into the room, they stopped and each stepped to the opposite side, leaving a path between them.

The music shifted, becoming a more uplifting and hopeful tune. Seri wondered where Ixchel had found this particular piece. Her bodyguard had been so busy preparing for this day, Seri hadn't had much time to speak with her. Regardless of where it came from, it created a perfect mood. The music elicited feelings of grandeur, majesty, and triumph.

Marshal entered the throne room. He'd seen it all the previous night, so he wouldn't be staring in awe at everything now, but... the size of the crowd made his eyes go wide. He recovered quick enough, and resumed his walk down the carpet. Victor and Talinir waited until he passed them, and then fell in behind him. Together, the three of them approached the throne.

Master Korda waited for Marshal to reach him, and then raised his hands. The music came to a stop. The crowd stayed silent, waiting for what came next.

"We are gathered here today for the coronation of Marshal, King of Antises. If there is anyone here who disputes his right to this throne, let them speak now," Master Korda boomed.

Seri held her breath. She didn't want to think anyone would go so far as to object now, but neither did she think it impossible. The moment passed, and no one spoke.

"Very well," Korda said. "Your eminence?"

The high priest stepped forward and looked at Marshal. "Kneel," he instructed. Marshal obeyed. "You are not kneeling to me," the high priest explained, "nor to the Master mage here. You are kneeling in honor of the unseen witness to our ceremony: Theon himself. He watches us now, and he approves of this proceeding.

"Marshal, son of Aelia and descendant of Akhenadom, are you prepared to take the throne of Antises and rule its people?"

"I am," Marshal answered.

"It is well. But the question goes deeper, to the heart of sovereignty. Are you prepared, then, to take responsibility for the people of all six lands, showing partiality to none, discriminating against none, but treating all as equal in the sight of Theon?"

"I am."

Seri knew the questions had been rehearsed in the past few days, but the weightiness of the inquiries gave her pause. How could

Marshal—how could anyone—possibly fulfill all of this?

"Are you prepared to listen to wise council, accepting that you alone cannot possibly know all there is to know?"

"I am."

"Are you prepared to ensure both justice and mercy are promoted within the six lands of Antises, as seems fit to you, your wise council, and Theon's guiding?"

"I am."

"Are you prepared to oversee the six Lords, while allowing them to lead according to each land's laws and customs?"

"I am."

"Are you prepared to give all that you are and all that you ever will be for the people of Antises, holding nothing back and devoting yourself to their welfare?"

Marshal hesitated only a second longer before answering this one. "I am."

"Do you vow to do all that I have listed, by the sacred name of Theon above, to hold fast to this vow, come what may?"

"I so vow."

"Then by the authority of the priesthood of Theon, I proclaim you King of all Antises."

"And by the authority of the mages of Zes Sivas," Master Korda intoned, "I proclaim you King of all Antises."

The Lords stood and recited together: "And by the authority of the six Lords, we proclaim you King of all Antises."

"It is done," the high priest announced. He lifted his hands and looked skyward. "Great Theon, Lord of all the world, we have done as you commanded. Bless this King in your sight." He lowered his hands and looked to the Eldanim. "Where is the crown?"

Indala stepped forward, holding a wooden box in her hands. Seri craned her neck. No one had seen the crown yet. The ancestral crown of Akhenadom was long lost, either through neglect or the earthquakes. The Eldanim had offered to craft a new crown, and of course, everyone had been thrilled with the idea.

"Your Highness," Master Korda said, "would you like to request someone to crown you?"

"I would."

"Please name them."

Marshal lifted his head, but remained kneeling. "Because the salvation of Antises was accomplished largely through her work and determination, I request that Seri-Belit, Master Mage of Arazu, place the crown on my head."

Seri gasped. How dare he not warn her of this in advance! Everyone was looking at her now.

"Go, my child," Lady Lilitu whispered. "This honor belongs to you."

Feeling like her legs might collapse under her at any moment, Seri walked to Indala. "Should I take the box, or—" she whispered. Indala flipped the box lid open.

Seri went from unsteady legs to feet rooted in place. She couldn't move. She could hardly breathe. The sight of the crown took everything away. She couldn't possibly touch it, let alone carry such a thing of beauty. What if she dropped it?

The crown consisted primarily of a band of gold between two rounded bands of a silvery metal Seri knew must be warpsteel. At its very front glowed a transparent crystal about the size of a sword pommel, filled with purple flame like the space between worlds. Six stars floated to either side of it, three on each side, shining with multicolored light. Seri could not see any form of connection between the stars and the crown itself.

"Will they... do they move with it?" she whispered. She heard a stirring from the crowd, growing impatient.

"Take it and see," Indala whispered back, smiling.

Seri reached into the box and grasped the crown by the sides. The stars gleamed so brightly, she feared she might burn her fingers on them. She lifted the crown out into the air and held it high. The stars, as she hoped, stayed in their place, moving with the metal. The crowd gasped in awe, and murmurs swirled around the entire room.

She turned and walked to Marshal. Master Korda stood aside and allowed her to move in front of the kneeling King. He winked at her. She'd get him back for this, somehow.

"Let this crown symbolize the union of our six lands and the sovereignty of the house of Akhenadom!" the high priest proclaimed. He gestured to Seri to proceed.

She stepped forward and lowered the crown onto Marshal's head. She wasn't surprised in the least to see a perfect fit. As she took her hands away, the purple flame of the gem flickered and she almost reached for it with her magic senses. Instead, she took a quick step backward.

"Stand, King Marshal of Antises, and take your throne!"

Marshal got to his feet and stepped onto the throne's platform. He turned to face everyone, and lowered himself into the seat. With that, the crowd could keep silent no longer. Loud cheers and applause erupted throughout the room. Seri clapped as hard as she could and felt tears welling up in her eyes.

"Long live King Marshal!" Victor shouted at the top of his lungs.

And the crowd roared its approval.

(((57)))

For Marshal, the entire coronation was a surreal experience. For much of the time, he felt like it was all happening to someone else. Only during the vows did he feel truly a part of it all. He could not take those words lightly.

After the crowning, each of the Lords knelt before the throne and pledged their service. Even Lords Meluhha and Rajwir said the words without difficulty. The Masters then knelt together in a group and pledged their service as well. With each action, the crowd cheered wildly.

When all was said and done, the doors were thrown open and Marshal walked back down the red carpet. As he passed by the Rasnian delegation, he paused and beckoned to Tich. At first she pretended not to notice him. But as the crowd around her realized what was happening, they screamed with delight and pushed her forward. She rolled her eyes and joined him. Together, they exited the throne room, followed by raucous shouts and cheers.

Some of the Lords and Masters had suggested a formal ball after the crowning, but Marshal turned it down. He had never learned to dance, and wasn't about to reveal that to the entire world. Instead, he agreed to a massive celebratory banquet. At least there, his only responsibilities would be eating and being polite.

They walked a short distance down the hall to another huge set of double doors leading to the banquet hall. Marshal called it the banquet hall in his mind, anyway. No one knew if that had been its actual purpose. As he took ownership of this citadel, he would need to start naming things. Maybe one room named after Aelia, another for Nian…

His musings came to a stop along with his forward progress. He and

Tich both stood and stared. Unlike the throne room, Marshal had not gotten a sneak peek at this room. The banquet hall had been decked out with dozens of banners along the walls, depicting the six flags of the lands, along with a seventh flag interspersed among them. The seventh flag bore the flying creature featured prominently on all of Akhenadom's relics.

In the center of the massive room sat six enormous tables in a star-shaped pattern. Each of them was piled high with foods distinctive to each land and culture. As he walked past them, Marshal recognized Varioch and Rasna's, which weren't very different from each other, and Kuktarma's, which he'd sampled before. The other three were completely unfamiliar to him.

"I wonder if I have to eat something from each table," he whispered to Tich. She snorted.

A blue-robed mage escorted them to a table set on an elevated platform at the far wall. Marshal and Tich sat beneath one of the Akhenadom banners. Victor and Talinir flanked them as the only other occupants of the table.

"How many of the Lords are going to count the banners to be sure they're in equal numbers?" Tich asked.

"All of them," Marshal answered. He kept his eyes on the doors as the Lords and their families began to enter. He barely noticed as servants filled his chalice and placed a plate of food in front of him.

"You didn't tell me you were going to make me do this," Tich said a moment later.

Marshal looked at her and smiled. "Who else could I persuade to sit with me?"

"I could make you a list." She waved toward the families spreading out into the hall. "But they'll all make their way up here at some point, I'm sure."

Tich wasn't wrong. One by one, after they'd claimed their own tables, the Lords came to wish Marshal well. They brought their families with them, and Marshal struggled to keep track of all the names. Most of them made a special point of introducing and praising their marriageable daughters and nieces and even some relatives Marshal couldn't work out. All of the women did their best to impress him, some more blatantly than others. Without fail, at some point in each conversation, they frowned or scowled at Tich.

"Is it me or does the amount of jealousy in this room keep climbing?" Victor asked after Lord Meluhha and his daughter left their table.

"You mean toward Tich?" Marshal asked.

"No, I mean my jealousy toward you." He gave an exaggerated sigh. "Some of them are paying a little attention to me, at least."

"You're a decent second choice," Tich said.

"Ouch." Victor pantomimed getting hit with an arrow.

"Maybe this will brighten your mood," Marshal said, pointing. Seri and Ixchel approached their table.

"Theon's burning pillars," Victor murmured, staring at Ixchel.

"Is there a problem, Victor?" Seri asked, eyes wide with innocence.

"No, not at all." He cleared his throat. "Ixchel, your hair… it's, ah, beautiful."

"Smooth," Tich said. "Quite the ladies' man, you are."

Ixchel nodded to Victor, but said nothing.

Seri giggled. "So, are we still having our own celebration afterwards?"

"Please, yes," Marshal said. "Can you make sure everyone knows. Meet in the throne room."

"Of course." Seri eyed the crown. "Can you believe that? I'm dying to study how it works."

The crown was so light, Marshal had almost forgotten its presence. He removed it from his head and examined it. "How do the stars stay in place?"

"That's what's so amazing!"

"Talinir, do you know how it works?" Tich asked him.

Talinir shook his head. "I am neither mage nor engineer. However, I find the symbolism as striking as the design itself."

"Six stars for the six lands, obviously," Seri said. "And the gem in the middle represents the King?"

Talinir opened his mouth to answer, but Seri gasped. "Oh! And the purple flame! Like the space that binds the worlds together. So the King binds the six lands together!"

Talinir smiled and nodded.

Marshal replaced the crown on his head. "It's a big challenge to live up to," he confessed. "I still don't think I can do it all."

"That's why you've got us," Victor said. "We'll keep you in line."

Masters Ganak and Tzoyet approached the table, interrupting any further discussion. After that came a steady string of well-wishers and admirers. Marshal couldn't help but notice their reactions to his scars, once they were close enough to see them clearly. Some tried to look him directly in the eye and pretend they didn't notice. Others flinched and looked away. But everyone, aside from those who already knew him, reacted in some way. Regardless of anything else that happened, here was something he'd have to keep dealing with his entire life.

As the meal progressed, each of the delegations also sent a plate of special foods from their lands. Marshal tried all of them to be polite, but he struggled with some of the spices. After the visit to Kuktarma, he knew to be very careful with their food, but Mandiata's plate caught him by surprise. He drank far more than he ate, working hard to keep himself from coughing any of the food back up.

"Poor country boy's taste buds aren't used to this," Tich noted.

"I won't have any after this is over," Marshal muttered before taking another long drought from his chalice.

Hours later, when at last the celebration began to wind down, Victor got to his feet and looked around. He nodded to Ixchel, who stood near the door, then turned back to Marshal. "It's time."

•••••

Seri entered the throne room to find Dravid and Jamana waiting. Jamana's smile seemed even larger than ever. Seri opened her mouth to ask him why, but Adhi entered just then. "I am excited," he announced. "I have not done this before."

"Nor I," said Jamana.

"It's an experience," Dravid said. "You'll love it."

"Who else is coming?" Jamana asked.

"Who do you think?" Seri smiled and looked to the door.

Ixchel entered, followed by Victor. Marshal and Tich came next, hand-in-hand. Last of all came Talinir and Eniri. Seri was somewhat surprised to see the Eldani girl, but she had been a crucial step along Marshal's journey.

"Is everyone here?" Marshal asked, looking around.

"Unless you asked anyone else I don't know about," Seri answered.

Marshal nodded and drew Akhenadom's sword. "I assume someone brought the drinks?"

Jamana held up a basket.

"Then let's go." Marshal held up the sword for a moment, then slashed it across the air just above his head. A gap appeared, a hole between the worlds. Seri never failed to marvel at this process. How she wished she understood more about warpsteel! It held amazing properties, perhaps far more than they knew.

Marshal continued to cut through the air, forming a doorway. When he stepped back, they could all see the strange light of the Otherworld waiting for them.

"Ah, we just step through?" Adhi asked. Here among magic and mages again, he seemed to revert back to his more nervous persona. So different from the commanding seventh son of the Lord Meluhha he'd been back in Kuktarma.

"Easy as that," Marshal answered, smiling. He stepped through the doorway himself, followed by Tich.

Seri and Ixchel went next, with Dravid and Victor close behind. On the other side, she turned back to give an encouraging wave to the others. Jamana and Adhi looked at each other, then came through, staring in wide-eyed wonder around them. Talinir and Eniri, Seri noticed, performed some sort of ritual, passing their palms down the center of their bodies, before coming through the doorway.

Marshal gestured and the doorway itself faded away. He spread his arms wide and turned in a circle. "Welcome, my friends," he cried. "Welcome to the Starlit Realm!"

(((58)))

Marshal stepped back to watch the reactions of the others. Jamana and Adhi had never been here, so their wonder was obvious. The others, with the exception of the Eldanim, had not been here since the Passing. A lot had changed since then.

The Otherworld bloomed. Or at least, things grew here now. Everywhere Marshal looked, he saw sprouts of plant life. Most of it clustered around a series of tiny creeks that now criss-crossed the land, or at least this area where Lake Litanu existed on the other side. The island of Zes Sivas still stood high above it all, but even here, he could see a few spots where grass or some other plant life was taking hold.

In addition, Marshal had enlisted the Eldanim in a new project. So far, they'd managed to clear all the ruined debris from the island. Marshal couldn't help feeling a little curious about what type of construction had been here hundreds of years ago, but it didn't seem likely he would find out. For now, he wanted new construction. A few foundational pieces had already been laid, and one partial wall had been built, only a few feet from where they now stood.

"What is this?" Seri asked. "What are they building here?"

"I want a citadel on this side as well," Marshal said. "A place where we can visit and stay sometimes. We can't shift our whole home back and forth like the Eldanim do, so this is the next best thing."

"So we can come here to hide from everyone else?" Tich asked. "Sounds good to me."

"Ah, didn't you say there were predators here?" Adhi brought up. "Should we be concerned?"

"Now that Intal Eldanir is in this region, the wardens are working to keep it clear," Talinir explained. "Plus, with the changes in the climate here, they're shifting their hunting patterns as well. We're working on understanding it all."

"It's all very exciting!" Eniri chimed in.

Seri walked around, examining the foundation layout. "It's not going to be the same size as the citadel in our world," she observed.

"No, I'm not aiming for that," Marshal said. "It's only for small visits, not huge gatherings. But…"

"But what?"

"I want more. We can maintain portals between Zes Sivas and the six lands with that device."

"Which still needs to be repaired somehow," Seri pointed out.

"Right. But you'll figure it out. And after that, I want a portal to here." He pointed at the ground. "A permanent one."

"Uh, didn't we just do an awful lot of work to close those kind of portals?" Victor asked.

"The big ones, yes. But I want a door, a single door, that we can walk through. It won't allow an army through, and besides, we'll then be able to maintain a presence here at all times."

Victor laughed. "It's not enough for you to change two worlds. You want to keep changing things!"

"I'm not just going to sit back on the throne and relax," Marshal said. "That's not me."

"You don't think you've fulfilled your purpose yet?" Seri asked.

"My purpose." Marshal shook his head. "I've done what I set out to do. But new challenges keep appearing, don't they? I never expected to be King, or to even survive. Or to find… so many friends." His voice broke.

"And you're stuck with us," Tich said. "We're not going anywhere."

Marshal swallowed and changed the subject. "Your new leg is amazing, Dravid," he observed. "I can't even tell it's not real."

Dravid bent down and tapped it. "Most of it is wood and metal, but it has some parts made of stuff I don't recognize." He looked at Talinir. "And they're not telling me, either."

"We can't give away all our secrets," Talinir said.

"Anyway, I just have to feed some of my magic into it each morning, and it binds to me for the next ten hours or so."

"You can maintain the magic that long now?"

"No, no. As soon as I feed it in, it dissolves. It's like the dissolving is what powers it." He shrugged. "I don't understand it at all."

"Neither do I," Eniri said. "And neither does Talinir. We're not magical engineers." She eyed Dravid's leg. "My father might have had a hand in it, but his magic is more direct."

"I'd love to study with them sometime," Seri exclaimed. "I could learn so much!"

"You are a Master now," Adhi pointed out. "You can choose your areas of study."

"I know! But there's so much!"

"Good thing you're starting young," Dravid said, "but I haven't shown you all of this leg's capabilities yet."

"What do you mean?"

"Well, it's not easy yet, but... Jamana, can I have a hand?"

Jamana obligingly gave Dravid support as he knelt on the artificial leg. He held out both arms. "See?"

"All right," Seri said with a bemused smile, "but you don't have to kneel to me. Marshal's the King."

"Enough of that," Marshal grumbled.

"But I do have to," Dravid insisted. "Because I need you to know what an incredible, wonderful woman I believe you are."

Seri opened her mouth, but Dravid rushed on, holding out one hand toward her. "And I need to ask you one very important thing: Seri-Belit, Master Mage of Arazu, would you condescend to accepting this poor, one-legged failed mage as your husband?"

All eyes shifted to Seri. Her mouth fell further open.

"If we were in my homeland," Dravid went on, "my parents would lead a procession to your home where a formal ceremony would announce our betrothal."

"In my homeland—" Jamana began. Tich elbowed him to shut him up.

"I, I..." Seri stammered.

Dravid's face fell. "Is it too soon? I thought—"

"No, it's not too soon!" she exploded. "And I don't have to condescend, because you're not a failed mage and I love you, you idiot!"

He tilted his head. "Is that a yes?"

"Of course it's a yes!" Seri grabbed his outstretched hand. Jamana seized Dravid from behind and pulled him upright. He barely let go before Seri threw herself into Dravid's arms. "You, you!"

Dravid kissed her then. Seri's face turned bright red, but she didn't pull away.

Everyone cheered.

"So when you were gone the past few days?" Seri demanded.

Dravid nodded. "I was visiting my parents, your parents, and Lady Lilitu."

"It is time for the wine, I am thinking," Jamana interrupted.

"Break it out," Marshal agreed.

Jamana reached into the basket and drew out a wineskin, which he handed to Adhi. Then he handed goblets to everyone. Adhi walked around and filled them, one by one.

"To the betrothed couple!" Jamana cried.

They cheered again and drank.

Dravid, his arm around Seri, held up his goblet. "To the future of Zes Sivas, in both worlds!"

"Hear, hear," Marshal agreed.

Everyone drank, and then fell silent for a moment. Victor lifted his goblet. "To the friends we lost," he said in a low voice.

Marshal lifted his goblet. "To Aelia."

"Nian. Topleb," Victor added.

"Albus. Gallus. Callus. Rufus."

"Kishin," Jamana said. Ixchel nodded.

Talinir opened his mouth, but then closed it without saying anything.

Seri hesitated, then added, "Volraag."

Marshal looked at her, then closed his eyes and took a breath. He raised the goblet higher. "To lost friends."

"To lost friends," the others echoed, and drank.

Everyone looked at each other. Then Adhi raised his goblet. "To found friends," he suggested.

"I found the best ones," Marshal agreed. They drank again.

"Anything else in that basket, Jamana?" Victor asked.

"Oh yes." He set his goblet down on the incomplete wall, and bent down. "We have some cheese and bread. A few things to snack on."

"We just left a banquet!" Seri exclaimed. "How can you possibly be hungry?"

Victor shrugged. "We traveled all the way to another world. I've got an appetite again."

"I could eat a little something," Ixchel admitted.

"You go right ahead," Seri said. "I don't know if I'll eat again for a day or two!"

Marshal smiled. He felt much the same, but didn't say anything. He set his goblet down and walked around behind the wall. There he found the pile of cushions he'd brought over the day before. He picked up half of them and carried it around to the others. Exclamations of surprise and delight greeted him. After retrieving the rest of the cushions, they spread them out on the fresh foundation stones and lounged about, watching the stars above and the new creeks flowing below.

Tich sat beside him, and he put his arm around her. She did not complain. Seri and Dravid sat together nearby. The others spread around. Jamana and Adhi remained on their feet, walking about, pointing things out to each other, and exclaiming over different views. This was all new to them. Marshal smiled, remembering his first view of these stars.

"Will it ever fill up to a lake, like our world?" Tich asked after a minute.

"What's that?" He pulled his gaze away from the stars.

"The water." She pointed down. "Do you think it'll keep growing and rising, Talinir?"

"We don't know," the warden replied. "We're not entirely sure where it's coming from, but most think it's springing up from below. A few wardens have been tasked to follow the water to its source."

"There are so many new and wonderful things to study and learn," Eniri said. "Everyone in the city is excited and eager to figure things out. I've never seen it like this in my lifetime."

"Nor I," Talinir agreed.

"There are new challenges and adventures everywhere," Dravid observed, a faraway look in his eyes.

"If there weren't, life would get boring," Victor said.

Tich reached up and traced one of Marshal's scars with a finger. "And all of this happened because of you."

"It all happened because my mother decided to lift my curse," Marshal corrected.

"And then you lifted all the curses."

"And broke all the bonds," Victor added.

"And the gods returned, and the stars fell," Talinir said. "The worlds changed."

Marshal nodded. All of that. Everything wasn't perfect, of course. He still had pains. There was work to be done. Tension between the six lands. Worries about other lands and nations. But someday, maybe, it would all be right. He remembered something he'd heard long ago.

"Eniri. What was that prayer or whatever that your family said before meals?" he asked.

"We who wait for the ransoming of all worlds, we thank you for your provision," she quoted.

He nodded. That was it. The ransoming of all worlds. Now there was something to look forward to.

Tich snuggled closer. He squeezed her shoulder. A lump rose in his throat and moisture gathered in his eyes. He never thought he would be in a place like this. Not the physical place, though that was incredible, of course. But in a place to gather with so many friends.

He watched them interacting with each other. Seri. Dravid. Victor. Ixchel. Jamana. Adhi. Talinir. Eniri. And Tich. He was surrounded by friends, people who cared about him.

"What are you thinking?" Tich asked.

"I am loved," Marshal answered, surprising himself with saying it out loud.

"Yeah," Tich agreed.

Marshal leaned back, his arm around Tich, surrounded by friends. He took a sip of his drink and sat back to watch the stars. Around him, his friends celebrated the day, each other, and the beauty of the Starlit Realm.

The End

For more information on Antises,
upcoming books, and more,
visit timfrankovich.com

(Sign up for the newsletter and you'll get access to free
short stories, such as the origin of Kishin, and bonus
materials, like an unused epilogue.)

If you enjoyed this book, please post a review on Amazon,
Goodreads, B&N, or wherever you find books!
There's no better way to spread the word.

Glossary

Caution: These listings may contain minor spoilers.

Aapo - Kishin's household servant

Adhi - A mage acolyte from Kuktarma, son of Lord Meluhha, studying on Zes Sivas.

Aelia - Marshal's mother who willingly sacrificed herself to lift his curse. Daughter of Evander.

Aharu - Sister of Akhenadom. Founder of the priesthood. First High Master Mage of Antises.

Ajaw - Lady of Ch'olan. Wife of Lord Rajwir. Commander of the Holcan.

Akhenadom - Called "the Great." At the time of the Great Cataclysm, he led six people groups from their original homes to the land of Antises. He introduced them to the worship of the one god Theon, and presented to them Theon's Book of the Law. In return, the six people groups proclaimed him the first King of all Antises.

Albus - A soldier in the army of Varioch. Cursed for murder and assigned to the curse squad. Killed in battle.

Alpin - Former Master Mage of Varioch. Murdered by Curasir.

Aluri - Daughter of Lord Tyrr of Rasna.

Amnis River - A branch of the Trebia River that flows along the western side of Varioch and its southern border with Rasna.

Antises - The union of the six lands of Rasna, Varioch, Ch'olan, Mandiata, Arazu, and Kuktarma. Ruled from the island of Zes Sivas in the middle of Lake Litanu, which borders all six lands.

Arazu - One of the six lands of Antises. Arazu is located on the eastern side of Lake Litanu, between Mandiata and Kuktarma. Arazu is the smallest of the lands, but claims the oldest culture and strictest traditions.

Arun - Third son of Lord Meluhha of Kuktarma.

Atzam - Captain of Kishin's ship

Bakari - The young Lord of Mandiata. Son of Sundinka. The first Lord of a land without possessing any magic power (due to Volraag's theft).

Balaes - A blacksmith in the village of Drusa's Crossing. Father of Careen.

Book of the Law - A compilation of the moral and ceremonial laws of Theon, written by Akhenadom.

Calu - The name of an ancient god of Rasna, associated with wolves.

Callus - A conscript in the Varioch army, twin brother to Gallus. Assigned to the curse squad. Killed in battle.

Candrama - A town in Kuktarma, near the border with Arazu, and not far from Lake Litanu.

Careen - A young woman of Drusa's Crossing. Daughter of Balaes. Was in a relationship with Victor prior to his departure.

Cassian - General of Varioch's army. Placed in charge of the war with Rasna by Volraag.

Cataclysm, Great - The event which motivated the six people groups to follow Akhenadom. Details about it are apocryphal at best. Descriptions range from earthquakes to volcanic eruptions to extreme weather events to floods, perhaps a combination of all of these.

Cato - A young man of Varioch who seeks out Forerunner.

Cautha - The name of an ancient god of Rasna. Brother of Laran. Associated with giantism.

Chimon - An elderly priest at the temple in Woqan.

Ch'olan - The northernmost of the six lands of Antises, bordered by Varioch and Mandiata. Ch'olan is known for its fierce warrior traditions and its stone monuments, especially pyramids.

Conclave of Mages - The organization of magic-using professionals based in the Citadel of Mages on Zes Sivas. The Conclave is led by six Master Mages - one from each land - and includes numerous lesser mages of varying degrees of proficiency.

Curasir - A schemer who at times has claimed to be Durunim or Eldanim. Exact truth unknown. A mage of significant power.

Curse-stalker - A large reptilian creature that is drawn to magic. Since the primary sources of magic encountered by most common people are those who are cursed, this gave rise to the idea that these creatures only hunted cursed individuals. Curse-stalkers possess two long tongues that excrete some form of acid while absorbing magic energy.

Cyra - Volraag's concubine.

Devir - The name of an ancient god of Arazu.

Diabol - The devil. Rarely mentioned in the religion surrounding the worship of Theon. Mostly used in epithets.

Djatan Desert - A large desert marking the eastern extent of Antises, primarily connected with Mandiata, but also bordering Arazu.

Dravid - A former mage acolyte who gained strange powers during an encounter with Forerunner. Lost his leg during one of the earthquakes on Zes Sivas.

Drusa's Crossing - A village in the mountains near the border between Varioch and Ch'olan.

Dursa - The name of an ancient fertility goddess of Kuktarma.

Durunim - Former members of the Eldanim whose physical form has been changed through an unknown process. They now wage war against the Eldanim on behalf of the so-called gods.

Edin Na Zu - A phrase of uncertain origin in Arazu. Used as an epithet. Has some connection to the Djatan Desert.

Efesun - A large town in Varioch, located on the shore of the Trebia River, near the Great Plains.

Ekur - Father of Seri. Husband of Ninsha. Merchant.

Eldanim - A magical race of non-human beings. Eldanim exist both within the primary world and the Otherworld (or Starlit Realm). This creates a strange dichotomy for human eyes, as their physical shape within each world is different. For their part, Eldanim can see both worlds at the same time. Their physical appearance within the primary world is similar to humans, though generally taller with much sharper, angular features. One eye appears all black, with tiny pinpricks of light. Their physical appearance in the Otherworld is several feet taller.

Eltaru - A member of the high council of Intal Eldanir.

Eidolon - An apparition, often seen as a misty human-like form. In reality, the eidola are Eldanim or Durunim who have shifted their primary essence into the Otherworld. "Eidolon" is the name used by residents of Varioch and Rasna. In Arazu, they are called **Gidim**. In Ch'olan, they are called **Tzitzimitl**. In Kuktarma, they are called bhoots.

Eniri - A young woman of the Eldanim who resides in Intal Eldanir, daughter of Harunir and Indala. She works in the healing profession.

Enuru - Current Lord of Arazu, husband of Lilitu.

Evander - Father of Aelia, grandfather of Marshal. Died in the Starlit Realm.

Forerunner - A mysterious man who possesses a strange magic unlike the usual magic of Antises. Sent to the land of Varioch.

Gallus - A conscript in the Varioch army, twin brother to Callus. Assigned to the curse squad. Killed in battle.

Ganak - Current Master Mage of Kuktarma. Part of the Conclave of Mages on Zes Sivas.

Gidim - *see* **Eidolon**

Gnaeus - A conscript in the Varioch army, cursed with a twisted hand. Assigned to the curse squad. Remained at Forerunner's old camp.

Great Plains - A wide, open area of land on the western side of Antises, bordering Varioch. Generally considered to be the location of Intal Eldanir.

Hain - Master Mage of Arazu. Part of the Conclave of Mages on Zes Sivas. Mentor to Seri. Died from injuries received during an earthquake.

Hanirel - A member of the Durunim, who can make himself appear as one of the Eldanim, or so he claims.

Harbinger - A mysterious man who possesses a strange magic unlike the usual magic of Antises. Sent to the land of Mandiata. It is probable that others like him or Forerunner were sent to each of the six lands.

Hauk - A boatman who works for the mages on Zes Sivas.

Harunir - A mage of the Eldanim, resident of Intal Eldanir. Husband of Indala, father of Eniri.

Haruta - High Champion of Intal Eldanir.

Holcan - An order of female warriors in Ch'olan, trained from an early age in multiple fighting techniques. Usually assigned to guard and escort the Lady of Ch'olan (wife of the Lord).

Indala - A member of the high council of Intal Eldanir. Wife of Harunir, mother of Eniri.

Inkil - A news broker in Woqan. Often employed by Kishin.

Intal Eldanir - The primary city of the Eldanim. While floating above the ground, it can be shifted from the primary world to the Otherworld (and back).

Ixchel - A young member of the Holcan. Assigned by Lady Rajwir to serve Seri.

Jamana - A mage acolyte of Mandiata. Serves on Zes Sivas under Master Korda.

Janaab - A name used by Evander during his wanderings in the Otherworld.

Junia - A young woman of Varioch who seeks out Forerunner.

Kanna - A small town in Varioch, near the border with Rasna.

Kawal - A man of Woqan. Kishin's second murder.

Korda - Current Master Mage of Mandiata. Part of the Conclave of Mages on Zes Sivas. Mentor to Jamana.

Kishin - An assassin of Ch'olan. Cursed with a form of leprosy.

Komadi - A mage assigned to the Lord's court in Tenjkidi, Mandiata.

Kombori - A port city of Mandiata, downriver from Tenjkidi.

K'uh - A word for magic in Ch'olan. An ancient belief (pre-Antises) connected magic with each individual's life force. This led to human sacrifice in some communities.

Kuch - Blademaster of Ch'olan. Responsible for training warriors, including the Holcan.

Kuktarma - One of the six lands of Antises, bordered by Arazu on the north, and the sea on the south. Known for its walled cities and the antics of the current Lord's sons.

Kumara - Daughter of Lord Meluhha, sister of Adhi.

Laran - The name of an ancient god of Rasna.

Lasa - A human slave of Vayan.

Laws of Cursings and Bindings - A set of magical laws put in place by the first Conclave of Mages. Anyone who willingly violates one of the moral laws of Theon, as described in the Book of the Law, receives a magical curse appropriate for his action. Magical Bindings are formed between family members and other close relationships. In addition, special Bindings are created when someone rescues another person from serious danger or potential death.

Lilitu - Lady of Arazu. Wife of Lord Enuru. Sponsored Seri's membership in the Conclave of Mages.

Lake Litanu - A huge freshwater lake in the center of the six lands of Antises, bordered by all. The island of Zes Sivas is in its center.

Lords' Betrayal - An event that followed the creation of the Laws of Cursings and Bindings by the Conclave of Mages. The first six Lords of Antises twisted the Laws to attempt to exempt themselves from the curses. Instead, curses for their actions fell on their children.

Lucia - A young woman of Varioch who seeks out Forerunner.

Mages & Lords - A card game popular throughout Antises (with some variants) dating back to the Lords' Betrayal. Small deck with limited cards. On a player's turn, he flips over the top card of the deck, then decides whether to play it or put it back on the bottom of the deck. Object of the game is to collect either six Lords & King or six Mages & High Master Mage.

Magnus - Current Master Mage of Varioch, appointed by Volraag.

Makaan - Former Blademaster of Ch'olan. Mentor to Kuch and Kishin.

Malena - A woman from Rasna who serves Forerunner.

Mandiata - One of the six lands of Antises, bordered by Ch'olan and Arazu. Known for exotic wildlife, elaborate architecture, and high respect for the dead.

Marshal - Son of Aelia and Varion (rape). Grandson of Evander. Half-brother of Volraag. Inheritor of the powers of both a Lord (Varion) and King.

Meluhha - Current Lord of Kuktarma. Father of seven sons, whose escapades have been documented (and exaggerated) in dozens of stories that his people delight in repeating.

Merish - A conscript of Varioch. Stole a sword and received some form of mental damage as a curse. Rarely if ever speaks. Assigned to the curse squad. Remained at Forerunner's old camp.

Mukuy - A man of Woqan. Kishin's first murder.

Murdak - The name of an ancient god of Kuktarma, leader of the pantheon, associated with justice and strength.

Namnirnu - The name of an ancient god of Arazu, leader of the pantheon. Associated with wind and water.

Ne'gal - The name of an ancient god of Kuktarma, associated with death and decay.

Nehesy - Son of Aharu. Second High Master Mage of Antises.

Nian - A priest of Mandiata. Decided to go on pilgrimage to all six lands of Antises. Never made it to Rasna.

Nijamu - Second son of Lord Meluhha of Kuktarma.

Nimruti - A member of the high council of Intal Eldanir.

Ninsha - Mother of Seri. Wife of Ekur.

Nummotem - The name of an ancient god of Mandiata, associated with nature.

Otioch - Leader of Varioch's Remavian Guard. Confidant of Volraag.

Otherworld - A parallel world separated from the primary world. Similar in shape/geography, but lacking most water and vegetation. No sun or moon, but lit constantly by enormous stars of varying colors, leading to its other name, the **Starlit Realm**.

Passing - An annual event on Zes Sivas, where the King and Lords of all six lands are instructed to surrender their magic power for one hour. The power returns to the land temporarily and seems to keep it from breaking apart.

Plecu - Current Master Mage of Rasna. Part of the Conclave of Mages on Zes Sivas.

Raeton - Capital city of Rasna. Known for spectacular pillars.

Rajwir - Current Lord of Ch'olan. Husband to Ajaw.

Ranir Stone - A stone given by Aelia to Victor. Aelia used it for sending a message to the Eldanim. The magic involved is unknown. Appears as an ordinary rock.

Rasna - One of the six lands of Antises, bordered by Varioch on the north, and the sea on the south. Known for the Pillars of Raeton, mining, and little else.

Rathri - An assassin employed by Volraag. Appears to possess a leprosy-style curse similar to Kishin, but claims to be one of the Eldani wardens like Talinir.

Regulus - One of the three Consuls who control the economic power of Varioch.

Reman - Capital city of Varioch.

Remavian Guard - Elite warriors of Varioch, recognized by their red capes. In service to the Lord and his household.

Rufus - A conscript of Varioch. Once stole food from his neighbor and received the curse of a twisted foot, causing him to limp. Assigned to the curse squad. Tried to kill Marshal under threat from Rathri. Killed Topleb, was cursed again, then killed by curse-stalkers.

Sakouna - The first Lord of Mandiata, from the time of the founding of Antises. Apparently, he had a monkey.

Sandu-Emuq - Capital city of Arazu.

Sebittun - The title of a group of seven war gods of Arazu, defenders of Namnirnu.

Sekou - A Master Mage who wrote extensively about wild magic.

Seri-Belit - Mage of Arazu. Prefers just Seri. Possesses the unusual ability to "see" magic due to a "star" in her eye, a result of her unusual parentage.

Simbala - Capital city of Kuktarma.

Simmar - Former Master Mage of Kuktarma. Murdered by Curasir.

Sipak - A legendary beast of the sea, described in stories of Ch'olan.

Siratel - An elderly woman of the Eldanim. Appears to have the ability to foresee a person's future to some extent.

Starlit Realm - *see* **Otherworld**

Sundinka - Former Lord of Mandiata. After his power was stolen by Volraag, he was murdered by Rathri.

Talinir - A warden of the Eldanim.

Tatiska - Sister of Lord Bakari of Mandiata.

Telra - A high councillor of Intal Eldanir.

Tenjkidi - Capital city of Mandiata.

Term - The name of an ancient god of Varioch, associated with messages.

Tezan - A wild mage who, under the control of Lord Tyrr, attempted to convince everyone he was the lost King of Antises. Fell under the control of Volraag, who used him to steal power from Lord Sundinka.

Theon - The god worshipped (or at least acknowledged) by the majority of Antises.

Thrummers - Insects about one centimeter in length. Bites like a mosquito, but less painful. Mostly harmless. Especially attracted to those with magic, as it absorbs tiny amounts of magic when it bites. The insect's abdomen glows in response with an intensity and color based on the magic's potency.

Tich - A young sailor on Kishin's ship. Originally from Rasna.

Tiranel - High Warden of Intal Eldanir.

Titus - A young man of Drusa's Crossing.

Tiur - A human slave of Vayan.

Topleb - A conscript in the army of Varioch, originally from Ch'olan. Assigned to the curse squad. Killed by Rufus.

Trebia River - A river that flows on south along the western edge of

Varioch, next to the Great Plains.

Tunaldi - A ferocious beast of the Otherworld, comparable in size from a hippopotamus to an elephant. Carnivorous. Attracted to magic.

Tungrorum - A small village near the border between Varioch and Ch'olan.

Tyrr - Current Lord of Rasna.

Tzitzimitl - *see* **Eidolon**

Tzoyet - Current Master Mage of Ch'olan. Part of the Conclave of Mages on Zes Sivas.

Varioch - One of the six lands of Antises. Bordered on the north by Ch'olan and the south by Rasna. Known for aggressive leadership.

Varion - Former Lord of Varioch. Father of Marshal (by rape) and Volraag. Murdered by Rathri.

Vayan - The name of an ancient god of Kuktarma, associated with pain and wind.

Victor - A young man from Drusa's Crossing. Best friend of Marshal.

Volraag - Current Lord of Varioch. Son of Varion. Half-brother of Marshal. Stole power from Lord Sundinka of Mandiata.

Wolf - A conscript in the Varioch army. Assigned to the curse squad. Later revealed to be **Calu**.

Woqan - Capital city of Ch'olan.

Zes Sivas - An island in the center of Lake Litanu. Center of magic and authority for Antises. Most of the island is covered by the Citadel of Kings and the Citadel of Mages, two interwoven fortresses.

Zeyus - The name of an ancient god of Varioch and Rasna, leader of the pantheon.

Ziv - Eldest son of Lord Tyrr of Rasna.

Retrospective & Acknowledgments

This is really the end of the story. For me at least, that's very hard to believe. I've spent so long with Marshal and Seri and their friends, it doesn't seem like it could all be ending now.

Some of those friends became so much more important than I ever realized at the beginning. When I first introduced Dravid and Jamana, they were intended to be casual friends of Seri's age, so she wouldn't be alone among the Masters. I had no idea at the time how crucial their roles would become. I knew the basic outline of the story, and the major events. But characters can surprise an author, adding new elements you never thought about. I never saw the romance between Tich and Marshal coming. I didn't know Rathri's origin at first.

As I'm writing this, it's been twenty-seven months since I first published *Until All Curses Are Lifted*. In that short time, I think I've grown as a writer in significant ways. The first two books of this series could have been better. Regardless, I'm proud of it all. For my entire life, I've wanted to write an epic fantasy series, and now I've done it. It's complete.

But is it really over? There's room for so many more possible stories within Antises. So many questions that could be answered. So many ideas that could be explored. Will they be written down, or forever be a part of our collective imaginations?

I won't say no. I love these characters, and I'd love to write more about them. But it would have to be a story worth telling, not just "another adventure." I have ideas simmering in the back of my mind. Maybe I'll realize one (or more) of them is the beginning of something big.

At the moment, I'm rushing through my science fantasy series, *Dragontek Lore*. If all goes well, several books will show up next year. And I'm brainstorming another epic fantasy, completely unrelated to anything previous. I'm not sure I'm ready to write it yet, but we'll see. Beyond that... who knows? Marshal and Seri may have more stories to tell.

* * *

I've been blessed to have a supportive family throughout all of this. The fact that they tolerate my sitting at the computer for so many hours is amazing. Thank you, thank you, thank you!

Stephen Tallman and Allen Perkins have been my most dedicated and helpful beta readers for the past two years. These books are much better because of them! I've also gained much in the way of encouragement and growth from the Apex Writers Group and the 20BooksTo50K group.

To the Creator of all, I owe everything. Thank you for letting me be a sub-creator.

As always, you can keep track of my writing progress and other stuff on timfrankovich.com or my Facebook author page. But the special people who sign up for my newsletter get the best stuff, including short stories and other bonus material. There's an unused "epilogue" to this book that I believe I'll be sharing with them sometime soon. So go sign up on the website! You won't regret it.

Thanks again for coming on this journey with me. What do you say we go on another one sometime soon?

www.ingramcontent.com/pod-product-compliance
Lightning Source LLC
Chambersburg PA
CBHW021241200726
48288CB00014B/172